MW01253560

"*What He Left Behind* is a compelling, heartfelt debut, announcing Benjamin Bradley's welcome arrival on the literary scene. This whodunnit expertly weaves the dangerous secrets of past and present in small-town Appalachia, delivering a jaw-dropping conclusion that's well worth your time. Bradley has the goods, and I can't wait to see what he cooks up next." —**Scott Blackburn, author of** *It Dies with You*

"Dark, atmospheric, and utterly gripping. *What He Left Behind* will keep you up all night, peeling back Oak Hill's layers of lies and heartbreak. Benjamin Bradley writes with fire and grit—you won't put this one down until it's burned itself into your soul." —**Eryk Pruitt, author of** *Something Bad Wrong* **and** *Blood Red Summer*

"Master storyteller Benjamin Bradley pulls you into a beautifully-written, compelling tale with his latest, *What He Left Behind*. It has all the elements mystery lovers want: an intriguing locale, powerful characters, and a puzzle that won't let go. A must read!" —**Lisa Towles, award-winning author of** *Terror Bay* **and other books**

"Benjamin Bradley has his finger on the pulse of small-town life: the thorny relationships between the haves and the have-nots, the currency of gossip, the distrust of outsiders, and the casual familiarity everyone has with the details of each other's lives . . . Bradley uses the conventions of a murder mystery to conduct his own autopsy of Oak Hill and its residents, and no one is spared. A worthy addition to the Southern Gothic tradition." —**Christopher Swann, author of the Faulkner Family Thriller series**

"*What He Left Behind* masterfully blends the past and present in a small-town setting with chilling prose, a multi-layered mystery, and unforgettable well-rounded characters. With page-turning mysteries like this, Benjamin Bradley is an author you'll want to come back to again and again!"
—**Caleb Wygal, award-winning author of the Myrtle Beach Mystery series**

WHAT HE LEFT BEHIND

WHAT HE LEFT BEHIND

BENJAMIN BRADLEY

CamCat Books

CamCat Books

2810 Coliseum Centre Drive, Suite 300

Charlotte, NC 28217-4574

Hardcover ISBN 9780744311969

Paperback ISBN 9780744311976

eBook ISBN 9780744311983

Library of Congress Control Number: 2024944068

Book and cover design by Maryann Appel

Interior artwork by Bokasana, Chronicler101, Fraserd, George Peters, Victor Metelskiy

5 3 1 2 4

FOR MEGAN

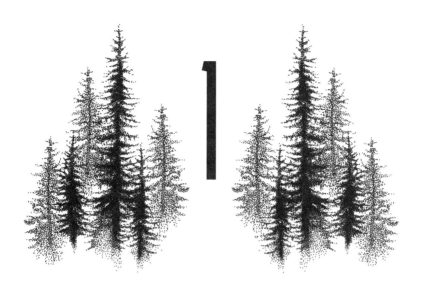

ray drizzle clung to my raincoat as I pressed myself against the centuries old door to Oak Hill Grocery and said a silent prayer to no one. The scripture on the dimly lit sign out front opined about the valley of death, a threat or a promise, I wasn't sure. Pushing inside, I navigated the cramped aisles and let raindrops tumble from my shoulders onto the scuffed linoleum floor. When I'd assembled enough for a hearty dinner, I moved toward the counter where Margo Locklear, the biggest gossip in all of Oak Hill, North Carolina, waited with a frown.

"Jacob Sawyer is back in town," she said.

The name hit me like buckshot, even though I knew it was coming.

"You hear me, Grace?"

"I heard you, Margo."

Silence hummed as rain trickled down gutters and gurgled into the drain. I didn't take my eyes off the box of noodles in my hand, instead lifting it to the counter to lie next to the massive jar of marinara. If I combined all the rumors I'd heard sneak out of Margo's lips, there stood a good chance that it was every combination of words and letters possible.

"Hell," Margo said. She lifted my handful of groceries from the counter and swiped them across the register. "He doesn't look half bad for an outsider."

"Just because he left town doesn't mean he's an outsider," I said, half-hearted.

"He came in searching for some medicine." She let out a throaty laugh. "As if he doesn't know that's not something I shelve. Like that big ole pharmacy sign three blocks down ain't lit."

"Medicine?"

Parmesan cheese took two swipes and then toppled onto the rest of my dinner ingredients.

"I guess he came back to take care of his ma. Willa's sick, didn't you hear?"

My throat went dry. I did my best to force a smile. "I heard. Everybody heard."

"Beats hospice care. Those bills. Unimaginable."

"Right," I said. "Hope she recovers quickly."

"That's not how cancer works, dear."

I rarely stopped to listen to the talk that swirled around town like hawks overhead. Not that I was above swapping stories about the failures of other residents. We all have that instinct. But I could never risk the idea of hearing a whisper with my name attached.

"Sometimes it does."

"Once death gets its grubby little fingers on you, it's over."

I didn't need to ask why she knew that. There were no secrets in Oak Hill. I had firsthand witness accounts of her late husband Henry's diagnosis, downfall, and death. He stood in the background of stories and memories like a leaf on a tree.

"That's some lullaby, Margo. I hope you tell that to the grandkids."

"Sawyer's been gone since the accident. I remember when your daddy came in here and told me the news like it was yesterday."

"Nat's always had a big mouth," I said.

"Even so. That's a long time. Fifteen years since you folks graduated high school and went into the woods. Fifteen years, Grace."

My body tensed, pushing away memories that were nudging their way into my mind. I said nothing. I simply laid my cash on the counter and fixed my eyes on Margo's until she broke the stare.

"Why don't you seem interested, Grace?" She picked up the bills and held them between her fingers like a cigarette. Her hand fell to the counter-top.

"I'm only interested in getting my dinner started. Nat's probably waiting for me back at home and wondering what the holdup is."

"Isn't that part of your job? Protect us from the outsiders? From the trouble that creeps in and takes root in a small town?"

"Who says he's trouble? It's been a while. Maybe he—"

"Fifteen years. He's spent his entire adult life outside the city. That makes him as good as gone. He doesn't know this town from Adam."

I kept my eyes on the counter, willing Margo to punch the keys in the register and collect my money so I could run home. She stared at the cash as if checking the serial numbers against some mental database. I heard the cheese growing warm. My stomach growled.

"Heard you had a big interview today," she said, palms flat on the counter.

"Just the first round," I lied. "Mind if we—"

"Right," she said. "Hope it went well." She ripped the receipt off the printer and handed it my way. I stuffed it in my bag and hurried out the door.

It would be a matter of days, hours even, until word spread that I'd fumbled my words and botched the opportunity to become Chief of Police. But that was tomorrow's problem. And Jacob Sawyer's arrival in Oak Hill seemed like fate doubling down on my misery.

No matter how hard I shut my eyes and willed myself to forget, memories of the last time I'd seen Jacob Sawyer raced through my frontal lobe like floodwater. To be honest, I thought he was gone forever. But nothing truly lasted forever. The grief of losing a second parent, this time to a vile disease that no saintly woman such as Willa deserved, must've been enough to beckon him home. And now, sneaking up on fifteen years to the day since he left, I walked through downtown and lingered on the silhouettes in the distance, wondering if I'd recognize his shadow among a crowd.

I made it to my car without glimpsing the ghost from my past and raced home, taking the long way to skirt around Sawyer's street and avoid pushing my luck. I worried that if my gaze strayed from the road for a second, I'd see the contours of my youthful stride as I scrambled out to meet Sawyer in some shoddy, rough-hewn structure we'd built with fallen timber. Those ghosts were best left alone in the forest.

Nat's house, and by default mine, was an unspectacular slab-on-grade with a wraparound porch and windows in the bedrooms that leaked when it rained. Weeds had overgrown the walk. Crabgrass crept beyond the borders and onto the well-trodden path that led to our front door. Unless I found the time, Nat would be down on his knees, picking the roots of each dandelion by the weekend. Come Monday, he'd be bedridden and aching, lamenting about a younger version of himself with dreams and hopes and a working spine.

My loyal tabby Agatha watched me enter from the armchair, too comfortable to greet me, until I entered the kitchen where her food waited. Water boiled. Noodles softened. Sauce gurgled. I tugged at my hair, neat in a topknot, and let it fall to my shoulders like curtains at the end of a play. In the fridge, I spotted the unmistakable logo of Mickey's Bar and Grill, a clue about Nat's night. No doubt his supper had included red meat and deep-fried somethings, two food groups his cardiologist requested he avoid. It was always those who took tremendous care of others that couldn't take care of themselves.

I flipped on the TV and let the hazy flicker wash over me like a balm. I uncorked a bottle, poured a glass of red, and drained it faster than planned. Agatha sniffed at my plate but opted for the warmth of my lap over the scraps of my pasta, enthused by the familiarity of our routine and the banality of my life.

Nat squirmed in his bed; blankets coiled around his legs. I tiptoed over and shut the door to let him rest. Hinges howled—an ailment Nat had maintained that he'd fix by the next weekend for thirty-something years now. By the time tiredness crept in and replaced worry, I had relived that humid June day sixteen more times with no inkling of what was to come. I'd warned my younger self that feelings and instincts are two different things, and you can't listen to both at the same time.

I carried Agatha, purring all the while, into the bedroom and dragged the door shut. She leapt onto the comforter and nestled herself in the corner as I changed out of work clothes and smiled at faded photographs tucked into the edges of my mirror. Nat and I looked younger than possible in the top shot, adoption certificate in my hand and a wide-eyed smile on his face. In another, I stood stubborn and surly on the front steps as Nat snapped a photo of my first day of work with Susan Orr and the Dockery Center. In the corner rested one that I'd avoided for some time. Cliff, Sawyer, and I stood with a background of sprawling pines. Our lanky limbs fell onto one another's shoulders and our smiles were wider than the Murphy Road drag. I let myself linger for a moment. Just long enough to wonder what he looked like now. Then, I tucked the memories back into their spot and fought Agatha for room on the bed.

I plugged headphones in and let my head fall onto the pillow. The wine helped usher sleep in with crimson waves that calmed my mind long enough to crash. When sleep arrived, it was fitful and discomforting—like ants crawled in my bedsheets and tickled my bare skin. Maybe it was a warning. A nudge from the world to keep me half-awake. Whatever it was, it worked. I jumped to my feet when the phone rang.

I heard the words on the other end but struggled to comprehend. There was seldom an event in Oak Hill that required the emergency response team to wake the ranking officer and beckon them into the darkness. But like that June evening, things changed in a millisecond.

"Grace?" Patty Glassmire's voice came through hushed and immediate.

"I'm here," I said.

"We need you out on Ray Cove Road. Lionel Sutton's place."

"Break in?" I asked.

"No," Patty said.

A long pause followed.

"There's a body."

2

Oak Hill loomed deserted and dim, my headlights the only flash of color in the night. Murphy Road cut through downtown like a river, but my foot hovered over the brake expecting nature's nightly takeover. Coyotes and foxes slinked around under the moonlight and scavenged for scraps that humanity left behind.

I sped through the stop sign and veered onto Ray Cove Road, thankful the rain had quit. A flicker of red stung my eyes through the sycamore and oaks, some interstellar hue that stained the stars above and clouded everything with panic. Even after ten years of service, my heart still galloped when I heard a siren. It meant something was wrong. And by the sound of Patty's voice on the other end, I knew I was walking into a mess.

I eased onto the shoulder behind a cruiser and dug my flashlight out of the glove box. Crisp winds pushed through stands of loblolly and caressed my bare neck as I walked, a rare occasion for North Carolina in late May. Officer Miguel Munoz stood in the brush, alone, staring down into an illuminated stretch of knee-high cornstalks. He held a handkerchief over his mouth with one hand and a flashlight trembled in the other.

"Munoz?" I called out from the roadside.

He turned to me, pale as a shut-in. "Over here."

"You all right?"

"I'll be fine."

"Where'd you vomit? I don't want to step in it."

He pointed off to the side. "Out of the way. Didn't want to disturb the scene."

"Wise of you," I said, high stepping toward him. The thick air hung on my shoulders like an overcoat.

As I approached, the first thing that came into view was the worn sole of a boot. Then a second. I set my feet and crept close enough to get a full glimpse. Munoz stepped back.

"Who is it?" I asked.

He shifted the light toward the head where blood streaked the forehead and matted in the untamed brown hair. I swallowed the sick in my throat. "Don't know."

"Huh," I said. "Me either."

The smell hit me like a wave and wretched something awful inside me. It was only then that I realized I'd never seen a dead body, let alone a murder victim. I kept a brave face and directed my eyes to the patchy weeds around the lifeless limbs.

"I stopped by the store for coffee before my shift. Margo said there was an outsider in Oak Hill," Munoz added. "Maybe our victim is who she meant."

"No," I said. "She's just starting a commotion about Jacob Sawyer being back in town."

"No shit?"

Those two words summed up Munoz's philosophy on life. He was a no-nonsense kind of person. And I couldn't blame him. Juggling a budding family and a full-time job was inconceivable from my vantage point. Hell, I couldn't keep up with Nat's appointments and medication, let alone tussle with the sleep schedules of toddlers.

"No shit indeed," I said.

"You seen him?"

I glared at him.

He raised his hands in surrender. "Point taken."

"Who called this in?"

"Lionel Sutton heard a car door slam and tires squeal as he was getting ready for bed. Sent his dog out to shoo away the threat and found the pup by the body."

"Lucy okay?"

"She's fine. I gave her a belly rub when I pulled up. Sutton is inside settling down. He agreed to keep the news under wraps. I asked if it was one of his workers, but he shrugged it off and changed the subject."

"Smart of him to look out for their best interests, although we're not ICE."

Munoz stared down at the body. "I don't know if she's illegal. Could be. Lionel outsources sometimes."

I snapped on a pair of gloves. "You check the pulse?"

"Yeah. Sutton said he didn't see the point, but I confirmed his notion."

"Gloved up first?"

"Of course."

"Good work, Munoz. If you need a minute, go catch your breath. She isn't going anywhere." I studied her face once more, hoping for a sense of recognition or a trace of family resemblance.

"Thanks, Grace," he said. "Want me to call Macon?"

"Might as well," I said. "But it'll take some effort to get the coroner out this way."

Munoz looked up and down the road. "Might need directions."

"Nobody has reason to come out this way. Let alone somebody from the county."

"We'll see." Munoz stepped away, and I held my breath as I knelt next to the chest of our victim. In the commingling of hazy moonlight and powerful fluorescent bulbs, I jotted down a few rudimentary observations in my notebook. She didn't look older than fifty, maybe younger, but I couldn't say for sure. She wore faded blue jeans with tears on the knees and a long sleeve checkered flannel, red and black. No undershirt or bra. I gently turned her body with one hand and reached into her back pocket. No wallet.

"Munoz, did you take the wallet?" I shouted.

"No wallet," he said. "No ID."

I cursed under my breath and dug around anyway. With tender hands, I raised her skull and examined the wounds. Something big and heavy had come down on the back of her skull. Another blow had hit the crown of her head. Blood had oozed out of both wounds and pooled in the surrounding soil. The crimson color looked blacker than the sky.

Maybe that was normal. Maybe not. I had no sense of what was normal in a murder scene.

I'd never been to one.

I stood and snapped a photo of the woman's face. Lord knows that nobody wants to stare into the lifeless eyes of a dead body, but somebody in Oak Hill would recognize that face. The flash from my phone's camera lit her in an ugly, unnatural light. I felt for her. She wasn't just a woman. She was somebody's daughter or mother or cousin or aunt. That much was certain. Somebody would cause a fuss, right?

Munoz tramped back with a bottle of water before I could finish my thought. "County is on the way."

"ETA?"

He looked at me blankly.

"Lovely," I said, kneeling back down beside the body.

"What's the procedure here?"

I shrugged. "First murder we've had here in my lifetime."

"Wonderful."

"I took a photo of her face. I'd like to show Susan Orr."

Munoz tensed in the corner of my eye. "You think she's a vagrant?"

"She prefers the term unhoused."

"You think she's unhoused?"

"She's got ratty hair and a film of dirt on her skin. Add in the grime under the fingernails and the faint scent of urine—it's clear she'd fallen on hard times. And when you fall hard in Oak Hill, Susan finds you."

"What's the female version of a saint?" he asked.

"I should ask you. I haven't darkened the doorstep of a church on a Sunday morning in years."

"I know." He paused for a moment. "If you want to go . . . after seeing this, they'd welcome you back with open arms. We all would."

"Thanks, Miguel."

"Anything else you need me to do?"

I crinkled my lips. "Once Macon County gets out here with their team, they'll push us to the sidelines. Odds are you'll never see another murder victim before you quit the force, so if you were ever curious or anything—"

He chuckled, but it was half-hearted. "No, thanks."

"You'd drink for free at Mickey's. Probably for life."

"Sadie would love that," he said. "You planning to tell the tale?"

I stared into the woman's lifeless eyes. "You know me better than that."

"You never know."

Dawn spread through the sky like lavender and lilacs blooming in springtime. Munoz and I gawked at the watercolor painting above us, juxtaposed with the grisly scene on the ground.

I kept my eyes set skyward, at a loss for words.

Munoz prayed.

3

Sun painted the field and chased the fog away. I planted myself beside the body, with enough distance to avert my eyes out of some mix of respect and fear. After fifteen minutes, Munoz flagged me down from the road and jogged over. Sweat slunk down his tanned neck and painted a full picture of his emotional state, considering that it was borderline frigid out. The sun hadn't yet gotten to work to dry the morning dew.

"Mayor Rice is here," he said, the words careful and slow.

"Shit," I said. "Thanks."

Munoz smiled at the mayor and disappeared from view. Cliff stepped down from the jacked-up frame of his oversized silver truck and within seconds of his boots hitting the ground, he fussed with a toothpick in the corner of his mouth. "Some mess we've got here."

"You look like a cartoon cowboy, Cliff."

He transferred the toothpick to the other side. "Now isn't the time to be hitting on me, Grace."

That running joke had grown stagnant sometime in high school, but he still dredged it up whenever possible. Male egos, I guess. Carlos Clifford

Rice had gone nine rounds with Father Time and wobbled from the ring, having sustained more damage than most. Stress collected in bags beneath his eyes that, even in the hazy morning, seemed purple and puffy. A horseshoe of hair remained around the sides of his head, although he always hid it with a cap. Despite his heritage and Hispanic roots, he'd insisted on going by his middle name, Clifford. I never thought he was much of a Carlos anyhow.

I tapped the badge affixed to my belt. "That's Detective Bingham to you, sir."

"Right, and I should expect you to call me Mayor Rice, too? Pigs can fly, Grace."

"How'd you hear?"

"Patty rang."

"There some kind of secret arrangement you have with her?"

"No secret."

Despite warnings otherwise, Cliff had made a pile of promises during his inaugural campaign, and keeping a pulse on happenings around town had risen above the rest. You couldn't sneeze in Oak Hill without somebody hearing it and Cliff showing up to whisper, "God bless you."

"Right," I said.

"A man needs to be aware of what's happening in his town, Grace."

A man. His town. Like somebody handed him the deed to the city when he won the vote by a peck. Give a man an inch, right?

"What about the women? We're left for the buzzards?"

"You can park that feminist crap on the sidelines. You know damn well what I meant. Now, are we going to square dance or are you going to guide me to the body?"

"We're preserving it for Macon County."

"Who's our victim?"

"No clue."

Surprise sparkled in his eyes. I recognized the look from years back. Years when the world still could surprise us, more often in severe, cruel ways than the pleasant delights that youthful splendor brought. Like when your best friend sneaks out of town without a whisper of a goodbye or explanation. "And here I thought you could name every soul within city limits."

"I'd wager I could," I said, meaning every word. If Oak Hill was a *Guess Who* board, I'd clean up. One of the pitfalls of the job. Dirty laundry wasn't a secret, nor was it all that dirty.

"Then what's the issue?"

"An outsider, maybe." I hated myself for letting Margo's words sneak into my mouth. The very act of calling anybody an outsider validated the idea that insiders also existed. The world wasn't that simple. Neither was Oak Hill.

"From where?"

"Keep asking questions you know I can't answer, Cliff."

"Got ID?"

"I'm warning you."

He raised his hands in surrender. "I give. I give." He turned and stared down Munoz from a distance. "You advise him not to say a word to Margo or anybody in town?"

"Don't need to. He knows."

"It's a murder?"

I nodded.

"Then be sure and remind him, anyway."

"I'll consider it."

"How'd the interview go?"

I grimaced. "You already know the answer to that."

"Thought I'd hear it from you instead of the crows."

"It could have been better."

"Well then, this case is your best shot to earn the job."

My eyes widened. "I assumed they were going with somebody else."

"Your fellow applicants sputtered out when they learned the starting salary."

"Golddiggers."

"A quick win would go a long way to warming over some icy hearts, Grace. I did go to bat for you though."

"Figured you might. Thanks."

"Old friends. Can't make new ones."

"Speaking of, have you heard?"

"Yeah, I—"

"Reyna tell you?"

He turned cherry red. "No, we don't . . . uh. Hannah's on the hospice care team for Willa."

"Have you seen him?"

"No," Cliff said. "And I don't plan to."

"Can't be that bad. You've had fifteen years to let your grudge crumble."

"I'd say it's hardened more than crumbled. Heard anything about Willa?"

"Haven't been over since I heard the diagnosis. I was prepping for the interview, then Margo told me about Sawyer."

"And you didn't book a trip to Miami?"

"Look at my skin, Cliff. If I set foot in Miami, I'd come back a lobster."

"There's such a thing as sunscreen, you know. Hannah reminds me of that every time the sun peeks its head out. Think he'll stick around?" Cliff asked, shifting the toothpick to the other end.

"If you're asking the likelihood of you having to face him, it's high."

"Why?" he asked.

"I don't know. You've got words you've left unsaid for the better part of your life. Questions you want answered. Fate will give you that window."

He studied my face. "You don't have questions?"

"I did," I said. "Until I didn't."

"What changed?"

"That grudge got heavy. And Nat talked some sense into me after a while. Kept on about Sawyer's character and how that doesn't disappear overnight."

"But he did."

"Right," I said. "But Nat's point is that if the Sawyer we loved left without a warning, he must have had a good reason."

"Doesn't take a detective to link it to that night in the woods."

Munoz hollered from afar. In the faint dawn light, I saw the county vehicles steering down the road toward us. Tires crunched on gravel. Cliff pasted on his best mayoral smile and tossed in a new toothpick. Two tired faces frowned at us from inside the van. From the driver's side, a slender woman in her late forties stepped out and stretched toward the sky. She had sharp features with darkened eyes that seemed blacker than night. Shoulder-length black hair framed her face. Once she was limber, she tucked a hand into mine and shook firmly as she smiled. "Tessa Brown, sorry for the long wait."

"Detective Grace Bingham," I said. "And this is Mayor Clifford Rice."

"Mr. Mayor," Tessa said. She pointed to her teammate, who had disappeared behind the vehicle. "The worker bee over there is Blake Tucker. He's all business at this hour. Wait until he's two cups deep before you introduce yourself."

"Noted," I said. "Can I lead you to the scene?"

"Please. Later on, we'll need your boot prints for elimination," she said. "And the guy by the road, too."

It took everything in my power not to blurt that I'd never seen a dead body before and this was my first murder scene. Our first as a town as far as I knew. But I held it in check.

"Owner of the land lives a few hundred yards north," I said. "He heard something on the property. The kind old gent discharged his hound on the supposed intruder, but Lucy didn't return. When Sutton walked out to find her, the pup was sitting next to the body."

Tessa stared down at the victim. "And this is no dog bite."

"No, ma'am. I don't think so."

Tessa smiled. "No need to ma'am me. My sore back already reminds me of my age plenty."

"Head wound," Cliff said, the color drained from his face. The toothpick was gone.

"Two," I said. "One in the rear of the skull and one at the top. Blood streaks from both."

"Any ID?" Tessa asked, kneeling closer to the body.

I shook my head.

"That's okay," she said. "We'll find something to identify her. But for now, she's a Jane Doe."

"I'll alert the rest of my staff," Cliff said, before bolting away from the scene.

Tessa chuckled. "Ah, the fragility of masculinity. Detective, have you worked on a murder scene before?"

"I have not."

"That's what I thought. I want you to know you did everything by the book here. Aced it, Grace. We'll take over the scene and process everything we can. I hate to drown your hope, but without hard evidence, this will be a long shot. Your best bet will be to work backwards from the woman's identity and ask who benefits from her demise."

"Got it," I said. "Could this be an accident?"

"We don't work off possibilities. We focus on probabilities. You'll have our full report within seventy-two hours and a preliminary report by the end of watch today. But off the record, since we're spitballing in the morning sunshine, it strikes me as odd that there are two wounds. And the locations. I'd guess it was a sneak attack."

"She's ten feet off the road, too. Since I can't think of a single reason she'd be walking through this field, my thought was that she ran from a car."

"Could be," she said. "Hypothetically, she runs from somebody, they follow, strike her from behind and it's lights out."

"Damn."

"Damn indeed. Not your normal night in Oak Hill."

"That's the understatement of the century."

"No matter the how of it, it's clear that whoever did this wanted her dead."

-THEN-

UGLY THINGS CAN HAPPEN IN BEAUTIFUL PLACES. I learned that the hard way the summer I turned eighteen. Hell, the whole town did. Up until then, I'd seen Oak Hill in a certain light. Shaded by towering pines and friendly locals, danger never seemed within striking distance. Maybe we should've seen it. Maybe it was in the background of every childhood memory, of every risk that we took. But none of it felt real until we saw what happened to Sarah Price. After that, though, danger was everywhere.

Back when I was a kid, Oak Hill stood as the classic all-American example of small-town life. Now, a small town only left so much room for adventure and mischief. Youthful citizens, feeling the suffocation of the Macon County border and the yearning for new horizons to explore, turned instead to the untamed parts of the land.

Some packed into borrowed cars and drove far across the state line, bumping into trouble in Tennessee or Georgia. Others crisscrossed the state and parked themselves on the pristine beaches of the Outer Banks, or some lesser-known village. No matter the location, anywhere was more attractive than Oak Hill, North Carolina.

In my years of adolescent zeal, we stayed local. Lucas Franklin, three years our senior, was the first one to find the clearing. He'd been on a hunting trip with his father and some navigational blunders drove them into the scrub. The naked spot in the thick forests of Nantahala appeared like a blank canvas in front of him. Once fellow students got their brushes on it, the secret was out. Everybody painted their stroke.

Sawyer and I first visited in our sophomore year, after great insistence from Cliff that we were squandering our teenage years watching TV mysteries and playing board games. Cliff was drawn to the bright lights and hormonal buzz of the party scene and despite our differences, we traveled as a pack. Some wisecrack in middle school called us the tricycle, and we made a stink each time somebody dusted off that nickname, even though we secretly adored the label. The beauty of a tricycle was that all the wheels pulled their weight. Everybody supported one another. The danger was that all it took was one missing wheel, and the others fell obsolete.

The older crowd dubbed the clearing "the inferno," slapping an ominous label on an innocuous, picturesque gap in the woods. That first night, I gawked at the surrounding pines that safeguarded any activities from civilization. My feet rested less than three miles from Murphy Road, yet I felt like I'd stumbled through a portal into a new world. One without rules or adults or consequences. Soon, smoke from bonfires snaked into the treetops. Beer spilled over plastic cups and glee mixed with sparks in the air.

High school lumbered along and the three of us ventured to endless beer-soaked bonfires where we'd mingle with upperclassmen or gossip with our classmates. Cliff came for the lukewarm suds in his cup. I came for the backdrop and for the light show, where fireflies opened the first act and embers sent us home. I liked to think that all the trees in the forest watched alongside us. Virgin stands of sycamore getting their first taste of trouble. Yellow poplars dancing along to the music. And Sawyer, well, he came because I was there.

The crowd varied night by night. Recent graduates, stymied by the limitations of small-town life, often lingered and hung around with the younger crowd and attempted to keep their youth alive. Many bemoaned the burdens of blue-collar jobs and the pressures of adulthood. We ignored them. The inferno was no place for worry and long-term planning.

The only property within earshot of the spot was the palatial mansion owned by local tycoon Silas Dockery. The fence line of the family's estate stretched for acres along the edge of the Nantahala, but we never saw a soul. On the occasional night, Madison and Ethan Dockery, Silas's two kids, would appear with a gaggle of out-of-town friends and steal the spotlight. They were the closest thing we had to local celebrities, being the richest kids we knew. Ethan basked in the attention, but Madison tended to skirt into the shadows and mingle with whoever caught her eye. Once I returned from a bathroom trip in the trees to find her and Sawyer talking alone. He broke off quickly and snagged my hand.

"What was that about?" I asked.

"Oh you know. My dad works for their dad," he said.

I considered pushing him further. I'd seen the twinkle in Madison Dockery's eye. I'd also seen the fury in her stare as Sawyer walked away and held me. Maybe I thought Sawyer was too naïve to know what Madison's intentions were. Maybe I thought I was the naïve one.

By senior year, Cliff had a relationship with the organizers and thus, we had a standing invitation to join whenever we wished. Cliff had packed on the initial traces of a beer belly, but it suited him somehow. Sawyer and I, we didn't see the merit in joining every weekend. There was a life to be lived that didn't involve drowning yourself in booze and gossip. Cliff had a taste for it and joined whenever he scraped together enough cash for a few beers. He lived for the inferno. We didn't have dilemmas or trials. We were just kids looking to pretend to be wild for a night. Most of the time, it worked.

The police, as with most things that happened in our town, caught wind before long. Whether it was a pair of loose lips or a parent stomping into their son's room with demands about their whereabouts, we'll never know. Nat warned me one night after I returned with the palpable scent of smoke on my clothes that the party wouldn't last forever. Rumor had it that Don

Chamberlain was fuming about the transgressions happening under his nose and before long, his bark would become a bite. Like a million other things Nat and the town threatened, I shrugged it off.

That night after graduation, we slapped unearned cash into Cliff's hand and drove his truck out of Oak Hill's main drag. Ahead, headlights illuminated the dark entryway that dead-ended with a wrought-iron gate which led to the Dockery Estate, one of the few structures on that far side of town. Still, they were far enough away for us to feel safe and on most nights, the wind pushed westward. Cliff pulled off the road and nestled the truck behind a collection of six others. Heads bobbed in the fading moonlight and slithered into the bowels of the forest. What once stood as an emergency entryway into Nantahala, in case of fire or rescue operations, had become a sidewalk for us teenagers. The familiar path required limited navigation—a beacon of oranges and reds flashed ahead and invited us in. Voices swelled and celebratory shouts acknowledged each new arrival.

We were kings and queens, if only for a moment. Our whole lives stood ahead; futures bright like the flames that flashed in the pit below. Cliff snatched our cups and filled them with a foamy brew that tasted like freedom and bitterness. Arms raised in triumphant cheers; we drove our cups together. Beer sloshed over the rims and puddled in the untamed grass below. A holler and a hoot and with that, the party was on.

4

L ike a sudden burst of breath, the road pushed away from the bleak stretch of farmland and knifed into town. Two-story buildings, once bustling and hectic, stood deserted and grim along the road. The few that still churned up enough business to stay afloat weren't making enough cash to retire on, but that was life in Oak Hill. You found enough to get by and muddled through like generations before.

Oak Hill was a dot on a map in the most literal sense. Murphy Road ran through the center, and half-moon clusters of homes branched out on either side. Zoomed out, it's a near perfect circle. Although, that contradicts life within that bubble.

The saying went that Oak Hill had one of everything you could need. If you're drawn to the tint of neon and don't mind the crooning of classic country music, Mickey's is your place for chasing beer and regrets. If you're hankering for a damn good plate of breakfast food or a hearty sandwich, Emma Barnes runs a mean kitchen at the Empire Diner. If your legal troubles piled up, you could walk down to Bill Nickelson's office and pray he's still got some sense left in his elderly brain. Earl's is your best bet for gas and a cold drink. Scattered between those haunts were a handful of municipal and government buildings, the police station among them.

Back behind the uninspired stretch we called downtown, houses hugged sidewalks that hugged curbs throughout the surrounding six square miles. Farmers, like old Lionel Sutton and others, kept to themselves out in the spacious fields but still came into town for coffee or conversation. The only outlier within city limits was the Dockery Estate. And if I had half the money they did, I'd spread out on my own swath of land too. I leaned against the uninhabited intake desk of the station and glared into the oceanic eyes of Cliff as I choked down a mess of curse words and thought of a rational response to what he'd said. Damned if you do and damned if you don't.

"You're poking the bear," I said.

He stared back at me with tired eyes without an ounce of compassion. Cliff saw life in black and white. There was no gray in his world. You're either right or wrong, and that was judged by how much you agreed with his opinion. "He's a big city detective and this is a big city crime."

"Sawyer doesn't know the difference between Perkins Pharmacy and Margo's. Just five minutes ago you were talking about him like he was dead to you. What changed?"

"The Dockerys want him to consult," he said. "I can only push back for so long."

"Did anybody bother to ask Sawyer himself? Willa's dying. It's not like he's got time to roam about town and interrogate suspects. You really want to complicate things right now?"

"Remember when you said you didn't have any questions for him? I call bullshit."

"Having questions doesn't mean I want to ask them."

Cliff sat back and stared at the ceiling as if the words to convince me might appear on the microfiber panels above. Few things provoked me more than a prolonged silence, unless I was the architect behind said silence. That's the impossibility about working with old friends. They know you too damn well. But I wasn't going down without a fight.

"Give me twenty-four hours," I said. "If I don't have anything, you can bring Sawyer in."

Cliff scrutinized my face and stood. "Fine. End of the day. At supper time, I'm heading over to Sawyer's place. If you haven't made any headway, you're coming too."

He left in a dust cloud as Munoz crept inside. "Everything okay, Detective?"

Some people couldn't read a person's face if they were a billboard screaming to leave them alone. Munoz meant well. And if he didn't, I'd have still held my tongue out of respect for the chain of command. Not that there was much of a chain these days.

"Mayor Rice wants an old friend to help us out on the case."

"Already?" Munoz chuckled. "The blood isn't even dry."

"I bought us a day's worth of time. But you've been up through the night. Why don't you go get some rest?"

"Molloy isn't in until noon, I—"

"I can handle it," I said. "Give Sadie a hug for me."

Munoz snatched his lunch from the fridge and snuck out the back door just as a knock came on the pane of glass in the front. I inched the window open and glared at Margo's mug.

"Dinner was just fine, thank you. Although I miss that old spaghetti sauce you had last fall. The one with the red label."

"Hush now," Margo said. "Is it true?"

"Indeed. I do make the best pasta on this side of the Mason-Dixon."

"A dead body?"

"Margo, I advise you to not believe everything you hear."

"There's a van down off Ray Cove. The side of it says Crime Scene Unit. I've seen enough TV to understand what that means."

"It means somebody is having a much worse day than you are, Margo. Revel in that for a moment instead of trying to muddy the waters."

She blew a raspberry with her lips. "What gives you the right to keep secrets?"

"Everybody has a right to their secrets. And this one isn't mine to share. Somebody lost their life today. Rather than looking for an angle, look for empathy. Look for grace."

She scowled. I swallowed hard, realizing I'd tipped my hand and accidentally confirmed Margo's hunch. Where was this in all of my training? How do you calm anxious citizens without telling the world what happened? Thankfully, Margo appeared unaware as ever.

"This isn't a coincidence, Grace. Bertha Hawkins told me last night that she'd seen Billy Jenkins smoking a cigarette outside Mickey's. Add that to your old flame showing up out of nowhere and—"

"Margo, the longer I stand here stamping out your flames, the longer it is before I can get back to actual police work."

She snorted and walked away.

"Pleasure as always, Margo," I said to her back.

I observed the morning bustle of Murphy Road. The shuffle of cars in and out of spaces. A school bus roared past, hauling children to the edge of town to teach them about the world as if that would do them any good. All was quiet. All was normal. I thought of Margo's words to me the night before, which now sounded more prophetic than cryptic. An outsider in Oak Hill. She had that much right. But it wasn't just Sawyer. He was tumbling down the list of my problems.

Problems weren't a new concept to Oak Hill; they usually came disguised as petty casework or governmental busywork. Just like Mickey's, we had our regulars, but most of them were harmless. More often than not, I could solve my biggest problems by lunch time and revel in the midday commotion at the diner. Margo's mention of Billy Jenkins stirred an unsettling feeling in my gut.

Billy Jenkins was the reason for my first crime scene. He'd had a few too many down at Mickey's and instead of walking home, decided to shoot target practice by lining Miller Lite cans on my squad car roof. What compelled his logic that night, I'd never know. Don Chamberlain and I found him asleep in our parking lot on a bed of pine needles with a rifle by his side. I spent that day bagging bullets from my tires and trunk while Chamberlain filed paperwork.

Billy had once been a kid with a ton of promise but the demons of a small town warped his good nature and by the time he hit twenty he'd been arrested for nearly every petty crime in the book. Still, Jenkins wasn't violent. He was just an addict without the means to pay for his supply. And an idiot who was a terrible, terrible shot.

Jenkins famously skipped town some four years back after he was beaten to a pulp by a crowd of thugs in Moxville. Rumor had it that he was on a church kick somewhere in Georgia. I made a mental note to check his old property for signs of life, but it didn't seem pressing. The morning's discovery carried an unfamiliar weight. A discomfort rested on my shoulders like a rucksack thrust upon me by fate or fortune.

Back inside the station, I plugged my phone into the computer, printed out the photo of the victim's face, and tucked it into a folder, then steered north toward home in search of some answers and a hot shower. I hoped that the scalding water might scrub away the film of grime that clung to my skin. If that didn't work, at least I could turn to Nat and bounce theories off him until one had legs.

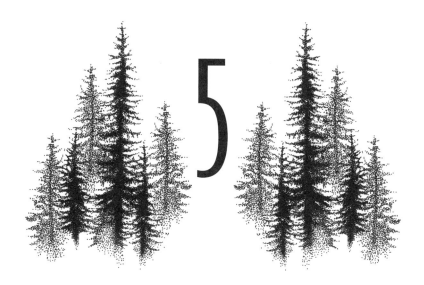

5

Before the state of North Carolina officially licensed me to drive, the three-mile stretch from my house to Upper Oak Hill felt like an eternity. Nat was never much for rules or regulations and such trivial things as a driver's license weren't important to him. But I still spent the better part of a decade using my own two feet to get around town. I couldn't keep a bike in shape. It would always end up with a rusted chain from an unexpected rainstorm or plucked by older kids who'd try to pawn it off for cash.

At age eleven, I spent my entire summer trying to bushwhack my way through vines and brush to create a shortcut through overgrown woods and fields. With a stolen machete from Nat's shed, I slashed at rhododendrons and new growth until it was passable.

No matter how long I combed and clawed, I couldn't clear the carpeted forest floor where wildflowers and ferns reigned supreme. Spiked balls from sweet gum trees seemed to reappear on the ground every time I turned my back. Acorns fell from red oaks and capsules tumbled from the overhead mountain laurels. I was fighting nature and losing. In a frenzied rage, I lashed out until there was no victim spared. Filament and anther scarred the

soil where flowers once bloomed. Hickory nuts toppled from the sky and raced sugar maple seeds to the ground.

After the shortcut failed, Sawyer started meeting me halfway and walking alongside, skipping rocks in the puddles and pools that bordered the gravel road after humidity broke into a hard rain. If I'd asked him, he would have walked all the way to Nat's simply to spend extra time with me. If I felt I'd deserved that extra hour, I'd have inquired.

Nat's double-wide jutted out from Upper Oak Hill down a precarious road where asphalt turns to gravel and tests your patience and the integrity of your shocks. Shrubs choke the end of the driveway and Nat liked to joke that it ensured that somebody had to pay attention if they wanted to track us down. We never had neighbors, aside from the sparrows in the pines and a gaggle of geese that seasonally filled the pond. Nat seemed to revel in the solitude and although we weren't blood, he'd passed that down to me as well.

He sat half-awake on the front porch, blinking away the drowsiness of his medication and the early morning blues. I'd seen Nat Bingham in every state of mind: worried, sick, happy, you name it. Most moods came with a toothy grin pasted across his face. Even on the harsh days, when age crept in and bewildered him, Nat was the definition of jolly.

"Young buck," he said, his narrow eyes following me as I approached.

"Big Nat."

"I missed you last night. You were late." One hand scratched at his bushy beard, which somehow remained the same length every day of my life. The man looked like he belonged in the wild, fighting a grizzly bear. Despite a hard life, he'd brought nothing but joy and wisdom since he'd made me kin.

"Got caught up," I said, taking a seat in the decades-old rocker with the chipped paint. "But I beat you up this morning."

He laughed. Nat loved early mornings like most people loved sleeping. "How was the interview?"

"Hell with air conditioning."

"Who is on the committee?" He spoke with his cheeks more than his lips.

"County Sheriff, a Dockery, and a consultant they hired."

"Which Dockery?"

"Ethan, on behalf of Silas."

The mention of the name roused memories in my head that popped like flash grenades. The snide look on Ethan's narrow face as he leaned forward and tore apart my resume, as he outlined all the qualifications I lacked. When I'd responded that I, in fact, did not have a college degree or a certificate in criminal justice studies, he smirked and jotted something in his notebook. And that was that. If that three-person committee were a jury, he'd be the swing vote.

Nat kicked a leg out and stretched toward it. "Where's Silas?"

"Under the weather."

"That's too bad."

The first thing I noticed about Silas Dockery was that he walked with a limp. It was the only thing remarkable about him from a glance and, as a young girl, it was what I'd noticed. Nat caught me staring and lectured me that night, reminding me that we should all be so lucky to escape life with just a limp. How most hands dealt were much worse. He didn't say how it came about, nor did anybody else around town. For all the gossip-hungry folks in Oak Hill, for whatever reason, Silas was off limits.

For my entire life, Nat's was the only landscaping company in town. He'd joke that on some streets he could ride his mower down each side, from house to house, without getting off for a break. Every Friday morning, without fail and regardless of weather, Nat would load up the trailer and spend the day working on the Dockery property. They didn't need him year-round, yet Nat didn't cut corners.

And I perceived mutual respect when I saw Nat and Silas speak. Whenever I mentioned the Dockery name, respect coated Nat's tongue. He didn't say the words, but I understood before I found the words: Silas was good people.

"This town's not ready for a female police chief, let alone one that's thirty-three."

"You'll be thirty-four in a month," he said. He tapped his finger on his temple. "And they say I'm losing my mind."

I hopped to my feet and leaned on the railing. "And I say you never had it in the first place."

He mimed a bullet to the heart.

"We had a call late last night. You remember Lionel Sutton? We found a dead body on his property. Doesn't look like he's guilty, but I'm still waiting for the crime lab to provide a report on the victim's identity."

Nat chewed on the words for a protracted minute before he responded. "Not many strangers in Oak Hill. And not many reasons to pass through."

"If Oak Hill ever needs a marketing consultant, you're the man for the job."

"Was he shot?"

I laughed. "What kind of question is that?"

"One you're going to get a lot, I'd imagine."

"No, *she* wasn't shot."

"Stabbed?"

"Nat."

"If you go around town using vague terminology like that, you're opening the door for these kinds of questions. You can't go running through life leaving doors open everywhere."

"I can't tell you what happened, Nat. You know as well as I do that I've already said too much. Even to you, old man."

"Who are you calling old? You're going to be thirty-four next month. That's old as dirt."

I shoved him. "How you feeling today?"

"Like a young chickadee."

"Oh yeah? Gonna finally teach me how to line dance?"

"I don't think people do that anymore."

"Yeah, but we're not people. We're Binghams."

"The strangest breed there is."

I stared into the breeze for a long moment before I found the next words.

"Sawyer's in town."

Nat gave a slow nod. "That's good."

"Good?"

"It's about time," he said. "And Willa's sick."

"Cliff's demanding that I let Sawyer work the case. He's a detective in Philadelphia now."

"What did you two used to call yourselves?"

"The Clueless Detective Agency."

Nat thundered into a throaty laugh. "Ah, I haven't thought about that in ages. You two were too much. Darting around with notebooks. I kept waiting for you to adopt a dog and name it Scooby."

"We were kids."

"You were friends," he said. "Old friends. Can't make new ones."

"Cliff said that today, too."

"It's from some old movie. The best wisdom is like that, just sticks with you like a catchy tune. What are you going to do?"

I shrugged. "Work the case. Find the truth before Sawyer steps in. I don't think he's going to want to anyway. He's got his hands full with Willa."

"You know Willa too well to believe that for a second. She'll give him the boot at the first mention of a case, especially if it leaves him running alongside Grace Bingham."

"Which is exactly why I won't let Willa hear about it."

"This is Oak Hill, young buck. She already knows."

"I need a shower. That smell," I said. "It's been clinging to me like a campfire."

"It'll cling to your memory too. The first dead person I saw was in Khe Sanh. I'll spare you the gory bits, but it was one battle where both sides claimed victory, even though they both lost. We were defending the base from the initial attack, just a small division. A soldier from the Republic was walking across the field and tumbled like he'd forgotten how to walk. Me and two others ran to check on him, but it was too late. And even though I had no part in putting him in the ground, I still see that man's face from time to time."

"How do you live with it?"

"The better question is, how does your killer live with it? If you feel that dreadful just seeing her lying there, imagine how the killer feels."

"Frankly, I can't," I said. "But I can't do much legwork smelling like I do."

I kissed him on the cheek before marching toward the bathroom. Agatha waited for me inside the door. When I'd first brought the mangy domestic short-hair home, she clawed at the doors and windows in a futile escape attempt. She'd have been fine living a hybrid life, bouncing between the wild and her cozy indoor home. It was me that couldn't handle the possibility that, without explanation, she might never return.

I contemplated Nat's words as scalding hot water rivered over my shoulders and tumbled to the drain below. *Imagine how the killer feels.* No matter how strong the soap, the smell persisted. Maybe it was mental. I made a note to ask Munoz and see if he'd shaken the sight. Then again, I recalled his pool of vomit on the side of the field and grinned.

Everything in the case felt backwards. In every case study I'd read, the detective and their team work to unravel the mystery and reveal the killer. There are libraries' worth of material on the inner workings of the criminal mind. Seminars on serial killers and more podcasts than anybody could listen to in a lifetime about dastardly deeds that nearly went unpunished. But none of that was useful yet. Instead of hunting down a killer, I was hunting down a ghost. Who was my dead woman in the field? And what secrets was she killed to protect?

6

I was two years old when Nathaniel Bingham took me in. The few memories I have before that glorious day are cloudy and shapeless. I don't know my mother's face or the sound of my father's voice, but I recall the first time I saw the tinge of love in another's eyes. And those hazel pupils belonged to Susan Orr.

Oak Hill leaned on Macon County for most social services and ancillary needs, according to any official document. To anybody in town however, Susan Orr and her overabundance of generosity were the sole service provider within city limits. Whatever you needed, she was the one to help. In a similar way that I'd latched on to Nat, there was a tacit kinship between Susan and I.

I sailed past the turnoff to Nantahala Forest trails and inched toward downtown. The northern border of the county stood marked by prodigious loblolly pines and red oaks that stood sentinel in a rigid line. Guardians of the Nantahala. The name's harder to say than it is to spell, and it's damn hard to spell. Most folks in Oak Hill simply called it the woods. I thought that was an undersell, but nobody asked me. Back when my hair was still brilliant blond and not split at the ends, I'd run into the forest as long as my lungs would allow. My cross-country coach would scold me, preaching precision and planning, but I only had one gear, especially in the forest.

The simple truth was that people who grew up in Oak Hill could trace trails in Nantahala like city kids learned the subway lines. The how was irrelevant. Perhaps a redneck uncle took them hunting too young or an armchair ornithologist aunt brought them to different perches to watch the robins and bluebirds whirr into violet blurs. Nat and I did little more than walk, the shrapnel in his knee limiting our pace to a trot, and peer up at the treetops with admiration. For all of his warts, Nat never preached about nature. He let it speak for itself and damnit if it didn't croon.

My sophomore year of high school, I was sitting on Sawyer's back porch when Cliff rode up on his Huffy and hollered about a lost man in the forest. We rushed to the trailhead and watched as search crews tramped through brush and pine straw for hours. They denied our offered assistance but we couldn't take our eyes away.

The hiker, later learned to be named Keith Downey, was part of a bachelor party camping trip in Nantahala. He'd stopped to take a pee while his friends all roamed on ahead. By the time his tank was empty, their voices were out of reach. He never met back up with the others, who doubled back to find him. A week later, a search and rescue team carried his body out on a baseboard. For outsiders, Nantahala carried a mystique that drew them in. To us, it was just the woods. A massive backyard we all shared and loved.

In white block letters, "The Dockery Center" lined the brick wall exterior of the building. Through the front window, I watched Susan tuck midnight black hair behind her ear and grin at something on a computer screen. The moment seemed too authentic to shatter. What business did I have walking in and uprooting everything to ask if she recognized a dead woman in a field? What kind of repayment was that for her saving my life?

Questions aside, I nudged the door open and winced at the clatter of the jingle bell on the doorjamb. "Gracey!" Her voice was sugar sweet, as if she could bottle it and sell it to Hershey's.

"Good morning. I hope I'm not interrupting anything important."

Stray strands of hair poked their way toward the overhead lights, most appearing as gray as the gravel road. Her broad smile, brighter than the fluorescence overhead, almost made me forget the troubles I'd lugged in. "Always with the formalities," she said, enveloping me in a hug that I held onto for a lingering moment. "Everything okay with Nat?"

"Of course. Nat's himself. That'll never change."

"That may very well be the problem," Susan said. "But that's nothing new."

"Sure isn't. I saw you giggling at something on your computer."

She blushed. "Oh no, that's nothing."

"I could use a laugh," I said. "What's the joke?"

"My love life. I've leapt into the precarious world of online dating. Have you ever tried it?"

"Once," I said. "This may surprise you, but Oak Hill doesn't have much to offer. It was sobering trying to decide how many divorces were too many for my taste. The few single men left in Macon County thought that a room full of deer mounts would be an aphrodisiac."

"Sounds like you've gone on a few dates then."

"A few first dates."

"The worst kind."

"You can say that again," I said with a chuckle. "But I bet you're reeling them in."

"I tell you, old men are just teenagers in wrinkled bodies."

"I pray that's not true but I don't think Nat is a great case study either."

"I met one acceptable fellow who I'm considering meeting in person. Although he's over in Chattanooga."

The constraints of small-town life allowed for little surprise in meeting somebody new. Nicole Wallace, a local two years behind us in school, spent a year working after school and saved every penny. Then she parked herself in Charlotte and didn't come back until she had a ring on her finger. The stories took on a life of their own, but there were only a few ways to get out of Oak Hill without a miracle dropping into your lap. Although there was always Sawyer's move. Run.

"Long-distance could be fun," I said.

She eyed me. "Is that what you're here to discuss?"

"Long-distance relationships? God, no."

"I thought because of Sawyer—"

"No," I said. "You too?"

"Margo has a monopoly on groceries. Your receipt comes with a pinch of gossip. Your name sprang pretty quick to her lips."

"I'm not here because of Sawyer. Margo is seeking to scorch my name because I've kept quiet about an incident that occurred last night." I heard Nat's voice in my head mentioning specifics, and swatted him off like a fly. He had a way of doing that, of worming his way into your mind like a conscience that perched on your shoulder. Some days, he was an angel. Others, he was the devil. "I'd like you to look at a photo and see if you recognize someone. But I'll warn you that this woman is deceased."

"Deceased?"

"We found a woman's body on the Sutton property. Indications are that somebody killed her last night. There's a wound on her head, but it's out of sight. Don't worry. Can you look and see if she looks familiar?"

"I never forget a face."

"Munoz and I were on scene first. We didn't recognize her face. And from her clothes, we thought she may have been living on the street or away from town for a bit."

I slid the photo on the table. She raised it with both hands and scrutinized it. Susan's hands were an extension of her heart: warm and unyielding. There wasn't an ache of the spirit she couldn't soothe. There wasn't a cold stare her smile couldn't thaw. Some folks have that power, but Susan used hers for good. I never stopped to ask or inquire about why Susan cared for the town the way that she did. That was how much the Center was an extension of her body. "I don't recognize her." She took another glance. "She may be from another town over. Do you want me to call the shelters in Asheville and Charlotte?"

"That's a long walk," I said.

"Bus passes are easy to come by for support staff. Back when I was working in Asheville, I had a handful in my pocket at all times in case I saw somebody in need. Although the nearest bus stop would still be ten miles from the opposite side of town. Not likely. Lunch is in thirty minutes. You can ask the guests downstairs if you'd like, although it's only a few. We've been lucky with permanent housing units across the state line. And Dockery has funded them all."

"I don't think it's the best idea to show them a dead person's face. Especially not before lunch, so let's hold off on that. I'm waiting for a preliminary report from Macon County. They might make an ID."

"And you're wondering if the timing is coincidental. With Sawyer arriving and now this."

Billy Jenkins too, I thought. I didn't much believe in coincidences after all. "Well, if I wasn't before, now I am."

"Me and my big mouth. I don't see how that would fit, but Oak Hill gets two visitors in one day and one ends up dead? That's strange."

"Strange is one word for it. Suspicious is another."

7

F resh air tickled my nose as I walked out of the Dockery Center and back into the serene life of Oak Hill. Every set of eyes on the sidewalk seemed to meet mine, as if fully aware of the things I'd seen and the burden that I carried. I considered passing around her photo, letting the inquisitive eyes put their wandering minds to good use for once. But I had too much reverence for the dead to allow that door to creak open. Cliff called seconds later.

"Mr. Mayor."

"Cut the nonsense, Grace. Any updates?"

"Susan didn't recognize her. I'm throwing up prayers, but unless Macon County comes through with a positive ID, I'm shit out of luck."

"Meet me at the station in fifteen."

"For what?"

"A few prominent citizens want an update."

"I don't have any more than I did this morning. What do you expect me to tell them?"

"Whatever it takes to ease their minds."

"Cliff, I—"

"Look, let's answer some questions and see if we can get you a little more breathing room. I doubt it'll do much, but we still need to try. If there's one thing a small town does well, it's panic."

"I'll be there in ten."

"Good, they're already on their way."

I placed my forehead against the top of my car and closed my eyes. The wheels were already in motion and I should have seen it coming sooner. Cliff handled pressure about as well as a house of cards and any threats to his re-election next year were a surefire way to light a match beneath him. Six minutes later, I waited in the lobby of the station and prepared for my undoing.

Car doors shut out front and I peeked through the window to see Ethan Dockery and Liam Price marching in. Liam looked like he could still make it through the ropes course at Basic Training at fifty-five. Most folks in Oak Hill treated public servants with an idle regard that kept society afloat. There was little reason to hate or hold ill will, but there was also little reason for grand excitement or appreciation. Liam Price was the exception. The steel chiseled military man strode around town with a perpetual smile that jockeyed with his ivory hair for brightness. People warmed to him. In short, he was the polar opposite of the arrogant, self-interested man he walked beside.

Liam's reputation and appearance stood in stark contrast to the horrors that plagued his past. Once a cheery family man with a daughter at the local school, he'd seen every hardship the world could think up and had his life torn apart. In the early years, back when his daughter's accident was fresh on people's minds, folks would ask him about her or tell him a story from her younger years. Lately, especially since his wife had moved out of town with Sarah and served Liam with papers, nobody had the gall to mention the name Sarah Price in his orbit.

Ethan Dockery, two years my senior, belonged on a billboard for smugness. He and his sister Madison were born with more wealth than they could spend in their lifetimes, yet often forgot that fact while strutting about town. Silas had ushered both his children away to private schools at the ripe age of nine, only for them to return for long weekends and summer breaks and pretend they owned the world.

In recent years, Ethan had stepped up as Silas's right hand, an extension of his awkward body, and in adulthood, he'd become a staple around town, although not always a welcomed one. Madison remained a conundrum, a Disney-style princess hiding in her ivory tower on the hill. She frequented town about as often as a bald eagle frequents the sky.

Ethan was long and lanky in all the worst ways, like a scarecrow that strayed from their field. His toothy grin was the heinous logo affixed to my memory of the job interview the day before. Cliff parked and hustled to join them, his ten-yard jog abducting the breath from his lungs.

I swung open the door and plastered on a smile. "Afternoon, gentlemen."

"Detective," Liam said. "Mind if we bend your ear?"

"By all means," I said. "The station is empty, but we can use the conference room for additional privacy."

In the drab conference room, Ethan installed himself at the head of the table with Cliff and Liam on his sides. I took the seat opposite Ethan and couldn't help but feel like I was in an adversarial position from the jump.

"I take it y'all aren't here to taste our coffee," I said, curious why my accent ratcheted up when talking to locals.

"What's the latest on the body?" Ethan asked, sipping his coffee. Call me petty, but I hoped it burned his tongue.

"This isn't the kind of thing that I can openly discuss with the public."

"We're not the public," Liam said. "And we understand the chain of command. Anything you say here stays in this room. Scout's honor."

"I'd bet," I said. "Y'all ever have a murder on Fort Sherman?"

"Military police would've handled it," he said.

I grinned. "Right, right. Leave it to the experts."

"Grace, you're not an expert," Ethan said. "Neither was Chamberlain, but he'd at least spent his entire life on the force."

"And spent half of that time drunk," I said and immediately tried to catch the words like butterflies that had escaped a cage.

Ethan didn't flinch. "Look, I'm beyond tired. I took a red eye home once Silas learned about this mess. So, let's cut through the smoke. Cliff said that the body is with Macon County?"

My stone wall was crumbling, and I saw Ethan Dockery's eyes scowling at me through the rubble. I locked eyes with Cliff, who signaled that this was a life raft and I'd better hop on. All of that in a nod. Old friends, huh?

"Correct."

"Have you heard from them?" Cliff asked.

"Nope. They said to expect a preliminary report later today. My hope is that we'll have her name before sundown, then tomorrow I can run down the rest of the answers."

"And what about Jacob Sawyer?" Ethan asked. "Have you agreed to let him consult?"

"Sawyer has his hands full. Willa's dying, Ethan."

"Nonetheless, Silas insists that we handle this in a timely manner," Ethan said. "He has concerns for the safety of the beloved people of Oak Hill."

"How is Silas anyway? I haven't seen him down at Emma's in ages," I said.

"He's a busy man," Ethan said. "And he demands we bring Jacob Sawyer into the fold. The risk is too great to not leverage every resource. We'll provide whatever funds necessary to convince him to assist." Ethan bent forward. "Grace, it's times like this that we expect you to act like the Chief around here. Especially if you think you're qualified for that job."

"I'm aiming to have a word with Sawyer around suppertime," Cliff said. "And Grace volunteered to come with me. So, if Sawyer agrees, we'll be ready to get him up to speed ASAP."

"You're on board with this?" Ethan asked me.

I nodded and swallowed the stinging words.

"Liam," I said. "Do you still have contacts at Fort Sherman?"

"Some. Mostly gray-hairs. What's on your mind?"

"Macon County plans to run DNA and fingerprints through their database. I stopped by Susan's to see if she recognized the victim—I thought maybe our victim passed through but no such luck. My latest hunch was that she was from the fort—got lost or something."

"Doubtful," Cliff said.

"Why?"

"If a soldier strayed from the base, they'd realize it."

"Not necessarily," Liam said. "If the soldier was out on leave or not expected back anytime soon, they wouldn't raise an alarm. Plus, if somebody was missing, they'd aim to handle that as discreetly as possible."

"I should keep an eye out for Humvees rumbling down Murphy Road then?" I said.

Liam chuckled. "You only need your ears for that."

"When you join the military, do you submit your fingerprints?" I asked. He nodded. "During intake after you enlist."

"And then they're digitally stored somewhere, I assume."

"There's a database. How old was our victim?"

"Mid-forties, I'd guess."

Liam thought for a long moment. "It's possible. They digitized the system in the early 2000s. If she joined before then, and if she's forty-five, she probably did, then Macon won't get a match. If they find anything on her person that indicates military experience, they'd have to coordinate with the MP for support."

"Sounds like red tape."

"An entire roll of it."

"She had untamed brown hair and a film of dirt on her skin, so it's been at least a few days since her last shower, if not a few weeks."

Liam shrugged. "Top brass are pretty strict about appearances, but we'll see. If that becomes the angle, I can get involved and grease some wheels."

"Anything else?" I asked the group.

"Silas would like to offer a reward," Ethan said.

"That's a bad idea," I said.

"Why?" He gritted his teeth. "That should be your best friend."

"I appreciate you boys rolling in here and offering your help. Truly. As I told Mayor Rice before, I'm comfortable raising my hand when I need support. But in the meantime, I'm the ranking officer for Oak Hill PD. So, until further notice, there will be no reward and no press conferences or anything like that."

"This is a small town," Ethan said. "People will panic."

I locked eyes with Cliff for a beat. "If there's one thing a small town does well, it's panic."

8

L ionel Sutton roared into the phone with such a fervor I hardly understood what he was saying. It reminded me of Agatha meowing as she tore
through her dinner bowl. Nonsense.

"Say that again, Lionel?" I said. "Slow down."

"Somebody is in my damn field."

I peeked at my watch. Too soon for a follow-up visit from Macon
County and too late for any of Tessa's staff to still be hanging around.

"What do you see?"

"Lucy is barking her tail off."

The idea of a pant-suit clad reporter standing in the weeds staring down
a growling dog made my stomach flip. "Don't let her loose. I'm on my way."

I zoomed through downtown, and in a flash, I was back at the crime
scene. There were no trucks or reporters in sight. If I hadn't been in that
very field hours prior, I'd never have guessed that a murder had taken place.
Stalks of corn sailed in the breeze as I hiked out to the clearing, still months
away from harvest.

Blood still lingered in the clay, but only a trace.

Far in the distance, the hazy outline of Lionel's barn rested atop the hill a few hundred yards away. I scanned the property and squinted to spot Lionel standing guard on his deck with his rifle on his lap. Even from my vantage point, Lionel would be hard to miss, but I saw no such mirage or shadow or figure besides him. Just a quiet pastoral farmhouse on the side of the road, miles from the commotion of Murphy Road.

A rustle of vegetation caught my ears. I closed my eyes as it sounded again. Whatever it was, whoever it was, they were directly behind me. Moving in slow motion, I dropped my hand, slipped it onto the top of my gun holster, and counted down.

On three, I whirled around and spotted a shadow sprinting away from the scene. *Shit.* I booked it after them, hurdling over weeds and cursing myself for wearing boots. The cornfield gave way to a barren stretch of soil, but I lost ground with every step. I squinted, but the distance was too great. I never got a proper look at the intruder.

They had made a sharp left and fled into a suffocating stand of sycamore, skirting past pitch pines and dissolving into the maze of rhododendron and creeping juniper that hung low. Nantahala skulked in the distance and I pulled up at the margin. There was no use in chasing somebody into that abyss.

I called Munoz and caught him on his way to work. "I found someone at the crime scene."

"Who?" he said.

"I don't know. They ran away."

"Male or female?"

"Not sure," I said. "But they can run like a rocket."

"Wait, why are you back on the scene? Did Macon County call?"

"Not yet. Sutton called in, threatening to send Lucy out into the field again. Mentioned he saw somebody creeping through the field. I assumed it was a reporter, but whoever it was, I chased them into Nantahala and out of sight."

"Maybe it was a lost hiker."

"Yeah," I said. "A hiker who got lost and found our crime scene. Some luck."

"That's why you're the detective and I'm not," he said.

For a long moment, I sat in my car and watched shadows and shapes dance in the mirror. If my visitor was watching, I willed him or her to return and announce their presence. But I was left talking to the trees. Whatever secrets they held would stay unsaid until I could shake them loose.

Once my heart rate returned to its normal trot, I hiked to Lionel Sutton's place and decided to withhold any mention of my sprint into the flora. Oak Hill didn't allow much patience for doubt and uncertainty. By the time news spread across town, I'd have a truckload of reports about suspicious people fleeting around backyards and silhouettes taunting geriatric residents from the bushes. People want to be part of something, even if it's mass confusion. Most folks don't have malicious intent; they just want an anecdote to rattle off when the topic floats to the surface next year. Sutton didn't strike me as the type to tally tales and spew them wildly, but I saw no reason to take the risk.

"Find anything?" he asked, red-cheeked, with Lucy close by his side.

"Not a thing. Maybe it was a doe?"

"You keep saying that like Lucy doesn't know a doe from Adam."

I swallowed a grin. Few things were more adorable than a cantankerous elderly man defending his pooch like it was kin. I didn't have the heart or interest to tell Lionel that I could never stomach the thought of getting a dog of my own. Not that I didn't have love for them, because I had that in truckloads, but because it didn't make sense to domesticate such a wild creature. Plus, Agatha was more than a handful in her younger days, especially when she was hungry. There aren't two types of people in the world. There aren't cat or dog people. That's somebody looking to start a fight and watch the world grumble at one another. I liked all the animals: the wild and the tamed. And from where I stood, well, humans were the true untamed beast.

"If anybody was here, I'd guess they were curious about the crime scene."

"Lord above."

"Worst case, it was a curious reporter looking for a scoop. But I don't expect they found much of anything."

"And they won't find squat. Except my buckshot in their backside."

"It'll pass," I said. "Things will be quiet soon."

"Somebody killed a woman on my property. Even if the visitors pass, I'll be sleeping with one eye open until you apprehend the person behind all of this. Now, I was patient with the trucks in and out today as those out-of-towners took photos and monitored the scene. I'm not going to wail about their slaughter of my field—I have too much respect for the dead to do that. But what the heck is happening with this case?"

"Look, the best I can offer you is the service I just delivered. You call in anything suspicious and we'll have an officer out here faster than you can blink."

"I can blink mighty fast, Grace."

"Then we'll have to be faster."

I wrote my cell number on a piece of scrap paper from the car and handed it over. "Direct line to me. Anything you need."

He raised the paper. "Cheers."

"Until next time." I stooped down and patted Lucy's head. "And good work out there, girl."

9

As I pulled away, gravel kicked up under my tires. Once I hit the street, Tessa Brown called.

"Bingham?" Her voice was boisterous like a carnival barker.

"Yeah," I said. "One second, let me pull over."

"Safety first, Detective," she said. Her maternal tone dripped from every word like an ice cream cone on a sweltering summer day.

"Please tell me you've got good news."

"You want good news? I can make something up. No problem. They're predicting a cool summer this year—I checked the Farmer's Almanac."

"We both know that's an impossibility."

"If you want my update, it won't be as heartwarming."

"What have you got?"

"Bupkis."

"Excuse me?"

"Nada. Zilch. Nunca."

"How many more synonyms you got? How is there nothing to make an ID?"

"It's not for a lack of trying, Grace. No match on fingerprints through AFIS or DNA through CODIS. No likeness found on the missing persons database—although that lags a few days. Unlike the movies, you can report somebody missing immediately if you file the right paperwork. But there's a period where loved ones assume their missing person will turn up with an explanation in hand, so they wait before taking that step."

"So that may not be useful until later in the week."

"Bingo. So, despite all the fancy abbreviations, it means we've got our work cut out for us."

"What about the murder weapon?"

"Garden variety shovel," she said. "That's our preliminary assessment. In a few days we'll have recreated the fatal blows and can report some basics about the chain of events. Things like the height of our killer. Whether they are right-handed or left. And a bunch more about the shovel too."

"I could run down the manufacturer and—"

"Don't waste your spirit. This bad boy is on the rack of every hardware store in the state. It could be decades old too. Folks hold onto things for a long time around here."

"So the shovel is another dead end."

"And the rest of the report is likely to be too. Everything will be a range of probabilities, but nothing concrete. Shit, most times we get the height range and it's anywhere between five and seven feet. That only tells us that we're not looking for Jack and the Beanstalk."

"I don't think Jack was the giant but I see where you're going with this."

She let out a long sigh.

"Look, I hate delivering bad news. Remember that I'm only the messenger here. And we're not done yet. Give me a few more days and we'll have a more detailed report for you. Sometimes, believe it or not, I'm wrong. We may discover something that makes this easier, but there are no guarantees in this life."

"Can you do me a favor in the meantime?"

"Probably, what's up?"

"Oak Hill borders the north end of Fort Sherman. My hunch is that she is a soldier or ex-military cadet that strayed from the property. I asked a local with military experience and he said they'd know if somebody was AWOL."

"Her appearance and clothes make that doubtful, but I can run it up the flagpole, so to speak. More often than not, when we mention a potential crime that connects to the military, they leave us flapping in the wind while they tie up loose ends that will come back on them."

"So I shouldn't hold my breath?"

"You should never hold your breath," Tessa said. "Especially for the wheels of bureaucracy."

"Thanks," I said.

"Call anytime if you've got questions."

I rang Cliff and told him the news.

"Have you changed your mind then?" he asked.

I stared off into the peripheries of Nantahala Forest and tried to summon my mysterious observer. Late afternoon sun veiled the hickory trees in a menacing tint of hazy black. Trouble had found its way to Oak Hill, and I'd let it in. And as much as I didn't want to admit it, I had no clue what to do next. Still, the thought of staring into Jacob Sawyer's eyes and trying to forget all the nights I sobbed myself to sleep felt like an insurmountable task. But it was an impossible time.

The nagging thoughts and whispers from town finally crept their way into my eardrum. Sawyer was back in town. Apparently, so was Billy Jenkins. Could one of them have returned with a secret? Could Sawyer have changed that much? Could he somehow be behind this?

I couldn't get the dead woman's face out of my mind. It was like a persistent fly that wouldn't relent. I burrowed into my heart for the words and they took a near full minute to traverse my body and make it through my lips. "Let's go see Sawyer."

S awyer's house, and most of the others I frequented as a child, sat in the middle of the northern semi-circle, known locally and nowhere else, as Upper Oak Hill. Nat always said that it started as a joke played on out-of-towners, making Oak Hill seem larger than life. Then, like a gag that runs on too long, it stuck.

Cliff drove from the station and we sat in silence for the entire ride. In the lane next to us, an echo from the past mirrored our every move. A left off Murphy, a few turns and then driving down Wilson Street until the second to last block. Sweat crept down my spine despite the frigid air pumping through the vents. Our bodies are terrible liars.

How was I supposed to approach Sawyer after all this time? How could I tell if this man was the same boy that I once loved? Should I look for traces of his early-morning creased cowlick that stuck out from the left side of his hair like a feather? Should I whisper lyrics to songs we once knew every beat and word and rhythm of? Or play a clip from one of the old infomercials that flickered on our TVs late at night, long after Nat had fallen asleep and shortly before Sawyer's stealthy exit? I had no way to measure the man that

I was about to see. And somehow in between all of that, I had to decipher if he was now a killer. Some reunion.

Cliff whipped the car around in the cul-de-sac and parked on the street beneath the towering magnolia in full bloom. He kept his hands on the wheel. The street stood empty, lampposts emitting pale yellow that illuminated the sidewalks.

"It's the same spot, isn't it?" he asked.

I nodded.

"At least this time we have enough cash for beer."

I smiled. "Billy Jenkins would have paid for me. I stand by that."

"And I'm sure your boyfriend would have loved that."

"Sawyer? No way. Billy Jenkins was never a threat."

"Who knew that you'd later be handcuffing Billy every other weekend until he left town?"

"Let's be honest, Cliff. Everybody saw that coming."

He smiled. "Maybe. But not everybody knew you'd upgrade from the Clueless Detective Agency into full-fledged law enforcement."

I glanced at Sawyer's bedroom window. "Some people did. You gonna tell him about Reyna?"

Cliff shifted in his seat. "Why would I do that?"

"Because you should. And she's his cousin for God's sake."

"I don't owe him that. And that's all in the past."

"Sure, Cliff. Can I check your message history then? I'm sure you haven't spoken to her today. Right?"

"He said we can talk on the deck. I don't want to disturb Willa," Cliff said.

"Me either."

"Ready?"

Questions filled my every fiber. Did our memories still rest coiled inside him? If provoked, either through words or scents or sights or sounds, would they spring forth? Did I hold that power? Did anybody?

I clutched the handle. "Nope."

"Tough," he said and pulled the latch on the door.

When I tiptoed onto the street, I glimpsed myself in the side mirror and cursed. There was no fraction of the eighteen-year-old spunky blonde who ran for miles without end and chugged beer with the best of the boys. My eyes hung lower for each of the fifteen years I'd lost since then. My hair frayed at the ends and splintered like an old board. I doubted Sawyer would recognize me at all.

Cliff walked in his usual trot, his middle-aged gut jostling with every step. I noticed his hands shaking. Nervousness isn't easily camouflaged for anybody. Before I knew it, we were on the front stoop. Cliff rapped his knuckles on the oak frame.

The house hadn't aged a lick. Deep maroon paint on the exterior hadn't yet chipped or faded in its brilliance. The front yard, trimmed with the precision of a barber with a straight razor, rested inside the most god-awful picket fence I'd ever seen. Willa had tried to implement her own form of Aunt Polly justice and persuade Sawyer to whitewash it when we were eleven. I don't think we pried open a single paint can.

When the door swung open, I expected the Jacob Sawyer from the bonfire, but he had changed in ways that time and age allow. The curly brown hair that once tickled his ears was less rebellious and more maintained, like a wild field somebody sheared. There was no cowlick.

I saw a dimmed version of his stormy eyes that once beckoned images of emeralds. But that smile. There was no apt description. Only the tingling sensation that spidered through my veins and warmed my heart. I tried not to meet his eyes again. Maybe that was a defense mechanism. Maybe I was just tired.

But there, in the hazy light of the corridor, stood a likeness of the ghost in all of my favorite memories. The sight of him opened old wounds and cut fresh ones. He smiled, dimples adorning his cheeks, and slid the door shut behind him. "My god, it's great to see you two. Willa's sleeping." He put his hands out on both of Cliff's shoulders. "Jesus, look at you."

"What's that supposed to mean?" Cliff growled.

"You're a walking, talking mountain, Cliff. Now I understand why Pearl named you that. Rolls off the tongue a bit better than Granite."

Cliff blushed a bit and scooped Sawyer into a hug. Just like that, all the talk, all the questions that Cliff had melted away. There were no hard feelings on that cramped doorstep. Just three old friends with too much to tell each other and no clue where to start.

When he turned to me, I avoided his eyes. His nose crinkled creating a canyon that would often trap sweat and salt traveling down his face. The knot in his nose formed a speed bump on the path downward. Somehow his nose, a bridge between two vessels of pure blue ocean water, always caught my eye the way certain songs worm their way into your ear. I glanced at the curl of brown that draped over the lines on his forehead. "Grace," he said. "My god."

"You don't have to call me God," I said.

He kicked his head back and cackled. "And here I was worried that you'd outgrown your sass."

"And here I wished you'd outgrown that damn laugh."

My first lie. Thirty seconds together and I'd already lied for no good reason. I loved that laugh like people love sunrises. How people tend to their pets. For the better part of my life, that throaty laugh was my favorite sound in the world.

"Can I give you a hug?"

I swallowed hard and forced a smile. "Of course you can."

His arms wrapped around my back and that unmistakable Sawyer scent tickled my nostrils long enough to knock me into a daydream. Simpler times. When the smell of lavender and Old Spice bodywash had curled itself into all of my favorite memories. I nudged myself loose and Cliff caught my eye.

"Let's go around back," he said. "This shouldn't take long. I know you're a busy man."

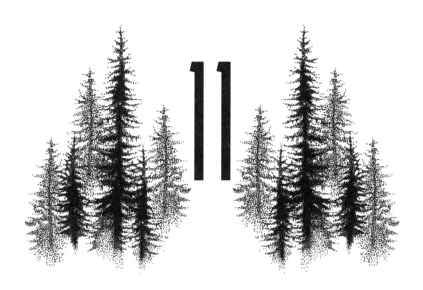

11

awyer led us through the side yard where scrub and dandelions choked the patch of soil that was once Willa's garden. He muscled open the back gate and brought us up the three rickety steps we'd stumbled down countless times as kids. I figured that if I looked close enough, there may still be a bloodstain from my knees on the bottom step.

Cliff maneuvered himself onto a wooden bench that bent beneath his weight while Sawyer and I sat in Adirondack chairs at opposite corners. "How's Willa?" I asked.

"She's fighting," he said. "Thank you for asking. And for all of your care. She mentioned that you two both come by often. And that Nat has been sneaking her takeout cheeseburgers from Mickey's."

"We try," Cliff said. I noticed him look down, a classic tell. I'd come by every now and again to say hi to Willa but it was like her to paint us with her brightest brush when Sawyer was around.

Not that we deserved that in the least bit.

Ulterior motives, perhaps. Too little, too late to save us, if you asked me.

"After what I did to you both, I'd say that's a miracle. I don't know what I did to deserve friends like you."

If that was an apology, it was underwhelming. I didn't sense an ounce of repentance or remorse within him. He had pity, more for his past self than for us, and a healthy dose of pain behind his eyes.

More than anything, it sounded like he'd spent his entire life trying to avoid the exact conversation that awaited him now that Cliff and I sat on his back deck.

"How's the big city?" I asked.

"Busy," he said. "But it's no Oak Hill. It'll never be home."

"Oak Hill is different from when you left," I reminded him. "Home has changed."

"Fifteen years will do that," Cliff said, remembering his grudge.

"Definitely," Sawyer said. "There's so much that has changed, but so much that is the same. I still smell the magnolias in bloom and the faint odor of cocoa from the plant in Moxville."

"How long are you in town?" Cliff asked.

"Indefinitely."

"I take it you're on call for anything Willa needs?"

He chuckled. "She's been trying to kick me out since I got here."

"Speaking of that, did you think any more about what I asked on the phone?" Cliff asked.

"I did," he said. "But I don't think that's my place or fair to Grace. She's more than capable. No need for another cook in the kitchen, so to speak."

"Thanks," I said. "Unfortunately, the higher-ups don't see it that way. Or at least those with sway around here."

"They'll come around," he said. "Did you mention the Clueless Detective Agency on your resume when you got hired?"

"I'm the only remaining member," I said. "So of course I mentioned it."

He paled slightly from my jab. "Can I get you guys some water or something?"

"We'll be out of your hair soon," I said.

"Then, I've got to ask. Is it true Cliff? You married Hannah McCullough?"

Cliff beamed. "Sure did."

"How in the world did you lock down the homecoming queen?"

"Have you ever heard of a shotgun wed—"

"Charm and grace," Cliff said. "But we've got our hands full with the twins now."

"Twins?" Sawyer asked. "My god, you mean to tell me there are more of you?"

"Scott and Todd. Eleven years old and filled with more angst than the three of us combined."

"Wow. I'm so happy for you. Both of you. I saw Reyna at a family wedding four years back and she was quick to spread the news."

"How's she doing?" I asked, just to watch Cliff squirm.

"Fine, I guess. We were never close except for those weeks each summer when her family would ship her east and she'd take up a part-time spot in our group. It always felt weird when the tricycle became a quad, but she had fun out here and Aunt Marie was grateful."

"She's good people," Cliff said.

"We should get going," I said. "Cliff wanted to try and change your mind and convince you to help out."

Sawyer studied Cliff's face. "Well, old buddy, as much as I owe you one, I don't want to overstep."

Cliff leaned forward. "How about I let Grace give you the skinny on our crime scene and victim? Then I can tell Silas Dockery that I did my part."

"Silas is still running the town, I see."

I wondered how that would sit with Sawyer, who saw Dockery work his father to the bone. George Sawyer was the only qualified and competent CPA in town up until his death.

By the time we were ten, George worked for Silas full time. I always wondered if Silas paid his respects to the Sawyer family after George passed. I didn't see him at the funeral. But then again, Sawyer wasn't there either.

"Mostly by proxy," Cliff said. "Ethan and Madison run the estate now. You should see those two."

"Ethan still look like a loblolly pine?"

"More than ever," I said. "Tall, straight, and bony. Madison is a shut-in. Doesn't even come down to Emma's for coffee or breakfast."

"Can't imagine those two running the show. When did Silas pass?"

"He didn't," I said. "But he hasn't been around much lately. Sends his attack dogs out when he needs something to go his way. You know, like the hiring of a new police chief and stuff."

"Got it," Sawyer said.

Cliff stood. "You two huddle up. I'll be out front. Holler if you need me."

He disappeared around the hedges. The metallic clank of the latch signaled that for the first time in fifteen years, Sawyer and I were alone.

12

The inside of my cheek remained pinched between my teeth as I gnawed the silent tension in the air. Crickets sang, too early for their normal show, faint and far off. Sawyer leaned back in his chair and craned his neck upward. I followed, either out of habit or discomfort. Part of me wanted to stare at him for an hour. To investigate every wrinkle in his skin. To trace his familiar body for scars, new and old. But in the persisting silence, we looked at the stars until the discomfort abated.

"I forgot how bright the stars are here."

"Same stars you see in the city," I said.

"But you can see so many more here."

"Still the same sky. It's not like the stars go into hiding or anything."

"Do you remember the question you asked Ms. Callahan junior year?"

I slugged him on the shoulder. "No, Sawyer. I didn't write down every word that came out of my mouth."

"Neither did I. But this one stuck with me."

"What did I ask?"

"You asked why the sky wasn't plural."

"The cloak of youth. People talk about skies all the time."

"Yeah, but it was kind of beautiful. And it helped me when things were tough away from here. It was the same sky. One vast, beautiful, expansive sky. Like a ceiling that we all shared."

"I guess that's a nice thought."

"I spent a lot of time wondering if we were both looking up at the same time. Seeing the same stars. Tracing the same constellations."

My heart rate doubled. There was the Sawyer I knew. He'd transform any banal topic into a deep, meaningful personal reflection on the ephemeral moments of life and love. I couldn't risk that snowball from rolling any further. "Cliff said you're a big shot detective up there. What's the biggest case you've solved?"

"Cliff has it all wrong. I know he's kept tabs on me since I left. He's about as subtle as a rhino. But I'm not what he thinks I am."

"You're not a detective?"

"I am, but before I got the news about Willa, I was interviewing for other jobs."

"Like a new precinct?"

He shook his head. "I don't want to be a cop anymore. When we were kids, I loved every minute. We solved puzzles, even if we created half of them ourselves. Answers were tangible and harmless. There's so much evil in the world. So much that they sheltered us from in Oak Hill."

"Not so much anymore," I said.

"Guess so. What's the deal with this case?"

"Remember Lionel Sutton?"

"Of course. He bought the beer the upperclassmen drank at the bonfires. And he used to wear suspenders to church. Willa would pinch my knee when I laughed at him."

"Right," I said, fighting off a grin. "You once lit a firecracker near his henhouse."

Sawyer's eyes widened. "That was him? Damn. We barely made it out alive. I thought for sure we'd need Willa to tweeze buckshot out of our ass cheeks."

"I've often wondered how none of us ended up in the hospital."

He exhaled. "The invincibility of youth."

"Vanishes fast, don't it?"

"So Lionel Sutton is dead?"

"No, but we found the body on his property. Macon County's team believes that it's a murder scene. A murder in Oak Hill; something I never thought I'd see."

"Maybe an unwanted trespasser?"

"Could be," I said. "But our victim has two head wounds. Lionel Sutton can't make it down the stairs without gasping for air. It's possible that he's lying, but not likely."

"Hm," he said. "Who's the victim?"

"That's the problem," I said. "We have nothing. Fingerprints didn't pop for Macon County. I asked them to coordinate with Fort Sherman but they warned that would take some time. Cliff and I both saw her face and neither of us recognized it. And not in that way where you can't think of their name, but in the way where I'd never seen this soul before in my life."

Sawyer glanced up at the stars. "Jane Doe in a field."

"So, that's where I'm at."

"What happened to Chamberlain?"

"Retired. Bought a condo in Florida."

"Figures. That asshole has Florida written all over him. Who runs the show now?"

"The job is open. You still looking for a new gig?"

"You'd be a good fit."

I swallowed hard. "I applied but they're giving me the runaround because I'm young and female. There's a hiring committee and to nobody's surprise, these three white men have little interest in any sense of diversity."

Sawyer shook his head. "That's not it. There's another layer, Grace."

"What?"

"Chamberlain was an easy mark. Dockery and other locals paid him off to look the other way. Probably why he could afford a condo in Florida in the first place. They want somebody who they can control and your reputation is no secret around here."

"When did you become an expert in Oak Hill politics in your fifteen years away?"

"My dad told me about Chamberlain. He'd always warned me that he was a loose cannon on a warpath. I didn't think much of it until the night of the bonfire. When I was in the back of his cruiser, he looked at me in the mirror and smiled. Between his crooked teeth, he said, 'It's about time.' Like I had been running from the law my whole life."

The mention hung like a hornet in the air and I didn't know whether to ignore it or swat it away.

"I can't believe neither of you have asked me about why I left yet."

I stared at him. "I assumed you had nothing to say."

He bit his lip. His eyes watered a bit. "I have so much to say but I don't think it will do any good. It's impossible to fight against the tide of fifteen years of pain."

I gestured toward the front of the house.

"Cliff hasn't forgotten. The vein in his forehead nearly burst when he heard you were back in town."

"I owe you both so much and I feel like I can't say no to him, whatever his agenda is. Maybe it's a push from Silas Dockery to clean this up fast, or at least make it look like he's putting all of his cards on the table. Although, there's nowhere for Cliff to go but down. But still . . ."

"But?"

"But I owe you too. If not more so. And the last thing I want to do is come in here and blow up your life."

"What life?" I asked.

"Oh, come on," he said. "I pegged you as married with a minivan full of kids by now."

"Who says I want kids?" I asked.

"You did. The night we snuck into Tommy Dekker's treehouse. We planned our life together. Big wedding. Three kids. A house on the edge of

Nantahala. You were worried about coyotes sneaking away with our chickens. It may have been ages ago, but I didn't forget that."

"We were just kids."

"I never felt like a kid though. We were on our own. Roaming around the woods. Solving mysteries. Causing trouble. I never felt like a child. But somehow, being here now, taking care of Willa, all I want to be is a child again."

I had no response or rebuttal. There were no words to address the idea that losing a parent was something I even remotely understood. That's not pain that you can imagine. So instead, I diverted.

"I'm not opposed to a second set of hands on the case. I'm understaffed at the station as it is and I don't want to burden them too much. But if you waltz in acting like you're Sherlock and I'm Watson, you're on the bench."

He smiled. Canyons appeared again. "That's a fair deal. But you ask me what you came here to ask, Grace."

I crossed my arms. "Think you've got me pegged after all these years?"

"No, but if this was a case I was working, I'd want to know if my arrival to town and this crime were intertwined."

"Fine. Where were you last night?"

"Home," he said. "I was with Willa through the night. She had a rough one."

"Anybody who can verify that?"

"Willa, although she was in and out of sleep. And Hannah was here for a few hours helping with some equipment setup."

"Cliff's Hannah?"

"As hard as that is to believe, yep."

"I take it Willa is happy to have you home?"

"She is," he said. "But it seems she's made a list of wrongs she has to right before the day comes and I can only handle so many visits to the past."

"The past wasn't so bad."

"I know. It's not. It's, well, you ever find that everyday things take on the ghosts of things you left behind?"

Every day, I thought, but nodded instead.

"Driving back here was a tour through a graveyard of ghosts. The same old turns. The narrow road up by the forest. I checked out for most of the drive but then, in a flash, I'm staring down the same tattered brown shutters that my father swore he'd replace the entire last year he was alive. I think Willa left them because they'd always remind her of him: his brown eyes and rough, calloused hands."

"That doesn't seem like a ghost. It seems like a memory she needs."

"Maybe. How's Nat?" he asked.

"Classic Sawyer. Dodging the tough talk. I was just giving you space to talk about your ailing mother, but—"

"I'll answer in a minute. How's Nat?"

"He's Nat."

"Could you sit by and watch Nat die?"

"No," I said.

"That's part of it."

"And Willa kicked you out."

"That too. But that shouldn't surprise anybody."

"Something else then?"

"Maybe," he said. "But that's neither here nor there."

"I'll leave it to you to break the news to Cliff," I said.

"That's fair. Where will you be?"

"I'm going to see Willa."

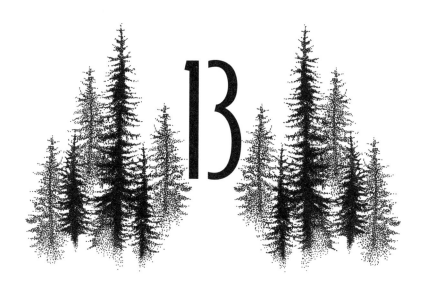

I n fluid movements, Sawyer walked into the front yard and I slid open the back door. Tiptoeing into the hallway, I was sixteen again and Sawyer's curfew had come and gone like a shooting star. I'd waited until Nat's snores reached their chainsaw pitch and pedaled past pines and their threatening shadows until I reached the back deck, stepping up undetected. With my shoes in my hand, I inched the door shut and smiled at Sawyer's goofy grin. We'd slink through the long hallway, past Willa and George's room, and tumble into his bed.

Too young to care about much else besides each other, nobody had an eye on the clock. Neither of us counted seconds or breaths or kisses. At some ungodly hour, I'd bolt back home and slip through my back door undetected. Back in bed I'd collapse with a full heart and fall asleep smiling. The next day, somehow surviving on such little sleep, I'd ignore the curious eyes of Nat and rave about my dreams, never sharing that reality was better than any vision I could conjure.

My mind flipped back to the present. I was not sixteen. I was old and weary and burdened by the weight of the world. Nothing lurked or waited for me. I was a welcome guest, but I still felt like I was on tremulous ground. I inched open the bedroom door and stuck my head inside. Willa looked up from a book of crossword puzzles and smiled. "Amazing Grace."

"Hey, Willa."

"My boy's back," she said.

"I noticed."

"You look tired," she said.

"Leave it to the dying woman to scold me about getting enough sleep."

Willa chuckled, which turned into a raspy cough. "Who says I'm dying?"

"Margo, for one."

"That hag," Willa said. "She's chasing headlines. I always had the mind to plant a story in her ear just to watch her credibility fly out the window."

"Not the worst idea I've ever heard."

"But I couldn't bear the idea of how much that would hurt her. Hard to understand where some people find their purpose, but who am I to judge?"

"Sawyer seems to think you're doing fine. Maybe he's working to disprove Margo's whispers on your behalf."

"That boy has optimism oozing out of his ears. Can you keep him busy? I don't want him doting on me all day and night. He shouldn't have to sit around and watch me fight time."

"Then why'd you call him to come?"

"Me?" Willa grinned. "The doctor called him. I'd told him I sprained my ankle."

"Was he mad? When he learned how sick you were?"

"At first. But did I mention the optimism oozing out of his ears?"

"Once or twice," I said. "I can't promise you that things will pick back up where they were back then. We're different people now."

"In a way, yes. But in another, you're still the same kids that dug up my lawn."

"That was one time," I said.

"And it took a full season to grow the grass back. But I suppose the fallout of a mistake shouldn't color the intent."

"Well, I just wanted to say hi. I'll check in later in the week."

"You don't have to go."

"It's late, and there's a huddle on your front lawn that concerns some trouble that's brewing around town."

"I'm not as connected to the grapevine as I once was. What's on your mind?"

"We found a dead woman over on Lionel Sutton's farm. Haven't been able to identify her yet but it's definitely murder."

She shook her head with vigor. "I'll pray for her."

"You do that," I said. "And I'll try to pin down whoever did it. If I'm capable, that is."

"You're Amazing Grace," she said with a gentle smile. "Who could be more capable?"

"I don't know, probably somebody who has worked a single murder case before. Or a single case. Oak Hill life doesn't exactly prepare you for a whodunit. My few investigative skills have oxidized and don't seem to be of much use."

"I believe in you," she said. "And I wish you'd believe in yourself too."

"I know myself too well for that," I said. "But I do need to ask . . . Sawyer said he was with you all night."

Willa nodded. "Not my finest hour. But he never left my side."

"That's enough for me. Now let me go holler at your son some more. Take care of yourself, Willa. And please call if Nat or I can bring you anything."

"Thank you, Grace."

"With pleasure."

I turned to face the door when I heard her stir. When I turned back, she smiled up at me. "I suppose part of dying is that you get to ask favors from all those you loved."

"Is it now? I don't remember hearing that at mass."

"You at mass?" She snorted. "Like a wolf in the chicken coop."

"I remember the basics."

"You don't have it in your heart to deny a dying woman, Amazing Grace. You don't."

The nickname never failed to bring a smile to my face. Every time Willa Sawyer called me Amazing Grace, I felt part of me believe it was true. She was right. I owed her as many favors as she could summon.

"I need you to do something. Something that may be the hardest thing you've ever done."

"I'm not washing your feet, Willa."

She cackled and when her breathing restored, she dug her hand into the top drawer of her nightstand. I watched her move like she was embossed in water, a slow, flowing movement with purpose. I didn't notice what she held in her hand until she looked up at me.

"This belongs to you," she said.

"Me?" I asked, looking over the crisp white envelope that looked worn and weathered. "I don't recognize it."

"Take it with you, but don't open it until I'm gone." She paused. "It will help you make sense of things. I hope. Maybe not."

I stared at the envelope. "Well, I hope I don't open it for a few decades then."

Willa smiled, but her look was resigned. "We'll see, dear."

I kissed her on the cheek and slid the note into my pocket, as if putting it out of sight would erase it from my mind. No matter the tricks I tried, the envelope would nag at me like a pebble in my shoe. But a promise was a promise, and Willa Sawyer deserved every ounce of my word. No matter the cost.

14

B eside the front door, I stared up at the staircase that led to the second
floor and wondered if it held the same ghosts it once had. Although the
stains were scrubbed away and Willa had bleached every board, they
still held a glint of red.

A tinted reminder of the catastrophic accident that happened there.
Like many things in life, once I saw it from that angle, I'd never seen it the
same again.

I snuck down the front steps to join Cliff and Sawyer in the yard. "She's
a fighter," I said.

"To a fault," Sawyer answered.

"You boys mend fences yet?" I asked.

"I've decided to let sleeping dogs lie," Cliff said.

"Haven't seen a dog around here in ages," I said. "I'm sure Sawyer told
you that I've acquiesced."

Cliff chuckled. "See, what did I tell you?"

"What?" I asked.

"Ten cent words," Cliff said. "When a nickel would do."

"Easy now," Sawyer warned. "I remember how you two used to go at it. Like cats fighting over scraps."

"Some things don't change."

"But most things do," I said. "Because if Oak Hill were the town we all knew back then, there would not be a murder to solve."

"I don't know if we'd have been up to the task back then," Sawyer said.

"I fear you're underselling the capabilities of the Clueless Detective Agency."

"That dumb name again," Cliff said. "Never made sense to me."

"You named us! But that is why you were never a member."

"I wasn't a member because I had a social life and I was busy making friends while you two hid in bushes and saved cats from trees."

Sawyer furrowed his brow and looked at me. "I don't remember a cat in a tree."

"Me either," I said. "I guess Cliff didn't pay such close attention and forgot the time we found the seventeen dollars he lost by the pitch pines."

"I still don't think you found it."

"Then where did we come up with seventeen dollars?" I asked.

"Sawyer stole it from Willa."

"Skeptics. Couldn't win them over if you tried."

Cliff shook his head. "I can't believe you asked Sawyer for an alibi. You really thought he killed that woman?"

"He volunteered it," I said. "And said Hannah would confirm."

"She has," Cliff said. "Sawyer's not our killer. You can cross him off your list."

Sawyer broke the awkward silence that followed. "Cliff mentioned that you had a visitor at the crime scene."

"Indeed," I said. "But I didn't get a good look at them."

"Guess you can't run like you used to."

I nudged him on the shoulder. "I will race you down the block right now. Boots and all, Sawyer."

"I'm retired," he said. "I'd pull a muscle before we hit the mailbox."

"Likely story," I said. "But I don't know what to make of the visitor. Nosy neighbor, I suppose."

"What's your next move?" he asked.

"Crack open a box of macaroni and cheese and try to watch an old episode of something if Nat isn't snoring too loud."

"I meant with the case."

"Same answer. I need to let things simmer. The wheels are in motion, according to my buddy Tessa Brown over at Macon County. I plan to do another canvas of the scene tomorrow and if worse comes to worst, I'll check in with Margo and see what she's heard."

"You could consider that reward from Silas Dockery," Cliff said.

Sawyer shook his head. "That has bad news written all over it. It's too soon."

"Good luck telling that to Silas," Cliff said. "That family is ready to go to war with whoever disturbed their sleepy little village."

"Sutton's house is on the opposite side of town as the Dockery estate, right?"

"Correct."

"Then they should be safe as can be. Last time I checked, they fenced their entire estate in as if they were guarding nuclear codes."

"Same as ever," Cliff said. "When I first ran for mayor, I had a meeting with Silas Dockery in his office. The room was about the size of my damn house. Marble floors. All that. Like something out of a movie. But I'm glad they stuck around after Norma died. Their money is the only thing keeping Oak Hill out of dire straits."

"Everything comes with strings attached," Sawyer said.

"I don't want to disrupt the moment, but I realize that I never had the chance to say this in person, Sawyer," I said. "I'm so very sorry about your father."

"Thank you."

"Truly," Cliff said. "We went to the funeral. Kept Willa company. The town was stunned that you left before the services."

Sawyer sighed. "I was too young to face that reality. Too young and scared to face a lot of things. Willa told me that you two took care of her and checked in after he passed. Whenever she came up to see me at Aunt Kay's, I had a million questions about what you two were up to. She stopped answering after a while. That was good for me. I assumed that you two forgot I was ever here."

"Impossible," I said.

"Yeah," Cliff added. "Who else would steal vodka for us from their parents' cabinet?"

Sawyer chuckled. "Maybe Billy Jenkins. He always had a thing for you, Grace."

"I was hoping you'd forgotten that."

"Keep hoping," he said.

"You busy tomorrow morning?" I asked.

"Willa has a visiting nurse that comes around eight. I'd like to hear what she thinks about Willa's progress, but after that, I'm free."

"Good," I said. "Want to meet me at the diner?"

"That place is still in business?"

"You bet. Emma Barnes bought it. Still officially named Empire Diner but most call it Emma's. Food is as greasy as ever, but the coffee is topnotch."

Cliff snorted. "If you like the gourmet crap. Which I bet you do, city boy." He slugged Sawyer on the shoulder.

"You only get so many free shots, Cliff. Soon, I'll start swinging back."

"Bring it."

"Emma's at eight thirty," Sawyer said. "See you there."

After some awkward goodbyes, I saddled up into Cliff's truck and he dumped me at the station. I leaned through the passenger door window and smirked.

"Like old times, huh?"

"For now, at least. How long until he disappears again?"

"Send Hannah my best."

He sped out of the lot. Under the haze of the streetlamp, I strolled to my car and collapsed inside. The youthfulness that our reunion brought forth exhausted me like a trail run. Too many curves and bumps. Still, there was a beauty in the ability to pick up as if Sawyer had never left. And on the lonesome drive home, I tried to fight my meandering mind's interest in whether he was single.

-THEN-

I REMEMBER WARMTH. My hands hovering over the flames as conversation and chaos around me drifted to background noise, giving center stage to the towering blaze that stretched toward the sky like a spirit soaring to heaven. Sparks jumped, some floating into the sky and becoming stars. For years since, I became convinced that stars resulted from youthful bonfires in the woods. When I looked up, I speculated which ones we'd generated and traced constellations that always came out spelling Sawyer's name.

Our relationship didn't fit the structure of any contemporary ideal. We were best friends quickly devoured by love. That's what most descriptions leave out about true love, especially first loves. It is all-consuming. It wraps its fingers around logic and reason and grinds them to bits. My every movement and thought and word aimed to put a smile on his face. I'd argue life doesn't get simpler than that.

After all of our firsts were out of the way, I worried the glow would fade, but it didn't. My lips were drawn to his like magnets to steel. A chemical reaction. When Cliff would look away, we'd sneak into the bushes and make out or strip to our underwear and splash around in the waist-deep, algae-filled lake a half-mile down the trail. He would take my hand and we'd wander through a proverbial tour of Oak Hill, where everybody stood euphoric, carefree, and drunk. When I conjure those memories now, my mind pushes Sarah Price into the forefront like a spotlight beamed down from the moon and onto her jubilant face. Her bouncing curls backlit by the glow from lightning bugs. She'd sip her beer, foam tumbling over the edges, and dance to songs I can't bear to listen to anymore. Billy Jenkins stumbled with his step. Emma Barnes made eyes at Nate McGuire. All was right. All was normal. I thought it could last forever.

A pop sounded, soon followed by a sizzle and a flash of brilliant light in the sky. We all looked up in delight, reveling in the spark of yellow and white on the star's stage. The spectacle continued on for some time. Maybe ten minutes. Maybe thirty. Nobody spoke. We stared upward until our necks were sore.

Somebody handed a Roman candle to Cliff, who shoved it into my hand. I'd never seen the kind, never been one for the dramatic display that fireworks brought, instead preferring the spark in the eye of the boy next to me. Still, I knew how it worked. I observed Billy Jenkins, who lit one in his hand and hoisted it upward. The pop exploded out of his hand and he cackled with delight. Sawyer leaned in close, wrapped my hand around his, and we did the same.

When the spark hit, a burst of heat bit both our hands. We let the firework fall to the ground. Cliff stamped out the ash with his feet. "You idiots," Cliff said. "Supposed to put those in the ground."

"Live a little," I scolded Cliff. He raced off in a huff.

When I think back to that night, to the bursts of color in the sky and the heat between our hands, I realize I should have known. A subtle warning from fate that if I held onto this magical thing too tight, I'd get burned. But if I let it shudder and rattle and have its moment, there may just be a flash of beauty.

In the fifteen years since that night, I've heard the story from just about everybody who was there. I've run through the same list of attendees that gave statements to the police and their parents. The same list that fell on a spectrum from suspect, to bystander, to victim. Every single name on that list represented somebody whose path changed because of what happened. It may have been minor, like the flap of a bird's wings in the scrub, but it rippled through our lives, especially my own. There wasn't a day I didn't think of that night or Sarah Price or the terrible things we heard.

Nobody remembered who first heard them approach. It just happened. Like the Big Bang or whatever disturbed the dinosaurs, nobody saw it coming. The whine of sirens. A cacophony of voices. Panic pushed through the floodgates. The crowd scattered like cockroaches in light, except everybody escaped into the untamed wilderness that encircled the clearing. Lost to the world. We're lucky everybody came back—in one form or another.

I don't remember running. I don't have any memory of my legs kicking up and forcing my body away from the inferno. But I fled. Sawyer's sweat-stained T-shirt became the map to my freedom. I followed his every move. When he halted, he pointed toward a fallen trunk that smelled of rot. We knelt behind it. Sawyer's head cocked back and studied the tree line.

"Where's Cliff?" Sawyer asked.

"I don't know. I saw him at first and—"

"I'm going to go find him."

"Wait," I begged.

Sawyer paused just long enough to turn back, kiss me hard, and bolt out of sight. It would be the last time we'd perform the sacred act. The last time I had his taste on my tongue, left to sip it for the next fifteen years. Even if I'd boxed it and preserved it with all my might, it would never have been enough. We never know how close the end is. We never feel the fire beneath our feet until it's burning.

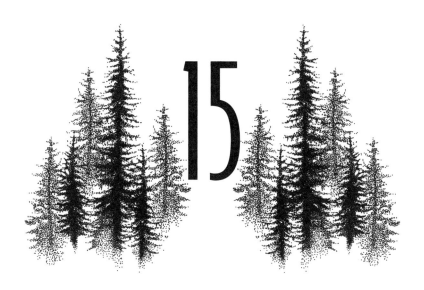

15

The next morning came swift and fierce. Nat clanked pots in the kitchen and I nudged Agatha out from the crook of my arm and hopped in the shower. The smell of sweet coffee, Nat's magical elixir, slithered into the cloud of steam and coaxed me out. I buttoned up dark jeans and snagged a plaid red button down from the closet, sniffing it more than once to make sure it didn't stink.

"You sure look nice," Nat said from the kitchen counter.

"I've got a hot date with justice," I said.

"Coffee?"

"I need to stop by Emma's."

"My coffee isn't good enough for you?"

Someday I'd find the heart to tell him that adding a pinch of nutmeg to his brew didn't qualify as a special recipe. But we sacrifice for those that sacrifice for us.

"Hey now," I said. "You'll live."

"How's the case?"

"No name of the victim. No suspects. A bunch of dead ends. But I saw Willa last night."

That perked Nat's ears. "Oh yeah? How's she?"

"Fighting," I said.

"Good. And Sawyer?"

"He's fine. The city hasn't altogether broken him, from what I gather. Although I did have to check his whereabouts on the night of the murder. Just to be safe."

"It's a reasonable ask," Nat said. "People change. Sometimes it's right before your eyes. Sometimes it's all the way off in Philadelphia. I take it he's accounted for?"

"Twice over, so I've agreed to let him look at the crime scene and the report I'll get from Macon."

"Good."

"That's it? No warnings for me to heed? No fatherly advice?"

He shrugged. "I'm not your father and you've had about enough of my advice."

I kissed him on the cheek. "You are my father. Blood is just a liquid. You are my kin."

He rolled his eyes as I left. Nat had refused paternal labels since I was knee high. I don't know which locals shook their finger at him for adopting a wayward child, but he'd let it slip that there were a few. In my firsthand account, Nat was the best and only parent I'd ever had, no matter if he was there when I took my first breath or not. We shared a last name, and I didn't take that lightly. Most days, Bingham was a badge of honor that I wore with more honor than the shield of OHPD.

Murphy Road in Oak Hill was one of those blink-and-you'll-miss-it spots. There are plenty of storefronts, most standing as relics of the past with family names affixed to the entryway, but few still rest in those hands. Like the rest of the country, Oak Hill fell victim to low-quality yet low-price options and half the town turned to the Walmart in Moxville instead of Margo's or Lieber Hardware. Loyalty was a price paid only by those that could afford it.

A decade prior, Empire Diner fell into disrepair. Grime and dust speckled the shiny brass door that marked its entryway. The menu fell off, and the cooks got lazy. When the owners walked away, the beloved Emma Barnes took the reins and never flinched at any of the criticism. If you ask Margo, she may think Emma was deaf.

Emma, a former Oak Hill High student just a year older than me, hadn't aged in the past fifteen years. Her deep brown eyes were as vibrant as back in her teenage years and she wore the faint outline of crow's feet with a likelihood of making it fashionable. The station rested a block away from Emma's, so Munoz, myself, and even Chamberlain, when he was sober enough, did our part to keep them afloat. Some more than others.

I walked through the front door and Emma Barnes looked up from the counter with a pen and a notepad. "Grace, if Nat finds out you're here for coffee, he'll gnaw a hole in the wall."

"He knows, and he's already chewed my ear."

"To what do I owe the early pleasure? Gretchen isn't in until eleven, so your BLT isn't quite on the menu yet."

"I'm actually here to arrest her. Did you know that she only put two slices of bacon on my sandwich last Tuesday? Two."

"Times are tough," Emma said with a delicate shrug.

"For her, they're about to get really tough."

Emma slid a mug of steaming coffee my way. "Margo has been talking."

"I didn't know you started listening to Margo. You forget your earplugs?"

"Any of it true?"

"Probably not, but depends what you mean."

"A dead woman on Lionel's fence line?"

I didn't move a muscle.

"But no name?"

"We're working on it."

"We?" she asked.

"You see anybody pass through town that doesn't belong?"

Emma flipped a switch on the coffee pot. "Nobody comes to mind. Bertha Hawkins was in here yesterday whispering loudly with Margo about Billy Jenkins, although I'm starting to think he's like our local bogeyman. It won't be long before parents are telling their kids that if they don't finish their chores, Billy Jenkins might visit them in their sleep."

"I heard he may be in town. But what about women? Anybody new stop in?"

"Same old crowd," Emma said. "This dead woman, she's not a local?"

"Seems that way."

"Huh," Emma said. "The only folks that stumble through those doors without an Oak Hill address are from Sherman. And that's made obvious by their tacky uniforms. But I'll keep my ears open. You know how people around here are. Although, one other stranger comes to mind."

I leaned in. "Who?"

"Is it true that Jacob Sawyer is back in town?"

"He's taking care of Willa."

Emma paused and leaned in close. "Then why is he walking through my front door right now?"

16

The bell chimed, and I whirled around to see Sawyer strut in with a black notebook tucked under his arm.

"Morning."

"Hi there, have we met?" Emma said with a grin.

His eyes widened and his smile dimmed the lights of the room. I had a hard time taking my eyes off the stubborn patch of hair sticking up from the back of his skull. I hid my smile.

"Well, Emma Barnes. It sure has been a minute," Sawyer said.

"Your math is a bit off if you think it's just been a minute."

"Blame Miss Dickens."

"It's rude to speak ill on the dead," I said.

Sawyer's eyes bulged. "I didn't even think about that. Oh, no. Miss Dickens passed?"

Emma laughed from the kitchen. "Only ten years ago, Sawyer."

"She was as old as the sidewalks."

"Geez," Sawyer said. "I should go write calculus equations on her gravestone. I hope she still accepts late homework."

I tried so hard not to let that seep through, but I couldn't help but laugh.

"Can I get you something?" Emma asked.

"Your coffee is famous around here," Sawyer said.

"Coming right up." She disappeared into the rear of the building.

Sawyer inspected the empty diner. "This place is a ghost town."

"Oak Hill, North Carolina," I said. "Where time moves like molasses until somebody winds up dead. Then everybody wants instant answers."

"Right," he said. "Look, I don't want to step on any toes but I'd be interested in seeing the crime scene."

"Sure," I said. "I want to ask Lionel Sutton if he saw anything weird overnight anyway. Maybe my mystery spectator stumbled back out of the Nantahala."

Emma arrived, handed Sawyer a mug, and leaned on the counter. "How's Willa?"

"She's fighting," he said. "The nurse said she is strong as ever."

"Damn right," Emma said. "That's the Willa I know and love. Swing by later and I can put together her usual lunch order to go. On the house."

"I appreciate it," he said.

I eyed the door.

Timing had never been Sawyer's strong suit but if Margo or Helen or any other wandering soul caught a glimpse of us sipping coffee and catching up, well, there was no silver lining to that cloud.

"Mind making these to go?" I asked, nodding toward the mugs.

Emma scoffed. "So much for the pleasure of my company."

Ten minutes of awkward conversation later, I led Sawyer through Lionel Sutton's field. We ducked under crime scene tape and I halted. "This is where we found her," I said. "The cornstalks were higher, but Macon County must've cleared it out to scan for evidence."

"She was face up?"

I slid out my phone, swiped to the photo, and handed it over.

"I should warn you that this is graphic. But I took it to show Susan."

"Susan Orr?"

"Yeah, she still runs the Dockery Center. It's grown since you left. It has short-term housing and rehab services for those in need. It's incredible, but it appears Mrs. Doe never came through."

He tapped the phone and smiled. "And who is this?" He pointed to my wallpaper, a photo of Agatha. "Did you become a cat lady, Grace?"

"I have one cat and her name is Agatha."

"No comment," he said.

"One cat does not make you a cat lady."

"Where does she sleep?"

"No comment," I said.

The blaring ring of my cell phone disturbed the moment. Munoz's name flashed across the screen. "What's up?" I asked.

"Just got a call from Margo. She says somebody just robbed the store."

"Crap. Secure the scene, then take her statement."

Sawyer watched my face transform. "Everything okay?"

"No," I said. "Somebody broke into Margo's. Since I'm your ride, you'll have to tag along."

"Perfect," he said.

As we veered back onto Old Murphy Road, Sawyer stared out the window. "When's the last time there was a robbery in Oak Hill?"

"Before we were born," I said.

"Weird."

"That's one word for it."

"You think it's related to the murder," he said.

"One and one makes two."

"It also makes eleven."

I rolled my eyes. "Down here, there's no such a thing as coincidence. The entire town was already up in arms thanks to Margo's big mouth. This will only make things worse."

Minutes later, we parked in front of Margo's store, behind the idling cruiser Munoz left by the curb. Margo leaned against the storefront with a cup of water. Her hand shook as we neared. "You all right?" I asked.

"I will be."

"Where's Munoz?"

"Inside," she said. "Looking for any evidence he left behind."

"It's a he?"

"Ain't no doubt."

"Want to walk us through it?"

She stared up at Sawyer and smiled. "Hi Jacob. Did you find your medicine?"

"Hi Margo," he said. "I did, thank you."

I shot Sawyer a look. If he was with Willa all night, when did he find time to drive downtown and pick up medicine?

"Tell Willa that whatever she needs from the store is on the house. You hear?"

"Mighty kind of you," he said.

I pulled out a notepad as Munoz emerged from the store. "Anything?"

He shook his head. "Nothing useful. I can't even tell what they stole."

"Margo, even if you already told Munoz, mind walking me through it?"

"I opened at ten, a few customers came through. Lots of folks talking about the incident out on the Sutton property. Anyway, maybe half past the hour, the bell chimed, and I looked up but didn't see anybody inside. Then I heard a rustling in the canned food aisle. I worried that a stray dog had wandered in. We'd had that happen in '08 and it took four hours to get the mutt out of the store."

"But this wasn't a dog?"

"No, when I rounded the corner and looked down the aisle, a very human face looked up at me. Messy hair, filth on his face. He had armfuls of fruit, chips, and some pasta. I hollered, and he bolted for the door."

"No attempt at the register?"

"No," she said. "In and out. Like a professional."

"Did you recognize him?" I asked, hoping Margo might catch my leading question.

"No," Margo said. "Never seen him before."

For once, Billy Jenkins was in the clear. Maybe he was just Oak Hill's bogeyman.

"But I saw his face plain as day," Margo continued. "When I saw his eyes, I saw madness. It was animal-like. It sent shivers up my spine. He looked so out of place, maybe because he was so young."

"Young?"

Margo nodded. "It was a boy."

17

One of the benefits of life in a small town was that you knew everybody's warts. But then again, what sliver of our selves we let society see rarely matches the iceberg beneath the water. Still, when I pictured the culprit of the bloody crime scene in the field, the furthest thing from my mind was a child. There had to be more to the equation that I hadn't yet discovered.

"A boy?" Sawyer asked.

"He was in rough shape."

"What kind of rough shape?"

"He was filthy. With hair all over the place. His clothes were ratty too."

I glanced at Munoz, then put a hand on Margo's shoulder. "Well Margo, you did an outstanding job. Not everybody could handle something like that. Have you ever had a break-in before?"

"Just shoplifting kids back before I put the fear of God himself in them." Margo let a trace of a smile appear. "You think you can find him?"

"If he's still in town, we'll find him within the hour," Munoz said. "But if he's fled, we'll have our work cut out for us."

Sawyer drew out his wallet. "Can I pay for what he took?"

Margo stared at him. "Why? Is the boy your son?"

"No. But when Grace tracks the kid down, I'll get my twenty bucks back and we'll be square."

She crumbled the twenty from Sawyer in her hand. "Did he kill that woman?"

"What makes you ask that? Was there blood on him?" he asked.

"Not that I saw," she said. "But I didn't get a full view. Just . . . what are the odds?"

"The best way for us to uncover the truth is to track down the burglar," I said. "I like to think there's a simple explanation for everything. Maybe he stole food because he was hungry. Maybe he has family to feed somewhere. Either way, we'll be on it until we figure out what is going on. Don't you worry."

We let her ease back into the store, and Munoz agreed to remain around for a while in case our visitor returned. Sawyer leaned against my car and watched while I peeked around the rear of the store and investigated the adjoining vacant storefronts.

"Find anything?" he asked.

"Just dust bunnies and relics of the past."

"But you've got an idea."

"Why do you say that?" I asked.

"I can see it in your eyes."

I scowled at him from over the top of the car. "You think I haven't changed a bit in fifteen years?"

"Tell me I'm wrong."

I slipped behind the steering wheel. "You're wrong."

"Fine," he said. "But at least tell me what your gut is saying."

"My gut's yearning for another cup of coffee, but there isn't time for that. We've got our work cut out for us between the murder scene and this mess."

"What do you think about the kid?"

"I think he's the person I saw at the crime scene yesterday."

"Probably."

"And now I have a good excuse why he outran me. Youth."

"I bet a younger Grace Bingham could have run him down."

"Without breaking a sweat."

"That I believe," he said. "When we were talking to Margo, you shot me a look like I'd spooked you. What was that all about?"

"Margo asked you about medicine. When did you come into town?"

"Four in the afternoon," he said. "Before I'd even made it to the house. Willa called and asked me to pick some things up on my way home. Margo laid into me for confusing her store and the pharmacy."

"Makes sense." Sawyer had an explanation for everything, yet I somehow couldn't kick the idea that he wasn't telling me the full truth. "Thanks for clarifying."

"Sure thing. So, where to?"

"Dockery Center. I asked Susan if she'd seen our victim, but she may know of this boy. She's my go to for everything unknown. When I worked there, I realized she had the answer to everything."

"Willa mentioned that. What'd you do there?"

"Whatever she needed. Some days, I cleaned the kitchen so the cooks could go home early and see their families. Others, I swept and mopped the floors. Sometimes I checked people into the shelter and made sure they had everything they needed."

"Did you like it?"

"I loved it. It was the first time I felt like I played an important role in this town. Almost as if I was no longer a bystander but instead had been asked to jump in and get my hands dirty. There's so much need in this world. After a year, it was hard not to feel like my impact was just a drop in the bucket."

"The butterfly effect."

I shrugged. "I don't know how Susan does it. I could only bear so much time trying to mend the souls of the needy."

"You always had that nature to you."

"Maybe," I said. "But Nat fostered that. When he adopted me, he instilled a certain amount of appreciation for those in need. After all, they're my brethren."

"You're a good one, Bingham."

"It's nice to know that Willa passed along updates about our lives down here from time to time. Whenever she'd leave town to visit you up north, she'd return and never utter a word or mention of your new life."

He slouched in his seat and glanced out the window. "I know," he said. "I think it was to protect you all."

"Protect us?"

"I didn't know how one sided it was until recently. Death's premature knock on her door has made her a geyser of information I never knew."

"Such as?"

"Well, for example, I assumed you and Cliff knew all about my days in college and the police academy. It broke my heart when I learned she pretended I didn't exist once I left Oak Hill."

"It wasn't like that," I said.

"I wanted to say goodbye."

"Why didn't you?"

"Willa didn't give me the option. It's a long story."

"We've got time," I said.

"I'm not sure it matters anymore," he said. "Willa controlled the narrative and protected me in some twisted way she felt was necessary."

"What are you trying to say?"

"That there are a lot of skeletons in my closet. And Willa guarded the door like her life depended on it."

"Nat would do the same."

"I hope to see Nat before I go back," Sawyer said.

The acknowledgment of him leaving again awoke the volcano in my heart and it roared. "We'll have to make that happen. He was asking for you."

I shifted the car into park and unbuckled my seatbelt.

"You can come in. Susan won't bite."

"I don't want to step on your toes and—"

"I'll holler if that happens. In the meantime, I'll take all the help I can get."

18

My spirit remembered the linoleum floors of the Dockery Center more than my mind. There was a warmth that washed over me whenever I walked through the grounds, a familiarity that was bone deep. I was too young to recall my early days in the Center. Too overwhelmed by the bright lights and cooing adults to stamp the memory into my brain. But the memory exists. I felt it in the floating grace that followed in a wake behind Susan Orr as she glided from room to room.

She met my eyes. "Did someone forget to tell me you're working here again?"

"Somedays I wish." I gestured to Sawyer in the plush chair next to me. "You remember Jacob Sawyer?"

"Nice to see you again," Sawyer said with a polite nod.

"I take it you don't come bearing good news."

"Can we talk somewhere private?"

She nodded and led us into her office. In all of my days working here, I'd rarely seen her door closed. Sawyer and I sat in neighboring scratchy chairs of blue felt.

"Somebody robbed Margo's store."

"What? Do you know who?"

"We have a description," I said. "But it doesn't match anybody in my mental rolodex of Oak Hill. I figured you were my best shot."

"I'll do my best."

"Margo described our burglar as a white male, fourteen or fifteen, with unkempt, scraggly brown hair and traces of stubble on his cheeks."

Susan pondered the vision.

"Nobody jumps to mind. Do you think this intruder was living on the streets?"

"It's possible," I said. "We obviously can't know for certain but by the sound of the description, it's a reasonable guess. Which gave us all the more reason to come check with you."

"Right," she said. "I hate to think of the rumors spreading around town thanks to Margo's big mouth. We've worked so hard to house every individual that comes through our doors and yet we still have folks around here that turn their nose up at the issue."

Sawyer shifted in his chair. "I'm still playing catch up on all things Oak Hill. It's been fifteen years since I left town so pardon my ignorance but what does the Dockery Center do?"

I leaned forward. "Let me try and dust off my elevator pitch."

Susan waved me along.

"The Dockery Center was founded in earnest in 1984. Silas Dockery, homegrown business tycoon, urged the town to boost their services for the unhoused and at-risk. With a blank check from Dockery, the town hired Susan to run the show since she'd had great success in Asheville."

"I was hesitant because I'd seen how the locals treated any outsider. But I like to think I won most of them over."

"If not all," I said. "Susan built a foundation that has continued to grow and support those in need in the community. Downstairs there's a food pantry and a suite of studio apartments that are connected to shared services like a wellness center, on-call nurse, and social worker."

"That's incredible," Sawyer said. "You must be proud."

Susan smiled. "There's always more work to be done. Right now, we're at near full capacity for our housing units. They're meant to be transitionary, short-term, but we've only been able to find long-term housing across the border in Tennessee where there are units within our price range."

"Have you had to turn anybody away? Maybe that's where this kid came from."

"We've never turned anyone away. We have measures in place to prevent such a thing from occurring but people are free to come and go as they please. However, if this youngster came through our doors alone, we'd be forced to notify social services at a county level."

"Why?"

"Assuming he's under eighteen, there are different laws for children."

"Can I ask a stupid question?" Sawyer said.

"It's never stopped you before," I said with a grin.

"In my younger days here, I never saw a homeless person on the streets of Oak Hill. Maybe one or two, but they were often transient."

"That's fair," Susan said. "And I imagine your next question is why Silas Dockery would funnel money into a service that wasn't a dire need?"

"Bingo."

"I spoke with him before I accepted the job and asked the same question. He insisted that the very idea of somebody roaming the streets without a place to live broke his heart, particularly when he sat on six thousand square feet of property on the ridge."

"Maybe he's not the monster we thought," Sawyer said.

"That's one thing we got wrong as kids," I said. "Nat always spoke highly of Silas. I know your parents had their own opinions on the matter, but by all accounts, Silas Dockery is a good man."

"I can verify that," Susan said. "And I hate to bundle twenty years of catching up into one conversation but, Sawyer, I'm so sorry about the loss of your father and the news about Willa."

"Thank you."

"She's a fighter," I said, somehow needing to add that qualifier every time somebody made a veiled reference to Willa's demise. Sawyer studied his shoes.

"Look, I've got to run and check on a shipment of produce," Susan said. "You have my cell. Call if you need anything or if you locate a photo of your burglar."

"If we bring him here, how long before the state needs to be notified?" I asked.

"We can hash that out if it arises. I'm not in the business of putting anybody in prison or foster care."

"Good."

"Good luck with the case. I know everybody is itching for an update but let them simmer," Susan said.

I smiled as she left, but there was a difference between the common folk and the lead detective on the case. I needed answers immediately. With every passing second, I felt them fall farther from my grasp, like a leaf descending from a branch before it disappears into a world of camouflage below.

19

Sawyer planted himself in the passenger seat and stared at the building. I wondered if he was picturing a younger version of myself abandoned on the doorstep. The whole town knew the story. It wasn't a secret nor was I ashamed of it. It took years of Nat's preaching for the fact to finally sink in through my stubborn skin: none of it was my fault. My past was a blessing.

Memories still floated to the forefront of my mind if I stared long enough at that doorstep. Chipped concrete and scuffed stone transformed into an important mile marker in my life. Before long I'd remember Susan and Nat and the world that warmed me and I'd let it all out like an exhale that dissolves into the air.

"This case ever gets to be too much for you, just say the word," I said.

He lowered his window and rested his arm on the door and for a moment he was seventeen again. His hairline crept back where it belonged and the five pounds that hung around his waist evaporated. The lightness in his touch, his smile, returned with a vigor. And all of it, all those memories, soured my stomach. He wasn't just seventeen. He was a boy again. The boy that didn't say goodbye. The boy that ran from my words like they were wildfire.

"I'll drop you at your car," I said. "I need to head into the station and harass Macon for another update."

Sawyer checked his watch. "Willa is with the nurse for another hour."

"Shouldn't you be there too?"

"I'd rather not. Too many cooks."

"Are you running from something?"

"More than one something. But that's not going to change my plans."

"Fine. I could use some more coffee if you're willing to hustle down to say hi to Emma Barnes again. And since it's almost lunch, grab us some sandwiches to go."

"What kind?"

"Emma will know."

He rolled his eyes but stepped from the car without another word. I couldn't help but watch as he curled around the block and disappeared from sight. How many times could I watch him leave? On some level, I knew how this all played out. Willa only had so much fight in her. Fate would take over and walk her from this world. Sawyer would stick around just long enough to bury her, then bolt back to his new life. The more time I spent with him, the harder that loss became to face again. We can outgrow so much but we can't quite outgrow our first love. It's embedded in our skin like a tick. Once it has your blood, you and it are one and the same.

Munoz sat at the intake desk and greeted me with a smile. Bags beneath his eyes flashed like a warning sign for exhaustion. "How's sleep training going?" I asked.

"Don't ask."

"Well, thanks for your care with Margo. She would've lost her mind if you weren't there with a steady hand."

"Part of the job."

"Not an easy one," I said. "I know firsthand how it's easier to shrug off compliments and kind words like they're empty. So, try and absorb the goodness people send your way. It only lasts so long." I paused to let the works sink in, but he shrugged them off as usual.

"Any luck with Susan? I have my fingers and toes crossed that we find a simple resolution to this mess."

"Nope. This case is nothing but dead ends. Has Macon County called yet?"

Munoz shuffled through a few pieces of paper. "Not on my watch. Nothing left over from Josh."

"Then it's time I rang Tessa Brown."

"Good luck."

As I stepped into my office, I craned my neck back into the lobby. "If you see Sawyer return, only let him through if he's got two coffees and the right sandwiches."

He shot his hand up in salute. "Your wish is my command."

I lifted the receiver from its cradle and punched in the number for Tessa Brown. Within two rings, a breathy male voice answered. "Coroner."

"Hi there, I'm looking for Tessa Brown."

"In a meeting," the voice said. "This is Blake Tucker. Can I help you?"

"Oh hi, Blake. I'm Detective Grace Bingham from Oak Hill. We met yesterday morning and—"

"The body in the soybeans."

"Right," I said, not wishing to spend the next ten minutes explaining the differences between corn and soybeans. "I was hoping for an update."

"One second," Blake said. "Let me switch lines."

A series of clicks followed then Blake rejoined the call. "Okay, I've pulled up the latest report. Tessa and I are tag-teaming things since we've had a busier week than usual. What do you know so far?"

"Tessa said that the victim's fingerprints weren't in your system and that DNA had come back without a match."

"Right," Blake said. "Jane Doe. Mid-forties female. Blunt force trauma to the rear of the skull was the cause of death. Another trauma to the top of the cranium followed but it was mostly superficial."

"Tessa told me about the shovel too."

"A spade technically. We haven't narrowed in on a make or model but the fibers of steel indicate that it's likely a generic model."

"What's the difference?"

"A spade is flat edged while a shovel is rounded."

"I feel like I should have known that. Anything else?"

"Tessa submitted an official request for a release of information from the military fingerprint database, but it hasn't been processed. There are no promises there but I'd give that another day or two."

"Red tape, lovely."

"Two more things. First, the only food in the victim's stomach was rabbit meat and rice."

"Rabbit and rice?" I asked.

"Since the body was found just past midnight, I'd estimate that this was the victim's last meal, likely a late lunch based on the state of digestion."

"Where in the hell does somebody get rabbit and rice in the afternoon around here?"

"Not my expertise," Blake said. "But we're tugging at every thread."

"You said there was one other thing?"

"Right. This one borders on the strange and useless, but it could be something that cracks the case. There's a tattoo on the victim's upper left thigh. It says 'SII' in what looks like Roman numerals."

"Huh. I'll have to google that."

"No need," he said. "Each 'I' represents a one. But the 'S' isn't a Roman numeral, so that's where I get stuck."

"S Two."

"It's very faded. A decade old, maybe more. There's no use in trying to run that down with local tattoo parlors or anything."

"You ever been to Oak Hill, Blake?"

"Just yesterday when we came to the scene."

"Figured. Well, let me save you the trouble. There isn't a tattoo parlor in a fifty-mile radius."

"I've added the tattoo finding to the report that we sent over to the military liaison in hopes that it will be useful in identifying somebody. They don't log individual tattoos but they tend to remember significant ones."

"I'm going to guess that's a dead end too. Who knows what colleague has a tattoo on their upper left thigh?"

"Either way," Blake said. "Tessa or I will call with anything else. End of day tomorrow, we'll release our full report but you've already heard the gist."

"Thanks, Blake."

As I hung up, Sawyer stepped into the office with two coffees stacked on one another and a crinkled paper bag. "Your security guard inspected my sandwich."

"Better him than me," I said. "I was worried you'd pull some bacon off my BLT."

"Emma asked me to tell you that this is a peace offering from Gretchen."

I snatched the sandwich from his hand and unwrapped the foil. When I lifted the bread, I noticed two full layers of bacon, eight pieces total. "Offering accepted."

"What's the latest from Macon County?" Sawyer asked.

"I'll fill you in over lunch," I said, moving a chair to the other side of my desk. "Now let me get ahold of that coffee."

After I updated Sawyer, I plunged into the bowels of the internet looking for a clue on our boy. Stories of feral children and vagrants surfaced within seconds of my search. The most famous among them were the young brothers that emerged from the brush in northern Canada, only to be found out by an international news report that exposed them as spoiled runaways.

None of the incidents were starkly dissimilar to our mess in Oak Hill yet somehow none of it fit. The boy showed no indications of malice or danger. His desperate thievery at Margo's could be explained by the most basic of human needs: hunger. A greedy pilferer would have taken more or robbed the register or harmed Margo on his way out. But he bolted for the brush and a return to normalcy. I couldn't entirely say I blamed him.

Caffeine pulsed through my blood like medicine and I slowly felt energized. Sawyer chomped away at his sandwich as he pondered in silence.

"What do you think?" I asked.

"Rabbit and rice sounds disgusting."

"The better question is where in the hell did she get that."

"Maybe a fancy date in Asheville or Charlotte and on the way home, the killer stops in Oak Hill and murders the victim."

"So Oak Hill would just be a stop along the way."

"Maybe," he said. "But you're not getting a meal like that anywhere around here unless Oak Hill changed more than I could imagine."

"Putting that aside . . ."

"Not much to work with."

"That's being generous. We're basically at square one."

"Unless the kid is connected," Sawyer said. He sat up straighter in his chair and nodded toward the door. "Jesus, is that Mr. Price?"

"Liam?"

"Looks like him. He's marching through the parking lot on his way here. He looks like he's hardly aged."

I wiped crumbs from the table and tossed the foil wrapper into the trash. "He's been helpful."

"He's friendly with the cops after everything that went down with Sarah?"

I shrugged. "Like I said, he's been helpful."

The double doors of the front burst open and Liam rushed through. Munoz gave me a look as he blurred passed. "Hey Liam," I said.

"What's your plan of attack?" Liam asked.

"Attack?" I motioned for him to sit. "What do you want me to attack, Liam?"

"You've got an outsider wreaking havoc in Oak Hill, Detective."

"Havoc is a bit extreme, don't you think? For all we know this is a hungry kid that was passing through."

"There is another explanation," Sawyer said.

Liam paused to stare at Sawyer.

"Liam, you remember Jacob Sawyer?" I said. "Willa's son."

"You went to school with my daughter."

"I did," Sawyer said. "And I heard Sarah passed. I'm sorry for your loss."

Liam didn't react.

He turned back to me like nobody just mentioned his daughter's name in any form. "Willa always had good things to say about her son."

"All lies," I said in a desperate attempt to break the tension. "But go on, Sawyer. Let's hear your explanation."

"Well, look at it this way: For the first time in a long while, there's a dead woman in Oak Hill. Not just dead but murdered. And now we have a kid running around breaking into the grocery store."

"It's reasonable to assume the two incidents are related," I said. "But how?"

Liam stared at me. "C'mon Grace. Half the town has already made the very conclusion you're avoiding."

"Which is?" Sawyer asked.

"This vagrant boy killed that woman."

"Maybe. But there's just as good of a chance that this boy is related to the victim."

"What makes you say that?" Liam asked.

"Both were described as grimy and a bit unkempt."

"To be fair, I once walked into Margo's because I ran out of coffee and she told me I looked like death's cousin," Liam said. "I don't know if I trust her descriptions."

"I'm not saying that we should eliminate the possibility that this boy is our killer. Much the opposite. But what if he was with the woman when she was killed?"

"Then he'd be able to identify our killer," Sawyer added.

Liam leaned back and blew out a long breath. "Both scenarios are piss-poor."

"But it's clear that the answers rest with the boy," I said.

"Well, I had a plan to flush him out. If you're interested," Liam said.

"I'm open to suggestions."

"The boy is hungry, right?"

"He ran off with a decent haul from Margo's, so I don't know if he's still hungry now."

"When I was in the service, I took pride in the diversity of my unit. Not just men and women but where they'd come from. The joke is that there are only four kinds of people that join the military. There's a handful that have it in their blood; it's the family business. Others are desperate for a job; they'll do whatever it takes for a paycheck and stability. Then there are the natural born killers trying to find a legal means to slaughter. And last, there are those willing to live and die for their country."

"Are you saying you think the boy is military?" Sawyer asked.

Liam shook his head. "I had a sergeant once who told me a lesson about wanting. She was one that needed a job and a means to provide for her family. She grew up hungry and looking for a way out. And she told me that once you get that hunger inside you, there's a constant nagging feeling that you will always need more."

"So you think he'll be back for more."

"Maybe. But I think if we want to bring him to town on our terms, we set a trap."

"A trap?" Sawyer asked. "This is a child, not a rat."

"It's humane," he said. "We know that he's had eyes on Margo's before. She said he came in through the back door, right?"

"Right."

"Let's have her toss some perfectly good scraps out there and see if we can lure him back."

"I don't know about this," I said. "I'm with Sawyer. There are ways to treat him like a human."

"I have no ill will for this child. If your theory is correct, he's from the brush. Guess what you can see without binoculars from the fringes of Nantahala?"

"Margo's back door."

"Exactly," Liam said.

"Mind if I have a minute alone to discuss this with my consultant here?" I asked with a smile.

Liam excused himself from the room.

I nudged the door shut and leaned up against it. "What do you think?"

Sawyer pursed his lips. "This is one way to show the town that you're willing to do whatever it takes to keep them safe."

"Hard to tell if you're saying that as a positive or negative."

"I'm not sure it's either."

"We could send a search crew into the outskirts of Nantahala but it would take a few hours at minimum to coordinate a search crew."

"So do both," he said.

"Both?"

"We can post up with Liam and stake out Margo's in hopes that he comes back. In the meantime, work the phones and rally whoever you can to search. Oak Hill isn't that big. There are only so many places to hide."

"We found plenty," I said.

His cheeks flushed red. "You're right. Kids tend to find the spots that adults overlook. But I don't think he's necking with a cute girl in the clearing at the end of the fire road."

The casual mention of our old bonfire spot awoke something inside me. All of those dormant feelings rose to the surface and flushed my face. I choked them down. "Let's do both."

"I need to check on Willa, but I'll be back soon."

"Do what you need to," I said. "We're fine without you."

He took the punches without flinching, but I knew the words cut deep because as he walked out of the station, for the second time in fifteen years, he didn't look back or say goodbye.

21

The sun burst through the barrier of clouds for a whole fifteen minutes while I stood in front of the station and surveyed Murphy Road. I squinted at shadows in the distance, willing them to shapeshift into our missing boy.

All the fuss and formality that Liam would soon bring back downtown was unwarranted and unwieldy. Much to my disappointment, my sorcery proved futile and Liam's truck roared into the parking lot.

"Is your consultant coming back?" Liam asked, a hardly subtle undercut that reminded me of Ethan Dockery's interview questions.

"Eventually."

"I bought a bag of groceries from Margo's and I'll leave it on the sidewalk. She's going to take a bag of produce out back and set it by the dumpster in case our man is watching the rear exit."

"He's a boy," I said. "Not a man."

"Either way," Liam said. "Why don't you hide somewhere with a view of the dumpster?"

"Nothing I love more."

He slapped a plastic yellow walkie talkie into my hand. "Chirp if you see anything."

"I haven't seen one of these since I was a kid."

"You use one before?"

"Of course," I said. "How else do you think we spied on half the town?"

Liam grinned. "I'll bet you raised hell. But we should get going."

"Before you go, you know anywhere you can get a dinner of wild rabbit and rice?"

"I do," he said. "You'd just need a snare and a pot to boil it in."

"Huh?"

"Nantahala. I've had worse meals while backpacking and hunting. That's what my mind went to."

"Right," I said.

I watched him depart and gripped the handle to my car door before pausing. There were only so many places to park a police car downtown and not raise suspicion, especially if our visitor was watching from a crow's nest somewhere. I slipped through the alley and into the back door of Emma's Diner.

The frowning face of Gretchen Klein blocked my path into the dining area. "That bacon was a peace offering," she said. "Not an invitation."

"Offering accepted."

She held one arm up over the doorway and studied me. "You look like crap."

"You know, I was just about to ask what you thought I looked like. Thanks for letting me know."

"Is it true that there's a vagrant robbing stores left and right in Oak Hill?"

I couldn't help but laugh. "No, it's not true."

"But the dead woman—"

I ducked under her arm and pushed open the door. Turning back to Gretchen, I smiled. "Stick to your bacon. I've got the detective work covered."

Emma Barnes looked up from the register. "You again?"

"Me again," I said.

"Now this is becoming a strange trend. Is this about the order I sent back with Sawyer? I swear we—"

"It was perfect."

"Good," Emma said. "Now if only that spread around town like the rest of this gossip."

"In due time." I parked myself in the corner booth and scooted toward the window. "Mind if I wait here for a while?"

Emma shrugged. "Not sure what you're hoping to see but the seat is all yours."

I stared out the window and studied the green dumpster that lurked in the alleyway like a monster with open jaws. On cue, Margo strolled through the back door and tossed a bag of produce onto the ground. Potatoes toppled out and trickled onto the hard concrete below. The sun disappeared again, back to its normal resting place.

Emma slid a glass of water onto the table in front of me. "My father used to have this saying. Never pass up a chance to drink, piss, or sleep."

"Why do I feel like that wasn't about drinking water?"

"Some things got lost in the translation. I blame my youth."

"Thanks."

"Where's your sidekick?"

"Checking on Willa."

Emma put her hand on her hip. "It's a damn shame. That woman is revered in this town."

"A mighty fine human," I said.

"Speaking of mighty fine," Emma said with a grin. "Is Sawyer single?"

"I don't know."

"What do you mean you don't know?"

"I haven't asked."

"Why not?"

I stared into the glass of water.

"Because it doesn't matter. He'll leave town soon."

"Then what's the problem?" Emma said. "Still enough time to make his return to Oak Hill memorable, if you catch my drift."

"Consider it caught."

Emma smacked her lips. "If they gave out medals for dodging questions, it'd be you and Nat on the podium alone."

My phone vibrated. Sawyer. I texted him my location and checked my reflection in a spoon. Hardly impressive. My younger self would have spent the next five minutes in the bathroom trying to coax water into making my eyes pop again. But there was little point in the matter now. Sawyer had seen me at my best, and he still chose to leave.

He strolled through the front doors and sat across from me. "Any luck?"

"Not a creature was stirring."

"Good, then we have a few minutes to talk."

I eyed him. "Why do I suddenly hope we get a visitor?"

"Can I ask a question? It's been on my mind for years but, well, you know."

I swallowed hard. Was I ready to have this conversation? Here? In a diner that I'd made so many pleasant, flavorful memories? Sawyer had already taken half the town and stamped it with his scent. Fifteen years had been just enough time to erase the faint outline of his memory on every sidewalk, street, and fire road. Could I let him take this from me too?

"Go ahead," I said, the words escaping my mouth like cigarette smoke.

"What made you become a cop?"

I flinched. Of all the questions, this wasn't what I'd anticipated. Or hoped. The question lingered like smoke in the air until it dissipated in the light above. "Wasn't much else I was good at."

"That's not true."

I turned it back on him. "Why did you become a cop?"

He stared at me. "The Clueless Detective Agency."

"You parlayed those childhood adventures into a spot in the police academy? I'm guessing you fibbed about our solve rate."

"When we were solving mysteries and piecing together puzzles, I felt alive. In a way that science or history didn't quite match. In college, I started off as an education major."

I considered mentioning our plan to make a long-distance relationship work. I wanted to dig out the calendar that we drew up with weekends that I'd visit him up north and breaks from class where he'd return to Oak Hill. But I'd shredded and burned it ages ago. "I remember."

"Teaching felt like a clear path. But it wasn't in the cards. I joined this amateur sleuth club on campus and found my people."

"Your people?"

"Don't worry, none of them were half the detective you are."

"I hope they were twice the detective I am."

"You still didn't answer my question."

"I don't have a good answer. There's no superhero origin story here. Nat raised me with a sense of justice. I worked with Susan at the Dockery Center long enough to see that the world was full of injustice. Something in my head connected that to police work."

"And now you're interviewing for Chief of Police," he said. "That's huge."

"There's a big difference between an interview and getting hired. The selection committee knows that. It's why they agreed to interview a mid-thirties woman with no college degree. They can check that box and hire some mirror image of Don Chamberlain to keep them safe."

"Who is this committee?"

"Three white men," I said. "One Dockery, one county bureaucrat, and one outside consultant."

Sawyer leaned back in the booth and stared out the window. "And Ethan Dockery. The worst of the worst."

"That family wants to hold their puppet strings and know that whoever fills the role will dance."

"And?"

I narrowed my eyes. "In all of our years growing up, did you ever once see me dance?"

Sawyer immediately went stone-faced. "Look!"

I turned to the alleyway and saw the scruffy image of a boy peering around the corner and heading toward the dumpster. Sawyer jumped to his feet. "I can block the alleyway if you go to the front of Margo's."

I wanted to bark at him about giving me orders but there was no time. Our suspect had arrived and the plan was sound. I bolted through the back door. Within seconds, the jingle bell on Margo's door sounded. I put a finger over my lips and looked at Margo, who went white. I drew my pistol and double-checked the safety.

Approaching the back door, I glanced through the pane of glass and saw the boy creep toward the bag of produce. A shout echoed off the alley walls and dissolved into the clouds. The boy froze, turned, and his eyes met mine. Without a moment of hesitation, the boy bolted away from us.

I burst through the back door just in time to see the boy duck under Sawyer's grasp and sneak out into the streets. Sawyer's body folded onto the pavement. "Are you okay?" I shouted.

"Fine," he groaned. "Don't wait for me."

Before I moved another muscle, a gunshot rang out.

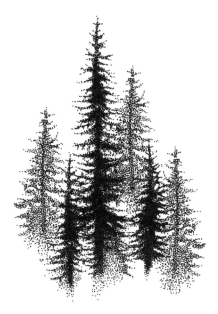

-THEN-

Before allowing time for a rebuttal or response, Sawyer ducked under a branch and disappeared from sight. Frantic footsteps sounded around me. The forest's nighttime harmonies mixed with the human interruption that seemed unnatural and unwelcome. A twig snapped behind me. Panic pulsed through my bones. I flipped around to see Emma Barnes, hands locked with Nate McGuire. She glared at me, then slunk out of sight.

Cliff burst into view a moment later. He stood in front of the log, panting like he'd just run the mile in gym class. Sawyer appeared behind him. I waved my hand from behind the trunk and they both scattered my way.

"You see anyone?"

Sawyer hoisted me to my feet. "We need to keep moving. They're close."

"They're harmless," Cliff said.

"My dad will murder me if I get arrested," Sawyer said. "Said he wouldn't pay for college if I got in any trouble this summer."

"All talk," Cliff insisted.

"We can't have that. You'd be stuck in Oak Hill forever," I said. Hope lurking behind every word.

"We've made it this far without getting arrested," Sawyer said. "I don't want that lucky streak to end on graduation night."

"Who said it was luck?" I asked.

Sawyer smiled and I saw moonlight bounce off his teeth. He squeezed my hand. "Let's run a little more." He pointed toward a faint light in the distance. "I think that's the way out."

It was not. We ran for what felt like a country mile. Decayed logs and spiky shrubs scraped at our bare legs. Sweet gum trees dropped small obstacles for us to navigate and avoid. Sweat streamed down my spine and splattered onto the soil below. Puddles of panic. Perspiration soaked my shirt through.

Cliff staggered and paused with his hand on the trunk of an oak, his gut heaving in and out as he choked down breaths. Sawyer shoved us out of sight. We toppled onto one another like fallen leaves and stared into the distance. The bonfire was just ahead. Shadows shimmered in the waning light of the inferno.

We squatted behind a stand of pines, Cliff to my left and Sawyer on my right. In the hazy light from the bonfire, we watched the police comb through the scene. Don Chamberlain, young and brash, shined flashlights into the trees and hollered. His voice grated my ears like a razor blade.

"Go home," he said. "If you don't go home, we'll take you down to the station and book you. Nobody wants that. So just go home, kids. Don't make us ask again."

Twigs snapped. Kids ran. It was a game. The ultimate moment of freedom before adulthood wriggled in and forced youth to its knees. Sawyer was the first to stand.

"What are you doing?" Cliff barked.

He hissed back to us, "Wait here."

"Sawyer, I—" I wanted to speak but the words didn't come.

"Just wait here," he said, more pleading than ordering.

Cliff and I did as instructed. Our fearless leader disappeared into the night.

I held my breath the entire time he was gone. Cliff belched. I contemplated the shadows by the fire pit, but they petered out of sight. We had to move. Fast.

Sawyer reappeared and, without a word, tugged at my hand. I grabbed Cliff's. We tumbled and hurdled our way through another thicket. Thorns scraped at my flesh until my feet landed on a bald terrain that felt familiar yet foreign. A footpath. One I'd never seen, but just like the millions of others that snaked their way through Nantahala. We hiked in silence for a long moment before Cliff interrupted. "They won't have parties like this in Philadelphia."

Sawyer laughed. "I sure hope not."

"Big city life," Cliff said. "No time for redneck bonfires."

"You'll just have to make time for them when you visit," I added.

Sawyer didn't respond. His silence gnawed at me like a pack of gnats.

"Who do you think called the police?" Cliff asked.

"Silas Dockery," Sawyer said. "That rich prick."

"A prick?" I asked.

"He sends his kids to special schools. Doesn't even let them associate with the common folk. And his kids are spoiled rotten. They think they are entitled to whatever or whoever they want and if you refuse, you're screwed. Besides, have you ever seen Ethan or Madison at any ordinary town function?"

"Church," Cliff said.

"Besides that," Sawyer said, rolling his eyes.

My eyes checked the forest for signs of life. "Nat cautioned me that Chamberlain had an itch to take down the bonfires. I should have listened. He'll never let me live it down if we get arrested."

"And you didn't tell us?" Sawyer asked, betrayal coating his lips.

"You know how parents are. They exaggerate so we'll listen."

"Maybe," Sawyer said.

"I guess he was right. Or somebody called," I said. "Hey, are we going the right way?"

All three of us froze and stared into the surrounding forest. Sawyer glanced back, then forward. "I'm not sure. I'll run ahead and find out."

Sawyer pushed through the trees. In the hushed moments that followed that confusion, Cliff and I heard something that forever altered our lives. A noise that marked the end of a chapter and the start of a new one.

The crack of a gunshot reverberated through the forest.

Followed by a full-throated scream.

Fibers in my legs screamed in agony as I rounded the corner and sprinted down Murphy Road. Sawyer was three feet in front of me and all I thought of was how disappointed Coach Pico would have been after all those long mornings of cross-country runs. Sawyer yelled and pointed ahead to where Liam stood with a pistol raised in front of him. When we neared, I saw a stunned look on the boy's face. My heart rocketed into my throat.

"Easy now, Liam," I said. "The warning shot scared him plenty."

"Got cuffs?" he asked.

"I do," I said, turning to the boy. "But I'd rather not use them."

"Who are you?" Liam shouted.

Sawyer inched closer and examined the boy with care. "Mr. Price, he's scared."

"The whole town is scared," Liam said. "I'm not about to let this happen again."

"Liam, I understand," I said. "But we can all agree to be civilized here." Dropping my pistol back into its holster, I edged closer to the boy. "Hey, bud. What's your name?"

The boy had big chestnut eyes that flitted back and forth. Sweat dripped down his forehead and traveled like a river down the tip of his nose. His eyes returned to Liam's gun.

"Lower the gun," I said.

"I don't think that's the best idea, Grace."

"Nobody wants to have a conversation with a bullet looking back at them. Lower the gun."

Liam lowered the pistol, pointing it at cracks in the sidewalk. Sawyer glanced backward. "There's a crowd forming."

"Shit," I said. "All right, we need to go to the station. Don't worry, you're not being arrested at this point. You're not in trouble. We just need to talk to you."

The boy quivered and shook, but he detached himself from the concrete wall and shuffled his feet beside me as we walked. Liam dawdled behind, no doubt clutching his pistol with careful excitement. Sawyer forced our way through a small crowd of familiar faces that I refused to acknowledge or tally. In two blocks, we pressed through the front doors of the station.

The boy squinted at the harsh fluorescent glow of the overhead lights like it stung his eyes. Sawyer gently nudged him forward and guided him into the bullpen. I nodded toward the conference room.

"Can you bring him in there? Shut the blinds too," I said to Sawyer.

Munoz peered up from the break room. "Doesn't look much like a killer."

"We'll see. For now, I'm confident he's our burglar. But don't go telling Margo just yet. I'd like the boy to explain himself before public opinion becomes judge and jury."

"My lips are sealed."

"And can you do me a favor?"

"Anything that doesn't keep me here past four. Sadie has a laundry list of chores for me to tackle."

"Grab a sandwich from Emma's. Juice too."

"Aye, aye."

Liam scowled from the lobby. "You're being too sympathetic. That's a criminal in there. Everybody is in danger, Grace. Everybody."

"Thanks for your help today. We're always short-handed here, so I'm thankful we could bring him in without anybody getting hurt. I know you've seen firsthand how dangerous this town can be, and I promise you that I think of Sarah often in this job. But this is under my control now. I'll ring you if I need any help or if I decide to dig into Fort Sherman any further."

"Grace," he said. "You need to—"

"It's Detective Bingham," I said. "And I've got it from here."

"I'd like an update when this is all wrapped up."

I grinned. "Have a lovely night."

Liam stormed out as I slipped into the conference room and sat across from the boy. I flicked off the lights and let the faint light that snuck through the blinds serve as our illumination. The boy seemed to appreciate it because he dropped his hand from his forehead and looked up.

"You two friends yet?"

Sawyer shook his head. "We were just taking a breath."

"That's all right. Strangers can be scary. This guy here, Mr. Sawyer, he's your friend. And so am I."

The boy's eyes followed me but he didn't so much as make a sound. I'd heard mice louder than him. As he sat across from Sawyer, I watched for signs of terror. If this boy had seen Sawyer hurt our victim, he didn't show it.

"That's right," Sawyer said. "And we just want to ask you a few questions if that's all right."

"Have you been here before? To Oak Hill?" I asked.

The boy paused for a long moment before nodding his head.

"Good," I said, pasting on a mile-wide smile. "It's not such a terrible place. We've got lunch coming for you. They're cooking it up now just around the corner. But that food comes with a price. We'd like to know your name."

The boy pushed curls away from his forehead. The shaking halted, if only for a moment. Sawyer bent forward. "Do you live in Oak Hill?"

Another head shake. Sawyer met my eyes and transmitted the message. Yes or no questions only for now.

I met eyes with Sawyer. The rabbit and rice. Whoever this boy was, I had a connection to explore. My gut didn't think he was a killer. Not unless it was a matter of survival. And by the timid nature of the kid, I wondered if he was the real victim here.

"Do you live in the forest?" I asked.

He nodded.

"That's a beautiful place to call home," Sawyer said. "I've been lucky enough to hike through a few times and loved it. You're a lucky guy."

I leaned back and considered the next steps. There were many directions to take things, but few allowed us to eliminate or confirm the boy as a suspect. I studied his hands from the table. No blood. Just dirt caked on and dug into the fingernails. He had faint traces of a mustache but little other facial hair. My best guess was fourteen, maybe fifteen years old. If our Jane Doe was forty-five, their relation wasn't hard to extrapolate.

"Do you live there with your mother?" I asked.

Sawyer shot me a look, but I ignored it.

The boy nodded.

"But you haven't seen her for a few days?"

His eyes widened, terror and panic stretched across his face. The scarce color that filled his skin evaporated like a puddle in the summer. He shook again. Nervous energy enveloped the room. Sawyer leaned over and whispered, "We can't show him that picture."

"I know," I said. "I've got an idea."

Moments later, we had a pen and piece of paper in front of the boy. "We want to help you find your mother. So, I'll need to know a little more about her, okay? Does your mother have a tattoo?"

He nodded.

"Can you draw the tattoo?"

He clutched the pen in a shaky hand and drew for a long moment as Sawyer and I watched. When he placed the pen back on the table, I slid the paper my way. In shaky handwriting, the boy wrote 1 1 5. Sawyer furrowed his brow. I turned the paper around so the numbers were upside down. He mouthed the letters "SII."

I swallowed hard and fumbled for the words. How do you tell a boy that his mother is dead? How do you break a heart with care and tact? How do you choose those words? That's not something that the training covers. There's no 101 on devastation and disruption. My tongue became too thick for words to form, like I'd gargled molasses. Maybe the interview committee was right. I wasn't cut out for this.

"Is she dead?" The boy's voice was muted, almost like he hadn't spoken in ages.

I nodded. "I'm so sorry."

The boy slumped back into his chair and wept. When the food from Emma's arrived, he didn't so much as look at it. Instead, his eyes remained fixed to the window as tears puddled on the ground. Sawyer and I sat speechless.

23

hildren required experience. Most folks bump into youthful cousins or nephews or neighbors by the time they're considering a family of their own. But not me. Nat was grown and distant from what little family he had left. The only adjacent children to my life were Cliff's twins and Munoz's pack, and although I had offered my babysitting services on many occasions, I was met with empty nods. So when the boy didn't say another word for the next few minutes, I had little to dig through to find a connection. Thankfully, a stir of voices swelled to a mild roar outside as Munoz pushed back inside and mimed wiping sweat from his brow.

I forced a smile to Sawyer and excused myself from the room. I eased the conference room door shut and glared through the front windows at a raucous crowd of adults who all should have had something better to do with their time. "Damnit. How do they hear everything so quickly?"

"How do vultures find roadkill?" Munoz asked. "Is he talking?"

"No," I said. "But he says he lives in the forest. And that our victim was his mother."

"Holy crap."

"Indeed," I said. "I'm trying to decide if that news would calm that crowd or notch things up to a full-on riot."

"There isn't a sentence you could string together that would calm them down, Grace. Our best bet is to drive them away and move the boy somewhere else."

"I want to bring him to Susan."

"Smart," he said. "I've got thirty minutes until Sadie starts fuming. How can I help?"

"I'll clear things out. Wait here for Molloy and give him the update?"

"Aye aye," he said.

I let breath fill my lungs then pressed into the front of the station. Oak Hill couldn't muster up a volunteer crew to pick trash off the medians, but something peculiar sure drew a crowd. Margo stood with two other women flanking her side, Bertha Hawkins and Helen Poole. Bertha was broad-shouldered and strong with narrow eyes that screamed condescension. The last time I bumped into her downtown ended with her rattling off the reasons that my biological clock was ticking. Helen Poole filled out the third role of the terrible threesome. She was a whisper where Margo was a shout.

"Grace, if there's a dangerous person in this town, we need to know," Margo said.

"Immediately," added Helen.

"We have apprehended a suspect that may have been Margo's intruder. By all accounts, it was an act of desperation, not of malice."

"Aren't all criminals desperate?" Margo asked.

"Some are looking to wreak havoc and get rich quick," I added. "But that's not the case. And he won't be stealing from your store anytime soon."

"Because he'll be in prison?" Bertha asked.

"What would happen if I decided to come by and tell you how to price oranges at your store, Margo? Or if I came by the taxidermy shop and told you how to mount a buck, Bertha?"

"This is different," Bertha said.

"How is this different?"

"Our safety is at risk," Margo added.

"If I have to spend half of my day out here trying to squash the rumors you're spreading, I won't be able to focus on putting criminals behind bars. Can you trust me to do my job?"

"We can try," Helen said.

"This is why they won't make you chief," Bertha said.

My face turned cherry red but I forced a smile. "Everybody's entitled to their opinion. But I'd like you all to leave this property."

I looked at Margo and flashed every ounce of sympathy I could in my eyes. Margo seemed to catch on. "Come on, let's make sure the store isn't in tatters."

The three strolled around the bend with only a few nervous glances backward. Back inside, I shrugged at Munoz. "They'll be back."

"Death, taxes, and gossipers," he said.

The sandwich was untouched. Same with the juice.

"Not hungry?"

"Not quite," Sawyer said. "Maybe we should get him to Susan's."

"I'll give her a heads up," I said.

Sawyer sat with him while I called Susan and briefed her on the situation. As expected, she urged me to bring the kid over to make sure he's protected and cared for. She laughed when I told her we tried to give him a sandwich to no avail. With little protest, the boy slid into the back of the cruiser as Sawyer and I fell in the front.

"He'll be okay," Sawyer whispered.

"Susan is the kindest woman on earth," I told the boy in the rear-view mirror. "She'll make sure you're taken care of while Sawyer and I here sort out what happened to your mother."

The engine roared; stale air pumped through the vents and filled the car. I cracked open my window and fumbled with the radio. Sawyer shifted in his seat and craned his neck forward. Pointing out the window, he said, "Is that smoke?"

The smell of char punched into my nostrils. I vaulted out of the car to follow Sawyer's finger. A billow of smoke snaked into the clouds from downtown. I dug my cell from my pocket. "Munoz, you hear anything about a fire?"

The radio crackled. "Just came through. Nickelson Law is burning to the ground."

24

N at taught me how to build a fire when I was six. I plucked kindling from the ground, stacking it into my arms and rushed back to his spot in our backyard.

"More," he said and I rushed away, happy to have a task to own.

Nat hauled split logs from our woodpile and tossed them next to a ring of rocks. He snapped twigs from the kindling pile and nestled them into the center.

"The little things catch first," he said. "So they're the most important. You did a good job collecting them."

"When do we add the logs?" I asked.

"We start small. There's no wind tonight and it's been dry all week, so we're not fighting the elements." He drew a matchbook from his pocket. "Here, take these."

I held the flimsy cardboard box in my hand and extracted a single match.

"Go ahead," he said. "Once it's lit, move slowly and light the bottom of the pile."

I scraped the match against the strike pad and watched it flare to life.

Inching it toward the fuel, it suddenly extinguished. Nat smiled. "Try again. It takes practice."

The second attempt was successful. I lit the bottom of the pile then whipped the match onto the ground and stamped it out. Nat leaned back and watched the kindling light. When it flickered into a flame, he stacked wood in a box around it and tossed small twigs in the center.

"You built your first fire, young buck," he said. "You're a natural."

"Better than you?"

He laughed. "Not yet."

Nat and I lit a fire most weekends. We'd watch the flames dance until one of us clamored for bed. Early on, I was the first to retire. Later, I was left alone with the cinder and smoke. I only saw fire in those settings. In the enclosed ring where fire belonged. Even at the bonfire pit down the old fire road, the inferno was restricted to a boundary that it didn't dare to cross. But as I stared into the billowing smoke and felt the sting of its scent punish my nose, I understood that not all fires followed the same rules.

"Shit," I said. I hurled the keys at Sawyer. "Take him to Susan's. I'll be there as soon as I can."

Without another word or a second for him to protest, I sprinted around the corner and toward the inferno that once was Nickelson Law.

Bill Nickelson was a local celebrity who was born in town then navigated the state's political minefield, eventually serving as a state senator for the great state of North Carolina.

Once his moment in the sun dimmed, he put his tail between his legs and settled back into Oak Hill to collect paltry sums from the common folk to keep their transactions, estates, and businesses in proper standing. Nickelson grew old and he hardly made it to town.

So, when Nickelson Law stood aflame before me, I faced a drought of explanations.

Fire engines trudged in, making good time on the urgent request and barging through traffic down the road. The team was off the truck and on their feet in milliseconds. Each individual moved like a member of a Broadway play—no bickering over who did what. Everybody played a part and did it seamlessly.

Munoz appeared seconds later and shook his head. "Shit," he said. "Want me to take crowd control?"

I turned to see a gaggle of inquisitive faces in the street. "Stay here in case they need anything from us."

With my fingers tucked into my belt loops, I walked toward the crowd. "That's far enough."

"What's happening here?" Bertha asked.

"The building is on fire, Bertha!" Margo yelled.

"I meant why? Why is it on fire, Grace?"

"I bet it was that boy," Helen said.

"You think?" Margo asked.

"I saw them pull a gun on him earlier!" Helen shouted. "I bet he did this before they caught him."

"Maybe that's why they arrested him in the first place," Margo said.

"The young man is not a suspect, nor has he been arrested," I said.

"Says who?" Helen asked.

"Says I, Helen, and in matters of law and order, my words are the only ones that count." I stared her down. She didn't flinch, but didn't challenge me either, so I pressed on. "Why is it that you insist that this is a deranged criminal instead of a helpless, abandoned boy? Instead of whispers and stories, maybe you could offer help and love. Even a prayer, if you still believe in that kind of thing."

"I'll pray for our safety," Helen said.

"Good thinking," Margo said. "Grace, how can you explain these terrible things happening as of late? Don Chamberlain walks away from the job and a month later, we've had a murder, a robbery, and a building on fire. That falls on your shoulders."

I forced a grin. "I appreciate your opinion. But I'm more interested in facts. Now, you can focus on what's gone wrong or you can help us try to reconcile things and find answers."

"I can post on the forums to see if anybody saw anything," Margo said.

"That would be a tremendous help," I assured her. "Did any of you make it here before the fire department?"

Heads shook, and shoulders shrugged. "Seems that most people weren't on the street. So, Margo, let me know privately if you get any messages, okay?"

Munoz shouted my name, and I retreated toward the blaze. He stood with a uniformed man with a thick gray mustache that curled up at the ends. Straight out of firefighter central casting. "You in charge?" he asked me.

"Detective Grace Bingham."

The man smirked. "Don't tell me you're Nat's kid."

"Don't hold it against me."

"I'm Captain Brian Holderbaum. Folks around here just call me Cap, though," the man said. Charm burst out of him like sunbeams. "Your old man used to mow my lawn. Although he spent more time barking at me about my Yankees decor."

"Sounds like Nat."

"We're still clearing the scene. It will be a little while before we have it secured. But if you're curious about the cause, this one is pretty open and shut." He pointed at a charred, half-melted fragment of red plastic. "This is your smoking gun, so to speak. A gas canister. One of those plastic jugs you can get at any hardware store."

"This was arson?" I asked.

"No doubt."

"Any initial theories on where the fire started?"

"Back room. The blaze moved rapidly from there since there was accelerant soaked into the carpeting."

"I hate to do this to you but can I throw a hypothetical your way, Cap?"

"With pleasure."

"Could somebody have set this fire and run off?"

"They could have," Holderbaum said.

"How long ago?"

"Maybe fifteen minutes," he said. "Give or take."

"And if you were looking for that individual . . ."

"Use your nose. They'd reek of gas. You can't just pour that much without getting the odor baked into your clothes."

"Thanks, Cap."

He tipped his hat at me and pointed toward his team working the fire. "We'll be here a bit, but you can tell the crowd over there that it's contained. We'll close off the rest of this block until we can get an engineer in to inspect the guts, but other buildings nearby should be fine."

"Appreciate your speed," I said. "I'm surprised you got the 911 call before we did."

He shook his head. "Slow day. I'll take a walk over to dispatch later today and see if they've got anything to share about the caller. Probably just a concerned citizen, but you never know."

"Thanks," I said. "I won't hold my breath."

Munoz glanced down at his watch. "Sadie is going to have my head."

"You can go," I said. "Molloy should be in soon enough. Not much we can do here besides wait."

"Don't have to tell me twice," he said. "Keep me in the loop, okay? I can come back out after the kids are asleep."

"Can you do me one favor?"

"Lay it on me, boss."

"First thing tomorrow, can you go talk to Bill Nickelson and see what he's got to say about this fire? Maybe it's random."

"Or maybe it's all connected," he said.

"Bingo. Have a good night," I said. "Let's hope I don't need anything else. But based on how this week is going, keep your phone on. Send Sadie my love."

T hirty minutes later, Holderbaum secured the scene and confirmed that his team wouldn't need Oak Hill PD for the foreseeable future. I offered to wait but he rebuffed my every word. He warned it would be a while before anything useful came out of his report. A familiar refrain. I wondered if he knew Tessa Brown.

A crowd of worried and dismayed faces followed me as I exited but I paid them no mind. There were more vital issues than the charred remains of a law office that hadn't seen steady business in nearly a decade. The abbreviated drive left insufficient time for me to process the events of the last few days. Helen was right. Since Don Chamberlain handed in his badge, Oak Hill had seen their first robbery, fire, and murder in decades. Unlike Helen, I saw little use in casting culpability on the only crusader for justice left in this desolate wasteland of a town. I was just easy prey for the wolves.

The smell of smoke adhered itself to my skin. There wasn't time for a shower, but I kept the windows down to let a breeze rush through and defuse some of the stench. I'd once cherished the aroma of fire in my clothes and hair. Countless adventurous nights with Cliff and Sawyer ended down that old fire road where steady hands brought a flame to life. By the time I'd reached my pillow, exhaustion would overwhelm my body, and I'd crash harder than a rotted pine. No matter how hard I scrubbed the next morning, Nat would scrunch his nose like a dog in the wind as he stuffed breakfast in his mouth.

I hardly had time to regain my footing before walking toward the Dockery Center and straight into another round with fate. Sawyer sat on the front steps. "Was anybody hurt?" he asked.

"Doesn't look that way. But it was arson. That much we know for certain."

"What the hell is going on?"

"I was about to ask you the same thing. You pull in from Philly and this whole town falls apart at the seams."

His face went pale. "Grace, I would never."

"I know," I said, slugging him on the shoulder. "Timing has never been your strong suit. Just thought I'd test you one last time."

He swallowed hard, but had no rebuttal. "Susan is with the boy."

"Let's see if she's shaken anything loose."

We pressed through the double doors and knocked on her office door. She inched it open and waved us over. The boy sat in an orange chair, his foot tapping on the ground. "I heard there was a fire," Susan said.

"Nickelson Law burned down," I said. "No injuries or casualties though. How's everything over here?"

"We're working through it. But I can at least provide a proper introduction. Jacob, Grace—this is Cedar."

The name fit like a lid on a pot. I couldn't help but smile and whisper the name to myself. "Cedar."

He nodded, but his nature was still timid. Sawyer knelt and extended a hand. "Cedar, I'm Jacob but everybody calls me Sawyer. It's a pleasure to meet you." Cedar stared at his hand but didn't take it. "That's okay. You've had a hell of a day."

"Heck of a day," Susan said. "No need to cuss around the boy."

Sawyer raised his hands in surrender. "I don't want to catch hell for it." He winked at Cedar, who let loose a smile.

I ratcheted my voice down an octave and spoke at the pace of a snail. "Cedar, I'm the person in charge of finding who hurt your mother. And I'm so sorry for your loss. That's a terrible thing to happen to somebody your age. Or at any age."

"I'd like Cedar to stay in one of my apartments tonight," Susan said. "Would that be all right with you, Cedar?"

He stared out the window.

"Maybe when you're rested, we can talk more about your mother. But in the meantime, do you know your mother's name?"

"Lark," Cedar said quietly.

"That's a beautiful name," I said.

"And I bet she was a wonderful woman. And a great mom too," Sawyer said. "We'd be happy to help arrange a funeral and—"

"These are topics for another day," Susan said, whisking us toward the door. She edged out and closed it behind her. "This boy is overwhelmed. I understand why you asked him about his mother at the station, but he's struggling to process what happened."

"Did he say anything about the murder? Did he see something?"

"He's said two words. His name and his mother's. It'll take time before he trusts any of us enough to open up beyond that."

"But if he saw something, he—"

"Time will reveal everything. It always does," Susan said. "I'll call if anything comes up, but he's safe here. I'll have one of the residents keep an eye on him downstairs to make sure he's taken care of."

"Thank you, Susan," I said.

I watched the boy through the office window and hoped he'd look my way. I wasn't sure if I wanted to apologize or interrogate him more. Everybody had some secret they were tucking away in their back pocket. Even if Cedar's wasn't malicious, it could be the crowbar that opens the vault that holds the answers. I sighed and let hope fall to the ground. Sawyer led me through the front doors. As we walked, I saw his hand dangle at his side and some animalistic part of me wanted to grab it. To hold it. To see if my fingers still fit in their familiar grooves, like walking the hallways of an old home you once frequented. Temptation faltered and I convinced myself that I felt relieved.

26

We lingered in the parking lot like strangers after an awkward first date until I shattered the silence. "Can you drive the cruiser back to the station? I can drop you at home from there."

"Sure," he said. "I'm sure Willa is already asleep, but I should be with her."

I followed behind him as he navigated the streets like an old pro. Memory has that way of imprinting on our brains and although we let it collect dust, it's natural to fetch those familiar feelings and instincts. He fell into my passenger seat a few moments later. "Part of me genuinely thought you'd still have Yvette."

I pictured Yvette, my old Jeep Cherokee, with the dented rear corner panel and the passenger door that only opened from the inside handle. The fire-red exterior paint chipped away from nearly every bend in the metal. Somehow those imperfections only served to boost Yvette's character.

"If only," I said. "She was like a part of my body."

"I thought the wheels would fall off each time you drove."

"And yet they never did," I said. "You should be grateful for old Yvette."

"Can I make a confession?"

"You can."

"My younger self would never believe these words, but I think you somehow became even more beautiful over the years."

The motor hummed for a long moment. Ambient noise cluttered my eardrums like plugs. I flipped the indicator and turned right. "How are you doing with Willa?"

"You mean with her being sick?" he asked.

"With her dying, Sawyer."

"I feel a lot of things about it, but somehow the loss is still unthinkable. I can't summon the grief that I know will crash like a waterfall after she's gone. She's at peace with it, as you'd expect, but I'm terrified enough for the both of us."

"I wish I had some wise words to share. But all I can say is that Willa is a great human. They don't make people like her too often and this whole town knows it. I never had parents to lose, so I don't think I'm qualified for advice, but I've had my fair share of loss and heartbreak. My two cents? Don't run from the pain."

"Unfortunately, that's what I'm best at," he said.

I slowed to a halt beside his driveway and turned to him. "I know."

"Call me if there's a break or an update?"

I allowed him enough time to step out of the car. There wasn't a fiber in me that could watch him disappear, so I hurried back to the station before the radio could end its commercial break. I could only bear so much reminiscence.

When Sawyer and I severed the ties of our relationship, it wasn't much like anything I'd seen in film or pop culture. We didn't have a teary-eyed goodbye or a one-sided plea for another chance. It left me to sort through our memories alone, divvy them up and decide what to keep. When I thought I'd buried the past, a whisper would catch my ear as a scent or song or street or shiver. The radio seemed to only play our favorite songs, which hit me like food poisoning. I never thought it would end.

Then one morning, without declaration, memory packed up overnight and pranced into the forest. The radio stopped singing our songs, instead turning to today's tunes.

The smell of cinder and sweat no longer recalled indulgent nights staring into his eyes.

Eventually, like weather wearing down the tread of a trail, matters changed without notice.

Officer Josh Molloy, the yin to Munoz's yang, stood with a cigarette pinched between his fingers, the smoke melting into the darkened sky above. Where Munoz was muscle and tone, Molloy was doughy and cherubic. Both were capable officers, neither with great interest in climbing the ranks. I'd lucked out. Molloy and Munoz were kind and cordial toward me, even in the wake of Chamberlain's retirement.

"Not your average week in Oak Hill," he said.

"You can say that again."

"I left a few papers from Captain Holderbaum on your desk. He said he'd call when there's actionable intel. Whatever that means."

I leaned against the brick facade next to him. "It means we're a rudderless ship for a bit longer."

Smoke snuck through the gap between Molloy's front teeth. "But we've got a hell of a captain."

"Sadly he's fighting gators and tan lines in Florida."

"Ah, hell, Grace. I meant you. Chamberlain was a straw man. Everybody knew that. Even if they don't offer you the job, they'll prop up some other puppet in his office and you'll still run the show."

"What a charmed life," I said. "You been by Margo's?"

"Nah, but I heard the scuttlebutt. A surprising number of people are turning their attention to your pal Sawyer or asking about Billy Jenkins."

"Is that so?"

He shrugged. "Lots of talk without a lot of evidence. I don't think they'd make skilled detectives in the court of law." He held the cigarette pack toward me. "Want one?"

"No thanks. But the air feels good. Plus, I should get home soon."

"Look, I'm the lowest ranking man here, but if I were you, I'd get Sawyer's name out of the mud before it's too late. However you need to."

"I've considered Sawyer's potential involvement. He's got an alibi for the night of. Besides, unless Sawyer is a serial killer up north, I don't see him stopping for company on his way to take care of his dying mother."

"Men can do terrible things out of embarrassment."

"What are you saying?"

"I'm saying that if she's from the streets, maybe he used her for something else. Then, tried to wipe his hands clean. Same goes for Jenkins."

"I've spent years cursing his name, but Jacob Sawyer doesn't strike me as the type to hire and kill sex workers."

"Probably not. But Billy Jenkins has a reputation."

"Most of which is history," I said. "But he's on my radar. Don't worry."

"What did the boy say?"

"Not much," I said. "And like Holderbaum and Macon County, he'll test our patience."

The distant roar of sirens broke the hum of crickets. Both of us froze and listened as they grew louder.

"Your radio on?" I asked.

He nodded.

The wail filled the air. Molloy extinguished his cigarette on the wall. "Only one family with a direct line to the EMTs around here."

The Dockerys. "Shit," I said. "We should go."

"They didn't call us," he said.

"We're the police. It's our job to know what's going on in our town. Even on the ridge."

Molloy snatched keys from his belt and tossed them to me. "Not sure that the Dockery Estate qualifies as our town, but whatever."

In the car, I zoomed out of the lot while Molloy dialed the direct line for the EMT dispatch. He spoke a few words then went pale and hung up. "You should call Mayor Rice."

"What's going on?"

"Silas Dockery is dying."

27

The wrought-iron gates swung open and let our car through like a whale swallowing a fish. Sirens glistened off the brass light fixtures that peppered the courtyard and highlighted the painted brick exterior of the enormous estate. I'd seen the Dockery estate up close just twice: both times for a fundraiser where white-gloved staff escorted guests in. I saw none of those folks around now, just the hurried movements of uniformed EMTs charging in and out of the enormous double-doors.

Curiosity won out, and I tiptoed inside the estate, pilfering a glimpse into what felt like a foreign country. Stout oak beams lined the ceilings. Portraits decorated the hallways. Embossed lights adorned the walls and quivered as the unwelcome visitors zipped by. A gurney's wheels screeched as EMTs propelled it through the hallway, clearing the path like a battering ram. I scanned their faces, curious if they felt the magnitude of the loss or the weight of Silas's legacy. They were all stoic, except for one vaguely familiar face to the left who looked pale as a ghost. Who could blame him?

I scattered into the adjacent room and looked up to find myself in Silas Dockery's office. A cherry oak desk sat diagonally in one corner, wall-to-wall bookshelves behind it filled with scriptures and classic literature. The bottom shelves were more recent. Nonfiction from the last century. Many covered military tactics, espionage, and true crime. Along the far wall a gigantic baroque painting of a shirtless man scuffling with a steer seized my attention. He had it by the horns. I concluded Silas Dockery wasn't much for subtlety.

A coldness drenched me upon realizing that just hours prior, Silas may have been in that very room. I was following his ghost. I was an unwanted visitor in a moment of agony. Worry prickled my skin alongside goosebumps. I tried the door that I entered through, but the knob didn't budge. Better luck awaited me on the westward wall, where the doorway dumped me into a cramped corridor lined with whitetail deer mounts, trophy cases, a glass enclosure filled with hunting rifles, and a collection of framed photographs where Silas Dockery posed with prominent politicians. I counted five portraits adorned with the name Dockery, mostly wrinkled men with round features and determined eyes. There had been a Dockery running the town since it was first established. I wondered if knowing your family's past made it easier or harder to echo it.

In one, he sat with his arm around George W. Bush. In another, he stood suspended in a prolonged handshake with a spry Jack Welch. On the top shelf sat a photo of the Dockery Family at their full capacity: Norma, Silas, Ethan, and Madison, smiling with their backs to the imposing mountains of the Nantahala. Family above all else, or so it seemed.

Pressing through the other door, I came face to face with a homegrown medical suite. Machines moaned. Monitors murmured. Guardrails rested at the side of the bleach-white bed. The sterility of the mansion, or the medicinal stench of death, lifted something raw into my esophagus. I hurried outside through the hallway and gulped fresh air like I'd emerged from the tumult of the sea.

A slender woman leaned against the corner wall and held a lit cigarette in her hand. I nudged Molloy and snagged one from his box, then shuffled over and joined her. "Hi Madison," I said.

"We didn't call the police," Madison Dockery said.

"It's a package deal. Us and the EMTs."

"There's no crime to solve here, Gracie. Just an old man that took his last breaths. Give us some space."

"The call made it seem like he was still alive."

She took a drag and let it out with a heavy exhale. "Ethan's wretched optimism."

"I'm sorry for your loss."

"Thanks."

The dim lighting somehow obscured the already angled lines of Madison's face. Where Ethan was slim, she was bony and sharp. Nat often commented that she was an echo of Silas Dockery in his younger days. Most days, I liked Madison.

Or maybe I just felt bad for her.

"I'm going to go check on things so we can get out of your hair."

She stared up into the starlit sky. I conferred with Molloy and caught an update that matched the one I'd received from Madison. Silas Dockery was dead.

The next car through the gates made me wish we'd already left. When Cliff emerged from the vehicle, he inspected the scene and stormed inside, only to be escorted back out by the EMTs. I waved him down. "You may be the Mayor of Oak Hill, but Silas Dockery calls the shots here. Even from the grave."

Cliff's eyes lit up. "Oh no. I heard he was sick but . . . Nobody knew how sick. Ethan alluded to the idea that Silas may not be around much longer, but I thought he meant years. Not days."

"The EMTs told Molloy that Silas had twenty-four-seven hospice care."

"Shit," Cliff said. "This isn't a surprise then."

"Not here. But out there? It will be. Oak Hill is going to tremble as if an earthquake struck," I said. "But you're good at damage control."

Cliff straightened his posture. "I could use some practice."

I cupped my hand into a microphone and held it in front of my lips.

"Mayor Rice, we heard the news about the passing of our beloved Silas Dockery. Will the town ever recover?"

"Silas Dockery and his family have been a pillar of this town for decades. We all mourn a loss of his magnitude, but his philanthropy and support of this town will not disappear. The family goes on. And so does Oak Hill."

I smiled and clapped three times, but Cliff's face went cold.

A nasally voice growled at me. "I don't think that's an appropriate response to my father's death, Detective."

I whirled around to find Ethan Dockery. "Ethan, I'm so sorry for your loss. I was trying to lighten the mood for Mayor Rice here."

"He was very sick. But I understand that the town will feel this loss greatly. Madison and I are still working through everything, but we're grateful for your discretion."

"Of course," I said.

Ethan stepped aside and locked eyes with Madison. "Excuse me, Detective."

Cliff let out an exhale that clouded in the nighttime air. "Ready for some good news?"

"Always," I said.

"Your murder moved down the list with this."

"Because of the fire?"

Cliff's eyes lit up. "There was a fire?"

"Where the hell have you been all day?"

"Marriage counseling."

"Say no more." I put a hand on his shoulder. "Let's catch up tomorrow morning."

"Fine. You heading home?"

"Yeah," I said. "Molloy is on call tonight, so ring if you need him. I'll need some rest for what's coming tomorrow."

"Let's hope not," he said.

Like hope mattered.

28

By the next morning, I'd concluded that a reckoning was coming. Oak Hill, for better or worse, was erupting at the seams with change. And the fire that burned beneath my feet, lit by the townsfolk, had simmered to embers and ash.

All eyes were on the latest inferno.

The sudden death of Silas Dockery.

I scarfed down granola and scrolled through the Oak Hill Next Door page, hungry for something I'd missed. Word spread, as it always did, from lips to ears and so forth. Rumors swirled about Silas hiding a cancer diagnosis from the town.

I scoffed at the phrasing, like him not broadcasting a death sentence was a slight to the town he had given so much. The third post from the bottom suggested Billy Jenkins may have poisoned Silas over an old unpaid debt. Emma's comment about Billy's urban legend status seemed more and more right by the minute

Susan texted that although he didn't touch his dinner, Cedar was safe at the Center. Despite her assurances, I planned to stop by anyway. Susan was one of the few in town that actually had a personal relationship with Silas, so I'd have bet good money that she was reeling from the loss and concerned about the future of the Center.

Nat hobbled from the front porch and leaned against the doorjamb. "Is it true?" he asked.

"Somehow, in the dead of sleep, even you heard?"

"I've got a phone too, Grace."

"I thought that was just a vehicle for your games of solitaire."

He sighed. "That's a tremendous loss for Oak Hill. Is that where you were all night?"

"I dropped by with Molloy. Dockery didn't call 911, but we saw the ambulances whirr and followed. When we learned what happened, I can't say that I believed it."

"He was an old man," Nat said, swinging open the fridge door. "Old people only have so much time on this earth."

"Don't even make a joke."

"Funeral is tomorrow. Seems Silas had it all arranged just in case he passed. I'd bet he was a lot sicker than anybody knew. Makes sense why Ethan was on your committee."

"I guess. I saw him and Madison last night. Both were business as usual."

Nat tossed a carton of eggs onto the counter and dug a frying pan out of the drawer. "Nobody knows how to handle grief, Grace. Even the experts are lying."

"Why do I feel like you're talking about more than just the Dockery kids?"

"Old and wise," Nat said. "That's what they'll put on my gravestone when I bite it in a couple weeks."

"I just said not to make a joke, Nat."

"It's the truth. Someday, Grace, I'll die. But it won't be today. So you can rest easy."

I mimed wiping sweat from my forehead and tossed my bowl into the sink.

"If you keep eating three eggs each morning, that day will come sooner than you'd like."

He growled at me. "How's Willa?"

"Hanging in, I guess. Sawyer was with me most of the day."

"Remember what I said about processing grief?"

I rolled my eyes. "Subtlety would go a long way for you, you know?"

"You two civil?"

"Most of the time. But sometimes I look at him and he's eighteen again. It's a slap in the face."

"Imagine how he feels."

"I'd bet he just feels awkward."

Nat cracked an egg onto the pan, and the sizzle filled the room. "Awkward isn't the right word. You need to work on seeing things from other people's perspective. Pause for a long moment. Consider everything on his plate. His mother is dying, and he's back in town for the first time since his father passed. He's forced to face down the people he left behind and a town that he abandoned."

"I'm not saying that I don't feel bad for him but—"

"But you condemn him for his choices."

"Right."

"Sometimes Oak Hill feels like a foreign country. We lean into that feeling too. Protect our borders like any outsider will threaten the status quo without questioning whether that change might be a good thing. We like routine. We like what we know."

"Well, Sawyer's not the only visitor to town. I still haven't cracked open Cedar. He may never talk."

"Here's some unsolicited advice: the boy is an outsider. If you want him to talk, it won't be with you. We take care of our own," he said. "Outsiders do the same."

I set my hand on his shoulder and stood on my toes to kiss him on the cheek. "Sage wisdom, Big Nat."

"Stay safe, young buck."

I rang Sawyer from the car while I let it warm. He agreed to meet me over at Susan's. There was no mention of Silas's passing. The bliss of ignorance. When I asked about Willa, he went silent and hurried off the line. At least some things weren't changing.

The leisurely drive provided enough time for Nat's lecture to sink in. What the hell did I know about being an outsider here? I'd spent practically every second of my life in Oak Hill and had little to show for it besides a ferocious loyalty to a town that had given me squat. Sawyer had walked away, started fresh and only returned when death was at his doorstep. Cedar stumbled in, lost his entire world, and faced a new life alone.

In the parking lot, Sawyer pulled up next to me and I met him outside. "How does it feel to be back in Oak Hill after all these years?"

"I've been waiting for you to ask that since I showed up," he said.

"Well, I'm asking now."

"It's like a garden that I left behind. There was nobody to tend to my plot of land, so the weeds grew in and encroached until there wasn't any space for me left. It's suffocating. The change. Everything is different. Like a new movie with the same cast."

"Good," I said. "I want you to talk to Cedar alone. And remember what you just said. Maybe you could explain that you're not from here either."

"Maybe," he said.

"Also, I don't know if you heard, but Silas Dockery passed away last night."

"Willa saw it online."

"How'd she take the news?"

"Like it was an election result from Peru. I never got the full story, but she held a grudge for all those long hours that kept George away from us. He was just doing his job but it . . . well, those hard feelings grew when George died. Like Silas stole something from our family."

"Makes sense."

"I had a thought, if you're open to it . . . The tattoo. I wonder if that's an ID number or something important."

"An ID?"

"We had this case in Philly, maybe four years back. Young woman who was barely twenty-five jumped from her balcony into oncoming traffic below."

"Jesus."

"I drew the short straw and had to coordinate with the family to get her affairs settled. It wasn't a homicide, but her father kept asserting that something had killed her: the scars from her deployment."

"She was military?"

"Yeah. I don't remember where she did a tour, but the fall had badly disfigured her face. We ended up making the positive ID using a photograph of a tattoo on her bicep."

"Was it roman numerals?"

"No, just the outline of a fox and a hound. But if Lark's are numbers, maybe it's a date. Like when she enlisted or her birthday."

"Fort Sherman," I said.

"Run that by our good pal Liam, maybe. Give him something to chew on that doesn't involve a gun."

"I keep thinking that once I get a name, things will be easier. But what if that's wrong? What if it'll only get more complicated?"

"Everything will get worse before it's cleaned up. But don't let me slow you down. I'll go spend the day with Cedar. At the very worst, I hope to walk away with a new friend."

I watched him walk to the door as I retrieved my phone from my pocket and rang Liam Price. He picked up after the second ring with a brusque hello. I explained Sawyer's theory and Liam grunted in approval.

"Lots of tattoos in the military, though. There's no index for you to look through," he warned.

"I'm wondering if the combination of the photo of her face and the tattoo would be enough for somebody at Sherman to make an ID. My best theory is that she has ties there since there are few other reasons to end up near Oak Hill."

"Reasonable. I'm tied up the rest of today, but I can make a few calls and vouch for you. Not sure how much good it will do, but it's better than trying to beat down that door alone."

"Thanks, Liam. I'll head that way now."

"Stay alert," he said. "Trouble is around every corner."

I'd never heard words more truthful in my life.

-THEN-

FIGHT OR FLIGHT. That's what Ms. Callahan said were the two human re-
actions to stressful events. Some humans find themselves ready to knuckle
up and take down whatever is threatening them. The others are already six
feet out the door and a lifetime away. But there's a third reaction, one that I
hadn't felt until that very moment when we heard that terrifying scream and
its resulting echoes through the treetops.

My body trembled like an earthquake shook the soil. I followed every
tremor of shadows in the trees and waited for another sound. Another shot.
Cliff reached for us both and tried to drag us down but I was too stubborn
and Sawyer was too strong. Before the sound had even faded, Sawyer bolted toward it. Fight or flight, right? He was gone before either of us moved
to stop him. We were too busy trying to thaw our bones enough to get a
move on anyhow. And even if I'd tried to stop him, I don't think he'd have
listened.

Nat had long ago told me that guns weren't the tools they once were
back when life depended on your ability to hunt game and feed your family.
Back then, a gun was a necessary part of the equation like shoes and socks

are today. Everybody had them. And despite millennia of stories where man fights man for land or goods or greed or whatever, none of that mattered at first. At first, it was about survival.

I didn't have to ask to know that Nat didn't like guns. There wasn't a rifle or handgun in our house and instead Nat had often preached the value of a wooden baseball bat as if it was a secret weapon. No matter my family's feelings on guns, you couldn't travel far within the forest without hearing a gunshot.

Hunters frequented the forest and ignored the posted signs outlining the parameters of the season. We never had any run-ins with the like, although stories ran rampant about self regarding hunters driving through Oak Hill with a carcass in tow. But this sound was closer, as if somebody plucked at my ear and let it reverberate through the woods and more than anything, it was unnatural.

"We need to help," I said.

I stepped forward but Cliff pulled me back. "It's not safe."

"Sawyer isn't safe either. That was a gunshot."

"We need to turn around."

"I'm not leaving without him."

"Fine. But don't run. We'll walk carefully. Keep an eye out for anybody in the woods."

"Why would they shoot somebody?" I asked. "And who was it? "

"They? What do you mean?"

"The police."

"I don't think that was the police," Cliff said.

"What?"

"I'd rather not find out. But if it was the police, they had a reason."

I squinted into the night. Silhouettes danced near a stand of trees. I pointed and Cliff nodded. "Careful now. Step by step."

We inched our way closer until we heard Sawyer's voice. He stood in a tiny clearing, one I'd never noticed, backlit by the crisp night sky above. "Help," he shouted. Before we could run to him, a dark figure appeared out of the brush and tackled Sawyer to the ground. A whack of something metallic crunched and Sawyer howled. Cliff snatched my arm. "No," he said. "Wait."

The figure lingered over another shape on the ground then darted into the forest, obscured by the camouflage of night and pine. I kicked back at Cliff. He let me go. Sawyer looked up, bruised and dazed. More movement ahead. Shadows and voices. I couldn't track anything. Sawyer seemed within reach but within seconds my body collided with the ground. A thump of my knee against a log. I winced and hobbled to my feet. But it was too late. Like a wind from the forest, the police burst out of the trees and surrounded Sawyer.

Cliff knelt next to me. "You okay?"

"They have Sawyer."

"They'll drop him at home," Cliff said. "He'll be fine."

"But it wasn't his fault. He was with us. Somebody else—"

"Let's wait for him at his house."

A crumbled mess of something sprawled on the forest floor. "What's that?" I pointed. Chamberlain stood over it like the shadowy figure had before. He shook his head and then dug a radio out of his pocket. From our vantage point, we couldn't hear what he croaked into the other end. Officer Chuck Agnew stood next to Chamberlain, starlight glinting off his fresh-out-of-the-box badge. I'd seen Agnew at bonfires when they first started. Maybe he was the instigator here, some twisted form of revenge or a rite of passage into adulthood. But when Chamberlain knelt down, Agnew dropped Sawyer and stepped closer.

"My God," Agnew said.

"Ambulance is on the way," Chamberlain added. "She's still breathing."

"We should pray."

"Jesus," Chamberlain said. "What a terrible accident."

"Accident?" Agnew asked. "How could you—"

"Chuck, run down to the clearing. Flag down the ambulance when they come. I don't think she has much longer."

"What about the boy?"

"Did he take the shot?"

Sawyer grimaced from the ground. "No, I heard—"

"Hey, aren't you George Sawyer's kid?"

"Cuff him and drag him along. We can ask questions later. If he's the shooter, he'll pay," Chamberlain said. "But I think this is just a good old-fashioned accident."

"Jesus Christ," Agnew uttered. "What a mess."

"Keep your eyes out for witnesses," Chamberlain shouted.

Agnew dragged Sawyer out of sight. Cliff and I remained frozen. Furniture in the background of life. My heart galloped in my throat. Every muscle tensed. Then we watched as Chamberlain stroked back Sarah Price's hair and whispered, "Hang in there, Sarah. Hang in there."

29

When my phone rang, I closed my eyes for a second and yearned for progress. Anything. A trivial turn that would yield any type of result. I prayed, for the first time in my life, that Sawyer was on the other end with good news. When Munoz's name popped up, I sighed.

"What's up?"

"Somebody is here to see you."

Munoz didn't say another word about the visitor. I took that as a damning sign that more trouble was hovering on the horizon. When I parked out front and noticed the same SUV that had parked beside our fire scene, I knew what awaited me.

Holderbaum leaned against a pillar in the lobby with his thumbs in his belt loops and a Cheshire smile across his face. "Morning, Detective. Can I steal a few minutes of your time?"

Munoz glanced up from the desk, but I couldn't discern what to make of his glance. "I thought your report would take a few days."

"We aim to underpromise and overdeliver. Plus, this one is rather cut and dry."

He tugged a file folder out of his bag, and parked himself at the end of the conference table. I took the bookend seat but left the door open. "What's the story?"

"Is it true you've got an unsolved murder case here?" Holderbaum asked.

"It is," I said, seeing little use in fighting the truth and rumors. "But at the moment, there's no apparent connection between the fire and the murder. Except timing."

"Right," he said. "I was just surprised. You know, the things you hear about Oak Hill, I assumed it's as sleepy as a narcolepsy study."

"We're full of surprises," I said. "But I'm sure you put that together, seeing as you're here to talk about a fire."

"Fires happen. They're a natural element that when the wrong things combine, poof. Now, in this case, somebody forced it. But a fire and a murder are two entirely different things."

"Can you tell me more about the fire? I'd love an easy win."

He flipped open the folder. "Wouldn't we all? I'm afraid that's not the case."

"You said cut and dry."

"Meaning that I've got an explanation for how the fire started and where. I don't have a who, and I think that's what you're hunting for."

"Nothing is easy lately," I muttered.

Holderbaum slid a photo my way. The charred remains of a room that looked like somebody took a sledgehammer to the walls and layered on black wallpaper.

"This is a room on the southwest side of Nickelson Law. Toward the rear. Our team concluded that the fire started somewhere in this room and spread to engulf the entire building. Accelerant of choice was gasoline, lugged onto the site in a red five-gallon Scepter jug."

"The back room? Was that his office?"

"Our team spoke to Mr. Nickelson who said the room was an empty office used for file storage. His knees don't allow him to climb up and down steps like he used to, but that room once held case records and other documents. Our hypothesis is that the amount of paperwork looked like a tinderbox to our perp."

"Makes sense. Easy fuel."

"The place lit up like the Fourth of July."

"How would the arsonist have sparked the blaze and gotten out in time?"

"Ten feet away is an emergency exit. They could have tossed a match into the room and snuck out with time to spare."

"Did Nickelson mention any enemies?"

"He's reviewing the cases from that room now but I wouldn't hold your breath. The man is nearly eighty and was exhausted after our brief conversation. Whoever wished him dead would have to wait in line behind old age and disease."

I sat up straighter and glanced at the window. "So you're here to tell me that this case is likely to go cold unless we find something that breaks in our favor."

"Correct."

"But you all will stay on it in the meantime?"

He shrugged. "It'll be on our plate until something or someone pushes it off."

"Someone?"

"Politics, Detective. If you want this to stay as our top priority, you'll need to urge your mayor to fight for it. Even then, the decision rests with Macon County and you never know what that means. Did your team turn up any eyewitnesses?"

"I'll check. Excuse me for a moment."

I eased the door shut behind me and found Munoz in the break room staring down a coffee pot that dripped hot brown liquid into a carafe. "You all right?" I asked.

"Can't sleep lately, but I'm fine. How's it going in there?"

"Fine. Nothing promising. Did you find an eyewitness?"

"No," Munoz said. "Molloy ran down everybody he could and I asked around. Nickelson Law has a back door that lets out into an alley that spits onto undeveloped property. Easy escape."

"Then what is it?"

"Holderbaum came in here and had a few choice words about you. I think he saw me as a disgruntled employee annoyed with my female commanding officer, you know?"

"Do I even want to know what he said?"

"I don't think it bears repeating. He's an asshole with some misogynistic views about women and police work."

"Surprised he wasn't on my selection committee then. Fits the bill nicely."

Munoz winced. "Shit, I'm sorry. I forgot about—"

"All good. Thanks for the heads up."

"I did stop by Bill Nickelson's house before I came in today."

"Holderbaum hadn't given me much hope for news there. Anything promising?"

"Well, he's an old man so it shouldn't surprise anyone that he had next to nothing digitized. What burned up was pretty much his life's work. He rambled on for a while about legacy and what that means, but the interesting part to me was one name he mentioned in his rant."

"Spit it out already."

"Silas Dockery."

"Why would Silas Dockery use a local lawyer when he's got high-priced firms on retainer? That doesn't add up."

"I got the sense that Dockery used Nickelson for some unofficial business. Things he wanted to hide from the rest of the world. But I'm just trying to decipher the old man's mumbles, so who knows if it holds water."

"Lovely," I said. "So in a matter of twenty-four hours, Silas dies and every sin he's tried to litigate out of existence goes up in flames."

"And the case gets that much weirder. Don't freak out but there's one more thing," Munoz said. "We need to call Mayor Rice."

"Why's that?"

Munoz pulled the carafe from the machine and poured coffee into a mug. "There's an appeal on your desk from the Dockery Estate. They want to shut down Murphy Road tomorrow for a few hours to allow the funeral procession to go through."

"And we're already at our overtime cap," I said. "I'll call Cliff."

Back in the conference room, Holderbaum handed over the folder and insisted he'd be in touch with any updates. After Munoz's insights, I doubted Holderbaum would rush to help a female detective, but I prayed for a surprise. I led him toward the door and gritted my teeth as we said goodbye.

Cliff said he'd be over in five minutes, but burst through the doors in four.

"This about the funeral?" he asked.

"Nice to see you too, old pal."

"When did our lives get this complicated?"

"I was about to ask you the same thing. I take it you heard the Dockery request?"

"Yeah. Make it happen."

"That's up to you, Mr. Mayor. I need your blessing for the overtime. Me, Molloy, and Munoz."

"Whatever you need."

"I respect the Dockery family as much as the next gal, but why do they need to shut down the entire town for his funeral? People have died in Oak Hill before and nobody asked for special circumstances."

"Money talks, Grace."

"So do people."

"Any luck cracking open the lost boy?"

"Sawyer spent the day with him."

Cliff leaned back in a chair and stared at me. "Is that the best idea?"

"They're both outsiders here."

"They're both runaways," he said.

"Does the devil know you're up here advocating for him?"

Cliff chuckled and pulled a toothpick from his pocket. "I'm just trying to stay involved. Speaking of which, I have a few timely mayoral requests to trade for that overtime approval."

"As if that was something I was pining for."

"Fire squad left a genuine mess around Nickelson Law. You need to secure that scene and make it look like it's under control. There's crime scene tape flapping in the breeze."

"We can manage that."

"Lionel Sutton wants the crime scene tape down at his property, too."

I nodded. "Maybe if we're lucky and take down enough tape, this town will forget that anything bad happened here in the first place."

"I doubt that," Cliff said. "But I'll pray for it."

"Save your breath."

"Lastly, there are . . . whispers. It's above my head. You know how these things go but—"

"Spit it out, Carlos."

"The SBI plans to take over the case."

"Lark's murder?"

"Correct."

"And how long do I have before these whispers get louder?"

He shrugged. "Nothing happens around here on the weekend. And despite the tragedy, Silas's passing may have bought you an extra day or two."

"You're saying if I don't have this wrapped up by tomorrow, I'm off the case?"

"Grace, I—"

"And you're going to stand by while some out-of-towner comes in here and pokes around Oak Hill as if he's got a sense of our spirit?"

"I never wanted—"

"You should go."

"Grace, you're being unreasonable."

"Have a good night, Cliff."

Once he stormed out, I got my first real moment of solitude since the evidence piled up and clouded the case. No matter Cliff's mumblings about the SBI and the alphabet soup that he thought was better suited for the case. This was my hometown. The Oak Hill that I knew better than the switchbacks of the Nantahala. But why did none of it add up? The answers seemed far out of reach.

W e muddled through our to-do list and, afterward, I wasted an hour in the station trying to wash the blackened char from my hands before giving up. Molloy shifted on for Munoz and they passed the proverbial baton with little fanfare. I explained to both of them about the Dockery family's request, my overtime approval, and how we'd block the streets the next morning.

When my phone rang, I expected Sawyer. But Liam Price's gruff voice accosted me. "Got a minute?"

"I do," I said. "What's up?"

"I'm in the parking lot. Come out for a second."

I hung up and walked to meet him. An unfamiliar man sat in the passenger seat with a bald head and wrinkled neck. He wore a crisp navy-blue collared shirt with the name EARL written on the patch. "I don't have time for field trips."

"Any update on the fire?" he asked.

"Arson. Beyond that, we don't have anything." I regretted the words the second they escaped. *Loose lips sink ships, Grace.*

"Common thread."

"One could say."

"I heard you're having trouble with the Fort. They're tough. That's their nature. Protective of their own."

"Aren't we all?"

"But Earl here knows the right people."

Earl leaned forward. "This the gal?"

Liam nodded. "This is Grace. She went to school with my daughter. We've got a case that might involve Sherman."

"I don't mess with ghosts, Liam. I thought we were going to the VFW."

"We found a deceased woman's body in Oak Hill. Signs of foul play, but she's not from town."

Earl scratched at his beard. "I heard about that. You think she's a soldier?"

"Or once was. It's the only angle we have left to explore. Sherman is a brick wall."

"As it should be," he said.

"So we thought . . . " Liam started.

"If she's been through the VA down here, I'd know her, or at least be able to provide a handful of possibilities."

"If we gave you her fingerprints and a photo, could you ask around?" Liam asked.

"I could. And for a friend of Sarah's, I will."

"Good." Liam flopped an envelope onto Earl's lap, which he whisked off and into his jacket.

Earl handed a business card my way and tapped the front. "Send over what you've got. I'll have an update by morning."

"Send him what you can," Liam said to me. "This favor is on the house. Consider it an apology for how I handled things with the boy."

"Apology accepted."

I studied Liam as he idled and did some quick math. "Should I be thanking you or the Dockery family for that payment?"

Liam smiled. "Let's hope the juice is worth the squeeze."

Inside the station, Molloy played a game on his cell phone and insisted that I head home. I didn't have to be told twice. On the drive, I rang Sawyer and when he answered, I sensed hope in his voice.

"Tell me you've got good news," I said.

"Maybe. Depends on your definition."

"My definition is anything that is not more bad news."

"Then I'm your man."

I'm your man. The phrasing echoed like a pebble in a puddle in a cavern. I let it linger for a moment, but despite my best intentions, I couldn't choke down the words that came next.

"Want to come see Nat?"

"More than anything," he said. "But I don't want to intrude."

"Nonsense. He's been asking after you anyhow. Bring some wine over and he'll light up like Nickelson Law."

"Timely joke."

"Somebody's got to make light of this mess I'm in."

"I'm with Willa now, but I'll be over in an hour or two. Does that work?"

"See you then. I take it you remember the way."

"I couldn't forget if I tried."

I burst through the door like a tornado, and Nat hardly flinched. Agatha stretched out her torso, clawing forward and limbering up. I knelt to her and scratched her chin.

"You're going to meet a new friend tonight."

"Do I get to meet the friend, too?" Nat asked without peering up from the newspaper.

"You do. But he's not new to you."

He lowered the page and smiled. "I better start cooking then."

"And I need to take the first of many showers. I smell like an incinerator."

"You've smelt worse," he said.

I spent the better part of the next hour with scalding water running over my shoulders and a litany of body washes, soaps, and creams that all somehow failed to remove the scar and stench of my ashy afternoon adventure. In a way, I'd been trying to wipe ash and cinder and smoke from my body for fifteen years. But it persisted.

Sawyer rapped his knuckles at the door and peeked through the screen. Nat swallowed him in a big hug and held on so long that Sawyer's face resembled a red grape. I yanked the wine from his hand and popped the cork. "Since when do you knock?" Nat asked.

"Felt odd to barge in after all these years, Nat," he said.

Agatha's hackles raised as she eyed the newcomer. Sawyer knelt down to say hello but Agatha's ears pinned back and she hissed at him before sprinting away to hide under my bed.

"She takes a while to warm up," I said. "But don't let that interrupt Nat's lecture on knocking."

"He's allowed to knock if he wants," Nat said, licking butter from his finger. "It's a different day, but we're still the same people."

"Maybe," Sawyer said. "But only one of the three of us looks like we did back then."

"Who says I don't look better?" I said.

Nat raised his hand slowly and shrugged. "Sorry, young buck, it's the truth. Maybe if you actually got a full night's sleep and didn't stumble home smelling like a bonfire."

"Our illustrious mayor had me clean up the debris from the fire. But nobody wants to hear me complain. Sawyer, how was Cedar?"

"He's still reserved, but we spent the day walking on the edge of Nantahala and he showed me a few things. I figured taking him somewhere he felt comfortable may do the trick, though Susan nearly had my head for the impromptu field trip."

"Smart," I said. "And he didn't bolt?"

"Nope. Much the opposite. Now, that clamshell is still shut, but he let out a few pearls."

"Anything that helps with his mother's case?"

"Breadcrumbs mostly. Cedar said that he and Lark would come into town occasionally. Lark would leave Cedar at an intersection of trails and return an hour later. Then they'd hike back into the brush for a day and surface on the other side of the forest where Lark would grab groceries and food that they couldn't forage or hunt."

"So they lived in the forest?" Nat asked.

"Seems that way. I don't know how long they'd been in there, but Cedar seemed unfamiliar with most modern technology."

Nat nodded. "You all remember that mess with Eric Rudolph?"

"Don't remind me," I said. "That was all people talked about here for a full year. It was the first time I prayed for the Braves to win the World Series just so people would shut up about Eric Rudolph."

"That was after I left," Sawyer said. "But it turned out he was living in the forest, right?"

"For six years. Nobody spotted him. Madman planted those bombs at the Olympics in Atlanta, then fled into the forest. They caught him in Murphy because he was pulling day-old tacos from a dumpster."

"What's that got to do with Cedar and Lark?" Sawyer asked.

"Only other person on record that ever lived inside Nantahala. At least in my memory."

"Nat's saying that maybe Lark was on the run."

Sawyer leaned back in his hair and sipped his wine. "Maybe, but I didn't get that sense. Lark was careful, but I'm more curious where they were getting the money to get groceries. It's not my area of expertise but I know in Philly sex work came in many forms. It would be one way to make a quick buck and it's not like they regulate the industry around here. It's dangerous stuff."

"That's a hell of a life," I said.

"What if she had the money stashed around town?" Nat asked.

"Doubtful," I said. "If you found a stash of someone's money, you'd take it when nobody was looking and bolt."

"She could have found D. B. Cooper's fortune out west and hid it in Oak Hill," Nat said.

I stuck my tongue out at him. "Are you done showing off yet?"

He shrugged. "History is never done, young buck."

"We could run down a list of people we think would indulge in the services of a sex worker but that's not a path I was expecting to pursue," I said.

"Nothing about this case has been business as usual."

"You can say that again. Cliff told me I've got until Sunday night."

"Then what?" Nat asked.

"It falls into the lap of the SBI."

Nat whistled.

Sawyer groaned. "Maybe they'd let you stay on the case."

"And pigs may fly," I said. "But we always did work well under pressure."

"Well, you'll need to put the shop talk aside for a moment because this chicken is about ready," Nat said. "And we've got some serious catching up to do in the meantime. I didn't know I'd be an honorary member of the Clueless Detective Agency tonight."

Sawyer and I met eyes and smiled.

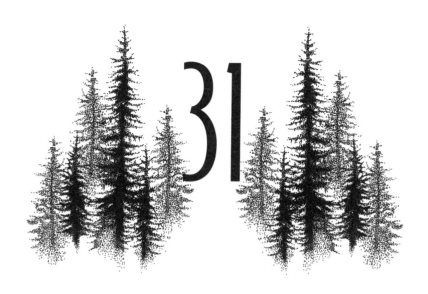

31

The Clueless Detective Agency began with a whimper of a case. One evening, Sawyer, Cliff, and I ate burgers on the deck with Willa and George. Willa told us all about her day spent in the garden and the hope she had for a boon of herbs in a couple of weeks. George chomped away and fussed with the grill. I worried that the silent males at the table were leaving Willa disheartened, so I piped up and mentioned how I loved to play in the dirt.

Willa promised to show me the finished product but after some gentle-arm twisting, she decided to bring us kids over for a sneak peek. The far side of the house hadn't been touched in years. Once upon a time, Sawyer and I played catch while Cliff did push-ups in the grass until his arms felt like Jell-O. Now, soil littered the ground boxed in with railroad ties and small statues. Willa pointed to a stone formation that resembled two hands. In the palms rested a large glass blue ball.

"What's the ball for?" Sawyer asked.

"Good luck," Willa said.

"Is it glass?"

"Yes, and it should never move," Willa said. "If any of you break it, I'll have you weeding out here until you earn enough to buy a new one."

"Yes ma'am," we said in unison.

Later that week, I scampered through Sawyer's backyard and noticed the side gate wide open. I didn't think much of it but when I went inside, I let Willa know. She rushed outside, whispering about rabbits and deer, then returned pale as the moon. "The ball is gone," she said.

"Gone?" Sawyer asked.

"Somebody stole it."

Sawyer and I met eyes, marched outside and examined the scene. We'd been burning through George's VHS and DVD seasons of *Columbo*. Willa watched in horror as we studied the soil, staring at boot prints in the flower beds.

The name didn't come around until later. We had our fill of Scooby Doo and the Mystery Machine and although we didn't have the license or means to procure a van and drive around the country solving crimes, we got a sense of what it required. Answers came shrouded in mystery until the very last minute. No friendly on-looker or well-wisher was innocent. There was always an explanation for any bad happenings. And this was no different.

Aptly enough, Cliff was the one that gave us our name. We'd badger him on his front porch and try to convince him to chase down ghosts with us to no avail. He'd scoff and call us clueless. And that was enough for us. Life as a child is simple in its needs. We saw no reason to puff out our chests and claim we knew everything. And looking back, we were clueless. Hell, we still are.

The mystery of the missing ball took a twist by the next morning. The sun had barely risen when Nat burst through my bedroom door and tossed the phone onto my bed. Too groggy to ask anything, I raised it to my ear and whispered hello.

"There's been a development in the case," Sawyer said. "Come over as fast as you can."

When I arrived back at Sawyer's, Willa sat at the kitchen table with a note in her hand.

"It's a ransom note," Sawyer explained. "They want a thousand dollars."

My eyes bulged out of my skull. "That's more money than Nat's truck costs!"

"It's also ten times the price of a new orb," Willa said.

"So you're not going to pay it?"

She eyed me. "Whoever wrote this note is a child. One aiming for a life of trouble."

"We'll find out who did it," Sawyer said.

Willa rolled her eyes and left the room. I slipped into her chair and examined the note closely. Sawyer read over my shoulder and grinned. "Tonight," he said.

"But how will we get a thousand bucks?"

"We won't," he said. "But we'll throw some books in a bag and make it look like we did."

"That's stupid! What if we get caught?"

"Once we know who is behind this, we'll be able to go to the police."

I shrugged. That's how little it took to convince me when Sawyer was the one doing the convincing. Magic words from magic lips. I had no rebuttal nor did I want to find one.

That night, Sawyer swiped a duffel bag from George's office and met me on the front steps with the fake ransom. He nearly toppled over six times as we rode our bikes downtown but somehow neither of us fell. I perched myself around the corner while Sawyer slid the bag beneath the bright blue post office box near the Empire Diner.

We lurked in the corner for less than five minutes before somebody showed up. When we saw who it was, neither of us pursued. Instead, we marched around the corner to the police station and bolted through the doors.

"You two lost?" a snotty voice asked us when we entered.

"We'd like to report a crime," Sawyer said.

Don Chamberlain didn't rise from his chair. He moved his eyes from his crossword puzzle and looked each of us up and down. "What kind of crime?"

"Robbery."

He raised a single eyebrow. "You don't say?"

"Billy Jenkins stole a glass ball from Willa's garden and tried to hold it ransom."

Chamberlain grinned. "Ransom?"

Sawyer forked over the note, and we both sat in nervous anxiety as he read it. Chamberlain nodded, tucked the note into his pocket, and smiled. "Thanks for the tip."

"Aren't you going to do something?" Sawyer pleaded.

Chamberlain pointed to the clock. "Maybe tomorrow. I'm off in ten minutes. And I think your precious ball can wait another day. This isn't life or death, kid."

Sawyer fumed but I tugged his shirt and pulled him out of the station. He huffed the whole way home and slammed his bedroom door shut so hard it rattled the walls. I rode my bike home in silence, feeling responsible for the weight of the words that Chamberlain wouldn't say.

Two days later, Chamberlain appeared on Willa's front door and handed her the orb, stating that he tracked it down as a favor to George. She politely thanked him. He didn't so much as mention Sawyer and I and our investigative work. When we pleaded with Willa that we were the ones who cracked the case, she smiled and nodded along. But the world was reset to its natural setting. The orb was returned. The garden was complete again. And largely, that event held no significance other than that it forged a bond over a common interest between Sawyer and I. We became a team. And we'd remain one for years to come.

Grease jumped from the pan as Nat set it on the table between us. Sawyer craned his neck and stared at the dish, unsure of what to make of it.

Nat grinned. "It's too late to say you don't eat fried chicken anymore."

"I can handle it," he said.

"Good, because Grace here puts up a fight every damn time."

I filled my plate without another word, just a glance to Sawyer to convey my dismay with the slander that filled Nat's cup. Back when the world was full of hope, when every day seemed fresh, I reveled in the magic transmitted from one set of eyes to another. How did we learn that language? When did his emerald greens train my ocean blues on the inner workings of the brain? It hadn't taken all that long for the skill to return. Old friends, as Nat and Cliff had said, you can't make new ones.

As the dinner progressed, Sawyer shared more about his life than I'd heard in the past four days. Nat's ignorance of Philadelphia provided a boon of topics, including whether there was indeed a crack in the Liberty Bell and if the Phillies stadium looked as good as it did on the TV. I left space for Sawyer to pivot into more personal details, knowing all too well that he would avoid it like the mayonnaise bottle on the table.

I learned little about my old friend that I couldn't have read online if I'd ever taken the time to search. Eventually, Nat let him off the hook and started complaining about a coyote that was creeping on local farms. I swear Sawyer nearly floated out of his chair once the pressure lifted.

When the moon rose to its peak, Nat sipped from his glass, stood in a stupor, and smiled. "It's time that I call it a night."

Nervous eyes met one another and as Nat drifted into the bedroom, Sawyer and I sat alone, fighting the pull of ghosts and muscle memory nudging us closer.

32

ew things aren't improved by fresh air. After we cleared the plates, I
nudged open the front door and told Sawyer I'd join him in a second.
He topped off his wine glass and offered me more. I nodded, although
every fiber inside screamed for rejection. I moseyed toward the bathroom,
demonstrating the casual, glib nature I hoped to exude. I hardly think it
worked.

In the mirror, I was faced not with the youthful, pigtailed version of myself that Sawyer knew but the wrinkled mess of a woman without a direction
in the world.

I splashed water on my face but nothing I did brought out the girl I
once was. Although I wasn't even sure she belonged here, sitting on the
porch drinking wine with Jacob Sawyer like he didn't abandon me and this
town fifteen years ago.

When I rejoined him, he smiled, lifted his glass, and clinked it with
mine. The seat he chose, out of all the options, parked him next to me. When
I sat, our knees grazed beneath the table. Sawyer leaned back and looked up
at the stars. "How long has Cliff been cheating on Hannah?"

"Since the twins were three," I said.

"Always with Reyna?"

"How'd you know?"

"She alluded to it. Not in so many words, but it wasn't my place to say anything."

"He swears it's over."

"But he's said that before?"

"Right," I said. "I feel for her. She's waiting around for him to wise up and leave Hannah but that'll never happen."

Sawyer shook his head. "Crazy. If you told the high school version of Cliff that he'd be married to Hannah McCullough, he'd say he won the lottery."

"People always want what they can't have, right?"

"Maybe," he said. "But this town . . . Everything is different yet the same."

He pushed a swath of curls away from his forehead but they kept falling, and so did I.

"That doesn't make sense."

"It does in my head," he said. "It's like Nat said. The same people in a different world, kind of. I never imagined that you'd still be living in this house."

I smiled. "I left for a bit. Rented a house over on Murphy, but Nat needed somebody to look after him."

"Is he all right?"

"He's fine. It's nothing damning or fatal, just age tapping him on the shoulder from time to time. His mind is sharp on most days but when it's dulled, well, dealing with him isn't a task that I felt should be outsourced. It's my penance."

"Penance for what?"

"The life that Nat gave me. I owe him the world."

"You are his world, Grace. He doesn't think you owe him a thing."

"I know."

Crickets chirped and sang their nighttime symphony. We paused to listen for a long moment before Sawyer broke the ice with a sledgehammer. "Somedays, I wish we'd never gone to that bonfire."

"Yeah?"

"I dream of the timeline where you, Cliff, and I drank skunked beer that we stole from our parents and stared up at the stars. That was how we should have celebrated graduation. We were never part of that scene."

"But we went."

"We did," he said. "And my life fell apart."

"You can't blame yourself for an accident, Sawyer. Your father would have—"

"I can and I will."

"Fine," I said.

He smiled and leaned forward. "Has anybody ever told you that you should listen to your own advice?"

"There are moments when I feel free from it all. Like a cloud in the sky that gets to watch the world from above. But if I don't pay careful attention, if I don't consciously focus on it, I begin to evaporate and dissolve."

"Somedays, evaporating doesn't sound all that bad."

"Since we're dragging skeletons out of the closet, I think I owe you an apology," I said.

He looked shocked. "Apology?"

"I shouldn't have said that I loved you that night. I know it scared you and—"

"No. What? Why would you apologize for that?"

I shrugged. "I figured—"

"Because I left without saying goodbye?"

"Right. But that's because of what I said. You were too kind to break my heart."

He stood and extended a hand. "Come with me."

I took it and followed him off the deck. His warm fingers intertwined with mine like a needle on a groove. And soon a familiar song played. One that I'd let collect dust long ago. But I knew all the words and loved every note. That fateful night on the fire road, I tucked away the words I'd never have the chance to say in a journal in a box in my closet. No matter how many boxes and crates I stacked on top or in between, the words still snuck their way into my eardrums.

Sometimes they came in the words of a song on the radio. They'd hit like bullets, leaving me breathless and gasping for air but before long, they'd become a balm. There's a comfort in knowing that others have felt these feelings. That others have had these words bundled up inside. And somehow, they survived.

Other times, those regrets snuck up in the hot breath of another in my ear. The smell of another man. The possibilities and promise and future hopes and dreams, all crumbled into a dust that spelled out all those things I couldn't say.

There wasn't anybody else to blame. There wasn't anybody to tell. I bundled them up and carried them on my back for fifteen long years, knowing damn well that they'd never stay hidden in the closet. But now, as I blew dust from the lid and pressed my fingers to the lid of that box, I didn't know if I had the strength.

Those demons didn't die without a fight. There were scrapes and cuts and bruises that I never stopped icing down. Wounds that left scars that only I could see, or so I thought. Nat could see some. I could see it in his eyes when a story or a word or a rumor hit me like a punch to the gut. But he never tried to explain it away. He'd just swallow me in a hug and hold me like a child.

I'd always thought that the words we can't say wither away and die if left alone without food or water or sustenance, but they don't need our fuel. They feed off the silence, the lingering doubts that creep into worried minds. They feed off time, gobbling up seconds like a dog scarfs down dinner. And all the while, that silent, creeping, waiting beast lurked in the recesses of my brain—until the room was too cramped. Then, I was powerless. And the floodgates opened.

Far away from the house, Sawyer stopped and looked into my eyes like he was searching for the words to say. Soon enough, he found them.

"I left you a note that explains everything. But I learned this week that Willa never gave it to you."

"But you can't carry that around the rest of your life. You'll be so weighed down you can't even move."

The whole sky was velvet black. The stars receded into the distance and the only thing that shined was Sawyer's smile.

"Why do you think she did that?"

"I don't know, but I can't change that. I need to say something that's been lingering for fifteen years."

"You don't. I—"

"Grace, I love you too."

Crickets chirped before words filled my mouth. My cheeks flushed and I let out an exhale. The words tasted like vinegar, their acid burning my mouth until I let them free. "It's too late, Sawyer."

"I know but—"

"It's too late for all of this." I tugged my hands from his and held them at my side. He stared long and hard at me, a faint impression of the girl he once knew and rejected in the warm moonlight of summer.

An alien sound broke our trance and he dug out his phone. "It's Willa's nurse."

By the time he'd answered, I knew Willa was gone.

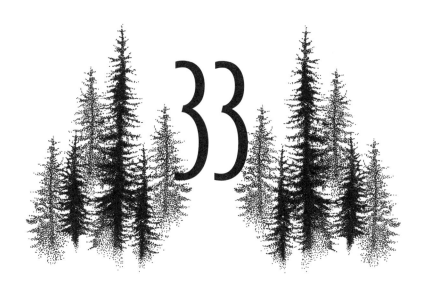

Quicksand exists. It lurks in disguise and hides in plain sight. It can be a relationship—somebody that drags you down bit by bit until you're under water and nobody can hear you begging for help. It can even be a place. Hallowed ground stolen from the Cherokee people centuries ago that today's Oak Hillians are forever attached to.

Upon graduation, four of my classmates made it out of Oak Hill. Sawyer made his midnight run and settled far away. Tamara Winkler snagged a basketball scholarship to NC State and trekked up to the big city, never to return. Her first year, they held watch parties down at the Town Hall not knowing she'd ride the bench until her junior year. By that point, her family had left town altogether and there was hardly any mention of her, even when the Wolfpack won the title. Selective celebration, that's what we called it. Once the family left, Tamara was as good as dead to half the town.

Gustavo Nunez joined the Marines. The first year after graduation, he returned to town, clad in his dress blues, and marched around town like he'd won an election. Hard times followed, as they tended to. Last I heard he was working his way through treatment and starting up on methadone to kick the habit. Some called that an escape all unto itself.

Billy Jenkins struggled to shake the trauma of the town turning against him after what happened to Sarah Price. Despite a lack of evidence, the locals served as judge and jury. Those thugs in Moxville that beat him to a pulp? Rumor had it that Liam Price had paid them to send a message.

The rest? Well, besides those brave four and Sarah Price, the rest were mostly still here. The fight only lasted so long. There were no twelve rounds. It's a slow, dogged marathon that you're designed to lose from the get-go. And I should know. Maybe I didn't take as many blows as the others. And seeing as how I don't frequent Mickey's like the rest of my classmates, it's a near miracle that I don't carry an addiction or vice around like a sign on my back. They still exist, don't get me wrong. We all have our vices. We all have our secrets.

I learned an important lesson from watching those folks that escaped, whether dead or alive. Nobody escapes life unscathed. And the only mark of success is how many lives you touch along the way. Sarah Price paid dearly for the town's sins. She never complained. Never moaned about the night in the woods and how it changed the course of her life forever. But when she died, it seemed like the ending to a movie that had stretched out longer than it had to.

Death didn't scare me. It crept around town and turned pitch pines into widow makers. It whirred through an ambulance down the road. But typically, it was unremarkable and predictable. Older folks taking their last breath. Addicts fighting their demons with one arm tied up. But people like Willa and Nat, well, they seemed invincible to me. Stitched with a different thread. Like kindness was a medicine that they'd made part of their souls. One that would spring eternal life if we let it.

My neck ached from staring up into the abyss above so I rocked myself in the chair and watched the cool evening breeze tickle the needles of the neighboring evergreens. When the door swung open behind me, I was hardly surprised to see Nat emerge and hand me a steaming mug of tea.

"You heard the news?"

He nodded. "Thought you'd be up grappling with it."

"Sawyer went to be with her."

"Good. That's where he belongs."

"It was weird to have him here tonight. If I didn't know better, I'd have thought he never left town."

"You've heard just about every story I've got in my memory banks over the years. Some probably more than a few times. But have I ever told you about the first time I fell in love?"

"No, I don't think so."

"I was sixteen. A young buck in my own right but not nearly as plucky and strong as you. But we share some of the same warts. I had little faith in myself or the notion that I deserved anything good in the world. I was two years from a life of military service, or so I thought."

"What was her name?"

"Mary Ann."

"So I take it she was from the South?"

"Oak Hill, actually. Now her family has long since packed up and left, but the summer after my sophomore year of high school, we both worked part time at a little day camp for local kids on the edge of Nantahala. It was heaven. The kids would frolic in the woods and we'd supervise them as we walked around together. Soon, we were holding hands. Conversation warms that connection faster than much else. We had more common ground than I thought possible. But soon she let the news drop that her family was moving. Her father, a military man himself, was reassigned after a tragic accident on base took his right hand."

"I'm sorry, that's terrible."

"Love doesn't operate well with a ticking clock. It needs time and space to unfurl and reveal itself in its entirety. So we rushed things. Talked about forever and how we'd write letters until somehow, we'd wind up in the same city."

"But you didn't?"

"Life got in the way. We wrote each other through the fall but I faltered and had eyes for a new girl in town, who ripped my heart into a million pieces. When life crept on, I always had her in the back of my mind but never thought I could bear the look on her face when she asked why I stopped writing, when she asked why I gave up."

"That's a heavy load to carry," I said.

"It is," Nat said. "But I don't have to tell you about what that's like."

"Sawyer is going to leave again," I said.

"Maybe," Nat said. "But I saw how he looked at you. Back then. Tonight. It's all the same."

"Looking and feeling are two different things."

"Our eyes are a window to our minds, Grace. We can't control them as well as we think."

I hesitated for a moment until the rocker stopped and the words came in their entirety. "When he left, you never rushed me along. I was a crumpled, broken mess and you provided a stable hand, a shoulder to weep on, and more patience than I deserved."

"It's what anyone would do."

"It's not but that's not my point. Back then, you acted like it was part of life. Heartbreak and devastation. And I see why, don't get me wrong. But now you're here, up past your bedtime, and singing a different tune."

"We only get so many second chances."

"You should tell that to Sawyer."

"He knows," Nat said.

unday morning mirrored its name and bright rays kissed my skin
through the kitchen windows. I whispered a goodbye to Willa and dug
into my nightstand. The envelope rested in my hands and stared back
at me with concern and worry. It took every fiber in my being to adhere to
Willa's request in the first place but now that I was faced with the reality of
opening the flap and releasing her final words to me, my stomach soured.
With a sharp inhale, I flipped it open and dug out the contents. Two pages
fell onto my lap. One in Willa's handwriting. The other in Sawyer's.

I read Willa's first. It was abbreviated and to the point. And by the time
I finished, I didn't even need to look at Sawyer's. I knew most of what it
said. By the time I was through, I had learned only two new things. First, I
learned that Sawyer had faced relentless pressure from Madison Dockery
after she'd asked him out. He'd said no, but she didn't accept that. It was
borderline harassment. Staying in town meant facing that down or addressing it. Neither was a realistic option. By the end, despite Willa's plea for
forgiveness and understanding, I nearly retched at the idea that the truth
had been kept from me for so long.

The second thing I learned was that Sawyer had loved me too. His note concluded with his Aunt Kay's address near Philadelphia and three crushing words.

Come with me.

The realization washed over me like the sun pushing through a cloud. The way I'd seen the world since that horrid day in June, all of it, was misinformed. A distorted reality that I created and Willa furthered. The feeling burned inside me. I hated how much I cursed her name on the day she left the earth. I hated how much I had to say to Sawyer. How much I had inside me.

I read over the notes once more and set them back into the envelope. When did Sawyer learn that she'd never given me the note? Did he think that I'd spent the last fifteen years ignoring his urges and wishes? No wonder he trotted into town like there wasn't a scar across his cheek. In his eyes, in his world and his memory, I was the one that never provided an explanation. I was the one that left him.

Embers woke inside me and heat pulsed through my veins. I'd never known rage, instead preferring to let small spurts of anger out with a long run or a shout in the woods. But I sat in my car, staring at the interior above and screamed at Willa Sawyer for obscuring the fork in the road and forcing me to believe I only had one path.

When the fire simmered, I wiped tears from my eyes and stared at myself in the mirror and saw the small, unknowing person that I'd become. Someone starved from the truth and left to reckon with a false reality. Gaslit into oblivion. And the conductor standing in front of the orchestra of lies had walked off the stage forever. A coward's exit.

My eyes hung low and gritty, and exhaustion weighed on my shoulders like a backpack that I couldn't set down. I sat in the kitchen and grappled with the realization that Willa Sawyer's sole mission in life was to protect her family. To protect Jacob Sawyer. And I started to wonder if I'd given her word too much weight when confirming Sawyer's alibi that night. The creeping realization hung over me like a fog.

Cliff arrived the same time that my coffee pot chimed. I emerged from the house and interrupted his friendly conversation with Nat. "Is she gone?" I asked.

"She passed early this morning," Cliff said.

The words riddled my heart like bullets. How could you know something was coming and still have it hurt so much? My eyes darted to Nat's who smiled as if somehow knowing I was trying to size up the enormity of his eventual demise. If losing Willa hurt this much, losing Nat would all but break me into pieces like a boulder into gravel.

Cliff forced a smile. "I figured we could go over together. Like old times. If you're not trying to bite my head off, that is."

"I haven't decided which part of you I'll bite," I said.

He shrugged. "You cut me off last night but I want you to know that I'll fight for you and do what I can. Even if it's pointless."

I retreated to the kitchen to fill another mug. On the porch, the steam clouded under the overhang and dissolved into the morning sun.

"She passed peacefully," Cliff said. "Hannah wasn't there, but a colleague was."

"How is your wife?" Nat asked.

"Good as ever, although she's devastated by Willa's passing. I think they grew close in these last few weeks."

"I hate to ask this, Cliff, but you're certain that she was with Sawyer the night Lark was killed?"

"One hundred percent," he said.

"Good. So, you and Hannah doing all right?" I asked.

He nodded. "Better, I think. In a way, Sawyer's arrival helped that."

"How so?"

"I . . . Nothing. It'll sound weird."

"That's never stopped you before."

He sighed. "Seeing him and how twisted his life is—how there are so many pieces left for him to figure out. I guess, it reminded me that I have it all if I want it."

"You can't make yourself want it," I said.

"No, but it's been a good reminder to cherish what I do have. Take care of my own."

"That's good. I'm sure Reyna will understand."

Cliff winced and turned away from me. "What's the latest on the case? Any luck with Fort Sherman?"

"It's like trying to run through thorn bushes."

"And if it turns out this woman has nothing to do with the military?"

"Sawyer connected with Cedar a bit yesterday. We've got another possible lead but it's a lot harder to pin down. Turns out Cedar and Lark would come into Oak Hill about once a month."

Cliff raised his eyebrows. "How come nobody ever saw them?"

"They'd approach down by the fire road. Over by the Dockery Estate. Then Lark would head into town while Cedar waited in the woods."

"Weird."

"Our guess is that she was in town to collect funds. Now, how she earned those funds is another question we have yet to explore."

"Prostitution?" Cliff asked. "In Oak Hill, North Carolina?"

"That's an outdated term, Mr. Mayor. But yes, sex work is entirely possible. Although we haven't the slightest clue who would be her customer base."

"If she's approaching town from that direction, she'd have to get a ride to end up over by Lionel Sutton's property."

"That's a good observation, actually. We hadn't gotten there yet when Sawyer heard the news last night."

Cliff downed the rest of his mug and I followed. "Nat, you want to come?" I asked.

"No, I think I'll sit here a while and remember warm times with Willa Sawyer a bit longer. I don't see a point in rushing that."

"Are you coming to Silas's funeral today?" Cliff asked. "Weird to have that service on the same day as Willa's passing but they say that tragedy comes in threes."

"Willa, Silas, and your victim," Nat said.

"See you at church?" I asked.

"Silas Dockery was a good man," Nat said. "But I'll say my kind words from this porch and wish his spirit well."

I jumped into Cliff's truck. We rode in silence on the way to Sawyer's, a shadow of the same drive we'd made many years back and then days ago. Yet somehow none of them felt the same. When we arrived and knocked on the front door, nobody answered. There was no movement in the house and Sawyer's car wasn't in the drive. Cliff sighed. "He's probably gone to arrange for her service."

"Or he's already back in Philadelphia."

Cliff eyed me. "Don't."

"A tiger can't change their stripes."

35

After our unsuccessful visit to Sawyer's house, by fate or luck or circumstance, I retreated to the station and was forced to face the actual reality before me. Liam Price sat in the lobby with a tan folder on his lap.

Liam wasted no time or breath in getting to the point. Before I was seated, he opened his mouth to explain his presence. "Earl is a man of his word," he said, gripping the file close and tight. "If our victim is not in here, we can drop the Sherman angle altogether."

"Can I look?"

He slapped the folder onto my desk and I slid the three photos inside into a row. Each of the women were white, brown-haired, and looked similar to one another.

In the center, a pair of eyes stared back at me that stole my full attention.

I focused on her and flipped it over.

"Lauren Blackburn," I said.

He grinned. "I chose the same one."

"You knew her?" I asked.

"No. We were on Sherman around the same time but it's a massive place. Thousands of folks are stationed there at any given moment. Can't say I knew her but something stood out."

"What's her story?"

"Enlisted in 1999. Officially AWOL from Fort Sherman as of June 17, 2004."

"Huh," I said. "2004? That would put Cedar at eighteen. He didn't strike me as much older than fourteen or so."

"Right," Liam said. "So, likely AWOL then pregnant."

"Shit," I said.

"Something you're not telling me?"

"We learned that Cedar and his mother would head to Oak Hill once every few weeks where they'd split up. Cedar would wait along the trails in Nantahala. Our working theory is that she was here earning some cash."

Liam nodded slowly. "And so the pregnancy . . ."

"Right."

"I can dig into her time on the base if you'd like. Now that we have a name, that makes this a lot easier to chase down. Or . . . Look, I'm not discounting your hypothesis about her way of earning a living. But maybe somebody knew her routine and that she'd have cash on her. Easy target."

"Doesn't fit with an attack from behind but anything is possible."

"Either way," Liam said. "I won't tell a soul about her identity."

I studied him intently. "Even Ethan Dockery?"

"Even Ethan Dockery. He's got his hands full as it is. And from what I've seen, you're more than capable, Grace. I know he's got a bone to pick with you, but he's putting on a show. Sarah always said kind things about you. That memory means something. I wish I had more pull, but a Dockery is a Dockery."

"I appreciate that."

"You know how to reach me," he said. "Keep the files."

Benjamin Bradley

As quickly as Liam left, Munoz filled his seat. He slurped coffee and studied the photo of Lauren Blackburn. "She looks a hell of a lot better than when we saw her. Life took a toll."

I looked up. "Can I send you on a wild goose chase?"

"With pleasure. What's up?"

"I'd like to try and chase down Cedar's birth certificate. The only trouble is that we don't have a name. Since Lark was a pseudonym, Cedar likely is too. I don't know how easy it is to pull a birth certificate without a first name but—"

"Say no more," he said. "I'll work the phones. I take it you're planning to run down what you can on Lauren's life before she was AWOL?"

"That's the plan."

"Better hurry," he said.

"Shit," I said. "If you see Molloy, have him start to put cones up downtown, okay?"

He nodded and marched out. I

fired up my laptop, blew dust off the keys, and dug into every database that I had access to, suddenly fueled with the newfound identity of my victim.

I had middling results, struggling to pin down the specific Lauren Blackburns from a sea of other North Carolina-born residents with the same name. Frustrated, I rang Susan.

I explained the situation and the newfound discovery, which was met with mild celebration.

"There's no birth date on the record from the VA?"

"I have her photo and a short bio. Doesn't say anything about her birthday or hometown."

"What years did she serve? 1999 you said?"

"Right. AWOL as of 2004."

"All right. Give me two minutes and I'll ring you back."

186

Like clockwork, my phone rang less than two minutes later. "Moxville," she said. "Born at the County Hospital there."

"How did you find that?"

"State Homeless Coalition works closely with the Veterans Affairs office. I called up our VA rep and had him look through his database. Questionable legality but we're in the business of helping folks."

"Birth date?"

"August 4, 1980."

"Doesn't a birth certificate usually list a mother and father?"

"Yes, but I don't have the actual paperwork. Only what the VA has in their records. Hustle down to Moxville and they can give you a copy."

"I don't have time to make that run. The funeral is shutting down every inch of the city."

"Speaking of, can you ask Sawyer to come pick up Cedar?"

Damnit, I thought. "Didn't you hear?"

Susan paused. "Oh god."

"Last night. I'm sorry, Susan."

"The dominos keep falling. My lord. Well, good thing I'm heading to St. Anthony's."

"I can take Cedar," I said.

"Meet me behind the church around nine and I'll give you a big hug as a thanks."

"I should be the one thanking you."

"I hope you can find out what happened to his mother. He's a good kid."

"I'm on it."

I scanned online for a number that would lead me to Moxville's County Records Office. Every record request form mentioned a three-week lag time.

Timing, as always, stood in the distance and laughed at my misery.

Munoz shrugged as I passed him in the office. "Dead ends."

"Sunday," I said. "We're up a creek."

"Molloy's at the north end of Murphy Road."

"Good. I've got to head over to St. Anthony's, but we'll position ourselves like we discussed yesterday. Holler if you need anything."

"Will do, Boss."

I rolled my eyes and pushed out of the station. In the car, I called Sawyer, but the voicemail sounded after two rings. Instead I texted him and Cliff our victim's name with an urging to call me when they were free. Suddenly alone again, I rushed to the rear of St. Anthony's and waited for Susan to arrive.

36

Downtown stood empty and vacant, a husk of the bustle that it held on a normal day. Sunday always brought a quietness to the streets and CLOSED signs into storefront windows, but the once-beloved stillness felt more eerie than blissful. I checked in with Molloy, who sat half-asleep in his cruiser with sports talk radio on as white noise.

On a normal day, I'd ignore any laziness but I nudged him awake and reminded him that we'd seen three terrible events in a matter of days. Best not make it four. He didn't grumble, instead a sober realization coated his face like sunscreen and he sat rigid and on guard, at least until I drove away.

I held my breath as I drove past the graveyard that bordered the rear edge of St. Anthony's and parked myself in the adjoining gravel lot. Susan arrived moments later and Cedar stepped from the car without much reservation. I let him sit in the front and accepted the aforementioned hug from Susan.

She stared at the church, which brimmed with life and Oak Hill folks in their Sunday best. The high steeple appeared to pierce the sky and rest with the clouds. Little town, big church, Nat used to say. I wondered if that was because Oak Hill needed the security that faith brings or if every small town in Appalachia funneled into similar doors on Sunday. I wasn't sure that it mattered.

"Did Nat ever take you to church?"

I stared at her.

"Right, I should know better. I take it you don't know the significance of each saint?"

"I do not."

"Well, to spare you a lecture, there's a little catchy prayer that people occasionally mutter. One specifically aimed at our Saint Anthony. *Dear St. Anthony, please come around: something is lost, and it cannot be found.*"

"If only the rest of the Bible was written like a song."

"Everybody connects with it differently. I'm not here to tell you what to believe."

"Good, because I'm not sure I'd listen."

"Do you believe in prayer?" she asked.

"I do," I said. "But I think it's about manifesting things more than asking for them. Putting a wish out into the world, whether it's a good intention or a prayer for security or safety, it breathes life into the words. It forces us to look for it in every minute of the day, waiting to see if our prayers and wishes are answered. And before you ask, no, I don't pray for much."

"Why not?"

"Most of the things I'd wish for aren't going to change. Nat will die someday. The world will still be a dark place. And the cinnamon buns at Emma's diner will forever make my stomach hurt, no matter what words I whisper toward the sky."

"Have you prayed for Cedar?"

I nodded. "Every day."

"Me too. And I'll do the same inside. Maybe when I'm in God's house he'll actually listen."

"I'll meet you at the Center after the service, yeah?"

"See you then." She craned her neck and looked into the window at Cedar. "Don't cause too much trouble now."

I settled into the car and turned the radio on long enough for two large black SUVs to crowd the lot. Cedar watched on curiously as a well-dressed crowd emerged and approached the church. Madison Dockery stepped out in heels, marching with one hand out to her side as she navigated the gravel and rocks below.

Ethan Dockery emerged last, took one step toward the church then looked our way. He marched in my direction with a cloud of dust gathering behind him in his wake.

"Hang on a second, Cedar," I said, then hopped out. Whatever Ethan had to say didn't belong in Cedar's ears.

"Are you insane?" he asked.

"Excuse me?"

He pointed to the car. "Bringing a vagrant to my father's service."

"No, sir. He's staying with me during the service. Susan Orr wanted to—"

"This is a wild boy. Why isn't he in the hands of the state by now?"

"We don't—"

"And if you say it's because you don't have a lead in his mother's case, then you're digging your own grave, Detective. There's only one person responsible for finding those answers."

"We have a lead," I said.

"One that you're willing to stake your job and reputation on?"

"That boy, the one scared out of his mind sitting inside that car, deserves answers. Whether they come tonight or next Thursday, I'm going to do what it takes to get those answers. He doesn't deserve the uncertainty. The unknowing. I understand the lack of patience but—"

"Chamberlain would have had this case closed last week."

I grinned. "Maybe. But I have no doubt that it would have been closed without resolution. Every day we're learning something new. I'd rather wait for the right answers than rush to the wrong ones."

"Then best of luck in your next career, Detective."

"And I'm sorry for your loss, Ethan. Your father was a great man."

"One of the finest. But he'd be furious that it took you this long to identify Miss Blackburn."

The name hit me like a gust of wind. Liam must've lied. He'd told Dockery everything already. I decided to pretend like I never heard the name.

"We have our best team on it," I said.

With a snort, Ethan stormed off in the other direction with shocked faces by his side. I didn't have to follow. I knew the makeup of the church and the people of Oak Hill well enough to paint a vivid picture in my mind. The funeral, like that of Silas's wife, would be a muted, stoic affair. A buttoned-up review of a laundry list of achievements and awards. A sober recounting of Silas's impact on the town. There may not be any tears from the audience, but nobody would move from their seat before a Dockery signaled for such. Fear and respect are brethren after all.

All that recounting of days gone by brought a flash to my mind that stuck for a long while.

37

I was thirteen when Norma Dockery died. Nat woke me early that morning, not with the news, but with a warning that the town may not bustle with the usual hum of activity. I rubbed sleep from my eyes and tried to make sense of the words but youth filtered the facts like a veil. At the breakfast table, I feasted on cereal and watched birds twirl out the window, waiting for Sawyer's bike to spit gravel from its tires and lurch into view.

"What happens when animals die?" I asked, thinking more of the goldfinch on the branch than of the infamous Norma Dockery. Nat futzed with a mug of coffee, rapping his fingers on the rim like a new drum kit. When he'd beat out a rhythm long enough, his mouth croaked open.

"I don't entirely know how to have this conversation," he said.

"What conversation?"

"It's important that you understand death. It will be a constant in your life no matter the path you choose, kid."

I held my spoon in the milk for a long moment, watching dyes from the sugary mix cloud the liquid. "I know that people die sometimes. And birds too. And all the animals. And that there isn't heaven or hell."

Nat grinned. "Who taught you that?"

"You did."

"These conversations always take me by surprise. I have no recollection of telling you any of this stuff, yet you absorb it like a sponge. Which at least explains why you know all your curse words by now. Hell, you're fully grown, kid."

"Why did Norma Dockery die?" I asked.

"It's not a question of why. But you'll hear people ask how."

"How did she die?"

"In her sleep," Nat said. He must've seen my eyes widen because he pressed on without missing a beat. "That's something that can only happen when you're much older."

"How old was she?"

"Sixty-three."

"Won't you be sixty-three someday?"

He nodded.

"So you could die in your sleep too?"

"It's possible."

"And then I'd be alone again."

"No," he said. "You're never alone. This whole town sees you as kin."

"If there's no heaven or hell, what is there?"

Nat exhaled and pointed to the back of his truck. "Let me try this a different way. You know how every spring I plant flowers for my customers? Well, there are two kinds. One kind is called annuals. They last one season and then they're gone. Others, they come back every year. We call them perennials."

"What kind are we?"

"Well, we're not flowers but people have different opinions on the matter. Some folks think our spirits are like those annuals. We're once in a lifetime. But I like to think that we come back every season. Slightly different forms. Maybe different faces. But I like the idea that life goes on."

Sawyer rapped his knuckles on the door and let himself in.

Nat waved him over to the table. "Did you hear about Norma Dockery?" Sawyer said.

I gestured toward Nat. "He told me the second I woke up."

"How are your folks?" Nat asked. "Haven't seen George in a few days now."

"He's good," Sawyer said. "Busy with work. Dockery has him working so much he's got to eat lunch at his desk. He was supposed to start teaching me to drive soon too."

"He'll get around to it," Nat said.

"Willa asked me if I wanted to go to church tomorrow morning," Sawyer said.

"Do you?" I asked.

He shook his head, curly brown locks rustling in the breeze. "I don't see the point. She's dead," Sawyer said. "What good will praying do?"

"You can pray for her to rest peacefully and thank her for the good she's done in the community. Did you know that Norma was born and raised here? She was Norma Boone back then; her family owned the store before Margo bought it and changed the name."

"And then she met Silas Dockery?" I asked.

"Somewhere along the way. He wanted to relocate the family closer to the city but she convinced him to rebuild the house up on the hill and make Oak Hill their home. We owe that woman a lot more than a prayer."

"Why?"

Nat shrugged. "Home is a special place. Some people can't leave it behind."

"How'd they get all that money?" Sawyer asked. "I asked my dad but he told me that was none of my business. Mumbled something about old wealth and new problems. I think he's frustrated that they're rich and we're not."

"Some people pass down trinkets and jewelry to their family. Others have dishes and diseases. And others, a rare few, pass down enough money for their kin to live a comfortable life. Somewhere in the Dockery family tree somebody worked real hard for that fortune."

"But they're spoiled," Sawyer said. "The kids at least."

"Privilege is like a bad haircut. You don't see the full image in the mirror but others see it when they look. It's not their fault they were born a Dockery. And it does no good to turn them away. They have every right to be here too."

"What will the kids do now?" I asked. "Do they go to Susan's like I did?"

Nat winced slightly but forced a smile. "No, Grace. They have their father to watch after them."

"Kinda like you."

"Yes, I'm the guard at your gate like Silas will be for Madison and Ethan. It won't be easy, but they'll work through it. And I'll pray for them regardless."

A phone rang in the kitchen and Nat jumped to his feet. He curled the cord around his fingers as he spoke quietly into the receiver. Sawyer leaned across the table and whispered into my ear, "I've got a case."

"A case?"

"For the Clueless Detective Agency."

My eyes lit up. "What case?"

"Norma Dockery. I think she was murdered."

Once Nat scooted into town and left us alone, Sawyer and I knocked down Cliff's door until his parents agreed to let him free. The three of us, riding in a perfect "V" like birds in the sky, cruised down Murphy Road and noted the silent nature of the hanging heads that wandered through. Cliff bought an orange soda from Margo's store but returned with little useful information on the case.

Norma's death had turned Margo's usual fountain of information off. Sawyer led us out of town where we tossed our bikes into the bushes beside the old fire road in a thicket of weeds and thorns. We hiked up the path of loose soil until the Dockery estate came into view through the foliage.

Sawyer pulled a pair of binoculars from his backpack and passed them around for each of us to look.

When I peered through the lenses, there was nobody in sight. I half expected to spot a sea of mourners in a line waiting at the doorstep but there was no activity. The estate mirrored town, a subdued quietness that chilled my bones and soured my stomach. Sawyer pointed toward a far window. "Look through there. I saw somebody sitting down."

Following his finger, the interior of the room came into focus. Ornate decor hung on the walls and surrounded a long oak dinner table. At the head, the gray-bearded figure of Silas Dockery sat and picked at a plate of food. His two children sat to either side of him.

Ethan opened his mouth and spoke but my lip reading was piss-poor.

"What are they doing?" Cliff asked.

A smile spread across Silas's face and soon his children mirrored the same.

"They're laughing."

"That's sick," Sawyer said. "Somebody just died!"

I shrugged. "Maybe it's like what you said about praying. What's the point in feeling sad? What good will that do?"

"When my grandma passed, Mom had us in our church clothes within a few hours and I don't think I saw a smile in my house for a week," Cliff said.

"Exactly," Sawyer said. "This is evidence. Something bad happened here."

"Evidence of what?" I asked.

"It's a conspiracy."

"I know what a conspiracy is but remind me anyway," Cliff said. "It's like a trick?"

"I read it in one of my dad's books. It's when people team up to trick others."

"Norma Dockery did nothing but float around town and smile at the people she passed," I said. "Couldn't it be that she got sick and died? They may not be telling jokes. What if they're sharing memories of her?"

"We'll never know," Sawyer said.

"Let's go home," Cliff insisted. "There's a game at noon at the sandlot."

"Sounds good," I said. "Sawyer?"

His eyes appeared from behind the binoculars, raccooned from the mark left behind. I knew he wanted to stay. I knew that he'd sit in that shrub all day and monitor the Dockery family until the proverbial cows came home. But I also knew that he'd listen if I told him to quit it.

"Sawyer, come play ball with us," I said.

"Fine," he said. "But tomorrow we come back."

We didn't go back the next day. In fact, Sawyer dropped the whole bit after his father caught wind of our espionage. The magnificence of youth was that each day presented a new glimmering distraction that stole our attention. We had new ghosts to chase down, although none were as vivid and real as Norma Dockery.

Normalcy crept back into Oak Hill like a shift in seasons, gradually, then all at once. The Clueless Detective Agency redirected focus onto the small-potatoes cases we were built for and Sawyer never uttered another word about Norma Dockery.

We never made another trek down that fire road. At least not until the bonfire the night after graduation, when our innocence and eternal bond were both shattered and scattered into the foliage, never to be found again.

38

own was so silent that I almost heard the strained prayers of the
mourning through the church walls. If I closed my eyes, there were
familiar hymns and movements, all brief reminders that their life provided membership to a special community. One that Nat never thought I
needed. And from the few times that Sawyer snuck me in with Willa and
George, I felt he was right.

I shifted my full attention onto the nervous energy in the seat next to
me. Cedar's arms hung at his sides; his hands gathered together in his lap.
Not in a display of formality but discomfort. I wondered if he'd ever been
in a car before. If he'd seen things this week that were only in books and
stories and words his mother told him. I couldn't decide if that was a gift
or a curse.

"Do you like to read?" I asked.

He nodded.

"Do you have a favorite book?"

"No," he said.

"Why not?"

He chewed on that for a full minute while I stared. "I like them all. They're all special."

"They are," I said. "Someday you can write one about your life."

He smiled. "No, I don't think so."

"I bet a lot of people would read it."

"No," he said. "I'm not a good writer."

"Did your mom teach you?"

"She did."

"Then I bet you're a great writer. And if it's something you like, you can work at it. Learn more. Get better. Someday you'll write a bestseller."

"What's a bestseller?"

"When books are popular, they make a list that we call the bestsellers."

"Like Mark Twain?"

"Exactly." I grinned. "What kind of music do you like?"

Cedar stared with an intensity that could bore a hole in the wall.

"Come on, I'm sure you and your mom sang songs. Right?"

He nodded. "Sometimes."

"I'll mess with the dial until you hear something you like, okay?"

The static broke and the twang of country radio blared. Cedar recoiled in his seat when the gruff voice started singing about a river bank. "Not my style either," I said.

Another turn brought about the scratchy voice of Bob Seger and the muted notes from a guitar. Cedar warmed a bit, or at least didn't actively buck against the beat. I pushed on anyhow and next settled on an AM station playing classical songs from many years ago. Cedar nodded. "I like this."

"Good," I said. "Then we'll listen until your ears bleed."

He reached up and touched his ears. "What?"

"It was a joke," I said. "Sorry, I make a lot of those. Did your mom like to make jokes?"

He shook his head. I lost him again to the stands of pines that bordered the forest, blurred into an abstract painting as we drove past. My phone buzzed and relief crashed over me like a wave when I saw the ID.

"How are you?" I asked.

"Hanging in there," Sawyer said. "Up to my ears in paperwork though."

"We stopped by this morning."

"Cliff mentioned you'd dropped by. I'm sorry, I had to head into the funeral home over in Moxville and—"

"It's okay, Sawyer. We just wanted to check on you."

"I appreciate it. It's weird. I'm sad at times but it comes and goes."

I pictured a tide, moving in and out, and I wanted to reply, *I know*. "I don't think that's weird. That's how sadness works," I said.

"When does the funeral end?"

"They told us to have the streets blocked until noon. So, another hour or so."

"That's rough. I'm heading back your way soon. How's Cedar?"

"He's good," I said. "I'm with him now. We're listening to the radio and hanging out."

"Where can I meet you?"

"Sawyer, I—"

"I know what you're going to say and I appreciate it. But I could use a distraction."

"You sure?"

"No, but I'd like to help. I care for the kid, even if he barely tolerates me."

I grinned. "That's the most we can hope for sometimes."

The hour passed with little conversation aside from a few gentle nods Cedar begrudgingly provided. How Sawyer managed to get a full story out of the boy was beyond my imagination. Their bond seemed infinitely stronger than my fickle connection. In a way, it felt like a failure. Two humans should be able to link up, especially when they both want for something. Cedar and I both seemingly needed answers about his mom yet we were speaking different languages.

Thankfully, when I pulled into the lot behind the Dockery Center, Sawyer was already there sitting on a bench by the forest and watching the birds frolic in the sky. He waved at Cedar, who remained emotionless as he joined Sawyer on the bench.

"Glad I beat the traffic," Sawyer said.

"Whole town is a frenzy now. Roads are open again."

"Nice of you to freeze life to commemorate the dead," he said. "Don't worry, I won't ask the same for Willa's service."

"I think the town will shut down on its own for her. Everyone loved her."

"Maybe," he said. "You two find anything to talk about?"

"Cedar likes classical music," I said. "And doesn't like country."

"Oh yeah? See, Detective Bingham has steered you wrong. There's plenty of great country music but it's not on the radio. Don't worry, we'll find something that you like."

He didn't take his eyes off the trees. "Cedar, can I ask you something?"

He nodded.

"Does the name Lauren Blackburn mean anything to you?"

He nodded again.

"Is that your mother's name?"

"Not anymore."

"But it was?"

"Before."

A question surfaced that I was ashamed I had yet to ask. "Cedar, where is your father?"

He pointed to the trees.

"Your father lives in the forest with you?"

"Sometimes," he said.

"Do you know his name?"

A quick shake of the head. That would be too easy.

"That's okay. Now, Mr. Sawyer here told me about how you and your mom would come to town every once and a while."

He nodded. "Before we got supplies."

"Do you know where she walked when she got here?"

He shrugged. "I stayed by the road."

"Which road?"

"It's made of dirt," he said.

The introduction of that ghost from my past hit me like a punch in the gut. Even after all these years, I held a grudge against that forsaken ground. That damn fire road.

"At the end of the road, would your mom go left or right?"

He thought for a second. "Left."

I smiled. "Very good. You're a natural detective, Cedar. Someday you'll take my job."

He blushed and looked at the ground. I glanced at Sawyer who grinned from ear to ear. I nodded for him to take over. "Cedar, has anybody ever tried to hurt your mom?"

"No. Not really."

"Not really? Did anybody ever yell or shout at her?"

"Sometimes. Hikers would yell if we stole their dinner."

Sawyer grinned. "That's a clever move."

"We only did that if we had to. But they were mad."

"Did you steal food recently?"

"No," he said.

Sawyer cleared his throat. "Are you sick of us asking you questions?"

"Yes."

"When all of this is over . . . where do you want to go?" I asked.

Cedar considered this for a long moment before responding. "Home."

"Will your dad come looking for you?"

"He thinks I'm with my mom."

"Do you want to go there now?" I asked. Part of me prayed that he said yes.

He shrugged. "I'm scared."

"Scared of what?"

"That whoever hurt Mom will hurt me and my dad too."

Sawyer pulled a book out and flipped it open. It took me a minute to realize he'd unearthed our high school yearbook. He pointed to Billy Jenkins's senior portrait and looked up to Cedar. "Do you know this person?"

Cedar shook his head. Sawyer shrugged. "It was worth a shot."

I agreed. I looked over the boy. "If you stay with us a few more days, we can try to make sure that whoever hurt your mom is in jail forever. Then, we'll bring you back to your father. No questions asked."

"Promise?" Cedar asked.

I nodded. "You ever hear of a pinky promise?"

"Pinky promise?"

I stuck my pinky out and motioned for Sawyer to do the same. We wrapped our fingers around one another and kissed our palms. Cedar watched intently. "This is how we lock in the promise. Want to try?"

He nodded and let my finger wrap around his. "Pinky promise," he mumbled and leaned down to kiss the base of his hand.

A jarring sound broke through the trees and ripped through the silence. A gunshot tore a chunk of pine out of a tree, the sound echoing into the distance.

Sawyer pushed us off the picnic table. Fear pinched behind my eyes. With our backs against the legs of the table, another shot rang out. In a blink, Cedar had leapt to his feet and disappeared into the brush.

39

Growing up, Nantahala lurked in the background of my every memory and experience like a monster waiting to strike. Stories, like all things in Oak Hill, spread like wildfire and you couldn't walk two blocks downtown without hearing about some urban legend or wild experience that somebody linked to the forest. Dark woods are like that it seemed. Their natural obfuscation was a cloak that few have the patience or interest to lift merely to discover there are trees, shrubs, and woodland creatures lurking beneath.

As I grew older, time and age both brought a newfound light to the twisty trails of the forest. Glancing at the towering canopies before me, I still believed in monsters but I no longer believed they lurked inside the forest. And by the events in town, it had become clear where the real monsters lived.

Sweet gum seeds, small and spiked, blanketed the trail. The path ahead abruptly ended and I stared around the thicket. With one ear cupped, I listened for footsteps in the brush or voices in the distance. Anything to lead me to Sawyer or Cedar. Anything to help me live up to my promise to protect him.

A crash of leaves sounded, and I ran toward it blindly, my arms covering my face to protect from the overgrown thorns that poked and prodded and clung to my skin. Blood crept down my forearm. I heard it again and picked up the pace until the muscles in my legs burned and screamed for a break. In the distance, I heard a voice. After a moment, I recognized it.

"I ran away once," Sawyer said.

I peered through an overgrown rhododendron and studied the scene. Sawyer stood with one hand stretched outward, an invitation to Cedar, who remained frozen across a dried river bank. Although the gap was hardly three feet, it looked like a canyon from afar. Cedar studied his face and retreated a step backward.

"A long time ago. I ran away too."

"Why?"

"I was scared. Something bad happened to my family and I was responsible. So I ran away. But it was a mistake."

"A mistake?"

"I should have stayed. I should have fought. I should have hung in there. And you should too."

"But the gun," he said, his eyes darting back and forth. "A hunter?"

"Detective Bingham will find out who shot at you. I promise you that. She's smart and kind. Don't you think?"

Cedar nodded. "She's nice."

"She is," Sawyer said, a smile wrapping around his face. "There aren't many people like her in the world. And she'll fight for you, Cedar."

"The woods are safer."

"But the truth isn't in there. And if somebody is trying to hurt you, that means that you saw something. It means that you are part of the puzzle."

"Why? I want to go home."

"We can take you home. I promise. But for now, I need you to trust me. Somebody out there did a terrible thing to your mother. From everything you've said, she seems like she was a great person. Is that true, Cedar? Was your mother great?"

Cedar nodded.

"Good," Sawyer said. "Now, let's go find out what happened to her."

———————

Hesitation held every critter in the forest. Cedar mumbled something under his breath but I couldn't make it out from my angle. I inched my body forward but a twig snapped beneath my boot. Cedar flinched and stared out in my direction. "Just me," I shouted and extricated myself from my spot. "You boys all right?"

"We're fine," Sawyer said. "Any luck on chasing down our shooter?"

"Nothing," I said. "I ran this way but now I'm thinking that the footsteps I followed were from you two."

"I—I don't want to go back," Cedar said.

"We need to find out the truth about your mom's death. Somebody needs to be held responsible, Cedar. And I won't rest until I can find out who."

Cedar examined my face, worry flashed and faded. I did my best to smile through it and approach through the brush. He nodded. When Sawyer approached, he didn't flinch. Didn't retreat. For a second, I thought we'd all return back to Oak Hill humbled, with a new perspective. But a familiar sound echoed through the forest.

Another gunshot. Birds flew off their perches and hid in the sky. When I looked back, Cedar was gone.

Sawyer sprinted deeper into the forest while I ran toward the shot. Running toward something or running away. The opposition stood stark even in that panicked moment. More importantly, the question rained down on me like precipitation from the clouds above. Who wanted Cedar dead? And why?

When my feet met a trail, I recognized the familiar makeup of the forest and listened intently. No hurried footsteps or crunching leaves. Just the wail of overhead birds singing songs and warnings that I couldn't translate.

I followed the trail, pistol held at my side, and strafed toward the entrance. As the hazy sunlight crept in and marked the fringes of the forest, I heard the distant sound of heavy breathing.

With my back pushed against the bark of an oak, I waited three long beats and then burst onto the trail, waving my pistol out in front of me and shouting at the intruder. "Don't move!"

Susan Orr raised both her hands in panic. Her shriek danced through the sky and mixed with the birdsong.

I lowered the gun. "Sorry, Susan."

She took sharp, stiff inhales. "I . . . heard . . . heard . . ."

"The gunshots?"

She nodded.

"Any idea who was shooting at us?"

"At you?" she asked. "My god."

"We were behind the center when the first shot rang out. If Cedar hadn't ducked down, he'd be dead."

"Cedar?" Susan's eyes widened. "The poor boy."

"Sawyer and I corralled him in the forest. Talked him out of running away again. Took just about all that we had. Then another shot came and he bolted. Can't say I blame him."

Moments later, Sawyer emerged, downtrodden and disappointed. "Did you see which way he went?" Sawyer asked, his head swiveling back and forth.

"No," I said. "But my guess is that he ran home."

"Maybe," Sawyer said. "But that means he's gone."

"I'm starting to think that's the safest place for him."

"He needs help," Susan said. "Especially now that his mother is gone."

"The bullet may have grazed him," Sawyer said. "But I can't be sure."

"Shit," I said. "Either way, we need to find him immediately. Let me call around. I'm not sure I can raise the same group that I had on call for the search."

"Search?" Susan asked.

"Before we found him. It was a back-up option. We'd send a small crew to search the edges of the forest for any signs of Cedar. Only now I'm afraid that even if they find him, he will bolt in the other direction."

"Not if he's hurt."

"True," I said. "And if he's hurt, there may be a blood trail."

"Lord, I hope not," Susan said.

We stamped back toward the Dockery Center, my legs shaking with every step. Cliff picked up on the second ring and jumped to action once he heard about the shooting. One of the few perks of having the mayor in my back pocket, I supposed. "I'd like to stay here and wait for them," Sawyer said.

Susan put a hand on his shoulder. "This feels like deja vu but I'm so sorry for your loss, Jacob."

He nodded. "Thanks, Susan."

"Will there be a service?"

"Eventually, maybe."

"Well you let me know if you need anything at all, okay? Casserole, prayer, whatever you need."

He grinned. "You're an angel."

"No, but your mother was about the closest thing this world has ever seen," Susan said.

On a normal day, I'd have nodded along but all that came to mind was the wretched note that was tucked into my glove box. The many-years-too-late apology and explanation from a woman that I trusted wholeheartedly. Angel didn't quite fit. Guardian, perhaps.

I turned to Sawyer. "When Cliff arrives, remind him not to tell a soul about the gunshots."

"Why?" Susan asked.

"Our shooter could be one of those volunteers."

"Then how do I explain that there may be blood?" Sawyer asked "That he may be hurt?"

"You say that Cedar is in the forest and might be injured."

"Fair enough."

"Susan, thanks for your help. And if any of your team saw anything . . ."

She nodded. "You're my first call."

As she retreated, Sawyer stared into the forest and then brought his emeralds toward me. "Grace, we . . . we need to talk."

"We do," I said.

"I don't know where to start."

"So don't."

"Don't?"

"Not now. We've waited decades to have this conversation. It can wait until we find Cedar."

"But I—"

I extended my hand and took his. "Look at you. You haven't slept. I can't imagine how much pain you're in and yet, you're still here trying to help somebody else. I can't tell you how much I appreciate that. How much Cedar will someday appreciate all that you've done here. But this is not the time to rehash the past."

"Then when?"

"In the future," I said with a shrug. "But make me one promise?"

"Anything."

"Don't leave town before we have the chance to talk."

When I was six years old, I crept out of my bed and woke Nat, urging him to check the closet for intruders and monsters. Every child has some instance of this experience. A momentary break from reality where you are the sole target of antagonists, whether that be because of your youth or innocence. Either way, even at a young age, we discern details from the world around us and decipher them as clues that despite lessons in school, we are likely the center of the universe. The world, for all of our experiences, revolves around our daily life. We make it spin and teeter and rock out of pattern.

I don't know if it was a TV show or a story Nat read or whispers I heard in school but I got it in my head that there was a constant threat lurking around every corner. My once everlasting love of the isolation and remote nature of Nat's house was replaced with a pulsing terror that radiated through my bones.

Then again, I was six.

Nat sat with me on the couch and tickled my feet until I calmed and crashed into a fitful sleep. When I woke, he sat next to me reading from a book and sipping a mug of tea. We repeated the pattern for a week until he forced a conversation that I'd long been avoiding.

"The world can be scary, but you're safe here, young buck."

"Then why am I scared?"

"Can I tell you a secret?"

I leaned in close. Secrets were my favorite.

"Everybody is scared of the dark, even if only a little bit."

"Why?" I asked.

"We fear what we can't see. What we don't know. That's the dark. But if you listen to your body, not your heart or your mind but your gut, you will know that you are safe."

"Huh," I said, pretending to understand.

Years later, although I'm sure I transformed the memory into a more comprehensive conversation than reality would provide, I started to understand everything Nat said.

I never stopped being afraid of the dark. I just got better at listening to my gut and knowing what it was trying to say, like a language only I could translate for my body.

As I retreated and left Sawyer alone by the edge of the forest, something awoke in my gut that I couldn't quite put into words. In my car, I unearthed a notepad from the center console and started scribbling until I made sense of things. I wrote WHY on top in all capital letters. On the first line, I wrote: *Why did somebody try to kill Cedar?*

I lingered on this thought for a long moment. Then I wrote three theories that would refute that notion.

Maybe it was a hunter. No, nobody in the world has aim that bad. And the shots started when we were out in the open.

Maybe it was Cedar's father. Then why would he risk Cedar's life with such a cavalier move. No, that's a long shot.

Maybe they weren't aiming at Cedar. That would mean that either Sawyer or I were the intended target. And with Sawyer's sudden arrival in town, I had doubts that he'd managed to make enemies that quickly. That put the focus solely on me. I shut my eyes and considered all the people I'd wronged. The list wasn't long but if we're honest with ourselves, we're not the person that needs to make that list nor the best person to write it out. Willa served as a perfect example. We never know those that we've wronged the most.

If the shot was aimed at me, that meant that my investigation was getting close and answers were within reach. Still, the gnawing sense in my gut told me that there was still a gap in my analysis. None of this brought me any closer to understanding who met Lauren Blackburn when she came into Oak Hill.

I unfurled a map from the glove box and it filled the entire front portion of the car. I folded the edges against the grain, knowing that Nat was cringing somewhere with that idea, and focused on the old fire road that Lauren/ Lark and Cedar used to access town. Tracing my finger over the dotted line that marked the unpassable path, I followed it toward town. When it ended, I remembered Cedar's earlier statement. Left. She went left.

Left wasn't a big help. It dead-ended a quarter-mile later and disappeared into another thicket. Following the path back to the end of the fire road, I traced the path if she'd turned right instead. The bisecting road, Maple Avenue, crept toward town parallel to Mill Stone Road before eventually merging together and heading back toward town. A mile down Mill Stone would have brought her onto Murphy Road and another three miles of twisty turns would lead her to Lionel Sutton's land.

The path was seemingly random but I noted each house and property that it passed and wrote down the family names in my notebook. When I finished, the list stood as half of Oak Hill but a few names in particular stood out to me. First, there was no getting around the fact that she'd have to walk by Margo's store. There was a roundabout way to avoid Murphy Road but it would have added another two miles to the trek.

Next, there was the shabby property that once belonged to Billy Jenkins before he skipped town. If the rumors were true, he was back. That would put a nice little bow on our relationship over the years but it felt too clean. Better safe than sorry.

I rung Munoz anyway.

"What's up?" he said.

"Keep this between us but somebody shot at Cedar, Sawyer, and I."

"What?" he shouted. "Is everybody okay?"

"We think so. Sawyer and I are fine but Cedar bolted into the woods."

"Can't blame him. Who was the shooter?"

"No clue."

"Damn. And here I was ready to complain about the dull morning I had watching paint dry."

I stifled a laugh. "Do you remember Billy Jenkins?"

"I couldn't forget if I tried," Munoz said.

"Rumor has it he's back in town."

"Interesting. I can run by his old place and see if he's there. I don't think he sold off the family lot when he split town, or at least it's been empty for years."

"Thanks," I said. "Last I'd heard was that he found God in AA and had put his past behind him, but lately it feels like nobody can truly outrun their past."

"I heard that too. Worth running him down if he's here. Want me to bring him in?"

"If you can find him, yeah. Can't hurt. Start with his old cottage off Creek Road. I doubt he'd hide in plain sight, but he wasn't the brightest bulb of the lot."

"On it. By the way, I'm still chasing down Cedar's birth certificate. Like you said, Sunday has put a wall between us and any answers."

"Thanks, Miguel."

"Hell of a week," he said with a laugh. "Let me know if I can help at all. Sadie would understand."

"Appreciate it. Let's touch base this afternoon and see if we've made any progress."

"Aye aye, Captain."

I stared at the last name written on my notepad. The other curious name that rose from my mapping of Lauren's supposed route from the fire road to the location of her death: Liam Price.

I toyed with the approach for a long while before deciding to wait. There was no subtle line of questioning to float to Liam about his possible involvement. All that I had was a possible connection. The easiest spark to light that fire would be somehow proving that Liam and Lauren knew each other when they were at Fort Sherman together. But every connection and resource I had to Sherman was filtered through Liam. Still, there was a creeping doubt that shadowed over my suspicion of him. Could a man that had tragically lost his daughter inflict the same pain on another man? And why would he help us ID her? I struggled with the dilemma and decided that I'd have to loop Sawyer in, unless Tessa somehow pulled through with a miracle, about which I remained skeptical.

I knew in my heart of hearts that my map exercise wasn't foolproof. Lauren's customer or friend or whomever she knew in Oak Hill may have picked her up at a pre-set time and place. She may not have walked anywhere. That alone would render all of my plotting useless.

I stared at the map for a moment longer then cranked the ignition and sped toward the end of Mill Stone Road where it met the fire road. I parked off to the side and stared down past the obstructing gate at the end. The barrier, once painted a bright yellow but now chipped and rusted, still blocked any car from passing through. An installation that occurred well after our bonfire nights and mischief.

Facing the road, I turned left and took ten paces before the road ended, transformed to gravel, then disappeared altogether. Pines choked one another and crowded the forest at the end. I poked my head in and glanced back and forth. I took a deep breath and pushed my way through, stepping through thorns and shrubberies that crowded my path. The pines hardly gave enough room to breathe, let alone pass, but I scraped my way through anyhow until the semblance of a path appeared. Following it, I worried that I'd blink and end up in the bowels of Nantahala but after a quarter mile or so, I saw light creep through the trees and what looked like a clearing appear. When I pushed through the last of the brush, I saw Cedar standing and staring back at me.

"Cedar!" I shouted.

He turned and bolted again into the brush. I darted after him, my foot catching on a vine and my body hitting the forest floor with a thud of pain and dirt. I crept to my feet but Cedar, like a cloud dissolving in the sky, was gone again.

Instead of chasing after him, I stood where he stood and looked around. Beyond the clearing, there was another crop of trees but this section was much easier to pass through. The obvious path meandered for another quarter mile and I took each step with a careful look around, hoping to see Cedar's home and father waiting in the brush. Having no such luck, I hiked on until the path ended again and a clearing appeared. This time, Cedar wasn't standing before me.

In a way, the only thing I saw in that open field was Lauren Blackburn. Her ghost made those same steps. The same hike. And I knew that all of my suspicions and hypotheses were wildly off. When I glanced up and beyond the rolling hills beside me, I understood a new wrinkle to the case. Lauren had made a left. She had hiked through these woods and made her way into this very section of forest. The only question left was why.

-THEN-

CLIFF AND I MARCHED OUT OF THE FOREST IN SILENCE, both reeling from the fallout of what we'd seen. I reassured myself that we would be fine. Sawyer would politely explain that we'd been with him until the gunshot. He'd outline his intention to help. He'd tag us as his personal alibis and witnesses. They'd find no weapon on his body and release him back to his house before the sun crept over the horizon.

No matter the positive thoughts I could conjure, I still struggled to process what happened. Sarah's name circled around in my eardrums like a drop of water I couldn't shake out.

I'd forever been afraid of my mind. Not in terms of intelligence but in how I was terrified to let it run free. When unchecked and unguarded, my mind could spiral like a sink drain and drag me down with it. My mind could think its way into any dark feeling imaginable. But that was only if I listened to the whispers.

I'd always wondered if there was a class or assembly that I missed, which told the rest of the world how to use their mind for good and taught them how to ignore those dark thoughts and redirect them into cherry-coated optimism and hope. I'd spent every waking moment trying not to let the drain pull me down. Some days, it was damn hard. That night, it was impossible.

By the time we made it to Cliff's truck, other stone-faced classmates had emerged from the brush and staggered toward their vehicles in half-drunken shock. Billy Jenkins met eyes with me and I recalled that he once dated Sarah Price. I let go of the door handle and marched toward him. "What happened?"

He stared at me. "What do you mean?"

"There was a gunshot," I said.

"Police sending up warning signals," Billy said. "All bark, no bite."

"Where's Sarah?"

"Hell if I know. She dumped my ass in May then hooked up with Ethan last week. She's dead to me."

"Ethan Dockery?"

Billy frowned. "Like I said, she's dead to me." He caught my wrist. "Wait, why'd you ask about Sarah? You jealous?"

I stared at him for a long moment. I wondered if I had an obligation to tell him since I'd seen her body on the ground and watched the emergency team haul her out like a wounded bird. What did I owe Sarah Price? If nothing, I thought it was the decency to tell her own story.

"I haven't seen her yet. We were supposed to meet up later," I said. "Whatever. Goodnight."

"Hate to see you leave, but love to watch you go," Billy said in a whisper.

"Bite me, Jenkins," I said. He let me go, shrugged, and retreated to his car.

Cliff studied me through the driver's side window and followed me until I joined him in the cab of the truck. "We shouldn't tell anyone what we saw," he said. "Not until we know Sawyer is okay."

"We've got nothing to hide. Innocent until proven guilty, Cliff."

"Maybe so," Cliff said. "But somebody shot Sarah Price and they'll raise hell until they find out who did it."

"The police will figure it out. You heard what they said. It was an accident."

"Guess so," he said. "Can we go wait for Sawyer?"

I nodded, swiped the snot from my nose and tried to fix my makeup in the mirror to no avail. We got stuck in a slow march of cars down the unpaved path out of the clearing, traffic crawling one by one. By the time we made it back to town, Sawyer had been with the police for nearly an hour. I wanted that hour back so badly.

Cliff drove us by his place, then Nat's, each time assuring our loved ones that we were okay and that we didn't have anything to do with the accident. Cliff's father had heard whispers of an accident in the woods. Nat was snoring so loudly I don't think he would have heard an earthquake. We told them what we knew. What we saw. But we never mentioned Sawyer and neither family asked about him. The unspoken could've filled a library.

Looking back now, I know the updates fell like dominos. The Price family caught wind and rushed to the emergency room. Talented doctors did everything in their power but the bullet would leave her paralyzed from the waist down for life. The Price family wailed. Sarah reassured them, reminded them it was better than the alternative. She exuded strength. And she'd need a hell of a lot more of it in the days that followed.

The questions surfaced as they always did. Slowly, then all at once. Who brought a rifle to the bonfire? Was the bullet meant for Sarah or was there another target? Who saw the shooter? Could it have been a terrible accident? As they continued to bubble up, Chamberlain held court around town, skirting from the nearby Dockery Estate to different parents' homes, starting with Sawyer's then moving through a list of miscreants that could've had a hand in the terrible accident. All for naught.

We arrived at Sawyer's when Officer Agnew had just left, the dust from his exit still in the air. Chamberlain stood on the steps and barked at Sawyer's parents in a harsh tone. "If your son had something to do with this, I will not rest until he's behind bars."

"He didn't do anything," George Sawyer said.

"We'll see about that," Chamberlain added. "I don't care what it takes, I'll find the truth."

Chamberlain spit at the ground and left. Willa stopped us at the door and told us to come back tomorrow. No smile, no pleasant assurances. Just a cold abruptness that I'd never seen before or since. So, Cliff and I waited, convinced she would relent and let us hug her son. We lurked in the truck and fought sleep.

Somewhere in the dead of night, once the adrenaline wore off, Cliff and I had both fallen asleep. We woke to scattered lights and frenzied shouts. EMTs and police filed in and out of the Sawyers' front door. I worried they'd come to arrest Sawyer for Sarah's accident, but when the EMTs lugged a gurney with George Sawyer's unmistakable outline strapped in, Cliff and I braced for the worst.

Word spread quickly. George had passed. Another accident. Cliff and I steeled ourselves to wait on that curb as long as we needed, just to see our friend.

Our stakeout lasted a grueling week. Then life and responsibilities caught up and bitterness crept in, at least for Cliff. There was no explanation that would suffice for him. He rumbled about friendship and the differences in how he'd handle such an event, even if we both knew that nobody could prepare for such a loss. Nobody could prepare for life to change at a moment's notice. When the monsters of anger and frustration and abandonment won out, we fed them. We simmered and raged, a vicious circle, until we decided that we'd waited long enough. And on that night, that first night we didn't sit by Sawyer's house and stare into darkened windows, he left town forever. That night tattooed itself on my heart and occasionally, I'd remember the scars and they'd rush to the surface.

ack in my car, I read through a smattering of texts with varied updates. Sawyer alerting me that they were heading into the brush. Cliff asking for an update. Two missed calls from Munoz and a text urging me to call him. I rang him first.

"Where have you been?" he asked.

"Chasing down a lead. What's up?"

"I ran by Billy Jenkins's. Peeked in an open window and saw food that looked fresh. My guess is that he's been in town. The Oak Hill rumor mill scores a rare win."

"Seems like it," I said. "Thanks for looking into that."

"Want me to stake his place out?"

"Not yet. I'll explain in a few. Can you meet me down at Susan's place?"

"On my way."

I cruised through the sleepy streets of downtown and parked beside Munoz's cruiser in the lot. He leaned against the hood with his arms crossed. Leading him around the back, we found Cliff seated at the picnic table with a large map of the Nantahala blowing in the wind.

"Gotta find some rocks to weigh that thing down," I said.

Cliff shot around the table. "Grace? I texted you. Sawyer told me, I—"

"I'm fine," I said. "I appreciate it though. Everybody went into the forest?"

He nodded. "Six men total."

"Good, then the coast is clear for me to find this damn bullet."

"Talk about a needle in a haystack," Cliff said.

"I saw it splinter into a tree. We just need to find the right one and dig it out."

Munoz glanced at me with a skeptical look.

"Follow me," I said.

Two feet into the forest, I pointed upward where the trunk of a pine was scarred and splintered. The entry point was low enough that Munoz reached it with his hand. He ran his fingers over the hole and looked back at me. "This was aimed at you?"

"Or Cedar," I said.

"If you were sitting at the picnic tables, whoever did this is a terrible shot."

"How easy will it be to get that bullet?"

"Got an axe?"

"No."

"Then I'll head home and grab mine. Give me an hour."

"You're the best."

Munoz put a hand out. "Not so fast. What's the deal with Jenkins? If he's in town, that's huge. The most notorious criminal in Oak Hill turns back up the same week as a dead body?"

"Jenkins was an idiot and an addict, not a killer."

"People change."

"Ain't that the truth," I said. "And that's also exactly why I want to get that bullet into a lab for comparison."

"Comparison to what?"

"The bullet Billy Jenkins fired into my tire my first week on the job."

Munoz grinned and nodded toward the tree.

"Let's do it. I'll be back in a few."

As Munoz retreated, I parked myself beside Cliff on the bench and looked at the map. "There's a whole world in there."

"It's the size of Rhode Island. There's no chance in hell that we find your boy in there."

"Nat used to take me into the woods as a kid and preach about the land. Over a hundred different types of trees. Five hundred something acres of land. But you know what I remember most? The name."

"Nantahala?"

"Land of the noon day sun."

"What?"

"It's a Cherokee word. Long before settlers came in and drove them off the land, they used the same name for the forest. Somewhere near the center of the forest there's a gorge. Nat took me once; we hiked for two days and moved at a hellish pace. But when we arrived, I was unimpressed. I expected the Grand Canyon but it was just a river bed with water that ripped through."

"Never seen it," he said.

"Well that's where the name is from. At the gorge, the sun only touches down at noon."

"I don't know why you're giving me a history lesson, Grace. This forest—"

"Whenever I think about that trip now, I wonder if Lauren Blackburn was in the woods watching us. If she was digging through our packs when we turned a blind eye. If I'd met her back then."

"Maybe."

"Do you think that we ever really know our neighbors, Cliff?"

He hesitated and let out a sigh. "Why do I feel like that's a loaded question?"

"We watch them grow old and see them at the diner around town. I've had more conversations than I can count with the citizens of Oak Hill. But I don't know that I know them."

"Everybody's hiding something," Cliff said.

"Yeah? What's your secret?"

"You know mine."

Reyna, I thought. "Hannah know yet?"

He shook his head. "No, and I know I need to cut it off. Be a better husband. But Reyna is fuel to a fire that I thought burned out long ago."

I rested a hand on his shoulder. "Rip the Band-Aid off."

"What's up with you and Sawyer?"

"It's complicated. Willa gave me a note, two notes, technically, the day Sawyer came to town. She asked me to wait until she passed to open it."

"And you listened?"

I shrugged. "Part of me was afraid of what it said. The other part was scared of the wrath of Willa Sawyer raining down on me."

"What did it say?"

"Sawyer wrote me a note the day he left town. Told me all the reasons he couldn't stay. Asked me to come with him. To meet him up north. Gave the address and all. Then he told me that he loved me too."

Cliff stared blankly and shook his head. "And Willa kept that from you?"

"She said it was for my own good. She said Sawyer wasn't in a place to be loved."

"That's cold."

"It is," I said. "And I have yet to comprehend how a person could hold such a secret."

"But it explains a lot." He leaned forward. "Sawyer put himself out there. Asked you to move away with him. For all he knew, you ignored him. Didn't so much as call."

"Right."

"So I see why he wouldn't dare set foot in Oak Hill again."

"We were both blaming each other."

Cliff sighed. "How many days have you wasted daydreaming about what our lives would have been like if we never went to that bonfire?"

"Too many but for all we know, George Sawyer still would have taken that bad fall and died. Maybe if Sawyer wasn't there to witness it he would have had the resolve to stay but he still would have left for college."

"Every time I talk to him I feel the grudge lift an inch. He's still the guy that was my best friend throughout my entire life. He's still the boy you loved."

"I'm just not sure that's enough," I said.

"Take it from me and my sins. If you two can resurrect even a semblance of what you once had, it's enough."

I grinned. "Damn Cliff, sitting this close to the forest has made you sappy."

"Easy now," Cliff said.

"Did you know that Madison Dockery asked Sawyer out?"

"I cannot confirm or deny due to the binding power of a teenage pinky promise."

I slapped his shoulder. "You knew? You ass."

"He asked me for advice. Me. The kid who wouldn't get a girl to look his way if his hair was on fire. That's how panicked he was."

"He made it sound like she wouldn't take no for an answer. My only memory of them together is at a bonfire, but even that was barely a blip on my radar."

"Sawyer did everything in his power to protect you from it. I used to joke with him that he was the first person to ever say no to a Dockery."

I sighed. "Look what good that did him."

The words hung in the air like humidity as my mind dug through those old bonfire nights for a sign. Instead, a flicker of a memory caught my attention.

Billy Jenkins's remark about Sarah Price and Ethan Dockery. In the chaos of the night, it hardly sunk in.

What if Sarah Price had also said no to Ethan? Somehow this all connected back to Sarah. Whether it was Ethan or Billy, time was too precious to waste.

When Munoz returned, he marched into the forest and cut into the tree. The bullet rested four inches in. Years of life and oxygen turned to pulp. I bagged the bullet and waved goodbye to the men. "Where are you going?" Cliff asked.

"To find some answers," I said. Then, I sped away toward the County Line and dialed Tessa Brown's cell.

42

The blur of passing scenery eased the panic seizing my heart and allowed for a momentary respite. All in all, Oak Hill wasn't a community equipped to handle murder and mystery. We couldn't comprehend it in the first place. The sooner I provided answers, the sooner Oak Hill could go back to sleep.

Creeping up 23 Northbound, I passed the old gem mine that once drew in tourists for day trips and camping weekends in Nantahala. Decades ago, Macon County shifted their headquarters from the heart of Oak Hill out to the riverbanks of Cullowhee.

Oak Hill may be a nothing town, but we've got a few stoplights and enough people to hold quorum. Cullowhee is a blink-and-you'll-miss-it roadside attraction that hardly deserved the employment the county offered. Locals called it a speed trap town.

I didn't have Tessa Brown sorted out entirely, but I guessed she commuted in from Waynesville or Bryson City—somewhere with more humans than cows. I hugged the riverbeds along the road as I wound through the city limits and parked in the near-empty lot outside Macon County

Headquarters. When I pushed through the entrance doors, a warm smile greeted me from behind a rotunda. "Morning there, or is it afternoon?"

"Hi, I'm looking for Tessa Brown."

"Sure thing," the woman said. She punched three numbers into a phone and whispered into the receiver. Mere seconds later, a back door opened and Tessa waved me through. She wore the same outfit she did at the crime scene—dark colored suit pants and a button-down blouse, cherry red. A badge hung at her waist along the beltline and jiggled as she walked.

"Nice little surprise," she said. "We don't get many visitors out here."

"Not since they moved you all out here."

Tessa grinned. "Oak Hill would've added another twenty minutes to my commute. So I'm fine with the riverbanks."

"Any updates on the lab tests?"

"We've supplemented our request to the military databases with your information about Lauren Blackburn. How'd you manage that magical pull?"

"Elbow grease and a few strokes of luck."

"That's how cases fall. I heard this case may be out of your hands soon though."

"Until they rip the file from my hands, I'm not resting."

"Good."

"I'm here for a favor." I tugged the bullet out of my pocket and handed the evidence bag to her. "The third day of my training as an officer focused on weapons. I remember hearing that all weapons have a listing on file if they're registered. What would it take for you to run that bullet through the system?"

Tessa parked herself in a chair behind an oak desk and motioned for me to take the neighboring chair. "Depends. Is this related to your case?"

"It is."

"Your victim wasn't shot, Grace."

"Right, but we've located the victim's son. He was caught scavenging around town and confirmed that the victim was his mother."

"Scavenging?"

"They lived off the land in Nantahala."

Tessa's eyes widened so much they nearly filled her face. She examined the bullet in the light. "And this?"

"We've had the boy around town as we sorted out what to do with him. At first, we thought he saw something. I'm still of the opinion that he did, but he hasn't opened his mouth yet. Long story short, I was with him sitting and talking when somebody shot at us."

"And why do I believe that you have a particular person in mind that you'd like to link this to?"

"Because I do."

I handed her a second plastic evidence bag that I'd pulled from evidence lock-up. This one was worn and wrinkled. "I'd like to start by comparing it to this. Then running it through the database."

Tessa grinned. "Do I even want to know?"

"Let the chips fall where they may."

"Tell me this, if you confirm a match to your mystery suspect, does it clarify or complicate your case?"

"I'm not sure I know anything at this point. It's a Hail Mary."

Tessa grinned. "Then I'll pray it's a match. Either way, I can make this connect to the crime scene we're working. That's all I need. Let me see if there's still a tech in today."

As she strutted out of sight, I studied the row of desks that Tessa's rested in. Nameplates on each indicated that there were only two women in the whole group of ten or more, Tessa the only one with any sort of order on her desk.

Maps pasted onto the walls hung with frayed corners. Papers stacked and teetered on each surface, filing cabinets letting the setting sun glint off their metal. On a pinboard in the corner of the office, a collage of photos and printouts hung in orderly rows beneath the word UNSOLVED. The photo of Sarah Price in the top right corner froze me in my place. At least somebody still cared.

When Tessa returned, she was empty-handed. "Call you as soon as I hear something, but it'll be tomorrow morning at the earliest."

"Great," I said. "Actually, can you run one more test for me while you're at it?"

43

The Dockery Center parking lot stood mostly empty when I arrived. Sawyer leaned against the picnic table where a map was splayed out and outlined with rocks to keep it from drifting away in the breeze. Cliff worked his phone in the corner, kicking at pine needles on the edge of the forest. Liam stood hunched over the map and picking at his ears. "Where's the crew?" I asked.

"Mostly left," he said. "Can't see a thing in those woods with the sunlight fading."

"We'll be back tomorrow," Cliff said, joining our group. "And maybe the night will draw him out."

"Doubt it," I said. "It just might kill him."

"It's only one night," Liam interjected. "A fresh set of eyes in the morning may do the trick. Nobody is giving up."

"I'll call the Forest Service," I said. "Ask them to keep an eye out for any smoke in the trees, even though they're as understaffed as we are."

"Grace, what in the hell happened to that tree?" Liam asked, pointing to the makeshift carving that Munoz left behind retrieving the bullet.

"Rot," Sawyer said a little too quickly.

"Rot?"

"Damn near impossible to see it from the outside, but sometimes things are rotten to their core. A cancer growing inside that eventually would take down neighboring trees too. Can't have that around here," I said.

"Guess you never know with nature." Liam shrugged it off and my body nearly collapsed with relief. "I'm going to head home and rest up," he said. "Grace, can I talk to you for a moment?"

I stepped away from the picnic table and Liam limped over to join me. "What's up?"

"I need to tell you something but I don't want to implicate myself in any crimes."

"I already know you told Ethan our victim's name," I said. "It's okay, I get it."

He stiffened. "I swear to you, Grace. I didn't tell him a thing. But that's neither here nor there. This is much more urgent."

"Gee, that sounds mysterious."

His face was stoic. "I trust you, Grace."

"Let's hear it."

"I have it on good authority that Billy Jenkins is back in town. It seems he's cleaned up his act, enrolled in some medical training program at Davie County College in Moxville."

"Liam . . ."

"I know. I know," he said. "I've kept tabs on him ever since he left town. I'll never know if he's the one that hurt Sarah, but I couldn't help myself."

"I assume this *good authority* is—"

"Don't ask me. Let's just leave it at that. Trust me. Do with that information what you wish. I just thought you should know."

I studied Liam Price for a second, then nodded. He headed toward the parking lot as I returned to the picnic area.

Sawyer smirked.

"Want me to call the Forest Service?"

"I already did," I said. "But I warned them that it might be a lost hiker or kids blowing off some steam. I believe they're aware that some hooligans used to host bonfires in the area."

"Oh, to be young," he said. "Why'd you lie to Liam and say you hadn't called?"

I made sure Liam's brake lights were out of sight as an itch surfaced on my skin that I couldn't ignore. Liam was the only common thread. And every person in the world has heard the theory that criminals inject themselves into investigations to keep an eye on things.

I picked up a pebble and tossed it into the brush. "Can I think out loud with you for a moment?"

"Please do." I didn't have to look to know Sawyer was smiling.

"Every time I turn around on this case, Liam Price is there. He was one of the concerned citizens that showed up at the station and insisted that I seek outside help on the case. Then he's the first person in town to show up and insist that we make a plan to bring Cedar in. And now he's at the search party. Champing at the bit to find Cedar and feeding me intel about Billy Jenkins."

"Intel?"

"He's back in town. Confirmed."

"Interesting." Sawyer stood. "I hadn't really considered him, to be honest. I figured that a man who had so much pain in his life wouldn't inflict that on others. But pain can also lead to anger. For Liam, I see two possibilities: First, Oak Hill is just a small town and retirement is too dull for Liam's taste. He's genuinely distraught to see such a heinous crime in town and wants to find justice, especially since he never got any for Sarah. If we look through that lens, everything has a perfectly good explanation behind it. He's actually trying to help. One of the few."

"And the other?"

"You know it as well as I do. It's what you were getting at in the first place. He's staying close to monitor the investigation. And if you get close to the truth . . ."

"Bingo," I said. "Besides, I know he's lied to me. When I saw Ethan at the funeral, he already knew our victim's name. Liam swears he didn't divulge it, but I know the Dockerys hold everybody's puppet strings here."

"Maybe it wasn't him." Cliff leaned back. "Liam Price is a good person. He's active at town council meetings and an advocate for progressive ideals within Oak Hill. We could use a handful more Liam Prices around here and a few less Billy Jenkins, if you follow."

"Good people can do bad things, Cliff," I said.

"Especially with their backs against the wall," Sawyer added. "Some people will push their way out. No matter the cost. But if our measure of the man is right, Liam would need a damn strong motive to kill. I can only think of one that fits. Could Lauren Blackburn be the person that shot Sarah Price all those years ago?"

"Anything is possible, but that feels like a stretch," I said.

"Think of where the body was dropped," Sawyer said. "Sutton's field."

Cliff drummed his fingers on the table. "They never proved he bought the beer that night. It was all speculation."

"Prove? No," I said. "But it's documented in the case file that he'd buy a case for his farmhands most weekends. Chamberlain just chose to let sleeping dogs lie."

"If somehow Lauren was the one behind the gun that took out Sarah, that's motive for Liam through and through," Sawyer said. "But I agree that it feels fuzzy."

"Tread lightly," Cliff said. "For now, you should be grateful for all Liam has done. Not suspicious."

"I am grateful for his help," I said, "And the fact that he made the ID of Lauren Blackburn is a mark in his favor. Why would he help identify his own victim when we were lost as could be?"

"He wouldn't," Cliff said. "Plus, Liam is the main reason you got an interview in the first place."

"What?"

"I fought to put your name in the ring, but Ethan pushed my insistence aside. He had some out-of-towner that he wanted to plop into the role, but Liam made a personal plea to Ethan. They spoke for a few minutes in private, and that was it. Next thing I knew, you had an interview."

I swallowed hard. "As the ranking officer in Oak Hill PD, you weren't even going to give me an interview?"

"This isn't a me thing," Cliff said. "You know that I am beholden to all things Dockery."

"Makes it clear how you see me," I said. "A friend and not a cop."

"Politics," Sawyer said. "You have never been one to play games, Grace. Why start now?"

"So I don't have to sit on my hands and watch some imbecile run the town into the ground and look the other way because somebody slipped him cash. I don't know why every damn man in this town has decided to remember Don Chamberlain like he was impeccable. I'm so sick of it all. I earned that job."

"You've still got a good chance. Like I said, the others bowed out because—"

"How corrupt was Chamberlain?" Sawyer asked.

Cliff shrugged. "Stories outpace reality, probably."

"He was the one that arrested me that night. Threatened to lock me up even though there was no evidence. It's partly why I steered clear of Oak Hill for so long."

"Yeah, but it was a poorly kept secret that he would take cash to look the other way on anything. Speeding, parking, neighborly disputes."

"And now he's living off that nest egg in Florida," I said.

"Makes you think though," Sawyer said. "About how much we might not know about that night."

"Which one?"

"The bonfire. The night Sarah was shot."

"Those secrets are long buried," I said.

"Maybe," Sawyer said. "Sorry, old memories creeping up on me. You know that was my only time in handcuffs?"

"And yet you went the other way with your life," Cliff said. "I'd have put money on you becoming a CPA or something boring, like your old man."

"Boring, eh? Like mayor of a Podunk town?"

He grinned. "You could only be so lucky."

"If we're linking Lauren Blackburn to Sarah Price, there's an elephant in the room that we haven't addressed."

"Jenkins," Cliff said.

"If Liam's intel is reliable, Billy is back. And that timing stinks to me, so I've got Macon County working on something that might break this thing wide open."

Cliff and Sawyer both eyed me. "That's all you're going to say?"

"More tomorrow," I said.

"Fine. I've got to get home or Hannah will have my head. Either of you want to come by for dinner?"

"I'd love that, actually," Sawyer said. "I'm not thrilled by the prospect of heading to an empty house and checking the cupboards."

"Come on over," Cliff said. "Grace?"

"Not tonight," I said. "On the off chance that bullet was aimed at me, I know where they'd turn to next."

"I'm sure he's fine," Cliff said. "He's a tough old tree."

"Y'all have fun," I said. "Let's get breakfast first thing tomorrow and crack this case open."

Sawyer put a hand out in each direction, landing it on each of our shoulders. "It's spooky."

"What is?" Cliff asked.

"How much this is like old times. Grace rushing home to tend to Nat. Cliff and I off doing our thing until Grace barks orders at us like our captain."

"I wouldn't call it a bark but—"

"It's a welcome one," Sawyer said. "I'm just trying to say that I missed this."

Cliff grunted. I nodded. Sawyer let go.

"See you all bright and early."

Despite the early hour, Nat snored so loud it shook the walls. I tossed a blanket over his torso and shut the door. Agatha curled up on my lap and held me prisoner until I sufficiently scratched the crook just below her mouth. Each purr lapsed over me like a wave of tiredness. And before I knew it, Agatha and I were both unconscious on the couch.

dreamt of the forest. Sweet scents of pine tickled my nose. Dead leaves flittered around my feet. The bonfire flickered in the distance, then it grew closer. Too close. I blinked, and flames surrounded me. All around me. There was no escape. In the darkness, hands reached out and scooped me away. Then I woke up to Sawyer and Cliff at my door.

Agatha hissed at Sawyer, who didn't flinch. "I'll win you over one day, Agatha," he said.

I shrugged. "We'll see about that."

Cliff and Sawyer waited at the kitchen table while I showered. I sniffed shirts in the closet and stared at the overflowing laundry basket that wobbled like a game of Jenga.

Minutes later, I was fully dressed driving Sawyer to Emma's while Cliff followed behind.

"How was it meeting Cliff's family?" I asked.

"Strange," he said. "There are ripples of Cliff in them. But Hannah is a verified saint. Their relationship is a mystery."

"If I understood the dynamics of relationships, I wouldn't be single."

"Maybe," he said. "But it irked me even then. I thought of Reyna and trust me, she's great, but why blow up your life when you have it so good?"

I turned onto Murphy Road. "Perspective."

"Huh?"

"From your perspective, a single man approaching forty, he's got it made. Kids, a house, a sterling reputation, a job with some regard. And then Hannah. Stability, charm, beauty. From where you're sitting, things look rosy."

"But not for him?"

"Guess not," I said. "Cliff and I stopped talking about the hard stuff when you left. For a long time, you were our sole focus. When we were shooting BBs out in the forest, your face was on every aluminum can. When we snapped twigs off trees and burned them into cinder, they were your limbs. Cliff and I carried a lot of hate for you. And it became a burden. So one day, we just quit talking about the hard stuff because it always led back to you or that night."

He shook his head. "That night," he said. "If you only knew."

"Willa's gone," I said. "So, whatever happened that night—whatever drove you to run like your feet were on fire—it's your story to tell."

"I can't . . ." he said.

I parked in a spot in front of Emma's. Clouds lurked above us, oppressive and unbearable. "Then you can't. Either way, we let it go," I said, unbuckling my seatbelt. "But while you're still here, let's get some grub."

We spent an hour in the cozy back corner booth of Emma's like we were all seventeen again, but the present beckoned us before too long. Sawyer split to tend to funeral arrangements.

Cliff alerted me that the SBI's takeover was delayed, but still inevitable, then he bolted to jostle up a search party for the forest. And just like that, we split up. It was high school all over again. Except the lurking carcass of Nickelson Law glared at me from a distance. The char stung my nose even from afar. My phone vibrated halfway through my walk and I lifted it to my ear. "Bingham."

"Morning, Grace," Tessa said.

"I pray you're bringing good news."

"You don't strike me as the praying kind."

"Depends on the day," I said. "Your tone isn't making me feel very optimistic."

"Your bullet does not match the provided sample," Tessa said. "Not even remotely."

"Shit," I said.

"Grace, what does the name Silas Dockery mean to you?"

I whispered into the phone. "A whole lot."

"Your bullet matched a Remington 700 registered to his name in 1988."

"Is there a serial number?"

"Already in your email," Tessa said. "Why do I sense worry in your voice?"

"Silas Dockery passed on Saturday."

"Well isn't that convenient," she said. "He's got a modern arsenal registered to his name. All hunting types. I'm guessing he liked to head out into the woods and make nature bleed. Maybe his death isn't such a loss."

"You don't know the Dockery name? Silas is revered. Basically kept Oak Hill afloat. Half the town has his name on it."

"Then it begs the question why somebody had his rifle pointed in your general direction."

"Mine or the boy's."

"I wish that bullet told a better story for you, Grace. But whoever has access to Silas Dockery's estate likely had a hand in whatever happened in Oak Hill. Now, I can't connect any of this to Lauren Blackburn yet but—"

"Me either," I said. "But lightning doesn't strike twice in a small town without there being a reason."

"That's a good approach," Tessa said. "I did that other test you asked."

"And?"

"You know, when I joined the County, I got an earful from locals about famous unsolved cases, including that mess from your neck of the woods way back when. It's sat on our open and unsolved board for years, even though your former colleague closed the case. Were you there that night?"

"I was," I said. "And it would mean a lot to the family if we had some answers . . ."

"Sadly, this ain't your day, Grace. The rifle that shot Sarah Price was a Winchester 70. The rifle that shot at you and your boy yesterday was a Remington 700. Different guns."

"That would have been too convenient," I said. "This town might've self-combusted."

"I had my fingers crossed. Sorry, Grace."

I hung up. The Dockery name clanged like a gavel in my brain. Another puzzle piece nestled into the border and a hazy image appeared. All I had left to do was figure out how the Dockery family connected to Cedar. A familiar face appeared in my mind and I ran with it until my lungs gave out.

In the station, Munoz had his feet propped up on the desk and didn't bother to flinch when I barged in. "Morning, Grace."

"I need a favor," I said. "Run down to Margo's and ask what she saw after the funeral let out."

"What's going on?" he asked, confusion furrowing his brow. The radio crackled. Car accident out on Old Mill Road. Munoz looked up. "I should go."

I followed him out and marched into Margo's myself. She grinned and waved me over to the counter. "I keep waiting for my picture to pop up in the paper," she said. "After helping the police, I expected a bit more, Grace."

"The untimely death of Silas Dockery cast quite a shadow over the town."

"I'll say."

"How long did you have to close for the service?"

Margo popped her gum. "Nearly three hours."

"Woof," I said. "I missed the end. How did things wrap up?"

"Muted affair," she said. "I hate to speak ill on such a service, but it was hardly anything emotional or personalized. The whole town was there, but to be honest, nobody knew Silas unless they were here decades back."

"Nat spoke highly of him."

"True," Margo said. "But unceremoniously, they let everybody out while the family snuck through the back."

"I'm worried about their wellbeing," I said.

"Who?"

"The family."

"Why?"

"That's a hell of a loss, Margo. He damn near built this town."

"I don't think you have much to worry about though. They filed into their SUVs and cruised out of town like they were trying to beat traffic."

"None of them came through or lingered to talk to the mourners?"

She smacked her lips again. "Not even the least. I squeezed Elsa Carter, their maid, for every morsel when she passed by."

"What'd she say?"

"Whole family split up after the service. Filed into different rooms of the mansion and busied themselves for a long while."

"I thought I saw Ethan walking downtown. Over by Susan's place."

"By the Center?" she asked. "I doubt he'd be over there unless he got lost. Nobody saw his car in town from what I gather. But I hate to be nosy."

"Sure you do," I said. "One last question. Did you see Billy Jenkins anywhere?"

"He wasn't at the service," Margo said. "Is he a suspect?"

"Look, you've been an incredible help for us. You know us police are short-staffed and so you've been pulling the weight of a dozen men. I promise we'll repay you."

She waved it off and tapped the paper. "I'd appreciate an inside scoop on the case."

"Don't push it," I said with a smile, not ready to reveal that I had no answers to share.

45

drew the shades in my office and waited for Cliff and Sawyer to make their way to the station. The early reports from the search party volunteers were grim. Not a trace or footprint or broken twig that would mark Cedar's path into the brush. I knew it was a fool's errand. Still, I held a hope that they'd stumble into something useful, perhaps a shelter or camp that Cedar and Lark used before making their way into town. Although, based on all of the evidence on the table, I had doubts it was as simple as we once thought.

Sawyer arrived first and parked himself across from me. "Everything go all right?" I asked.

He nodded. "All good. Just funny how their tone changes from one visit to the next. First, it was how sorry they were for my loss. How they shared my grief. Then it became dollar signs and payment plans. But it's taken care of."

"That's a lot to shoulder," I said.

"Willa did most of the heavy lifting before she passed. Bill Nickelson had buttoned up her will and estate years ago, but it's never as simple as we think."

"Life rarely is. Cliff's on his way."

"Good. I take it the search crews didn't have any luck? What about your secret plan with Macon County?"

"There's some news, but I want to check my conclusions with you two before I make any moves."

"Sounds ominous."

"You planning to sell Willa's house?" I asked.

"I guess at some point. It feels weird to be in there without her."

Cliff strutted through the double doors, and I took the moment when he was shooting the proverbial shit with Munoz to drop a bomb of my own on Sawyer.

"We should talk when this is all done," I said.

"I'd like that."

"Good." I waved Cliff inside. "Here's our party boy."

"Hardly a cause for celebration," he said. "What's this all about?"

"Shut the door."

He parked himself in the only remaining chair. I shifted my voice to a whisper. "There've been a few developments in the case which I've kept quiet. I trust that when you hear them, you'll understand why."

"Is that why we're whispering?" Cliff asked.

"When I'm through telling you what I uncovered, we can decide what to do next. Although, I have a feeling we won't agree."

"My ears are open," Sawyer said.

"First, let's summarize what we know about Lauren Blackburn. Born in 1980, entered the army at eighteen, went AWOL somewhere around 2004. Cedar, likely born around 2008, and her lived in Nantahala for some stretch of time. She came to Oak Hill monthly, left with cash, and went to buy goods for her family."

"Then she was killed and dropped in Lionel Sutton's field."

"Right," I said. "Struck with a spade from behind and bled out."

"Nothing new there," Sawyer said.

"Correct. Now, let's talk about the attempt on Cedar's life."

"What happened to your idea that they meant that bullet for you?"

I shrugged. "Still possible, but not probable. Bear with me. I had Munoz retrieve the bullet from the tree behind Susan's. When I brought it to the crime lab over in Macon, Tessa Brown ran it through the registered firearms database and we found a match, although not the one I was expecting."

"So you know who owns the rifle that shot at you?"

"I do," I said.

"And?" Cliff asked.

"One more pivot."

Cliff groaned.

"I withheld something important yesterday. I saw Cedar after he ran into the forest."

"You what?" Cliff barked. "And you had me searching?"

I raised a hand. "Wait a second. Okay? While the first round of volunteers went in looking for him, I tried to approach things from a different angle. It's been nagging at me that Lauren Blackburn approached Oak Hill by the fire road when she came to town each month. It would have left her out in the open for miles. Somebody would've seen her. Plus, there are trails that would have spit her out downtown."

"Maybe she wanted a remote spot to meet up with her *customer*," Sawyer said.

"Maybe. But I wanted to walk a mile in her shoes, so to speak, so I went up to the fire road and stomped around. I found a trail that snaked through the woods. It was barely passable. It almost looked like somebody covered up the trail on purpose. I followed it for a bit until I stumbled into a clearing. That's where I saw Cedar."

Sawyer leaned back. "So Cedar knows the path his mother took."

"That's my suspicion," I said.

Cliff scratched at his head. "I don't understand. What was in the clearing?"

"Another path. When you follow that, you end up butting up against a chain-link fence with a hole ripped through it."

Sawyer's eyes traveled to the map of Oak Hill on the wall. He cursed under his breath.

Cliff squirmed. "What am I missing here?"

"As Sawyer just pieced together, that chain-link fence is the border of the Dockery Estate."

Cliff's eyes bulged. "Wait a minute. Those are important people and—"

I raised a hand. "Now back to the bullet in the tree. Want to take a wild guess at who owned the gun that shot at us?"

"Silas Dockery," Sawyer said.

"Meaning the gun now falls into the hands of . . ."

"His children."

"Bingo," I said. "And there, we have a conundrum. I had asked Macon County to test the bullet in the tree against the bullet from Billy Jenkins's errant night of target practice in 2010, hoping that would put a bow on things. But this opens some new doors."

"Now wait a minute," Cliff said. "Let's not drag our wealthiest citizens through the mud."

"Here's my best guess," I said. "If we stay on our sex work angle, Ethan Dockery met Lauren Blackburn somewhere and solicited her for her services. They forged an agreement. Once a month, she'd stop by for a visit and he'd pay her off. Then something goes south. He drives her away from the estate and into Sutton's field, then kills her."

"And the shot at Cedar?" Sawyer asked.

"Since Cedar knew about the path, there's a good chance he knew where his mom went each month."

"So Ethan Dockery was trying to clean up the loose ends," Cliff said.

I nodded. "It fits. And it sure would be convenient for Ethan if the SBI didn't take over the case and bring in a team of investigators. You said it yourself Cliff. The Dockerys have connections with the SBI."

"What good would that do him? Buy him time?"

"Enough time to cover his tracks. Especially considering his views of my abilities as an investigator. He thinks he's got all the time in the world."

What He Left Behind

"These are some serious accusations, Grace."

"And here's another thread that I can't yet prove but feels related. Sarah Price and Ethan Dockery were dating just before she was injured. If we compare the two incidents, they're different, but both a power-hungry man lashing out when he doesn't get what he wants. Although the bullets are from different rifles."

"This is atomic," Cliff said. "If you swing and miss at this, you'll never work in this town again. Maybe not even in North Carolina."

"You say that like I've got a bright future here. Our prime suspect is also the chief reason that I'm a long shot for the job."

"Doesn't make it easier to burn that bridge," Cliff said.

"He's right," Sawyer added. "We need to be extra careful here."

I leaned back. "There is no we. At the moment, this is solely information that I, Detective Grace Bingham, ranking officer of the Oak Hill Police Department, own. Any blowback would come squarely on me. The two of you can walk out of this office and act like you never heard a thing."

"Fat chance anybody would believe that I'd be in the dark on this," Cliff said.

"You're sitting there chewing on all the ways this could go wrong if Ethan is not our man. What about the flip side? Justice prevails. Cedar is safe. The whole town sees Ethan for what he is."

"You'd be up to your ears in lawyers and court dates," Cliff said. "You are out-resourced and out-manned against the Dockery family. They will throw everything in the book at you and then some. So it's not cut and dry. This isn't a charge-them-and-walk-away kind of deal."

"The law is the law," I said. "It's on us to prove that he's guilty. And I'm not saying that I want to barge out of here and put him in cuffs. We need more."

"Like what?" Cliff asked.

"Like a witness," Sawyer said.

I smiled. "Like Cedar."

46

It took the better part of the afternoon to wind down the search party and double-check everything back at the station. Cliff marched home, allegedly to kiss Hannah and the kids, but more likely to distance himself from everything that was on the precipice. We all need an alibi sometimes. Sawyer milled around the station, looked over maps and reports, and confirmed everything that I had on hand. The puzzle was coming together. No more blurry images of our perpetrator and architect of disaster. I saw his face clearly now.

The afternoon swirled by like a haze, and once I'd navigated a pile of overdue paperwork and reports, I jumped for the door. Sawyer bolted through at the same time and we nearly collided.

"We should get dinner."

"Have I mentioned that I've become quite a cook?" he asked.

I should've said no. I should've dropped the topic and line of conversation and walked away. The icy wall around my heart fractured with the piercing look in his eyes. Maybe we all have our hearts broken and spend too long trying to recreate the impossible. Maybe we should aim for function over form. And by the thump in my chest, my heart was fully functional.

I knew where dinner might lead. I knew how it might end. I'd played it out a thousand times in daydreams and fantasies and could-have-beens. Every time I jumped at a call from a random number and waited to hear his voice on the other end. A part of me, creeping under the cloak of a memory, lurched forward with a vigor that I couldn't outmatch. The monster won. The yearning stole my tongue.

"How about your place?"

———

I took the long way, curving around downtown to avoid any chance of connection with Sawyer and Margo and the relentless rumor mill. Loose lips sink ships, or relationships, who knows? Maybe part of me wanted to avoid staring into the charred remains of Nickelson Law, to avoid facing the void where answers should fill, but nothing aligned.

As I drove, I thought about the weight of my decision and how the entire town would steer me in the opposite direction. Away from the truth. Away from the Dockery Estate.

But the killer did not give Lauren Blackburn that privilege. Some thug drove her across town and dropped her body on the side of the road, nestled into a field hoping vultures and crows would pick apart any remaining evidence. It was a minor miracle that Lionel Sutton caught wind of anything and let Lucy loose on the property. If it had been winter or another day of the year, we'd have never found Lauren's body. We'd have never found Cedar. And then lost him again.

When I parked beside the house on the street, I smiled up at the old magnolia that stretched downward and greeted me. An old friend, of sorts. Set dressing from memories I held close and then buried deep inside. It felt wrong to barge into the empty house, so I waited on the steps and said a silent prayer for Willa.

Even with the crumpled note in my pocket, I struggled to find the words to describe the woman I thought I'd known. Funny how one desperate act can change our perception of a person. The version of Willa forever imprinted on my mind was the look she gave Cliff and me at the door after the bonfire. The shake of her head. Hair tossing to the side. It was clear our arrival was not up for discussion. We weren't family in that moment. We were strangers. And she protected her son.

It took me two years on the force before I read the accident report and fully digested what happened to George Sawyer that night. Stories and gossip shaded my expectations into something vile when it read as vanilla as ice cream. Sawyer stomped upstairs and into his room. Willa and George followed. At the top of the stairs, he had a mild heart attack. Chest pain. Willa turned back and watched him topple down the hardwood and collapse onto the floor. She called 911. She and Sawyer knelt with George and whispered prayers that went unanswered. He was gone.

There was no autopsy. No need to dig into the tragic events that befell that family. Even Don Chamberlain had understood that much, even if he still suspected Sawyer had hurt Sarah Price. The police took the necessary statements and stamped the death accidental. The whole town fell into mourning, although it remained second fiddle to the very-real-and-present story of Sarah Price's harrowing accident.

I used to think of the gray clouds that so often gather above Oak Hill as warning signs. Beacons that trouble was on the way. But looking back now and colored with the recent events of that past week, I saw everything in a new light. Storms only came once every few years and with them, Oak Hill lost beloved citizens and trust slowly eroded further. At least I had the calm that followed to look forward to, although this storm seemed unready to pass.

47

awyer arrived ten minutes later and lugged in two paper bags of groceries, despite my offering of help. "How's Margo?" I asked as he unlocked the front door.

"Nosy. She asked who was eating the rest of this meal."

"You think she'd let a man grieve."

"She toed the line. I think that's her form of kindness."

"Willa never had time for gossip like that, did she?"

He shrugged. "Late in life, I understood there were two versions of my mom. The one I knew for eighteen years growing up and the one that I left behind."

"You didn't leave her behind. You just left," I said.

"I never understood why Willa didn't leave Oak Hill," Sawyer said, waving me into the kitchen. I glanced around the now-empty space and waited for a glimpse of her ghost. The stillness was unsettling. A bone-deep inkling that something was missing. "Once I left, she was alone. Her friends were second-rate, that wasn't the glue. I asked her once why she stayed and she didn't answer. Just gave me that look that mothers seem to know transmits more than words. And I understood in a way. It was a trade-off. She stayed because I left."

"I don't think life is that transactional. We can't go around keeping score and feeling like we owe somebody something if we want to live."

He snapped spaghetti into a pot. "Then what's your justification for staying here?"

"I didn't have anywhere else to go." I moved closer and took his hand. He broke his stare at the pot of boiling water and met mine. From my pocket, I drew out the note and slid it into his hand. "Sawyer, you should read this."

He stared at it. "What is—"

"Just read it," I said. "I'll take over dinner. Don't worry, nothing will burn."

He nodded and slid open the back door. From the window above the sink, I watched him read his mother's note. I wondered if he knew, if she'd ever told him how she'd altered the path of his life with a decision. From the way his body sank, I knew everything I needed to.

When he returned, red-eyed and frazzled, I sifted noodles through the strainer and prepared the rest of the meal. He sat at the head of the table in his father's chair and futzed with a cloth napkin, like the answers were stitched inside. I served the meal, and he reached for my hand. "I'm so sorry, Grace."

"I know you are. But that's not your fault. It's Willa's." I pressed on. "Can I tell you something?"

"Anything," he said.

"When I heard you'd left town, I knew why you'd gone. It wasn't George's accident or Sarah Price. It wasn't a summer camp to prepare you for college life in the city. It wasn't a trip to juvenile detention—no, all the stories that swirled around town were false. Because they didn't know the truth. That you left because it was easier than telling me you didn't love me back."

"Grace, I—"

"That was hard to stomach for a while. The raw feeling went and transformed into something different. A realization, maybe. Then one morning, I woke up and understood that it had nothing to do with you. It was my fault. My stupid mouth. So every time I thought of you elsewhere, I felt guilt. I wanted to run around town, to flag down Margo and shout from the rooftops that I was the reason Jacob Sawyer deserted us. Because I was undeserving of his love."

"But—"

"But that's okay. Those are the cards life dealt me. The same ones that weren't enough for my mother and father to give it a go. We can't change the hand we draw, but we can change the game we're playing."

Sawyer stared at me for a long moment, his jaw agape, his eyes wide like a portal into the forest of green behind them. I had nothing more to say. Even if it left him speechless, I'd done my part. I slurped noodles and let the sound of my chewing fill the suddenly cavernous space. It didn't bother me that Sawyer needed a moment to process what I'd said. Hell, it had taken me nearly fifteen years. When he did finally speak, it startled me. "Grace, I loved you too. I always loved you and—"

"I learned this week how you felt about me when we were eighteen. The other night, you said aloud the words you'd written all those years ago. Some part of me has accepted it, but a large part of me won't ever. Too little too late."

"Your metaphor, about the cards you're dealt? It's wrong. It's not always about how you change the game you're playing or making the best with the cards you have. Life is about finding somebody who has a shitty hand themselves that, when combined with yours, it's a damn near impossible match."

"We were eighteen. Everything has changed."

"Has it though?"

"It has, Sawyer."

He slid his hand onto mine and I let it rest there. The warmth felt nice. Comfort I'd pushed away for too long. Before I could move, he was up from the chair and guided me to stand. He gently placed his hands on my cheeks and moved in close, his hot breath mixing with mine like a chemical reaction in the air. He met my eyes. And he pushed forward to kiss me.

In a movie, there would have been sparks and starlight to surround us. Not a mediocre spaghetti dinner and a small town full of crime. Instead, the magic of the moment hung for all of ten seconds, before I broke away and stared at the floor. "Sawyer, I can't."

"This time could be different," he said.

"How?"

"We loved each other once. What's to stop it from happening again?"

"I . . . I should go."

I'd like to say that my mind played out fantasies and flashed forward into a frantic mess of bare skin between sheets. That I wanted him entirely, wholly, and forgot the world around me until we finished. But the first thing that jumped to my mind were stretch marks and soft skin around my belly I didn't have when we were eighteen. A different body than what he'd expect. Than what he'd want. We can't all stay young. And we can't all pick up where we left off.

"Stay?" he asked.

The word filled the room like the flick of a light switch, a big elegant spotlight illuminating my spot on the stage. This was the moment, I supposed, where I'd fall into his arms and let the past lie where it belonged. But his words. The choices. How dare he ask such a thing?

I glared at him. "Will you?"

"Grace, I—"

I dropped my hands and pushed him away. Our words intertwined, two conversations at once. One about tonight. One about forever. Neither went my way.

He stood there, nervous and distraught. My pride skittered away into the corner, hackles up like a stray cat.

"No, don't. It's not my place to ask and—"

"Grace, wait. I—"

Fifteen years ago, I would have been as spineless as a jellyfish. I would've shaken off the hurt and let optimism soothe my ache until it disappeared forever. But this was a different Grace. A week wasn't enough to wear down those grudges, even if the note and the circumstances changed the reality I once knew. In a moment of energy, I snatched my bag from the chair and dug my keys from my pocket. From the door, I looked back at him. "I can't watch you leave again. My heart can't take it."

I pushed into the temperate summer air and sat in my car underneath the magnolia tree, my tears falling into puddles that I'd formed fifteen years earlier.

48

Hope helicoptered to the ground along with the seeds of sugar maples. My feet hit the ground before I knew where I was going. Ankle-high clover swiped at my bare calves and left an itch behind. Tears fell in a frenzy from my cheeks and puddled onto the ground. When I reached the clearing, there was no fire ring. No outline of fallen logs for people to sit and talk. I planted myself on a stump and tried to make sense of everything.

Six days ago, I'd had a clear sense of life and Oak Hill and all the fringe elements around them. I saw my path forward, the course I'd follow until my dying day. Whether or not I earned a promotion, I'd sit and interlock my fingers and wait for the next opportunity. Sawyer's departure all those years ago brought many things, most of them vile, but one of the few good perks was an undying, relentless sense of patience. I could wait out the seasons. The year or the decade. I'd grin and bear it and nod my head along. Smile all the while. I could've done it.

Sawyer's fumbling for words, well, that moment could fill epics written a lifetime ago, but it didn't fit. No, those stories taught lessons. They showed the truth of humanity and the adventurous spirit of man. There was no through line here. No advice for future generations. Just a young woman that never outgrew the young man that outgrew her. Maybe Willa was protecting me, not her son. Maybe Willa was the smartest of us all.

When I looked at life, I struggled to see myself at the center of it all. I'd experienced everything through my worldview, through my two eyes, but none of it revolved around me. I was not the sun. I was a constellation off in the distance, observing the brightest spots in the galaxy as they flickered and faded and aligned to brighten somebody's day. Maybe that wasn't so bad. There were worse seats in the house. The world needs set dressing too.

The past twenty-four hours had proven just how wrong I had Oak Hill too. Silas Dockery stood high on a mountaintop, living on a literal pedestal above the common folk. Why did we all accept that he'd be like us? In reality, all signs pointed to his kin being a deviant killer that used women for their body and company. They knew Lauren Blackburn as a desperate, needing woman and they used that for their gain. Few things in life are more despicable than those that sit idly by while somebody else suffers.

I figured that if I waited long enough at the clearing, Sawyer might find me. It was a simple trap. A block of cheese for the friendly out-of-town mouse. After all, this is where our trouble began.

The entire world was full of closets where pathetic maybes rested and lurked, stacked in neat boxes ready to topple over when the world teetered. That's where they belonged. Tucked away and out of sight. A diary to be dusted off before bed when I wanted to will my body to dream of sweet possibilities that were erased by accidents and death and betrayal.

A rustle in the trees drew my stare. I feared a coyote might creep out and sweep me away from this world. Would I even bother to fight? At least I'd leave the earth as food for another creature, not an all-consuming furnace that churned out regret like it was a byproduct humanity needed. I flicked on my flashlight and headed down the path. At the gate, I heard it again. Footsteps. Somebody marching through the brush. My mind framed an image of Cedar, hungry and hurt. I whispered, "Cedar?"

Only the crickets responded. I held still for a long moment, but I didn't hear it again. The last memory I had of Cedar flashed through my brain. He stood in the small clearing, facing the chain-link, then bolted out of sight. If I wanted to find him, if it was him, I knew where I had to go.

I darted through the brush with my ear cupped. No sounds. Nothing. That didn't mean Cedar wasn't on the move. My feet traced old footsteps, pathways from when I was younger, and Nantahala was a playground to burn away the stress of teenage angst. The same trees hung as a stoic audience. The soil welcomed me with every punch of my feet into the clay.

I ducked under a low-hanging branch and stood in the clearing. Moonlight filled the opening, like a flashlight from the galaxies above. But there was no sign of him. My eyes caught onto the faint markings of the path that led to the chain-link fence that bordered the estate. I sprinted, lungs raw, throat burning with every step. When I neared, I saw a hole in the fence. And then a gunshot sounded.

I squeezed myself through the tiny opening, metallic spikes scraping at my shirtsleeves and scratching my arms. Blood trickled down my bicep, but I was already pushing onward into the hazy space before me. I moved toward the sound, following my gut more than I wanted to admit. The faint outline of the back deck of the Dockery Estate loomed in the distance. A shadow moved. I dove for cover behind a tree just in time as another shot fired.

Panting, I heard my breath echoing off the surrounding trees. Wait. No. I held my breath for a moment. There was somebody else here. Somebody in the foreground.

I whispered, "Cedar? Is that you?" Something shifted to my left. "It's Grace."

Still nothing.

Of all the times I needed Cedar to be a talkative teenager.

I craned my neck toward the movement and squinted until I saw him. Both of his arms stretched downward, holding his left leg. I inhaled a sharp breath and raced across the field toward him. He looked up at me as I approached, wincing and gritting his teeth. Blood trickled out of a wound on his calf. "We need to get out of here," I said. "We need to get you to a hospital."

He studied the blood pooling on the patch of grass below him and then nodded. Pointing toward the ground, I whispered, "Find a handful of small rocks."

"Rocks?"

"Trust me," I said.

We gathered up a small army of stones. I collected them in my hand and pushed the rest into his. "On three, we'll throw the rocks away from the fence. The sound will draw their attention away, then I'll carry you through the hole. Got it?"

He nodded.

"One."

My breath caught in my throat. This wasn't a case for the Clueless Detective Agency. This was life or death. An injured child lay wounded and in my care.

"Two."

The evidence wedged its way into my brain until I zoomed out and saw the answers that it held. Something clicked, gears shifting into place and turning to churn out a product that didn't entirely make sense. But what made sense anymore in Oak Hill?

"Three."

We heaved the rocks. A pitter patter a few hundred yards farther into the field. I clutched Cedar in my arms and limped toward the fence. The gunshot rattled the metallic fence as we pushed through and out of sight.

I lugged Cedar through the clearing, down the path and out toward the fire road. When we emerged, a flashlight turned in our direction and blinded me. I shielded my eyes and braced for impact.

But no more gunshots came. Instead, a warm, sugar-coated voice said my name. Despite all of my attempts to build a wall between us, part of me knew deep down that Sawyer would come after me.

And thank god he did.

wish I remembered the words we spoke. The taste of the air that clung to our nostrils on that humid summer night. The panicked, frenzied moments that followed our rush out of the woods and onto the fire road. Sawyer being there was a minor miracle. Sure, I knew he may rush out to coax me back to give him another chance. But his timing, never his strength before, had been impeccable.

Sawyer pressed the gas so hard the engine strained to keep up. We careened over bumps in the road and the rear of the car drifted when he turned onto Murphy Road. Cedar lay in the back seat, my hands on his wound, applying every ounce of pressure that my adrenaline-fueled body generated. Sawyer kept glancing back in the mirror.

"Am I going to die?" Cedar asked, fear shattering each word as it escaped.

I pushed away the hair that matted on his forehead. "No chance in hell."

He winced. It was dark and light flickered in from the surrounding landscape, but I thought I saw him smile too.

Blood crept down his leg and I pushed with all of my might against the wound. He didn't buck. He didn't so much as grit his teeth. But I watched his lips form the word and it fall from his mouth like a spent piece of gum. *Momma.* The small shards of my heart that had returned to form shattered all over again.

"One minute," Sawyer shouted.

Cedar's eyes flashed in panic as he saw the harsh lights of the emergency room. I scooped him under my arm, but he fidgeted and fought. "I don't..."

"Don't worry about a thing," I said.

He nodded, and I felt his body work with mine. Coordinated as a three-legged race contestant, we hobbled from the back seat. Sawyer hitched us up from the other side and we dragged Cedar into the harshly lit ER. He shut his eyes. Blood rolled over his shoelaces and onto the sterile tile floor. The intake staff moved like birds building a nest. Worried glances darted back and forth. A silent conversation between nurses and doctors. One I couldn't translate as good or bad or neutral or anything. I let go and trusted that fate or fortune or medicine would save Cedar.

A gruff woman blocked Sawyer and me at the double doors. She raised a palm and glared at us. "You can't go back there." She narrowed her gaze. "Are you his family?"

"We're the closest he's got right now," I said.

The nurse crossed her arms. "I need you to fill out the intake forms. Insurance information, medical history, the works. Can you do that for me, dear?"

"If I do that..."

"We'll see about getting you back there with him. But nothing happens without completed forms. Let's start there."

When I handed in the paperwork, I caught the fierce stare of a middle-aged woman behind the counter. "Can we speak a moment?"

I followed her around the corner into a small hallway, where she extended a hand. "I'm Paulette. I'm the Emergency Department social worker. I'd like to ask you a few questions about what happened to your son, if you don't mind."

"He's not my son."

Paulette's eyes widened. "I see. How are you related to the boy?"

"He's a witness to a crime that I did a miserable job of caring for."

"Excuse me?"

I dug my badge out of my bag and showed it to her.

"That boy is named Cedar. We found him after discovering his mother's body in a local farmer's field in Oak Hill. We're still working the case and although he's been quiet about it, I think he knows more than he's said."

"When did his mother pass?"

"Wednesday night."

"And you've cared for him since? The county will want to put him into the system and find a family and—"

"He's been with Susan Orr."

Paulette smiled. "Lovely Miss Susan."

"She's helping us navigate things until we know what his fate holds. If it's possible to hold off on calling the county, I—"

"I'm not going to be the first person in this county to go against Susan Orr. But the boy needs help." Paulette hesitated and jotted a note down. "And this injury . . ."

"He's been shot in the leg."

"By whom?"

I thought of all the angles. Of all the ramifications of dropping the Dockery name in a place like this. For all I knew, there was a wing somewhere with Silas's name on it. A ripple of a memory snuck up on me and I let it slip just as easily as Don Chamberlain did. "It was an accident. He was in Nantahala by the old fire road in Oak Hill and we think—"

Paulette put her hand on her hip. "You think I was born yesterday?" Her eyes shot to mine. "This isn't funny. That girl suffered for years. I worked in the clinic back then. God rest her soul."

"I'm not joking and I mean nothing against Sarah Price," I said. "The similarities are striking. You can trust me that I'm running it down."

Paulette sighed and passed me a form. "Write your name and badge number here. If he speaks up with a different story, I'll need to hold you responsible."

———————————————

I met Sawyer in the waiting room and ushered him through the sliding doors. We leaned against the concrete exterior of the building and blew out breaths that looked like little clouds. Sawyer spoke first. "My first partner in Philly and I liked to play a game when we reached a crossroads in a case. We tried to walk through every conceivable scenario. Every explanation. Then winnow the list down."

"Go for it."

"If I have the facts straight, Cedar believes his mom went to the Dockery estate when she came into town. And I can think of three straightforward explanations for what in the hell happened tonight."

"This doesn't feel like a game."

"One, somebody thought Cedar was a trespasser and shot at him. Two, somebody knew it was Cedar and wanted him dead."

"And is a terrible shot."

"And three, somebody else was there in the forest shooting at Cedar. Another trespasser or a hunter."

"I'll winnow. First, the shots came from the back deck of the estate. That eliminates theory number three."

"So it's whether they were guarding their property or guarding their secrets."

The phrasing put me back to a younger day. Sawyer had always tackled problems like they were a box of sugary cereal. Once past the construction of the rigid outer layer, each following step was easier. Less resistant. He'd pry open the bag and devour the contents bit by bit until there was nothing left but the truth.

I envied that. His nature.

How he would size up something and find the angle for approach, no matter the bearings it had on his life or the world. I admired that more than words.

"Here's my take: Ethan Dockery, who may have had an arrangement with Lauren Blackburn where he'd exchange cash for sex, decided that he had to dispose of any evidence of his improprieties, especially because his father was staring down death. So he kills her, then comes after Cedar, because he saw something."

"And now he's freaked. He's scared."

Sawyer hummed for a moment. "Then what's your move?"

"Arrest the prick and put him away for life."

50

Sawyer and I drove in silence away from the hospital. Fog crept through the early dawn, but our headlights cut through it like a knife. My mind clutched onto the last conversation we'd had. The threads left to dangle. In more ways than one, I'd wanted to have that conversation for half of my life, dreamt up words and questions and rebuttals that needed air to breathe. But when the moment came and stood in front of me, I recoiled like a cornered cat, hackles up, ready to strike. I'd primed my body for a fight, so when it didn't arise, it forced one.

"He'll be okay," Sawyer said, his voice hushed over the sound of the humming radio.

"I know."

"And what about us?" he asked. "Will we ever be okay, Grace?"

"I don't think anybody is ever really okay."

I searched for more to say in the blur of the pines beside the guardrails. In the mustard yellow lines that marked the center of the road. In the trickle of sunlight creeping through the canopies and over the horizon. Nothing came. "Do you think you'll stick around for a while?"

He gripped the wheel tight, his white knuckles a fitting reply to my refusal to answer his question. "Elaine Lincoln is coming by later today to take some photos of Willa's house. I can't afford to keep both Willa's and my place in the city. Something's gotta give."

My throat went dry. "Makes sense. That's a lot on a cop's salary."

"Part of me wants to sell both houses."

"Both?"

"A fresh start. In past generations, they expected a home to pass from one generation to the next and that I'd make a family and form memories around the ghosts of my own. But that feels impossible. That house will forever be Willa's. I had a good life there but the assumption that says I can just live beside memories from my past, it figures that all of my memories would be good ones."

"George?"

He nodded.

"I'm sorry, Sawyer."

"I've spent my entire life being sorry about it. And feeling pain and guilt and angst and all of the other emotions that come with such an accident. And you know what? It hasn't gotten me anywhere. I'm back in Oak Hill with two fewer friends than before and a world of unanswered questions. Maybe feeling sorry doesn't do anyone any good."

His brake lights tinted the world red behind us and I looked out of the window. I had parked my car just off the road, a stone's throw from the fire road and a world of secrets. I paused in the seat and looked back at my first love. "I wouldn't mind another set of eyes on the evidence as I piece it together."

He tried to hide a smile. "I thought you'd decided. Ethan Dockery or bust."

I gripped the door handle. "If only it was that simple. I know what Cliff is going to say. If I want to go after Dockery, I better be ready to hand in my badge."

"That's assuming you're wrong," he said.

"Haven't you heard? That's the prevailing theory around here, Sawyer. I think it's about time I proved myself."

He let go of the wheel, and his eyes lingered on me for a protracted moment. "I'll run to Emma's for coffee then meet you at the station.

"I'd love that."

Mere seconds after I cranked the ignition, before the engine turned over and pumped heat through the vents, my cell rang. "Munoz?"

"Oh, good. You're already up," he said. "Early bird gets the worm or whatever. A call just came in from Charlotte. I'll explain when you get here."

"Start talking now. I'd rather that than morning talk radio."

"You don't like that stuff? I like to put on the sports station and listen to them bicker about some twenty-something prospect in the minor leagues and predict his future. As if that kid isn't working his tail off and—"

"You're stalling, Miguel. Spit it out."

He sighed. "I just hung up with a switchboard operator named Collins from the Charlotte Police Department. Somebody called into their hotline and left an anonymous tip about Lauren Blackburn's murder."

"What was the tip?"

"The tipster said Billy Jenkins is hiding on the far side of town. Gave us an address and everything."

"And how does that relate?"

"They also said that he regularly solicited the services of a prostitute, specifically one that lived in the forest beside town."

"Jesus."

Something prickled my skin. Munoz let the lord's name hang in the air. "I'll see you in five."

When I turned eight, Nat handed me a baseball bat and helmet. We walked down to the sandlot near the edge of town and he spent a full five minutes showing me how to swing a bat before he heaved balls in my general direction. I cowered and shut my eyes with each approaching missile. Nat moved in closer. I flinched. Rinse, repeat.

Finally, I tossed the bat aside and hollered at him. "You're going to kill me."

"No, I'm not," he said. "But practice makes perfect."

"I will not get any better like this."

"Says who?"

I sat in the red dirt and kicked my feet. He knelt next to me. "My dad had me spend an entire weekend at the diamond. I mean, up earlier than the frogs and out past sundown. All that time, I wasn't swinging a bat. He showed me the mechanics over and over. I watched and observed, as if through osmosis I was supposed to learn the magic. When weeks later he finally handed me the bat, I could hardly hold it upright. He complained that it should be easy for me."

"So, you're doing the same here?"

"No, I want you to learn what took me years to understand."

"That baseball stinks?"

"That easy is an intimate feeling. What's easy to you may not be easy to somebody else."

Baseball was never easy, but I kept Nat's wooden bat beneath my desk at work as a memory and a weapon, although I wasn't sure there was a difference. Running was. Complex algebra equations, no matter how much I wrestled with them or studied, were never easy. But biology was. I'd navigated a series of events in life that taught me that easy, just like Nat had said, depended on the person. And I knew damn well when something was too easy.

Munoz needed the answers that arrived to be true. I couldn't blame him. Part of me did too. Anything to give the case a chance to break. But somebody placing an anonymous call to a switchboard hours east of us and hand-delivering the exact break that we wanted? Something about that irked me.

When I parked, I spotted Cliff's truck two spots over. With my palm on the hood, warmth radiated through my fingers. I took a deep breath in, let it out, and rattled loose any signs of tension. A fight awaited me inside. And I knew damn well it would be the biggest one of my lifetime.

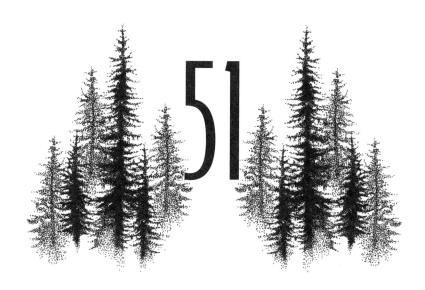

51

liff slammed his fist onto the table, and the thud echoed through my office. "You're being impossible."

"I just think we need to see this from all sides. We—"

"What makes you think the tip is bullshit?"

"Honestly?" I asked. "The fact that we've never had an anonymous tip in the history of Oak Hill coupled with the track record of Billy Jenkins. A drunk and a fool, yes. But a murderer?"

"Simple escalation," Cliff said. "Especially if you're in the camp that thinks he shot Sarah all those years ago."

"You know that was all bullshit," I said.

"What if it wasn't?"

I leaned back in my chair and willed Sawyer to hurry with the coffee and support. I knew he'd take my side. Knew that he'd provide enough clout for Cliff to consider things from my point of view. "Then, how do you explain the shooter at Susan's?"

"Billy Jenkins trying to curtail your investigation."

"Using Silas Dockery's rifle?"

"He's got a rap sheet that's longer than a country mile, Grace. It's simple logic. Plus, I remember the night after you'd spent the day cleaning up Billy Jenkins's little target practice in the parking lot. You said his aim was so bad you hoped he sat down when he pees."

"Cliff, I—"

"I'm over here making one and one equal two. I don't know why you don't listen."

Sawyer emerged like a mirage in the lobby, and I waved him over. Cliff seemed to shrink in his chair, knowing full well that his moment of leonine fierceness was over. There was another force in place now. Sawyer set a coffee cup on my desk and looked at Cliff.

"If I'd have known . . ."

"Had my fill already," Cliff said. "Grace was just telling me her theory about Ethan Dockery."

"Our theory," Sawyer said.

Cliff shrunk further. "Be that as it may, neither of you have the evidence to put Ethan Dockery in cuffs, let alone prosecute him in the court of law."

"But an anonymous tip from Charlotte is enough to drag Billy Jenkins through the doors?" I asked. "You weren't there last night, Cliff. Somebody on the Dockery Estate wants Cedar dead."

"By your own account, you found the boy trespassing on Dockery's property. Pretty easy to see that from the other side and explain it away. There's a murderer in town, Grace, in case you haven't heard. Everybody is up in arms."

Sawyer turned to face Cliff. "I take it you want to move on Jenkins?"

Cliff nodded.

"But beside the tip, what makes you think Jenkins is our guy?"

"Track record."

"And bad aim," I said, each word dripping with sarcasm. Sawyer stared blankly at me. I shrugged. "Long story."

"What the hell happened to him? He was pretty normal as a kid. Maybe a bit of an asshole, but still."

"The town turned against him when Sarah got hurt. Half the town still thinks he's the one that shot her."

"That's impossible," Sawyer said.

"Maybe," I said. "But if we're talking about his rap sheet, he has six arrests on record."

"For what?"

"Early days it was typically drunken disorderly. Bar fights at Mickey's. Then his parents kicked him out, and he started an unremarkable career as a thief. He'd rob somebody and try to pawn whatever he stole over in Moxville. Pawn shop owner didn't appreciate being a fence for stolen goods, so he rang the authorities right away. Last time I booked him was about four years ago and he skipped town afterward."

"And we've confirmed that he's back?"

"More or less. Liam said Billy is enrolled in a training program in Moxville."

"What's the harm in pulling him in and asking him some questions?" Cliff asked. "It's not like he's got a reputation we'd need to protect. Let's see what he's got to say for himself."

I looked at Sawyer, who gave me a subtle shrug. "I'll send Munoz to the location mentioned in the tip."

Cliff exhaled. "Thank you. It shouldn't be this hard to work together, Grace."

"Don't worry, you'll have a new puppet in place soon."

I waved over Munoz, gave him the rundown, and explained his marching orders. Cliff insisted he follow behind in his truck, just in case anything got out of hand. I didn't have the heart to fight it. They stomped out and left Sawyer and me alone again.

I slurped coffee and let the thick taste coat my tongue. Although I could practically feel it tinting my teeth brown, the warmth radiated from my throat and stomach and thawed the rest of my body.

"What are you thinking about?" Sawyer asked.

"What makes you think I'm thinking?"

"You stick your tongue into your cheek. You have since you were a kid."

I shifted my tongue back into the center of my mouth. "Force of habit." I shrugged. "Maybe we'll get lucky and find out Jenkins is our guy, but if that's the case, Munoz will be running this place before you can blink. My career ladder here is about to topple over. I've climbed as high as I can and this town decided that's the limit. Maybe Miguel has a decent shot here. He'd make a good leader."

"Ignoring that for a second, there's something I'm stuck on. Ethan dumping Lauren's body in a field brings more heat than if he just cut her loose altogether. Scared her away."

He was right. That was the wrinkle that continued to give me pause. Only one rational explanation came to mind, although I hadn't worked out the math yet. "What if Cedar is his son?"

Sawyer chewed on that for a moment, then reached for a notepad. He narrated as he wrote. "Let's say Cedar is fourteen. That puts his birthday in 2008. Ethan is two years older than us, so he would have been twenty."

"It tracks."

"How many twenty-year-olds do you know that solicit sex workers?"

"Not many," I said. "But since when has Ethan Dockery been the rule and not the exception?"

"Maybe. But that means he's out there trying to kill his son?" Sawyer asked. "That's a dark narrative, Grace."

"Nobody said we had to like the answers we find."

"Easy to test that theory," Sawyer said.

I snapped my fingers. "You're right."

With one eye toward the door, I punched digits into my phone and made a call.

Moments later, Munoz and Cliff returned empty-handed. I gave Munoz a list of tasks I needed him to accomplish. He studied it. "Do I want to know what your plan is?"

"Better you don't."

"Grace, I—"

"You can pay me back when you're in Chamberlain's old office. Buy me lunch or something." Munoz nodded and walked to the parking lot.

Cliff slid his phone onto my desk. "Hannah is still friends with Billy Jenkins on Facebook. Based on his posts, he's definitely back in town."

I glanced at the screen but the man in the profile photo was hardly recognizable. Far from the scrawny roughneck I'd once known. Almost an entirely new person altogether. I swallowed hard and pushed away the phone. That face. I knew that face.

Within seconds of searching "Billy Jenkins Training Program Moxville" online, I came across a press release about a training program for individuals with felony convictions. Panic pulsed through my every fiber. That face I'd seen and failed to fully recognize. The ghost-like look on the man's face beneath his EMT uniform, wheeling the gurney into Silas Dockery's house. Billy Jenkins.

Sawyer peered over my shoulder. "Billy Jenkins is an EMT?"

-THEN-

By the end of that long week, we had all the answers we'd have for the next two decades. Sarah Price ran from the bonfire pit just like the rest of us. She recalled heading east, but in the obscurity of the forest, the scene of her accident proved otherwise. She'd darted west, into the heart of the forest and away from the road. Brambles and thorny shrubs guarded her path. Shadows leapt out at her until fear took control. Sarah remembered running until her lungs burnt, then looking back and realizing she was alone.

She crept back in the direction she'd come from. Whenever she told the story, she'd stop and outline her fear of copperheads resting in the brush. The sting of nature's serpentine predator exceeded any human threat. All that worry focused on the brush drove her focus downward. Sarah didn't see the silhouette of her shooter. She didn't see their face or their rifle or the flash-bang explosion of the bullet exploding out of the barrel and into her spine. She remembered nothing aside from hurried footsteps in the leaves. Probably us kids running for our lives. Sarah simply felt the sting in her back as she collapsed onto the ground. Her body released a ghastly scream, primal and panicked.

Chamberlain's official report on the night, which I devoured the day I joined the force, painted a little more vivid picture but still left massive gaps in the timeline of events. Not to mention the shortage of explanations.

In his defense, he had followed protocol to start. He'd run the bullet—a .375 H&H Magnum—through tests, but it came back without a match, just a rough description of the rifle. Winchester 70. An affordable gun, a dime a dozen, most often employed to hunt big game. He left that thread to dangle, knowing full well that if he solicited a list of registered Winchester 70s in the town, he'd have every name in the phone book.

His legwork was unimpressive. His interviews with known punks around town, the addicts and the miscreants, yielded nothing but ironclad alibis and a laundry list of patrons that were within the walls of Mickey's tavern. All confirmed. All pardoned from the list. Hushed conversations swelled and rumors warned that Chamberlain planned to bring in every single bonfire attendee. Every knock at Nat's door caused me to jump. But he never came. I suppose that was too much work for the man. Or he'd already made up his mind.

Sarah had no known enemies. By all accounts, Sarah was a normal, small-town girl who sat in the pews of St. Anthony's each Sunday and led a weekly bible study for the younger crop. She'd dated Billy Jenkins and dumped him because he kept flirting with any girl in sight. Billy's whereabouts rose to the surface but multiple other graduates had him in their sights throughout the night, myself included. Many locals latched onto the idea of his guilt, even if it was largely unfounded. No matter his involvement, Billy Jenkins's reputation shifted permanently that year. Like a trail that saw its path overgrown by brush and weeds, the truth became murkier by the day.

Before long, word spread around town that Lionel Sutton had supplied most of the beer as payment to a few student farmhands that had earned their keep. That word never amounted to much more though, even if the whole town knew that Lionel Sutton's actions were the flap of a butterfly's wings that set the town into a spiral. Sarah's family contemplated a lawsuit against Sutton and then the national forest, but there was nobody to blame for what had happened. They sat buttoned up in stuffy chairs with Oak Hill resident legal expert Bill Nickelson as he warned them how long a case against the government would take. Margo let loose that Nickelson had told them to give it up and move on. They did as he recommended.

For Don Chamberlain and the local leaders, conclusions were easy to string together, even if they weren't altogether satisfying. Sawyer's name floated atop most of the paperwork for the early stretches of the investigation, but they never had much to work with. It broke my heart to think of Sawyer hiding in some big-city apartment afraid to come home and feel the wrath of Don Chamberlain's vendetta. Nobody ever seemed to tell Sawyer he'd been deemed innocent.

A theory surfaced like a bear after hibernation: Some imprudent hunter was out in the Nantahala using night vision and misfired. Confused Sarah Price for a buck. No soul ever came forward or fessed up to any nighttime hunting and Chamberlain didn't so much as pull hunting permits for that part of the forest, but it became a tolerable truth. One that fit the narrative. Simple as that. An accident.

When I read his notes and the orbit of his investigation, an old saying came to mind. A hammer finds a nail. Chamberlain had whispered to Agnew that it was an accident long before he'd analyzed the slug or taken witness statements. Confirmation bias, maybe. Don Chamberlain, as I learned firsthand, had a certain image of Oak Hill.

That very image and expectation was the impetus for his raid on our bonfire in the first place. Although he had surely cut loose after his high school graduation, Oak Hill was no place for escapades and antics like ours. By the end of his abbreviated investigation, he'd made sure that image remained unmarked.

In the years since, by the way Oak Hillians acted, you'd think Sarah Price fell down a ridge line or rolled her ankle. I don't know how folks ignored the creak of her wheelchair inching down Murphy Road and pretended like it was just part of life. Nat always told me that part of growing up in

Oak Hill was that you learn to have a selective memory. You choose what parts of your past and the world you want to hold on to and which you want to forget. Not me. I clung to every second of the past like it was a lesson blazing a path to my future. As far as Oak Hill was concerned, Sarah Price was the victim of a tragic accident. The Price family soldiered on as if the future would someday obscure the past. Maybe they were right. I suspect they weren't.

Oak Hill sacrificed to make sure Sarah and the Prices were taken care of but there were limitations on her life within city limits. There was only so much respite that microwave-ready casserole dishes and half-filled collection plates at the church provided. Funds dried up and along with it went the Price family's allegiances to Oak Hill. And soon after, the Price's marriage.

I remember the day the moving truck blazed through town. Bright and yellow like the sun. The Price family minivan sputtered behind, kicking up dust and whispers with each mile. Neither Sarah nor her mother stopped to wave. Their house stayed empty for a month until a shotgun wedding drove Chuck and Cathy Agnew to the courthouse. It was hardly a week before people stopped talking about Sarah Price. Even her father, who stayed local, stopped bringing it up. As simple as that, her name became a relic of the past. Nobody wanted to dig up those bones and surface a question without an answer. Especially Liam.

Whispers came through the grapevine eventually. A tragic life met with a tragic end. In some wicked twist, two years after moving away, Sarah Price was killed in a car accident on her way to a doctor's appointment. If her departure from Oak Hill didn't put her demons to bed, her death surely did. There was no longer blood to be washed from the town's collective hands. Damn near the whole town exhaled.

If you stitch together everything that happened that night, it paints a gruesome picture of Oak Hill. One innocent teenager was shot and paralyzed, later to die an untimely death. One bystander was tackled, arrested, and then released to his parents, one of whom later that same night passed after an accidental fall. Nat once said that he thought Oak Hill saved up all of its bad karma for a single night and I have to think he's right. Willa, God rest her soul, once whispered a quote under her breath that I tucked into my memory forever. We're tested by times when nothing happens at all and when everything happens at once. Everything with Lauren Blackburn felt like the latter.

52

illy Jenkins had been at Silas Dockery's house the night he died. If he'd managed to slip away for long enough, he could have lifted the rifle from the hallway—despite all of my denials, all of my insistence that Billy wasn't the violent type. Maybe we never know people how we think we do. At least there was light at the end of the tunnel. At least I'd be able to say we'd solved the case and brought justice for Lauren Blackburn.

I filled Sawyer in on everything as we raced out to the car and sped toward the location provided by our friendly tipster. Billy Jenkins's alleged hideout was about as impressive as the fort where Sawyer and I had our first kiss. Tommy Dekker, the resident high school loudmouth, had bragged about the wooden structure behind his house that his family had built years back. Dekker's intent was to announce that he'd felt up half the town in that cabin with hopes of adding a few more notches to his bedpost if time allowed. Sawyer and I heard a different message. It wasn't long before Tommy Dekker's family headed out of town for a vacation. Then, Sawyer and I snuck in through an open window and tossed blankets on the ground until we lay comfortably. The rest, as they say, was history.

From the looks of things, Billy didn't even have the same comforts we did. After a knock on the door, we peered in through the smudged windows and saw little signs of life beside a ruffled sleeping bag and a throw pillow. A plastic bag, snagged in the crack of the back door, blew in the wind and rattled like a maraca. "Nothing," I said to Sawyer.

Munoz rang me ten minutes into our stakeout but I sent him to voicemail. My wild goose chase was just that—a fool's errand. Sawyer sat beside me and chewed on his lip.

"What's on your mind?"

"It all lines up. But what's Billy's motive to kill Lauren Blackburn?"

"If the tipster is correct, he'd paid for services rendered. Maybe Cedar is his son and Lauren decided to confront him about it."

"Maybe. I guess the worst case scenario is that we bring him in and he walks. Plus, maybe we can finally press charges for stealing Willa's orb."

"Ah, the simple days when our cases were wrapped up by dinner time," I said.

"What was your secret plan before you put this all together about Jenkins?"

"The less you know the better," I said.

"Grace, seriously, I've got nothing to lose here. Whatever your hunch was, I want to know. If word gets back to my commanding officer in Philly, you'd be doing me a favor. It's the easy way out."

"You say that but I don't think you mean it."

"Despite what you think, people often say exactly what they mean, Grace."

"No, they say what they think other people want to hear. We're all guarded with our words. We know they can cut deeper than we intend." I turned to face him. He scrunched in the seat and shifted backward. A single curl draped down over the contour lines of his forehead. "Just trust me, okay?"

He nodded but I saw him bite his tongue. Instead, I let him off the hook with a subtle change of subject. "Sawyer, I'm sorry. I overreacted last night."

"No, Grace, I—"

"Let me finish. Nobody in their right mind would expect their old friend to return to town and have things return to the way they were. We were kids. We had optimism and youth and the world in front of us. Things are different now. We're different too. Our hearts and minds fell back into old ways, the easy imprint of a relationship that had been vacant for years. But there was a reason for that. If we'd been meant for one another, I don't think we'd have waited fifteen years to reunite."

"That's your big speech?"

I glared at him. "Nobody said you had to give feedback."

"I'm just saying, yeah, some of that is true. It's been a while. When I was driving down, I tried to imagine what it would be like to see you again. I pictured your face for the last fifteen years and dreamt of waking up next to you again. I wondered if my heart would shatter when I heard your voice."

"Did it?"

"Much the opposite," he said. "It skipped a beat."

"That's corny."

"When you spend half of your life trying to convince yourself that you are not the sum of your past experiences, parts of you start to believe it."

"So you're saying only part of you loves me?"

"Part of me knows how bad I hurt you and doesn't think I deserve to love anybody or anything."

"What are you trying to say?"

"That things picked up where they were fifteen years ago. Cliff is still trying to make his mark in the world and inflate his ego. You're still solving mysteries and spitting sass with Nat. I'm a bit older, balder, and out of shape but I'm still the same person. And I feel the same things."

"But—"

"And from the moment I saw you again, I knew that no matter how many times I told myself I didn't, no matter how many times I willed myself to let it go, no matter what, I never stopped loving you."

"Sawyer—"

"I mean it."

I swallowed hard. My lips curled. An invitation for him to bring his closer. He hesitated for a moment, then the flicker passed. I shrugged and faced forward again. "That's nice of you to say and all but it's not fair that you'd expect that I just forget the past and overlook the canyon between our lives."

"I'm not asking you to."

"Then what are you asking, Sawyer? Because last night, I was eighteen again. I stared into your eyes and imagined your lips on mine and for a brief second, I let my heart take over. So I asked if you'd stay and you stumbled like you did in the fifth-grade spelling bee."

"In my defense, nobody can spell rhyme."

"You and your diversions."

"I—" he said

"But now I know that I was wrong. Look how wrong I've been on this case. Everybody has pointed fingers at Billy Jenkins from the start and I was the only person to shrug it off. I don't deserve to solve this case. And I very much do not deserve anything as great as your company, Sawyer."

"That's bullshit, Grace, I—"

My phone vibrated in the cup holder. I flashed him a glare and lifted it to my ear. One long moment later, I sat it down and let out a deep breath. "Well?" Sawyer asked.

"I know who killed Lauren," I said.

"What happened to Billy Jenkins? Cliff will erupt if we return empty handed."

"Good," I said. "When he's done spewing lava, we can tell him that I solved the case."

Sawyer didn't respond. I followed his eyes and saw Billy Jenkins rounding the corner and strutting down the sidewalk with a soda in one hand and a cigarette in the other. "There's Billy. We might as well bring him into the station," Sawyer said.

I sped past Billy. "We've got bigger fish to fry," I said. "Because I'm about to put a Dockery away for the rest of his life."

———————————

When I stopped the car next, it was in front of Sawyer's house. I spent the brief ten-minute crawl through downtown explaining my maneuvering and the result. Sawyer nodded along until he saw that we were beneath the magnolia in front of his house.

"What are you doing?"

"Shut up and let me handle this. Meet me at the station in a half hour."

I saw protest coat his tongue but his gut won out. He slammed the door behind him but I was already speeding away toward the far end of the city. Away from the weed-infested field where Lauren Blackburn was murdered. Away from the hospital where Cedar sat in recovery, alone and abandoned. Away from Nat and Sawyer and all of the ghosts from my past. And toward the inferno.

53

slowed at the double wrought-iron gates and shoved my badge out in front of the camera. "Oak Hill PD," I said into the intercom. To my surprise, the gate creaked open and let me through. I blazed up around the serpentine bends, tossed the car into park, and barged through the front door.

Madison jumped out in front of me and blocked my path. "Nice of you to drop in, Gracie."

"Move," I said.

"I'd love to. Can I see a warrant?"

"I don't need one," I said. "But I can get one without any trouble."

"I'm not a lawyer but—"

"No, you're not. But you can just call Bill Nickelson, right?"

"I don't know who Daddy's lawyer was, I'm not one to meddle in his business. But you can't take another step in my house without evidence."

"This isn't your house. It belongs to Silas."

She didn't flinch. Didn't move a muscle. "How dare you say my father's name."

"I have nothing against your father," I said. "But if you don't let me pass, I'll arrest you too."

"What do you mean arrest me too?"

Ethan stepped out of the far doorway and crossed his arms. "What is the meaning of this?"

I sidestepped Madison and marched toward him. I swallowed hard and with a dry mouth uttered the words I'd longed to say. "Ethan Dockery, I'm placing you under arrest for the murder of Lauren Blackburn."

He went pale. "What the hell?"

"Anything you say can and will be used against you—"

"Maddy, call Nickelson and Dad's business manager."

She smiled at me. "With pleasure. And by the end of the day, we'll not only have Ethan back home, but we'll have your job too, Gracie."

"Good luck," I said. "I don't think Nickelson will fight for you two once he finds out Ethan here burned down his shop."

I nudged Ethan toward the door and lingered next to Madison for a long moment. Our eyes met, her icy stare reminiscent of a snow globe. She shook her head. "You're making a huge mistake," she said. "If you let him go now, we can pretend this never happened."

I cupped my ear. "Did you hear that? That's your father rolling over in his grave."

She spat at my feet but I was already through the front doors. I eased Ethan into the back of the car and sped toward the station, my heart rate outpacing the speedometer.

Ethan Dockery didn't say a word on the ride into town. The only sound I heard was the thump-thump of my heart as it slithered its way out of my throat and back into its cavity in my chest. I let out a breath I'd held for the last fifteen minutes and recounted the evidence in my head. By the time I was through, the station was in sight and I had no doubts about my maneuver. Ethan Dockery played a role in Lauren Blackburn's death, and it was my job to prove it. In the parking lot, I cocked my head back and forth but didn't catch any wandering eyes. Moving with haste, I led him through the double-doors and walked Ethan over to the holding cell. The door shut with a metallic clank. As I locked it, he gritted his teeth between the cold bars and let out a nervous whine like a scared puppy. Suspicion swarmed around him like flies on roadkill.

"My lawyer is already on his way."

"Old Bill will take a solid half hour just to get down the stairs. But when he gets here, I'll let him know who burnt his office down."

He turned away from me and faced the barren walls. "When you arrested me, you said murder?" He spoke with a deliberate pace and studied the empty station. "And I presume that the rest of your staff is elsewhere because they do not agree with your actions."

"We're a small force here, Ethan. You should know that better than anyone. And I didn't appreciate you trying to make it smaller."

He scoffed.

"We can wait for Bill if you'd like, but I have some questions for you."

"Why would I talk to you?" he asked.

"If you're innocent, you've got nothing to hide."

"I've seen innocent men put away before. I'm not looking to incriminate myself."

"The quicker you can clear your name, the less time the public has to catch wind of the fact that you're a suspect. You can preserve the Dockery family name. But we can wait for Bill if you'd like. That makes things rather formal."

Ethan chewed on the words like bubble gum. "Okay. Maybe we can settle this without him, then. Let me out of here and we can talk."

I wagged a finger at him. "See, this is an unusual spot for you. You're expecting to call the shots. To bark orders at the woman in front of you. But that's not how this goes."

I dragged a chair over. The high-pitched scrape of legs against linoleum nearly made paint crawl off the walls. Ethan stood, arms-crossed. "Get on with it then."

"How did you meet Lauren Blackburn?"

"That's the dead woman, right?"

"Your victim, yes."

Tension fell from his shoulders. "I've never met that woman in my life."

"She never visited you on the estate?"

"Never."

"You sure about that?"

He lifted a single eyebrow in response.

"Okay then. We'll circle back to her. Tell me, does your family own a Remington 700?"

"I'd have to check the gun locker. Silas was the one always marching into the woods at ungodly hours to hunt game. Madison and I never had much patience for his shooting lessons, let alone spending a day in the brush hunting deer."

His agreeableness left me off-kilter. The snarling rage had receded into a tranquil simmer. Then again, I didn't have the interrogation experience to know if it was all an act. I pushed on anyhow.

"We checked the registry."

He shrugged. "Good, then you're asking questions you know the answer to. Do we own one?"

"You do."

"Great. You said that the killer struck the woman with an object. So, what's this business about a gun? Was she shot too?"

"No, but Cedar was."

"That feral boy?"

I inched close to the cell bars and locked my eyes on his. "Ethan, that's no way to talk about the boy. You can drop the act."

"Feral isn't an insult. It's an observation."

"Nobody should make observations like that about their own son."

54

Ethan froze. "My son?"

"I can't decide what's more likely. That Lauren decided not to tell you to protect him from you . . . or that you were so ashamed you're pretending you didn't know."

"I . . . now wait just a minute."

"The DNA test proves it."

"Proves what?" he shrieked. "This is ludicrous."

"Did he see you kill her?" I asked. "Is that why you had to take him out? No matter the cost. No matter the blood. You saw a loose thread, and you had to snip it."

Ethan opened his mouth to reply, but hesitated. "Can I have my cell phone?"

"Fat chance."

"I won't make a call. I want to check something. It directly relates to this bombshell of a conversation we're having here, Grace."

I snatched his phone from my desk and brought it over. "I'll hold onto this. Tell me what you want to see."

He gulped. "Code is 2468. Open the Calendar App."

I held it out for him to see. "Now go to Wednesday."

"Last Wednesday?"

"The day of the murder."

I swiped around. A red block covered every hour on the calendar. It said "MIAMI". He pointed to it, horror still painting every inch of his skin. "I flew to Miami on Monday morning."

Hope waned. "You mean to say that you had a flight booked to Miami."

"You can check flight records. The airline will confirm that I boarded the flight on Monday out of Asheville. I was supposed to be there all week, but Dad caught wind of the murder and insisted that I come home early to sort things out. He was worried the local police would fudge the whole thing and the murder would be a stain on the town." Ethan let a smile drape over his lips. "Maybe he was prophetic after all."

"I saw you Thursday afternoon. You sat in our conference room and berated me about my ability to solve a murder case."

"I took the first flight back. Dad tells you to jump, you ask how high."

"I'll run that down."

"Wait," he said. "The DNA. I need to know if that was true."

"It is, Ethan."

"That's not possible. I never slept with anybody I wasn't in a relationship with, let alone a woman who lived in the woods. How does the DNA test work?"

"This is an interrogation, Ethan. I—"

"Grace, if there's a way to avoid the public fallout of my arrest, I think we both need to consider it because I swear to you, something stinks."

I slapped a piece of paper against the bars.

"I had Macon County Crime Lab compare the DNA of Cedar and your father."

"My father?"

"When they did his autopsy, they took a sample."

"Okay but then—"

"Your father and Cedar share roughly 24% of their DNA. That means that he is a second-tier familial match."

"Meaning what?"

"That he is your father's grandson."

Ethan gulped hard and shook his head. "That boy is a teenager. You're saying that I had a relationship with that woman when I was in high school?"

"You're thirty-five. He's maybe fifteen. It's not that hard to calculate, Ethan. And the sooner you come to terms with it, the easier this gets."

"It's not possible."

"Save it for the courts."

Ethan sulked into the shadows of the cell while I marched through the front doors and into the sunshine. When the door shut behind me, I let out the breath that I'd held the entire conversation. My body shrunk six inches as I slumped against the exterior wall and confronted the answers Ethan Dockery provided. None of which were what I'd expected or wanted. But nothing in life was easy.

I was so lost in thought that I didn't hear Sawyer's car pull up. His scuffed sneakers appeared in front of me, and he extended a hand to pull me to my feet. "How did it go?"

"Couldn't be worse," I said. "He's got an alibi for the murder. He was in Miami. I haven't checked flight records but . . ."

"That's a twelve-hour drive. It's possible, but not likely he could have driven up in the middle of the night. Sorry to rain on your parade."

"Great," I said. "Some friend you are."

"I was thinking though. You said in the car that the match came back as just less than 24 percent. We know they're related but not how."

"Correct."

"What if we have all the right evidence, but we're looking at it from the wrong angle?"

I looked up at him, waiting for more.

"Cedar and Silas Dockery share enough DNA to make them family. But Cedar could be his grandson without Ethan's involvement."

Gears clicked into place in my brain. "Then Ethan's innocence is not an act. And our best suspect is deceased."

"By Cliff's account, Silas was bedridden in the last weeks of his life. No way he could have done it."

"He could have paid somebody to do it. Like Billy Jenkins."

"Maybe. But I bet if we can figure out the connection between Silas and Cedar, we'll have our answers."

"We should go to Cedar."

Sawyer glanced back at the station. "Do we just leave Ethan here?"

"I've already lost my job. What's another hour in the cell for Ethan Dockery? If it's not for this crime, it's sure as hell for something else."

55

Maroon-padded chairs sat arranged in perfect rows, each facing forward and to the side of picturesque portraits of landscapes and mountains. We didn't take the risk of being told no and instead marched through the doors like we were staff. We found Cedar in the third room on our left.

Machines beeped and whirred all around us, like a mechanical orchestra working in tandem to keep everybody alive. Cedar sat upright in his bed, emanating the adage of a fish out of water. His wide eyes followed us as we passed through the doorway and stood beside his bed. Sawyer reached out his hand and caressed the boy's shoulder. "How are you feeling?" Sawyer asked.

Cedar shrugged.

"That good, huh?"

He nodded.

"We may know who hurt your mother," I said.

His eyes widened so much they nearly filled his face. "Who?"

"One step at a time," I said. "But soon. I promise."

Sawyer glanced my way, but I ignored him. I didn't need telepathy to recognize that I'd broken the secret vow of any investigator. Never promise answers. Never promise results. You only control what's in front of you. But I owed Cedar a promise. And he needed it. I didn't think we'd have a shot in hell of getting any answers from him unless he felt we were wholly, entirely, completely on his side.

"Okay," he said, a gentler tone to his voice.

"I need your help," I said, then pointed to Sawyer. "We need your help. On all of those trips your mom took into town, did you ever follow her?"

He nodded.

"Did she go through that same hole in the fence?"

He nodded.

"Who did she meet when she got there?"

"Nobody."

"Then what did she do?"

He hesitated, as if sifting through soil for the right words. "She took care of the trees."

Confusion creased my forehead. "The trees?"

"I only followed her once. She loved trees. She liked to point to her favorites and tell me the names, but I never remembered."

"Did she go where you went last night? The trees around the back of that house."

He nodded.

Sawyer stepped closer. "Cedar, your mother had 11-5 tattooed on her skin. Do you remember when we talked about that?"

He nodded.

"Is that your birthday?"

"Yes."

Goosebumps flooded my skin. How did Sawyer put that together? How did I miss it? Inadequacy and shock mixed for a dangerous concoction. Numbers flooded my brain and registered like a row of dominos tumbling one after the other.

"That's a great birthday," Sawyer said. "November is a beautiful time of year. The leaves are changing and it's cool enough to sleep outside."

He smiled.

"Cedar, how old are you?" I asked.

"Fourteen."

"So in November, you'll be fifteen?"

Another nod. That put his birth year in 2007. My throat went dry when I recognized our next steps. It couldn't be possible. It didn't add up. Yet somehow it pestered me like a pebble in my shoe.

"Thank you, Cedar."

Sawyer placed his hand over the boy's and held it there for a long moment. Then he leaned down and kissed Cedar on the head. "Thanks for your help. I promise we'll get you out of here soon."

I shot him the same look he'd sent my way before and he didn't blink. Cedar collapsed back onto the bed and watched us leave without another word. In the hallway, Sawyer set a blazing pace back toward the car. "We need to—"

"Why would she take care of the trees?"

"I don't know. It doesn't make any sense to me."

"Unless she wasn't taking care of the trees but checking her hiding spot."

His eyes went wide. "A perfect spot to leave a message for somebody."

"Or cash."

We tore past town and as we passed the station, I glimpsed Munoz standing by the door. "Shit," I said, under my breath, then fumbled for my phone. "Why are you at the station?" I barked.

"Madison Dockery appeared at my house. Told me that if I didn't let her brother out of the cell that she'd file a lawsuit and have me fired by the end of the day. I'm sorry, Grace, I—"

"No apologies necessary. Where did Ethan go?"

"Somewhere to talk with Nickelson. They drove out of town. Away from the estate."

"Thanks. I'll text if I need anything," I said.

As I hung up, we hurried through the wide-open gates of the Dockery Estate. There wasn't a person in sight. We parked and dashed around the back onto the grassy ridge where I'd found Cedar. I surveyed the grass for bloodstains or any record of our nighttime mayhem.

Nothing.

Sawyer and I split up the trees. I scanned each one, ran my fingers over the bark, unsure of what I was looking for. A yellow poplar in the far corner had a burr that looked like an abnormal growth, like a clogged artery. My hand slid along the bark, feeling every rough edge until it snagged on something smooth.

I waved Sawyer over and together we pried open a latch. Inside, there was a chamber, four inches tall and maybe nine inches wide. It was empty. "Cedar was right," I said.

"Does that mean Ethan was lying?"

What did that chamber hold? What secrets did someone stash inside beside a monthly mountain of cash for Lauren Blackburn? What did they owe her? And who owed it?

I glanced around the forest, hoping the trees would translate the evidence, so I shut my eyes and listened. The crackle of fire. The pop of sparks from timber. The silent yet thunderous roar of the surrounding crowd of teens, celebrating one last hour together. I smelled smoke, so strong that it stifled my nose. I let out a cough.

In that second, I put together the missing piece. I turned to Sawyer with delight. "What's the one thing we haven't been able to piece together?"

"The fire."

"Right," I said. "No matter which way I spin it, Ethan had no reason to burn Bill Nickelson's practice to the ground. But now we have this notch."

"I'm not following," Sawyer said.

"Lauren Blackburn wasn't coming to see anybody here. She wasn't a sex worker. She was a mother trying to take care of her son."

"And?"

"And she was a daughter, accepting a bribe to stay out of town."

"A daughter?"

"24 percent DNA. Cedar is Silas's grandchild. But not because Ethan is the father. But because Lauren was Silas's daughter."

"And he left cash for her each month."

"And he opened the Dockery Center around the time she left the military. Because he didn't want his daughter out there alone."

"Why not take her in?"

"Everybody guards their secrets differently, Sawyer. I can't explain everything, but it all makes sense."

"But then, who killed Lauren?"

I pointed to the massive estate behind us.

"Somebody who didn't want to share this place. Somebody who burned down the law office in fear of an unofficial record for another heir. Somebody who didn't want to share their inheritance with another sibling. Somebody who was here, in the shadows, all along. Somebody we overlooked."

Sawyer swallowed hard.

"The only heir left standing."

56

The pieces were coming together, and the picture was damning. Blue and red light danced off the immaculate white siding of the estate and marked Munoz's arrival. He emerged with a sheepish look, and only when Cliff stepped out of the passenger side did I understand.

"Sorry, Grace," Munoz said.

"How long has Cliff been bribing you for updates?" Sawyer asked.

"The whole time."

"Munoz, you're fine. I hope it supplemented your meager salary. Cliff, you're a prick," I said.

"Mind explaining what the hell is going on here?" Cliff barked.

I paused on the front steps and turned to Munoz. "Did you bring it?"

He extended a Manila envelope my way.

I pried the pins open and scanned the top, then handed it over to Cliff. His eyes sifted through the front page, color draining from his face with every word. By the time he tucked it back into the sleeve, he resembled a walking cloud. "What do you expect to find in here?"

"The truth," I said.

"First you go and haul Ethan Dockery into a jail cell. Now you're raiding his house?" Cliff barked. "Wait just a damn minute."

"The judge gave us the green light."

"I don't give a damn what any county judge said, Grace. This is a good family. A good man. Ethan Dockery isn't a killer. You could've at least informed me of your plan."

"You know, this whole time I've been trying to figure out how the Dockery family has been in lockstep with me with each new discovery of this investigation. I assumed Liam had leaked Lauren's name. But then I had a hunch that I hoped was wrong, Cliff. You were Ethan Dockery's mole. What do they have on you?"

"They don't—"

"Cut the shit, Carlos. This isn't the time for lies."

"They threatened to tell Hannah about Reyna."

Sawyer whistled.

"And?" I asked.

"And force my resignation."

"I knew I shouldn't have trusted you, Cliff. But what's done is done. You want to know the kind of people you are tangled with? Read the search warrant again."

His eyes scanned the body of the document and horror filled his pupils. "There's no way," he said. "Madison?"

"Now if you don't mind, I've got some evidence to find."

"What exactly are we looking for?" Munoz asked.

"The rifle," I said.

"That will only tie her to the gunshots. How do you plan to connect her to the murder scene?"

"Her car," I said, pointing to the garage. "We peered through the windows. It's in there."

"She left without her car?" Cliff asked.

"She was in Silas's car when she showed up at my front door," Munoz said.

"Then she may be on the run," Sawyer added. "Either way, we've got a case to build."

Munoz tried the front door. "It's unlocked."

"Good," I said. I cupped my mouth and shouted. "Oak Hill Police Department. We have a search warrant for the premises."

The walls creaked in response.

"Munoz, take the house with Sawyer. Look for anything that ties Madison to Lauren. Cliff, come with me to the garage."

Cliff followed along. The collective sound of footsteps danced off the cavernous space. We fumbled with the switch on the wall, but the garage roared open eventually. In the waning daylight, two cars appeared inside the concrete room. "That's hers," Cliff said, pointing to a white Tesla Model S.

I glanced at the search warrant. "That means Munoz was right. She has Silas's car. I'll need to put an APB out when we're through here."

Cliff disappeared inside and reemerged with a set of keys. I confiscated them and slid them into the envelope.

"What are you doing?" he asked.

"If Madison used this car to give Lauren a ride to the other side of town, I'd bet they will find trace DNA."

"Smart thinking," Cliff said.

"That might be the first time you've ever complimented me, Cliff. Let's see what they found inside."

Cliff led me through the labyrinth of hallways that I'd staggered down on the night of Silas's death. He called out for Sawyer, who beckoned us to the gun locker in the narrow path adorned with creepy portraits and family awards. "Did you find it?" I asked.

Sawyer shook his head. "Nope. There's no Remington 700 here."

"That would have been too easy."

"Maybe it's hidden somewhere else in the house?" Sawyer suggested.

"Maybe," I said. "Take Munoz and search the rest of the place. But leave the garage as is. I'll call Macon County now and tell them to hurry. This may be a long night."

Shortly after they disappeared, I made the call. Tessa and her team told us to expect them within the hour, and I sat on the steps and stewed over the barriers thrust in our way. For once, I had the path cleared before me. I knew who Lauren's killer was and with the right luck, I'd prove it, assuming Madison was as piss-poor of a criminal as she was a human.

I took Nat's age-old advice and considered the events from Madison's point of view. Her father, who had loved her and raised her with privilege and wealth, may have confessed to having a secret daughter in his dying days. He told Madison about Lauren hoping to add her to the family. Hoping that Madison could close the gap that Silas created. But instead of seeing it as an opportunity to grow the family, Madison saw it as an opportunity to dilute her wealth. And she manipulated Silas as a final act.

Maybe she saw it as protecting her family. I know little about bloodlines and inheritances, seeing as all I'll get from Nat is the creaky old double-wide. Still, the thought of taking your half-sister into a field and killing her sent shivers down my spine. Then the attempt on Cedar's life. Or mine.

I cracked open her closet and emptied her hamper onto the carpet. Sifting through the dirty clothes, the smell crept toward my nostrils and strung. Gasoline. Holderbaum had said whoever set the fire would have reeked. Madison burned down Nickelson Law. Another brick in the wall. But I still didn't have the smoking gun.

In all of my role-playing, I tried to imagine where Madison Dockery would hide her rifle. I walked to her room and unsurprisingly found bare walls and stuffy, antique furniture. I ran my fingers over the walls, feeling for a compartment like the tree hole in the backyard, but no latch caught my knuckle. The smooth impressions did not hide any secrets.

We keep our secrets close. Within arm's reach in case we need to bring them to the surface or run. I lay in her bed and stared at the ceiling, waiting for answers to come. The HVAC kicked on and conditioned air pumped through the vents and filled the room. I shut my eyes and let the cool air wash over me.

When the room was completely still, I heard the slightest rattle. An infinitesimal movement in a world of stillness. I followed the sound. Rushed toward it. The vent along the rear wall.

"Munoz," I shouted.

All three men appeared in the room. "What is it?"

"Got a screwdriver?"

He raced out of the room and returned a moment later, out of breath. I stuck the Phillips head into the screw and methodically removed every one. With a clank, I set the vent on the ground and stepped backward.

"Somebody take a photo," I said.

Munoz and Cliff both did.

Inside the vent sat a rifle tucked into the corner. "Munoz, can you film this? I don't want there to be any doubt."

He nodded. "Filming."

I slapped on gloves and inched the rifle out of the vent. Spiderwebs lingered in the punishing cold air that pushed through. When I set it on the bedspread, we all looked down. "It's not a Remington," Cliff said.

My breath caught in my throat as I made out the brand name on the side of the rifle. "No, it's a Winchester," I said.

"That's not the rifle that shot at you by Susan's place," Sawyer said.

I gulped hard, tears welling in the corners of my eyes. "No, it's not."

"Then why are there tears in your eyes?"

"Because this is the rifle that shot Sarah Price."

57

Tessa Brown arrived twenty minutes later. She winked at me as she lugged equipment through the front door and barked orders at a team of men with booties over their shoes. I led them to the garage and pointed to the car.

"Anybody been in?"

"No ma'am," I said. "Chain of custody."

Tessa grinned. "Smart cookie."

"We want to find any DNA that matches that of Lauren Blackburn. There weren't any signs that she was bound, so my guess is that she sat in the front seat."

"That's where we'll start."

"I'll also need your team to look over something else," I said.

Tessa raised an eyebrow.

"Two for one special?"

"This one is a winner."

After a half hour, Tessa reported that a luminol test had shown traces of blood in the trunk. They'd rush DNA testing, but we both knew what it would reveal.

She assured me her team had the scene locked down. Flooded with a mix of relief and disappointment, I rode back to the station with Sawyer. Munoz and Cliff followed close behind.

"Munoz, go home."

"I want to help," he said. "I want—"

I wagged a finger at him. "What does Sadie want?"

He deflated. "Help with the kids."

"Bingo."

Sawyer, Cliff, and I sat alone for a bit. The three of us were together again, yet somehow, we were still very much three parts of a whole. Even if time had eroded the foundations of our friendship, we still had enough of a bond to hold tight, although it was hard to look Cliff in the eye and overlook his betrayal.

"I owe you an apology, Grace," Cliff said.

"Save it for when we have Madison Dockery in cuffs," I said. "Besides, we're old friends. It's not like we can make new ones."

"I hope that day is tomorrow," Sawyer said.

"I should get home too," Cliff said. "Call me if anything surfaces?"

I nodded, but we all knew that we were in for a quiet night. It's funny how that feeling creeps in. How you just knew that the storm had passed. Maybe that's the beauty of life. Sometimes, it is predictable.

Sawyer and I sat next to one another and gazed into each other's eyes for a moment that felt like an eternity. Hell, it felt like fifteen years' worth of moments wrapped into one.

We'd made a stellar team.

And for all the faults and mistakes he'd made, he had my back when it mattered most.

Disappointment swirled in the ceiling fan and coated the room like a layer of dust. The long-awaited ending to a case that had more twists and turns than the Nantahala.

"We'll find her," Sawyer said, somehow seizing my thoughts from the spiral.

"We?"

"You know what I mean," he said.

"If you're going to leave, just do it already," I said, more exhausted than angry. I didn't have the heart to bear a goodbye. Maybe that's why Sawyer took that route back then.

"Grace, I—"

"Willa's body isn't even cold and you've got that old house up for sale. Don't try and spin this another way. You're leaving. Whether it's tomorrow or next week, that's beside the point. Before long, we'll be nothing but a memory again. A story you tell your city friends."

He deflated, his eyes turning wet. "I can't stand that house."

"I know."

"No, you don't. You don't have any idea. Nobody does. Every time I walk through those front doors and stare up at the wooden staircase, I see my father standing on the landing on top. I see his body bounce off the oak and crumble into a pile of bones on the ground. You have no idea what it's like to be suffocated by a ghost."

"I didn't mean to—" I said.

"If I pause for long enough, if I let myself linger on the landing, I can see my younger self standing there next to him. I can hear my words. I can hear his. The shouts echo off the framed family photos hung on the wall, a picture-perfect distortion of reality. His strained voice begging me to stay out of trouble. His harsh condemnation for the escort home from Don Chamberlain." Sawyer paused like he was tasting each word before he spoke them. "I can feel the rage that took control of my body. The angst that extended my arms and pushed him. The panic that filled my lungs as he lost his balance and fell."

We sat in silence. Sawyer had kept that secret so long we both had to make space for it in the world. Nothing I could say would help. There was no way to make it better or to tell him it was okay. I knew he'd tangled with those very words for so long that there was no more fitting response than silence.

"Willa never blamed me," he said. "No matter how much I blamed myself."

I swallowed hard. "And so, you left."

"I ran. Before the law or life could catch wind of what I'd done. Chamberlain was already after my head for Sarah Price. I was a wanted man."

"But Chamberlain recorded it as an accident. They—"

"Willa's words carried weight. Oak Hill was not a place where murder ran rampant and so nobody looked for one. Sarah Price's accident simultaneously wrecked and saved my life. It was the catalyst that provoked our argument. But it also stole the limelight long enough for me to sneak out under the cloak of darkness."

"And all this time, you've held that inside?"

He nodded. "I thought that if I said it out loud, it would make it true. It would give life to a memory that felt like a dream. Like somebody else controlled my hands. Like somebody else killed him. But I did it, Grace. It was me. And I deserved none of the love and affection and sympathy that came after, whether from you or a crowd of mourners at his funeral. I couldn't bear to live that lie. And I waited years for the consequences, but it's overdue."

"If you're asking me to arrest you, the answer is no."

"Grace, I—"

"That isn't justice. You've spent fifteen years wrestling with that burden. How you've survived, I'll never know. But you've imprisoned yourself more than any state judicial system could. And whether you pushed him or not, you never meant to kill George. Intent matters, Sawyer."

He was on his feet within seconds, wiping tears from his eyes. "Then I should go."

"Sawyer, wait. You can't just drop a secret like that and run away."

"It's been a hell of a day. We both need some rest. In the morning, we can find Madison Dockery and put her behind bars. Then we can revisit this conversation." He walked to the door with slow, careful steps. His body hung in the air like he was almost floating. "Goodbye, Grace."

"I'll see you tomorrow."

He looked back and said the words I'd needed so long ago. The words that once felt like the opening of a door. The words that left our future limitless. Full of possibility. But now those same words sounded like a door slamming shut. "I love you, Grace."

"I love you too, Sawyer."

He nodded and left. Part of me fell apart, shards of a future scarring my insides and scraping away any trace of hope. Sawyer would not be ready to search for answers tomorrow. He would be on his way back to Philadelphia to start his life anew. I was just a vessel to carry his secret. He'd passed that burden on to me with reckless abandon.

I filed paperwork away in the storage room and swept the lobby floor, willing my thoughts to scatter like the debris crowding the tiles. More times than I could count, I jumped at the slightest sound, tricking myself into thinking that it was the doorknob turning and Sawyer returning. When it was no use, I creaked open my office door, stepped inside, and flicked on the light.

The kiss of cold metal pressed against my neck like a raindrop on a sunny day. I didn't have to turn. I didn't have to squint at the reflection on the windows or crane my neck. Reluctantly, I exhaled and whispered.

"Hello, Madison."

58

My heart rocked against my rib cage. I balled my hands into fists at my side and gnawed on my lip as she eased the hair away from my neck and whispered in my ear.

"Brave little Gracie, you were always a bit too big for your britches," she said.

"Sawyer is outside. If I scream—"

"He left ten minutes ago, dear. If you scream, it will be your last breath. Choose wisely."

A chill raced up my spine. Muscles tensed. With great difficulty, I coaxed air out of my nose and choked down more oxygen. My eyes darted around the room. There had to be a way out. Madison Dockery would not be my downfall. Not today. Not ever.

"Sit down," she said, using the rifle to point toward my desk chair. A Remington 700.

I did as instructed. She sat on the table and pointed the gun at my chest. Visions of the slug tearing through my ribcage flashed through my mind. I saw my heart exploding. Blood dripping from the ceiling and painting the windows. Munoz or Molloy or some unfortunate soul would find me and never recover. I swallowed hard.

"It's not too late to—"

"If you'd just stopped looking, this could have gone away. I don't know what got into you, Gracie. You were like a dog on a hunt. And for a while, I thought you'd find somebody to take the fall. I gave you Billy Jenkins on a silver platter. But you just kept pushing."

"Even when you tried to kill me."

"Oh, hun. This wasn't personal. This was all business. Ever heard anybody say that the world is cutthroat? Well, that's an understatement."

"Killing your sister? That's just business as usual for you?"

"That woodland bitch was not my sister." Redness flooded her cheeks. "I don't care what my father claimed or what any DNA tests say. That whore was a mistake. One that nearly tore my family apart. But the Dockery family name lives on, thanks to me."

"That doesn't make her less of a human. You can't fault her for being born."

"Says who?" Madison asked. "Because from where I'm sitting, she was another brick in the wall. Another hurdle to clear as I lead this family into the new millennia. To hell with Ethan and his uppity nature. She had to die, and so do you."

"They'll never buy it," I croaked.

"Things work out for the Dockery family. Money talks. Old money shouts. Don't you fret. Nat will survive. I'll let you have that one because Daddy liked him so. Besides, time or disease will take him soon enough."

I choked back a shout, letting out a sharp breath instead.

"Sarah Price," I said.

Madison stared at me. "What about her?"

"It was you."

"Just piecing that together, dear?" She cackled. "Top-notch detectives we have here in town. That bullet wasn't meant for her. It was meant for that bastard child of my father's. Nature girl. I blame the rage that coursed through my veins while I was taking aim. In the dark, everybody looks the same. A shadow and a silhouette."

"How could you live with it?" I asked, already knowing the answer.

"Peacefully. It was an accident. Just like they said. We donated to her fundraisers. Daddy made sure that she was taken care of."

"He knew?"

"Aw, did you think Silas Dockery was a saint? It's okay. You and the rest of this godforsaken place needed a hero and he fit the bill. Yes, he knew. He made me promise that I would never try to hurt little nature girl ever again. But when his doctors warned us that his time was near, I had to tie up the loose thread before she tried to claim our fortune. My father had gone soft in his later years and I knew he'd been talking to Bill Nickelson about something. I couldn't take the risk and let that feral woman rob us blind."

"Her name was Lauren."

Madison tensed and I flinched but her finger didn't move. "If that's what she called herself, yes. The night of Sarah's accident, nature girl appeared at our front door, filthy and desperate and looking for my father."

"She was looking for help."

"A handout is more like it. From the second I saw her, I knew who she was. We looked enough alike back then. And my mother had alluded to her existence before she passed, but . . . to see her in the flesh was heartbreaking."

"Norma knew?"

"Stop trying to buy time," she said. "You'll have no use for these answers when you're rotting in the ground."

"I want to take my last breaths knowing full well how much of a disease your family is. Your mother shrugged off your father's illegitimate child. And when Lauren came to you, when your sister came to you for help, you ran her away and shot at her, critically wounding an innocent stranger. What kind of human does that?"

"I should've paid better attention when Daddy taught us to shoot. I never thought it would be of any use. Guns never appealed to me. I like a slow burn, not a big burst. But when I had her silhouette in my sights that night, I knew I had a taste for the hunt."

"Tell Sarah Price that."

"It took years to finish the job, but thanks to me that bastard from the brush no longer walks this earth."

"But why? Why did you—"

"Gracie, this has gone on long enough," she said with a sigh.

I flung my hands out in front of my face. "Wait!"

"No thanks." Madison closed one eye and aimed.

Something awoke inside me.

A beast that had lain dormant.

My body became weightless.

I dove to the side just as the gunshot ripped out. *Please let somebody be close enough to hear the sound.* Perhaps Oak Hill's cramped city streets would provide a chamber for the boom to echo through until somebody ran my way.

I rolled onto my side and leaped to my feet, using Madison's neck to pull myself upright. Sweat, either hers or mine, drenched my arm. She flapped at me, trying to create space to aim the gun, but I knocked it loose. It hit the wood with a crash, and I sent it skittering toward the door with my foot.

"You stupid bitch!" Madison dug her nails into my forearm, then sunk her teeth into the flesh. I wailed and pulled it loose. Free, she raced toward the door, but it burst open. Sawyer's face flashed with panic. Madison swept the rifle from the ground and raised it.

She smiled. "You always had such shitty timing, Sawyer."

He raised his hands in surrender, never taking his eyes from mine. Madison was close; I could track the path of beads of sweat as they trickled down her neck and disappeared below. Her arms shook as she caught her breath.

"Easy now," Sawyer said.

"Shut up," Madison said. "Just shut up. You were once a cute kid, you know that? Then you went and ruined it with your mouth. Nobody says no to a Dockery, Jacob. Not you. Not little nature girl. Nobody!"

I shifted my feet, aiming my shoulders toward her, and felt something hard against my right foot. Nat's baseball bat. Sawyer nodded slightly. A silent conversation between two old flames. He stepped forward. Madison's eyes widened as she shoved the barrel toward him. "Don't you move!"

In one smooth motion, I scooped the bat from below the desk, cocked it back and drove it into the base of her neck. She let out a guttural cry and slumped forward. Sawyer hopped to his right and snagged the barrel of the gun as she fell. He handed it my way. "Hell of a swing," he said.

I stood on wobbly legs. Then, the world around me went dark, and all I felt were Sawyer's arms wrapped around me. And I never needed anything more.

59

The collective lungs of Oak Hill exhaled as they wheeled Madison Dockery out of the station on a stretcher and loaded her into the back of an ambulance. Ethan surfaced moments later and stuck around to calm the worried cries of the townsfolk before rushing off to tend to his sister. I didn't see any of this happen, mind you.

Every muscle in my body froze in pure terror the moment the shot rang out. I lay wrapped in Sawyer's arms until the hum of spectators and scandal faded. A hoarse voice was the first thing I remembered hearing through the chaos.

Tessa Brown placed a hand on my shoulder. She whispered kind words that eventually enticed my muscles out of paralysis. Sawyer helped me to my feet, which dragged like there were cinderblocks in place of shoes. Tessa and Blake went on ahead, cleared the press and public out of sight, and moved my car to the rear door of the station. Sawyer drove me home. Nat rested with me on the couch as I told him everything through waterfalls of tears and weakened words. He kissed me on the head. Then Sawyer took over and helped me to my bed.

Propped up on pillows, I watched Sawyer stir about the room and take in the photos on the wall. A brief glimpse into the years he missed. When he settled beside me, Agatha tiptoed onto the comforter and nestled into his lap. He scratched her chin and I drifted off to sleep.

In a matter of days, the shock had worn down to a melodic whine. I wondered if that would be with me for the rest of my life. If there was any world in which I wasn't likely to coil up in fear at the sign of danger or threat. But we never know what our lives will look like down the road. We can only control today.

Cliff visited one day and inquired if I was still interested in the job. Sawyer steered him aside where he, Nat, and Cliff swapped whispers like schoolboys. I was grateful for the diversion. I didn't yet have an answer to Cliff's question. And part of me was unsure I'd ever have one.

I persuaded Sawyer to let me take a walk in the Nantahala alone on the third morning. The nagging feeling that I was a wounded bird unfit to fly put an itch in my skin. I thought nature might soothe me. And I wondered if Cedar's father might appear and smile my way, if only for a moment.

In the forest, I listened to birdsong and relished in their revelry. How much joy they got from the world around them. How much delight came from just a ray of sunshine. I'd never stopped to think of how lucky I was, never stopped to indulge in that ray and sing for the world to see. I'd spent my entire life fighting, but for the first time, I felt like I had enough perspective to look back.

Maybe that's the benefit of near-death experiences. Maybe I should have staggered into an alleyway in a roughneck city and waited for a mugging or a stabbing. Then I would have woken up long ago. Then I would have considered the people and world around me instead of viewing myself as background dressing for their show. Luck was a constant through line in my life. I was lucky that my parents gave me up. Lucky that Nat took me in and for the qualities he carried in his quiver. I was lucky to have Cliff and Sawyer and a million memories of an enchanted childhood in small-town America. And I was lucky that the bullet which paralyzed Sarah Price didn't strike me instead. And I was lucky that Madison Dockery was in the hospital and not me. In a way, I also felt lucky that I met Cedar. He reminded me of the wild, untamed world that I lived beside and neglected to think about.

When my luck perpetuated, it became a breeze to my sail. Something that carried me through. A blessing that would never die. That put me in a specific state of mind. One where luck and a strong support system would get me through the worst that life delivered. So I lived straight and along the path prepared by those around me. Desperate for stability. For security. For what I knew.

In all the falls of fortune and fact and fate, I finally understood: I'd spent my entire life reaching for lifeboats, but I never stopped to see if I could swim.

60

M unoz and Molloy managed for three days before they beckoned my support. They both looked like hell. Raccoon eyes and frazzled hair. In my office, I was unsurprised to see a sea of familiar faces. Cliff sat at the head of the conference room table with Ethan Dockery to his left and Liam Price on his right. A mirror image of where we all sat just weeks prior, before the storm struck town. The rigid, suit-clad county sheriff consultant didn't look up when I entered, but the smiling face of Tessa Brown drifted in from the break room.

"Coffee here is shit, Grace. I'd kill for a latte."

"Blame the mayor," I said.

"We'll put it in the budget," Cliff said. "Grace, have a seat."

I stayed with my back against the paned glass windows. Tessa parked herself at the table and glanced around at the sullen faces. "Some party this is."

Ethan Dockery cleared his throat. "I'll start. And preface this with an apology, Grace. You were on the right track and as much as it pains me to recognize what Madison did, I am pleased to see justice prevail. And I know my father would have been too."

"Kind words, Ethan," I said. "I'm sorry for pinning you in that cell. I should have handled it with . . . well . . . more grace."

"I've asked Bill Nickelson to amend the terms of Silas's will recognizing the new heir. We owe Cedar his stake of the family fortune. And he will forever have a place to call home if he so chooses."

"That's kind but Susan explained things to him. Cedar doesn't have much interest in your fortune, Ethan."

"I'd like to speak to him myself," Ethan said. "He is a Dockery after all."

"In blood only," I said. "I'm not inclined to force anything on the kid. He's been through hell."

"Look, it's no secret why we are here," Cliff said. "Grace, your actions have been nothing short of heroic. You led a dogged, determined, and comprehensive investigation. Miss Brown here provided a statement concerning your impeccable supervision of not one but two critical crime scenes."

"Few folks know how to stay out of their own way," Tessa said. "And I commend you for that."

"Considering that, this committee has voted unanimously to award you the job as Chief of Police, Grace. We can sort through details and compensation and all that when you feel ready. You've been through hell and the job can stay vacant for another week and—"

"Thank you, Mayor Rice. And thank you all for your support and endorsement, even if it's too little too late. I'd encourage you to consider other candidates. In fact, I'd like to withdraw my application altogether."

Cliff stared blankly. "Can I ask why?"

"I can't help but wonder what your decision would have been if trouble hadn't landed on Oak Hill's doorstep. Before, you all looked down your noses at me as if I was a kid with a badge instead of a senior ranking officer of the local police force. And your neighbor. So, it's nothing personal, but I don't want your job."

"You'd rather just stay a detective and work under whoever we hire?" Ethan asked.

I wrenched my badge from my belt and tossed it onto the table. The metallic clank reverberated through the tiny room like a crack of thunder. The four men stared at it with dropped jaws. Tessa Brown glanced up with a grin.

"Grace, you're not in your right mind," Cliff said. "We can—"

"I'm thinking clearly, thank you very much. Promote Miguel Munoz. He deserves the raise and he'll keep this town safe. He's the person I'd want in charge."

Liam Price captured my eyes and stood. I took his extended hand as he spoke. "Thank you for your service."

"Likewise," I said. "And I'm so sorry about Sarah. Truly. I've wanted to say that for years but never had the courage."

He bit back a smile.

I turned to the rest of them. "And thank you for your help. All of you."

In the bullpen, I hugged Munoz and told him the news. He didn't have any response. I didn't expect him to. Molloy offered me a vice-like handshake and a smile. "Best boss I've ever had," he said.

"Eh, find me again in ten years," I replied. "I'd bet I tumble down that list."

I left my desk alone and burst through the front doors. In the parking lot, my breath returned to my lungs, and I stood with my hands on my knees for a long moment. The door hinge squealed behind me.

"Hell of a show," Tessa said. "That beats basic cable any day of the week."

"Who still watches cable?" I asked.

"You did the right thing."

"Remind me of that when I stop convulsing."

"Come work with me," Tessa said.

"What?"

"You heard me. You're whip smart. A damn good eye at a crime scene and you worked that case like a dog on a bone."

"I just threw away my career in there," I said. "I'd be no help to you."

"Blake is taking a job in Raleigh. He leaves in a month. I want you on the team."

"That's nice but—"

"No buts. Think it over. If I don't hear from you by the end of the month, no hard feelings."

She extended a hand, and I slid mine into hers.

"Either way," she said. "It was a distinct pleasure working with you, Grace Bingham."

"Likewise," I said.

61

ilies and carnations speckled the exterior walkway that led into the church. Sawyer stood well-dressed and sleepy-eyed at the door and greeted every smiling face that ambled in. Cliff and I parked ourselves inside and watched the droplets collect into a flood.

Where Silas Dockery's memorial was laced with gaudy, stuffy displays of wealth and fortune, Willa's radiated authentic tenderness and grace. There was no police order to shut down the city. There were no requests for special circumstances or allowances. Just an open invitation to any and all that wanted to come and say a word or prayer or whisper about Willa Sawyer.

Once the formalities were out of the way, Sawyer white-knuckled the podium as he looked out at the audience.

"My mother always told me that the most important thing in life is integrity. Our capacity to do what is right. To perform what we preach. And it took years of maturity before I saw that she was the shining example of that value. When times were tough, she was a beacon in the storm. When good fortune came her way, she turned to make sure everybody else's cups were full. Although I can't say that I've been able to fill her shoes even in the slightest, I think you all being here today is living proof that her memory will live on for generations. Thank you."

Muted applause followed. Sawyer squirmed in his suit and stepped away from the microphone. The priest opened the floor to anybody who wished to speak or tell a story about Willa. At first, the crowd hummed with heads swiveling from side to side, waiting on the first volunteer. I took a sharp breath in and walked to the altar without a glimpse into the sea of familiar faces. When I looked up from the stand, the only faces I saw were those of Sawyer and Nat.

"I've learned a lot of lessons as of late. Some are about the realities and complexities of family. Some about justice and the deception of appearances. Sadly, in the past week, I didn't have a profound moment with Willa Sawyer. Lucky enough, I've had a lifetime of them to keep me afloat. One in particular comes to mind. I was young, with more freckles on my cheeks than years lived, and I was angry at Big Nat for something trivial, maybe an early bedtime or a snack I didn't want to eat. No matter the cause, I let a childhood fantasy swallow me and I bolted. I ran away from home. Back then, the only shelter I knew outside of my own home was one that Cliff, Sawyer, and I'd constructed with fallen logs and timber. It stood, swaying with every strong breeze, in the fringes of the woods behind Willa's house. She looked my way from the window and although I did my best to blend in with the tree trunks and hardwood around me, she found me. When she crept out and knelt beside me, she didn't ask what was wrong. She didn't offer a lecture or a collection of bible verses that may have made me wretch. No, she said, 'Life is a lot better when you're running toward something instead of running away.'

"Now, in my youthful state, the words were hollow and meaningless. But I've had the privilege of having them echo around my brain for the last twenty years. Willa was a classic example of a fighter. She fought for this town, for her family, and for her life. I like to think that in those last moments she was with us here, those words made their way back into my eardrums and danced around one more time. And I plan to do my best to heed the advice."

Subdued applause ushered me from my perch, and before I reached my seat, another speaker had taken the pulpit. Then another. The townspeople of Oak Hill sat in those rigid pews in their fanciest clothes for damn near five hours.

Every soul had a story about Willa. Sawyer absorbed them all, like a sponge in the sea, unable to comprehend or measure the magnitude of his mother's life.

When the stories ended, somebody hollered about a celebration outside and as the sun wriggled toward its evening position, the whole town howled and bantered around plastic card tables topped with black plastic tablecloths and potluck dishes from every corner of the city limits. I hung with Nat for a bit until I saw Sawyer walk to the pavilion alone.

"Heck of a service," he said.

"Heck of a woman," I said.

"I can't help but feel sad. Not so much that she's gone. I know she's not in pain anymore. But I'm sad that I'll never have a legacy like she does."

"Why not?" I asked.

He gestured toward the crowd. "She was here for her entire life. Her roots are deeper than most of the trees in the Nantahala. All of these people had a story about how she touched them."

"Maybe that's the lesson," I said.

"Huh?"

"It's not about where you are. Maybe it's about who you are instead."

"Way to turn that one around on me."

"I learned from the best." I paused. "You don't owe this town anything," I said. "Or the people in it. You did right by Willa with this celebration today. You did right by the town, helping me with the investigation and taking care of Cedar. I hope you can let that go."

"I don't know if I'll ever be able to let it go, but I can try."

"Trying is enough, sometimes."

"When I reflect on what Willa would want me to do, I get stuck. Part of me thinks she'd want me here. To build a life in that old house. To let my roots grow. But another voice is roaring for me to run."

"Nothing wrong with that."

"Grace, I've spent my whole life running."

"Running to or running from?" I asked.

He chuckled. "Running from."

"Then you've gotta find something worth running to."

He studied me for a long moment. His eyes were the same shade of green that I once watched the bonfire flames flicker inside like the roar of a wave on the beach. "Maybe I have."

62

"He's back," Margo said, her voice glazed with sugar and warmth.

I pinned the phone between my ear and my shoulder and hitched the box of junk into one arm. The random assortment of odds and ends pinballed around the box, but it was all I had to show for a decade as a cop. "He's leaving," I said.

"Not Sawyer. The boy."

I froze. "Where?"

"He's walking toward the station now. I thought you should know."

"Good," I said. "I'm there. I'll meet him."

"Grace?"

"Yeah?"

"He's not alone."

I watched from the front door of the Oak Hill Police Department as Cedar, as rumpled and grubby as ever, trotted around the corner. He held hands with an older man that I pegged for mid-forties. There was no need for an introduction. I knew it was his father.

They stopped before me. "Hi," Cedar said.

Benjamin Bradley

"Thought we'd seen the last of you."

"I had to get my father."

"That's okay," I said, extending a hand toward the father. "I'm Grace. You've got quite a young man there."

He tiptoed forward, watching me with vigilance. "Maxwell."

"Do you two want to come in?"

"No," Maxwell said. "I wanted to thank you for your help."

"I was just doing my job. I'm so sorry for your loss. From all accounts, Lauren was an extraordinary woman."

He nodded and his eyes went glassy. "Can I see her?"

"We buried her," I said. "With Cedar gone, we didn't want to delay anything. But I can bring you to her grave."

"No, that's okay. She's at rest now."

"Cedar, you left town before I could tell you what happened to your mom. If you both would take a quick ride with me, we can go to Susan's and talk through it all."

Maxwell turned to Cedar, who nodded. They rode in silence, sitting close in the backseat and peering out the window. I let the radio hum, flicking onto the old jazz station on the off-chance that Cedar was listening. He watched the town blur by and stepped from the car when we parked in front of Susan's.

After the events that shook the town, Oak Hillians dropped the Dockery name from the Center. Although Silas's funds kept the place running, there were wheels in motion to revamp it as the Susan Orr Center, a better representation of the heart and soul that ran it for so long. In the meantime, I'd taken to just calling it Susan's.

Warblers lingered in the branches and twirled in the breeze. The scent of pine washed over me as the sun dipped me in light. The clouds had moved on, blue skies were in the forecast again. Until the next storm, we were free. Susan joined me at the table to give Cedar and his father space to eat. "Thanks for taking care of them," I said.

"It's in my nature."

"The world is lucky to have you."

"And you, Grace."

"Maybe," I said.

"I've seen a shift in you over these past few weeks. A transformation. One that Willa Sawyer would smile at."

"Huh?"

"It seems like you're finally running toward something."

"A bit," I said. "Speaking of, I need to get over to Sawyer's. Call me if you need anything?"

"I won't. But thank you."

I waved goodbye to my friends from the forest and drove the long three miles to the Sawyer house. The ancient magnolia beside the curb seemed to prop up its posture, no longer scraping at the ground below but instead stretching toward the sky above. Neatly clipped grass framed the sidewalk. A "For Sale" sign sat in the corner.

At the door, I paused for a moment. There was a time when this door was closed. Forever. I didn't know what was happening behind the scenes, but remained convinced that I was the culprit instead of a bystander. Now, looking at those steps in the entryway, I saw them in a different light. Marred by loss. A gateway to a simpler time. Accidents happened. Life marched onward.

Sawyer stood in a sea of cardboard boxes and packing peanuts. Mountains of furniture and paintings filled the living room, each item labeled with stickers marking donation or sale. A small pile in the corner sat unmarked. The pile to keep.

In all the times we collect things in our lives, whether that be a wicker chair for the front porch or the ghost of a gunshot in the woods, we misjudge their significance. We regard the physical with the respect and reverence we should reserve for the old times. The old friends. Instead, when we pass, we end with stacks of physical goods to be dumped and donated to another family. The memories, well, they only live on if we had people to share them with in the first place.

"Cedar is back," I said.

"Good," Sawyer said without looking up. "He should get what is rightfully his. Ethan owes him that much."

"He brought his father."

This drew his eyes to me. Green dots like miniature forests. I wondered if they held the same secrets that Nantahala did. "Will they stay?"

"Susan recommended they find a house. If they want."

"I know one that's for sale."

"We'll see," I said. "I don't know if this is close enough to the forest for them. But those are tomorrow's problems. I'm still focused on today."

A car door thumped in the driveway. Sawyer peeked through the window. "Cliff."

"Did you tell him?"

"Only that I was leaving," Sawyer said. "I'll leave the rest to you."

When Cliff's barrel chest broke through the doorway, Sawyer's eyes welled with tears.

Cliff looked at the floor. "Leaving again, huh?"

They locked in a long embrace. "I'm sorry," Sawyer said.

"No hard feelings," Cliff added. "I'm sure glad I got to see you again."

"Next time it won't be so long between visits," he said, glancing my way.

"Good," Cliff said. He tapped Sawyer on the shoulder and looked around the room. "It doesn't feel real. I couldn't have imagined this past week if I'd tried. Murder, gunshots, a boy from the woods. And answers the town had been seeking since we were young. When you come into town, you sure bring chaos, Sawyer."

"I'd chalk that up to the combination of us three. The tricycle still works. And at least we know the truth about that night."

"I can't decide if knowing makes things harder or easier," Cliff said. "But something in all of this nudged me to be a better man."

"Yeah? You tell Reyna that?" I asked.

"I did," he said. "And she understood. I owe Hannah my full self."

"Good thinking, buddy," Sawyer said. "Now don't go running this town into the gutter while I'm gone."

Cliff chuckled. "No promises."

63

Worried eyes watched me collect my last paycheck. I assured Munoz and Molloy they'd survive and waved goodbye, a capstone on a series of celebrations and acknowledgments, and pushed through the double doors, suddenly a civilian. My waist, lighter than I'd grown accustomed to, thanked me for the change, although my mind remained uncertain about the decision. Sawyer picked me up from the parking lot and opted for the long way through town.

We passed the charred carcass that was once Nickelson Law, a smoke signal I failed to decode. In the distance, my eyes traced the outline of the Dockery Center, where recollections and anecdotes oozed out of every door and window like insulation filling a void. Sawyer drove slowly, more amble than march, and I didn't take my eyes off the scenery, as if seeing it all for the first time again.

When I looked at the town, I didn't feel heartache. No regrets floated to the surface to jab me one last time before I left them in the dust. The sun layered a warm coat of pink and yellow that brightened the dusty streets where people I knew and loved went about their lives. I worried I didn't have the words to say goodbye. That I didn't have the time or gumption to go from person to person and hug them for their microscopic nudge in the direction of my life.

After all, without every person who graced my life, I never would have taken that same journey. I never would have found my way. But old friends, as Sawyer taught me the hard way, didn't always need a goodbye. And something I'd come to know and appreciate, that a wise man once told me, is that you can't make new old friends.

Nat leaned back in his chair and stared at Sawyer while I put my life into bags and lugged them onto the porch. "Suppose I should say something paternal here," he said.

"That would be a first," I said.

"And something that warns you not to hurt my beloved," Nat said.

Sawyer nodded. "Consider it said."

"But I think a more fitting string of sentences would be a request."

"A request?" I asked.

"Don't hold her back," Nat said. "That girl is full of life. Don't you dare let that fade to ash."

I slugged him on the shoulder. "Don't talk about me when I'm standing right here."

He looked at me, eyes red-ringed and puffy. "You are full of life. Don't you dare let that fade."

"I'll do my best," I said.

"When will you be back?" Nat asked.

"I don't know, Nat."

"That's okay. Just felt like something I should ask."

"I love you, Nat," I said. "I could say that every second of every day for the rest of your life, and it still wouldn't be enough to fill the cupboards and walls and floorboards of this house. My love for you is eternal. You shaped my life and I can only hope to repay you someday."

A tear escaped from the corner of his eye. "There isn't anything to repay. Go live that life, Grace. And you know where to find me in the meantime.

Explore far and wide. I don't think you'll find another place like Oak Hill. It's up to you if that's a good thing or bad."

———

We kicked up a dust cloud as we drove away from Nat's, the tires shifting and relaxing as we lurched onto pavement. The same cracks in the concrete I'd heard every day of my life hummed their goodbye serenade. Like Nat said, they weren't going anywhere. But for once, I was.

Sawyer clenched the brake at the stoplight and looked both ways. His hand snaked around the console and found mine, a warm surprise in the uncertainty and angst of an immense moment. He paused and looked at me. In some ways, we were kids again, driving down the fire road with the world in our grasp. I hadn't decided what the future held for Sawyer and I. Fate hadn't been kind to us, but maybe it was our time. Maybe.

"Ready?"

"Nope," I said. "But I'll get there."

"Nothing is forever," he said. "Once I pack up my apartment, I—"

"Let's make decisions as they pop up. For now, I'm happy to be here with you. No hard feelings, no past regrets. Just Grace and Sawyer, the Clueless Detective Agency, off to see the world. I can't promise you much more than that just yet."

I caught a tear forming in the corner of his eye. He wiped it away. "That sounds like a dream."

We turned left, away from town, and approached the serpentine back roads that wound away from Oak Hill and eased us into the heart of the Carolinas. The town lurked behind us, tinted red by brake lights and the blood washing off my hands as we collected mile markers on the interstate. I had little doubt that Oak Hill would resume its normal hum within seconds of my departure.

We all want to believe we are the beating heart that allows a world to exist, but there's harmony in knowing that you are just a background dancer performing your moves as part of a larger whole. I hoped the feeling continued wherever this road ended.

The saying goes that you reap what you sow. The seeds you plant become the harvest down the road. But there's a great part of life that occurs long after we are gone. So often we measure a person by what they left behind. I'm not sure if it's fair, or if I'm equipped to judge the fairness. But I think of Sawyer and the wake of misery and heartbreak he left behind, only to right the ship and calm those waters. I think of how I'd convinced myself to see the worst in Sawyer's exit and how I'd nearly let that doubt and silence wreck any chance at a stable future. I consider Billy Jenkins and the tortured past of addiction he left behind, only to have it follow him forever. I conjure Silas Dockery's pristine reputation, shattered by a scandal and a decades-old mistake he buried. No man—or woman—is an island. We are all ripples of what we put out into the world and those around us are left to grapple with the wake. I suppose it's our responsibility to make that legacy one worth sharing, one worthy of the storybooks and tall tales that will someday be the only living echo of our names. If only we are so lucky.

-ACKNOWLEDGMENTS-

Above all else, thank you. Without readers like you, none of this is possible. I'm so grateful for all of the brave souls willing and excited to jump into this land of make believe and hang with these characters for a while. Your support is the scaffolding upon which all of these stories are built.

I'm forever grateful for the enduring support I received from my family. Megan, thank you for listening to countless ideas and what-ifs and for your relentless optimism. Mom, thank you for being the best beta reader of all time and for your everlasting support and cheerleading. To Dad, Kyle, Kelsey, and Ben, I'm lucky to have so many talented and creative people in my life to learn from and have cheering loudly in my corner. I'm eternally thankful for friends like Tom and Nick and so many others for thought partnership in writing and all the wacky things that come with publishing. Lastly, this novel wouldn't have been possible without the space to think that accompanied many walks with Harper or shenanigans with Fox.

This novel was shaped by so many talented people, but I especially want to thank Helga Schier and the entire editorial team at CamCat Books for their belief in this story and thoughtful edits. A massive shout out to

Maryann Appel for this incredible cover design. Early input from both Sara DeGonia and Sara Miller helped carve the path and I remain very thankful for their expertise. Finally, I owe a debt of gratitude to a cast of incredibly talented people, including Kim Lozano, Romy Sommer, Joseph Dowling, Lisa Towles, and more.

Benjamin Bradley was born and raised in northern New Jersey. His earliest exposure to writing crime fiction was a short story entitled "Mr. Frog Goes to Jail" written at the ripe age of eight. Through his teens and twenties, Benjamin put the craft on the back burner to explore the world through running, travel, and national community service through Ameri-Corps. In all of his experiences, he found a love for sharing the stories of misadventures, mischief, and mayhem from different pockets of the world.

Always a voracious reader, Benjamin turned back to writing crime fiction and mystery novels in his downtime as a way to process and control the harsh realities of the world he saw working in poverty alleviation and public health. This escape grew and with great trepidation, Benjamin began sharing his work with family and friends, eventually publishing a YA thriller and the Shepard and Kelly Mystery novels with an independent press.

His latest novel, *What He Left Behind*, the first with CamCat Books, is centered around experiences in many of the small communities across the South he has supported through his work. He cites Harlan Coben, Michael Connelly, Attica Locke, and S. A. Cosby as inspiration. His short fiction has appeared in esteemed literary magazines including *Reckon Review, Flash Fiction Magazine,* and *Rural Fiction Magazine.*

Benjamin holds degrees from Rowan University and NC State and now calls Raleigh, North Carolina his home, where he lives with his wife and their cat and dog. He continues to work in public health and housing alongside a dedicated team committed to ending homelessness and providing equitable healthcare for all.

You can learn more about Benjamin on his website:
www.BenjaminBradleyWrites.com

Or follow him on social media:
@benjaminbradleywrites on Instagram

@benjaminbradleybooks on Facebook

If you enjoyed
Benjamin Bradley's *What He Left Behind*,
consider leaving us a review
to help our authors.

And check out
K. L. Murphy's *The Great Forgotten*.

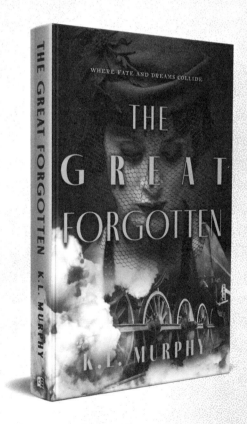

CHAPTER ONE

———— —— ———— —— ——

Summer 1988
Nashville, Tennessee

Ginny Campbell surveyed the boxes stacked in all four corners of the living room, surprised by how much she'd managed to bring to the new house. Footsteps sounded on the stairs, and she looked over her shoulder. The movers, their faces shining pink with exhaustion, marched down the stairs, arms swinging.

"That was the last of it, Mrs. Campbell," the larger of the two men said. A fresh bead of sweat dripped from his temple, and he mopped it with the sleeve of his coveralls. "What do you want me to do with the trunk?"

Her brows creased. "What trunk?"

"The one in the attic." He glanced at his partner and shrugged. "Probably left by the old owners."

The other man, as skinny as a pogo stick, chimed in. "Looks like it's been there a long time."

She thought about it for only a moment. The house was supposed to be empty, cleared of any items left by her grandmother that hadn't already been taken by friends and family, but this must have been missed. "Can you bring it downstairs?"

After they'd gone, she crouched down in front of the trunk, running her hand across the dusty surface. Wiping away the grime, she spied a set of faded gold initials. AMK. Ginny's teeth caught her lower lip and she frowned. Grandma Betty's initials were EJP, not AMK. She studied the curious case again. It was large enough for travel, but there were no stickers or anything to indicate where it came from other than those initials. From the look of it, the movers were right. It was old and had probably been in the attic for ages.

"Who do you belong to?" she asked the trunk, her voice a whisper. Reaching out, she caught the antique brass lock in her hand and drew in a breath.

The sharp trill of the phone made her gasp and fall back on her heels with a thump. Shaking her head with a laugh, she scrambled to her feet and hurried to the phone hanging on the kitchen wall.

"Hello?"

"Did they break anything? Movers always break something, you know." Ginny's grip on the phone loosened. "Hi, Mom."

"You have to watch them like hawks." Ginny couldn't help but smile. Her mother might be short on pleasantries, but she was long on opinion. "When we moved to Tallahassee, they broke an entire place setting of Grandma Betty's china. Do you remember it? The plates had those tiny pink flowers in the middle with gold trim along the edges. Maybe you don't though. I can't say I ever used it except when Grandma Betty came for Christmas which wasn't often—thank the Lord. It wasn't my style. Not modern at all. Please don't tell your father I said that. His mother was a dear when she was with us, of course, but we never did have much in common."

Ginny choked back a snort and dragged a chair closer to the phone. Her mother liked to imagine that she and Grandma Betty were quite different, but they definitely had one thing in common. Both women could talk and neither cared to whom—as long as the body was warm and even that wasn't absolutely necessary. It was no wonder Ginny's father was a quiet man.

"Anyway, I hope none of your china has broken like Grandma Betty's. Though I guess yours is plain enough that you could probably replace it with any old white plate, and no one would notice the difference. Now, if it were one of the Florentine patterns or the Scandinavian designs we considered, that would be quite upsetting. I really wish you'd gone with that Wedgwood. Can you imagine how gorgeous your table would be during the holidays? And with the crystal that—"

"Mom, stop." Ginny's fingers tightened over the phone again.

Maggie Piler made a clucking sound. "Surely, I'm entitled to my opinion, Virginia."

"I know your opinion." Ginny heard the sharp inhale over the line and groaned. "Please, Mom. Can we talk about something else?"

"Maybe you'd like to talk about that husband of yours. I swear, Virginia, I don't understand that man. Letting you move all on your own. He should have told his boss no, that it wasn't a good time for him to go to London. I still can't understand why he had to go halfway around the world. Couldn't they have done one of those conference calls? Your father did them all the time before he retired."

"No, Mom." Ginny raised a hand to her temple, massaging the soft flesh. "We've been over this."

"Well, in my day, a man would never let his pregnant wife move alone. It's not right."

"I'm not due for almost six months, Mom. I'm fine. Perfectly capable of handling a move by myself."

"It's still not right." The words were spoken in a way that made Ginny know her mother's chin was lifted to the sky, her red-stained mouth puckered in disapproval. "You can't tell me I'm wrong about this."

Ginny had no intention of discussing Shawn with her mother. "I'm hanging up now."

"Wait. I haven't even had a chance to ask how you're feeling or how the baby is."

"The baby's fine."

"You would tell me if anything was wrong, wouldn't you?"

Ginny looked up at the ceiling. "Yes, Mom."

"Good, because I would get on a plane if you needed me. I'd do it right now. All you would have to do is ask. Your father, too. We could be there in a few short hours."

Ginny's lips parted. "You hate flying. You're terrified."

"I'd still be terrified, but for you and the baby, I would do it. Promise me that if you need me, you'll let me know."

"I promise."

"Good." Maggie changed the subject again. "Well, how's the house? Is it as dreary as I remember?"

Ginny's gaze swept past the counters cluttered with half-emptied boxes to the large window overlooking the small backyard. The grass could stand to be cut, and the fence needed to be repaired, but there was room enough for a swing set and a patio. A huge oak shaded the front porch, and there was a fireplace. Now that her grandmother's heavy furniture and brocade drapes had been removed, the house felt brighter. The wallpaper would have to go, though. "It's not dreary, Mom. It needs a little updating, that's all. But you can help me with that when you and dad drive up next month."

"Will you let me help you with the nursery?"

Ginny hesitated. It wasn't like her mother to ask permission for anything. Maybe it was being a grandmother that was softening Maggie. Either way, Ginny wasn't one to argue. "I would love your help."

"I've got so many ideas. What do you think about pink and yellow with—"

"Why don't we wait until you're here?"

"Yes, we can do that. I've been going through boxes of your old things. Make sure you save room in the attic for the baby's clothes as she grows older."

"Mom, we don't know the baby's a girl."

"It's only a feeling, Virginia. Don't make too much of it. But I do have some dresses of yours I've kept stored all these years."

"That reminds me," she said and told her mother about the trunk.

"One of your grandmother's?"

"I don't think so. It has the initials AMK."

"AMK... AMK. I can't think who that could be." Ginny heard the clink of a spoon against a teacup over the line.

"Well," Ginny said with a sigh. "I guess I'll have to decide what to do with it."

"What's to decide? It's probably filled with spiders and mouse droppings by now." Ginny laughed imagining her mother shuddering at the idea. "Toss it in the trash before you regret it, Virginia. I'd do it today."

"But what if it's filled with family heirlooms or," she paused, her lips twitching, "very valuable china?"

"Well," Maggie said, dragging out the word. "I suppose you could open it and see, but I'm telling you, Virginia, if you don't find jewels or money, you need to get rid of that thing."

"How sentimental of you, Mom."

"Ha! Being sentimental is dead these days, or haven't you heard?"

"Whatever you say, Mom. I'm hanging up now. For real this time."

Ginny went back to the living room, stopping when she passed a small carton covered in pink hearts. Shawn had laughed when she'd drawn them, but she'd countered, "I'm being efficient. I could write wedding albums, but this saves time." He'd grinned and wrapped his arms around her. That had been three moves and three apartments ago. The hearts were faded now, nearly invisible. Her hand dropped to her growing belly, and her chin fell to her chest. This was supposed to be a happy time. The gift of Grandma Betty's house. Shawn's new job. A baby. So, why was she fighting back tears?

"Stop it," she said to the empty house. "You can do this."

Across the room, late afternoon sunbeams poured through the large window, spotlighting the leather-wrapped trunk. Sun-speckled particles of dust danced over the case, reminding her of fireflies on a hot summer night. She forgot about the heart-covered box, forgot about Shawn.

Falling to her knees in front of the trunk, she breathed in the musty scent of dried leather and dead flowers. In an instant, she was transported back to her childhood and playing in Grandma Betty's cedar closet. How many times had she hidden among the heavy woolen coats and perfumed gowns? Her heart swelled with the memory as she stared down at the old case. There was no telling what could be inside. Her mother was wrong. Sentimentality wasn't dead. It couldn't be. Besides, there were other reasons to value photos, books, or artifacts. Those things were someone's story, and more importantly, history.

She sneezed and knew her mother wasn't wrong about one thing. The trunk was dirty, and she leaned closer, inspecting the case for spiders or rotted wood or splits in the seams, but saw nothing. Hands trembling, she unbuckled the bindings. The leather straps split as they fell away. Dust clouds rose and tickled her nose again. Who was AMK? Had he or she searched for the trunk only to give up? Ginny considered whether the case could contain family heirlooms or valuable books or any number of things. Squaring her shoulders, she told herself there was only one way to find out. She turned the key.

Ginny pulled into the small lot, slowing at the sign. Welcome. Nashville Home for the Infirm. Hands resting on the wheel, she studied the three-story building. Dark streaks stained the concrete from the roof line to the lowest window. Cracks and broken pavement marked the lot and sidewalk. Dandelions pushed up through the weed-choked front lawn, their yellow faces the only bright spot to be seen. There's nothing welcoming about it, she thought. Not for the first time, she wondered if this was a good idea.

"Are you sure it's the right lady?" Shawn had asked when he'd phoned.

"Yes. Well, no. I suppose there could be another woman with the same name, but it doesn't seem likely."

"Well, let's say it is her. She's gotta be like a hundred years old though, right?"

"Maybe. I don't really know."

"Gin, I'm not sure this is such a great idea. I don't have a good feeling."

She'd wanted to laugh but thought better of it. "What do you think's going to happen, Shawn? I'm going to see an old woman in a nursing home."

It had been an easy argument to win, but she wasn't sure if it was because she was right, or because they were both too tired to make the effort anymore. And in spite of her brave words, she had doubts of her own. What if it was the wrong woman? Or what if the trunk did belong to her, but she didn't want to be reminded of it? After all, the old woman had left the trunk in the attic, forgotten. The images of the things inside flashed through her mind then. Everything in the old case had been so carefully wrapped and preserved. It didn't make sense that it had been abandoned. A new idea struck her. Maybe the trunk wasn't left but lost.

Ginny got out of the car and raised her sunglasses on her head. At the front doors, she peered through the glass. Inside, were a handful of empty metal chairs pressed up against the far wall and a table covered with magazines. A woman in a white nursing uniform sat behind the front desk.

"Good morning," the nurse said when Ginny walked in. The nametag she wore read Jean. "Visiting?" she asked.

"Yes."

Nurse Jean flipped a page in her book and pointed at a wooden clipboard. "You can sign in there. Who are you seeing today?"

Ginny picked up the pen and wrote her name. "Anna Mae Kennedy."

The woman's head came up. "Anna Mae Kennedy?" She closed her book and folded her hands in front of her. "Are you family?"

"Daughter." Ginny hadn't planned to say that, but the lie popped out of her mouth before she could take it back. The nurse lifted one brow. Realizing her mistake, she forced a laugh. "I mean, granddaughter."

"Granddaughter, huh? I've worked here since '82. Why haven't I seen you here before?"

"I just moved to Nashville. Earlier this week," Ginny said, relieved to speak the truth.

Jean pursed her lips and looked past Ginny to the mostly empty lot. "Are you alone?"

"Yes." Ginny's face flushed under the woman's scrutiny. It occurred to her that maybe she shouldn't have shown up without having sent a letter first. What if other family showed up?

How would she explain herself?

"Anna Mae doesn't get many visitors."

Ginny waited.

"Actually, she doesn't get any visitors. Ever."

"Oh." While Ginny was thankful that she wouldn't be running into actual family, she found the nurse's declaration sad. "Then I'm glad I came."

Jean tapped her fingers for a minute, as though considering. "She gets tired," the nurse said finally. "She's one of our oldest patients."

Ginny exhaled. "I won't stay long."

"Fifteen minutes," the nurse said, handing Ginny a visitor pass. "Second floor. Room five."

On the second floor, another nurse sat behind a larger desk. Ginny waved her pass in the air and kept walking. The door to Room One was open, the interior dark. A man in a wheelchair was parked outside of Room Two. Ginny slowed. The crown of his head shone pink and white under the unforgiving florescent lights. The hair he did have fell in a gray sheet to his shoulders, partially obscuring the cracked lines of his face. With his chin tucked close to his chest, he twisted his hands in his lap, half-talking, half-ranting, his words rising and falling in a droning hum.

"They're coming, I tell you. Coming. Watch for the night. That's when they come." His hands moved faster, his body rocking. "They're coming, I tell you. Coming." Spit dribbled down his chin. He repeated the same words and his head snapped up, his pupils searching, unfocused in the light. "Watch for the night. That's when they come." Ginny backed away and his head dropped down. "They're coming, I tell you."

At the door to Room Five, she drew herself up and tapped lightly on the door. Silence. She knocked again, louder, and pushed the door open.

An elderly woman sat in a wheelchair, her face angled toward the window. Wispy white hair like soft-spun cotton candy floated around her head. She wore a high-necked nightgown with pink lace trim and pearl-colored buttons. A colorful quilt lay across her lap. Pink slippers poked out from under the coverlet.

"Mrs. Kennedy?"

The old woman shifted toward Ginny. "You don't look like a nurse. Where's your white uniform?"

"I'm visiting." She lifted the pass again.

The woman in the chair blinked. "Oh, my. Did they tell you the wrong room?" She leaned her head to her shoulder. "Who are you here to see? I might be able to tell you the room you need."

"No. I'm in the right room." Ginny's arm dropped. "At least I think I am."

The woman's forehead wrinkled, her expression a mix of surprise and doubt. "Do I know you?"

"No. We've never met, but I live in your house—your old house—the one on Kensington. I moved in the other day, actually."

"I see." The lines that fanned out across her cheeks softened. "How did you find me?"

Ginny squirmed and she was reminded of her students in the classroom. All the doubts she'd had about visiting came flooding back. What if the trunk held unhappy memories? What if the woman didn't want the trunk anymore? What if she didn't want to be found at all? She pushed her thoughts aside. "I went to the library. They have all the old newspapers on microfiche."

"Why would you expect to find me in the newspapers?"

"I didn't. I was," Ginny hesitated, "I was reading through the obituaries."

The woman's lips almost turned up in a smile. "How resourceful of you, dear. And when you didn't find my name, you naturally thought to come here."

Ginny's face flamed. "No, not at first. I figured you could have moved out of town, but I decided to take a chance and call some of the nursing homes first. This was the third place I called."

"I see," she said again in a way that made the young woman unsure if she did.

Ginny spotted a hard chair in the corner. "May I sit down?"

"If you like."

Ginny pulled the chair across the room. "My name's Ginny Campbell."

"Anna Mae Kennedy, but I guess you already know that."

"Yes, ma'am."

"So, you moved into the Kensington house. What happened to the Mayers?"

"Mr. Mayer decided to retire. They moved to Florida."

"Ah. My brother lives in Florida. It's a nice place, I hear."

"Have you ever been there? To visit, I mean?"

"I haven't left Nashville in years, not since . . ." Her voice faded. "Well, not in a very long time."

"Oh."

"I don't understand why you're here," the woman said. "Is there a problem with the house?"

"Oh, no. It's, well . . ." Ginny took a deep breath. "I found something in the attic."

Anna Mae opened her mouth, closed it again. Her hands stilled in her lap, and her gaze drifted back to the window.

Ginny waited perched on the edge of the seat, but the old woman sat silent. Had the old woman heard her? Did she care?

"It's pretty out there, isn't it?" she said after a minute.

Ginny scooted forward to see better. A smattering of buildings hugged the roads. Beyond, she saw fields of wild grasses and a single railroad track cutting through the land, bleeding into the horizon.

In the near distance, a bridge stretched over the track to a busy road. As views went, Ginny figured it wasn't bad. "Yes, it's nice," she said, but she hadn't come to talk about the scenery. She wiped her palms on her slacks. "Mrs. Kennedy—"

"It's Miss," the old woman said, facing Ginny again. "But you can call me Anna Mae. Everyone does."

"Okay." She squirmed on the chair, trying to get more comfortable. "I wanted to find you because I found something in the attic that I think belongs to you. A trunk."

Anna Mae sighed. "I know what you found, dear. I left it there, didn't I? I thought for sure . . ." Before Ginny could ask what the old woman thought, Anna Mae continued. "The Mayers were nice people. I had high hopes, I suppose. I waited, but . . . well, it doesn't matter what I thought. I was wrong." She waved a hand in the air. "I'm an old woman now, and it's only a trunk. All of that was a long time ago," Anna Mae said, her voice husky with memory. "The world has changed. I'm not sure it matters much anyway. Not anymore."

Ginny sat forward, the hairs on her arms raised. "Maybe it does."

There was a swift knock at the door and Nurse Jean came in, shooting a dark look in Ginny's direction. "It's been fifteen minutes." Addressing Anna Mae, she said, "Are you tired? I could help you back to bed."

Anna Mae patted the nurse's hand. "I am a bit tired. Thank you, Jean."

"Why don't we say goodbye to your visitor then?"

"Yes, thank you for coming, dear," she said.

Jean kept her eye on Ginny as she returned the chair to the corner and exited the room. Ginny was almost to her car when the nurse called her name.

"May I have a word with you, Mrs. Campbell?"

Ginny spun around slowly, her heart pounding. "Is something the matter?"

Jean's hands went to her hips. "I know you're not Anna Mae's granddaughter or any other kind of daughter. Anna Mae didn't have any children. Makes it kind of hard to have grandchildren, don't you think?"

Ginny's face flushed pink. "I'm sorry I lied about that. I should have told you the truth."

"Which is?"

"I just moved to Nashville. Into my first house. And it turns out it's the same house Miss Kennedy used to live in." The nurse waited. "I found an old trunk in the attic that I think belonged to her. I came to see if she wanted it back."

"And did she?"

"She didn't say."

The nurse stared at her a moment longer, the marshmallow contours of her face hardening. "Anna Mae is my favorite patient. She's a really nice lady, and I don't like seeing her upset."

"I didn't mean to upset her."

"Make sure it doesn't happen the next time."

"Next time?"

"She wants you to come back. Tomorrow morning at ten o'clock."

Surprising herself, Ginny didn't hesitate. "Okay. I can be here at ten."

"Fine. For the record, I'm not sure it's such a good idea." The nurse squinted in the bright light. "There's one other thing. She said to tell you to bring the letters. Do you know what that means?"

The letters had been wrapped in paper and tied neatly with string. There was more than a dozen, each delicate envelope thick with pages. Ginny nodded. "I do."

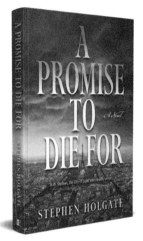
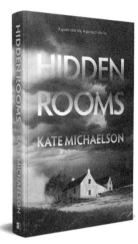
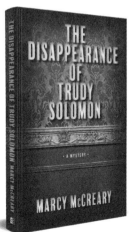